JOEL J. PAWLAK

Salter's Path

D1528132

First edition

ISBN: 9798845860477

This book was professionally typeset on Reedsy.
Find out more at reedsy.com

Preface

History

North Carolina fades into the ocean.

If one were to start in Western North Carolina, you would work your way down from the mountains, through the rolling hills of Statesville, to the piedmont of Greensboro, then the sandhills of Pinehurst, and finally to the coastal plain. If you continue further, you enter into the swamps and flooded forests of the North Carolina low country. Keep going beyond the marshes and to the shore, where you will find brackish water home to scallops, clams, oysters, shrimp, and many hatchling fish. If you have journeyed this far, you will see the barrier islands of North Carolina in the ocean.

These barrier islands are known by many as the "Outer Banks." When you speak to the locals, you find this connotation is more complicated. The traditional Outer Banks run north from Cape Hatteras, and the Southern Outer Banks run south from Cape Lookout. About ten miles from Cape Lookout along the Southern Outer Banks, you will find small coastal towns. Some date back to the earliest towns located in the continental United States.

Just across from the diamond-patterned Cape Lookout lighthouse, a Virginian painter named John Shackleford acquired the land in the early 1700s. Today, the low-lying sandy islands extending about ten miles long and half a mile in width bear his name. The islands are uninhabited, covered with low-growing trees and wild horses that trace their ancestry to sixteenth-century Spanish shipwrecks.

At one time, Shackleford Banks had a settlement. Through the 1700s and into the late 1800s, Shackleford Banks was home to an active whaling community. Whale oil was the fuel of the day, and a single whale could yield $1,000 (about $35,000 in today's money) in the oil value alone. The town became known as Diamond City after the pattern painted on the nearby Cape Lookout lighthouse, and its exact founding date is unknown.

Those who lived on the banks were a hardy bunch. They made a living working the sea and understood the cruelty Mother Nature could bring. They knew one mistake on the ocean could cost you everything.

In 1886, townsfolk watched helplessly as a ship called the *Chrissie Wright* ran aground and began to flounder on the shoals. The bitterly cold winter night and relentless waves broke the ship apart. Only the cook survived to tell the tale the next day. This event led to the creation of the U.S. Life Saving Service on the Banks. Today a U.S. Coast Guard Station is located across the Beaufort Inlet from Shackleford Banks and serves as a reminder of the dangers of the ocean.

Diamond City was lost to history in 1899 when a massive hurricane reduced the city to flotsam and jetsam, washing it into the Atlantic Ocean. The Diamond City residents were left to find a new home. Many of them went across the sound to the historic town of Beaufort, North Carolina, the legendary home of Blackbeard. Some moved to "The Promised Land," which is now modern-day Morehead City. At the same time, another group moved to Salter Path. Which at that time was a simple fishing village on Roosevelt Island.

Salter Path gained its name from the path that crossed the island from the Atlantic Ocean to Bogue Sounds. Roosevelt Island is about twenty miles in length and never more than a mile wide. In the early 1900s, the whiting fishery was alive and well. Whiting, also called sea mullet, were plentiful along the North Carolina Coast. Fishermen need to transport their catches from the ocean to the Morehead City, Swansboro, and Cedar Point processing facilities. It made sense for the fishermen in the center of the island to haul their catch across Salter Path to the Bogue Sound, where the fishermen could boat the catch to the processing facilities. Ultimately, the fish were packed into barrels and shipped to the cities in the Northeast.

Salter Path was a small fishing village that proliferated with residents relocated from Diamond City. Three families settled in this area. The original settlers were the Salters, who lent their name to the path crossing the island. The Jones, Willard, and Snow families traveled to settle in the island's center at Salter Path.

People use the term "settled" loosely. The island, at the time, was privately owned by the Roosevelt family. The families leaving Diamond City took up residence on land that they did not own. The families became squatters, building a life around fishing, families, and church.

As time went on, the Roosevelts decided they needed to reclaim their property. This reclamation was not as easy as one would think and a long battle ensued with the families settled in Salter Path. Eventually, the salty nature of the squatters in Salter Path was yielded to by the Roosevelts, and the families were granted eighty-nine acres of land for themselves.

Throughout the twentieth century, Salter Path mainly existed as a small peaceful beach and sound side fishing community. As the end of the century neared, developments began to reach Salter Path, and the town started to welcome vacationers from the cities of North Carolina and beyond. This influx of money and people grew the village, adding a police and fire department, a high-rise building, and many vacation homes.

Of the earliest developments was the trailer park. Purchasing about

150 acres on the sound side of Salter Path were the Blanchards. They established a vacation trailer park known as Paradise Bay. This location became the summer home for hundreds of people from the cities of North Carolina. The trailer park and new motels and beach houses swelled the village in the summers, breaking the streets' quietness. Before the vacation home developments, Salter Path was where sand crabs filled roads at night.

The town had grown, adding a drive-in restaurant known as the Big Oak, a gas station called Save-a-Stop, and a motel named The Oak Grove Motel. The permanent citizens had grown to 250, and the community's children attended school on the mainland. They rode the bus to the end of the island daily and took the ferry from Atlantic Beach to Morehead City for school. Salter Path established the first church on the island–Salter Path Methodist Church–and built the sanctuary in 1977. This church was the community's pride and the centerpiece of activity for many years.

Each of the families living in Salter Path grew and prospered in a low country kind of way. Success found them in fishing, boat building, service, and handiwork. The small town meant that families were close, and young people mostly found love on the island. Families grew closer and closer over time, living isolated on an island off the North Carolina coast.

The environment of Salter Path weathered the people in a literal way. They were blown from their first homes in Diamond City to land in Salter Path. Hurricanes regularly battered the coast, and one soon realized that building a structure to withstand a hurricane was a fool's errand. One should create a structure that can be rebuilt with speed after a hurricane.

The northern wind of the winter and the summer hurricanes shape the people and rhythm of life. The weather is unsettled. Summers are hot and punctuated by thunderstorms, and the winters are cold in a way one would not expect. The people formed in the weather were much the same. A Pather can be warm and inviting at one time, switching to cold and foreboding before destroying everything you have. Pathers are salt of the earth people. They are deeply loyal and deeply local.

The Club

In the early 2000s, North Carolina became a land of opportunity for many. Three major research universities form the Research Triangle. North Carolina State in Raleigh, Duke University in Durham, and UNC-Chapel Hill make up the triangle's three points. Located near the center was the Research Triangle Park. The Research Triangle Park attracted national and international businesses. A low cost of living and mild climate made it easy to move to the triangle. People from the northern cities of New York and Chicago flocked to Raleigh. As businesses grew, talent from California's Silicon Valley and Washington, DC moved to Raleigh. The population swelled with a million people living in the greater Raleigh area by 2010.

Communities sprang up around the city of Raleigh, each designed in a Stepford fashion. Cary, Apex, Holly Springs, and Garner became modern suburbs with sprawling development eating up the land with planned perfection.

Raleigh became the spot to live out the American dream. Well-paying jobs in the "information industry" with retirement plans, health insurance, and a neighborhood pool. If one could grab the ideal of the 1950 suburb and transform it in 2010, one would see the city of Raleigh.

There are classes within the middle-class suburbs. The stratifications are built into neighborhoods—vast tracts of cookie-cutter homes in various price ranges. Driving through the suburbs, it becomes easy to identify these subclasses by the amount of brick and size of the house. Those who occupy the upper slice of the middle class gravitate to the country clubs of North Raleigh. Houses snuggled between fairways with large pools and social events at "the club." Neighborhoods designed for leisure and relaxation at your back door.

High-minded people fill the country clubs. Doctors, lawyers, professors, and businessmen socialize, complaining about "crime" and suggesting ways to fortify their neighborhood with gates and guards, not realizing that they are talking about building their prison. This cloistering provides safety and comfort, allowing one to disconnect from the world's problems outside its bounds.

The Club ends up mainly being transplants from cities in the north. Fleeing the high taxes that destroyed the economies, these new settlers created entire communities and neighborhoods. Like those fleeing Diamond City, the people needed a fresh start as life became too difficult in those cold northern states. The good jobs, cheap housing, and outstanding schools were all hallmarks of the new southern land rush. Many coming here as married couples, these families begin to lay down roots, starting families, buying their first home, and rooting for the local college teams. These families will have transformed Raleigh from a quiet southern city to the highest concentration of PhDs in America within a generation. It will be a model for the growth of a city in the information age.

The children of these transplants take to the southern culture with ease. They embrace college football and the gentle ways of the south. They also find comfort in the legacy of southern society, where classes socialize within classes. The children find it easy to identify their class by their club. With all of its isolation, these neighborhoods provide a peaceful place to grow up in what appears to be a relatively carefree childhood.

1

A Little Bit Country

When most people get to know Ellie, they are always confused by the paradox of runway good looks and southern country charm. Ellie and I first met when our parents moved to the Brier Creek community in North Raleigh when we were just five years old. Brier Creek Country Club was the heart of social activity for the community. Ellie's parents were a northern/southern marriage. What that means is Ellie's dad, Clint Painter, was from New York City and her mom, Emily, was from High Point, North Carolina. They were a perfect mix of southern charm and northern ambition. They had moved around a bit, living in different parts of the country until Clint became a professor of Nuclear Engineering at NC State. The new job brought them back to the south, where they found the perfect city and southern living mix. When my parents moved to town from California, I was too young to remember anything different. And for me, I can think of myself in no other way than a southerner.

Brier Creek Country Club grew out of an empty field about twenty minutes north of Raleigh. The city of Raleigh kept its relentless growth outward from downtown, slowly engulfing farmland and small towns. In early 2000, ground was broken on the Arnold Palmer designed golf course. The golf course would be the center of the country club, with the first houses completed in 2001. Ellie's family and mine were some of the first residents of the new community. There were only about a dozen houses at that time, and it would take another seven to eight years before the neighborhood was complete. I still recall the first time I met Ellie. I was outside, drawing on the sidewalk with chalk. I was working on a giant heart as part of my "I love Bear" design. Bear was our family dog, a Shitzu-Yorkie mix. Emily and Ellie pulled into her driveway next door. Ellie jumped out of the car and ran to me, and said, "Can I help?"

I could not think of a better way to begin a friendship, or a better way to describe Ellie. If you are lucky, you get to have a friend like Ellie. She is the one who offers to share her cookies at lunch, makes sure everyone gets included, and will send a text message just to see how you are doing. We became fast friends, and I feel like we saw each other every day until we went away to college.

Ellie, as a child, was a little too tall and too thin. She was pretty, but as a youngster, she was physically awkward. As children, we couldn't see that Ellie would grow up, and her tall thin figure would transform her into a stunningly beautiful young woman. The funny thing about Ellie is that this never changed her. In some ways, you could hate her. Beautiful *and* a heart of gold. Sometimes it didn't seem fair that Ellie could be blessed with both of these attributes. But, if anyone deserved to have beauty inside and out, it was Ellie.

In high school, I can recall how girls became ruthless as they jockeyed for social position, how Ellie laid it all on the line for me.

Ellie, "Do you have a date for the Junior Prom?"

"No, I am not sure if I am going to go. Even if I have a date, I don't think I will get invited to any after-parties," I said.

"That's crazy! You know you can always come with me and my date. We are going to Michelle's after the prom. It will be fun!" said Ellie.

"I don't think you understand. Everybody likes you, but not everybody likes everybody. Michelle made a point to tell me she is having a party *and* made it clear that I didn't get an invite."

Ellie, "That won't stand. I am not like that. Why be fake? Why keep people away? The more, the merrier. You just need to find a date, and I will do the rest."

I later found out that Ellie told Michelle that she couldn't go to the party because I wasn't invited, and we already had plans. Everybody loved Ellie, and you couldn't have "the party" without her. Michelle backpedaled (lied) and said she never told me I wasn't invited, which I guess she technically didn't. Miraculously, I got a text asking me to the party, "AfTeR PaRtY – My house after prom – 10:30 - ??? – Bring PJ's and a snack to share." Once again, Ellie was there "to help".

The one thing Ellie never put a priority on was boys. While all of us girls went boy-crazy, she liked them as friends. Ellie went on a few dates but never had a boyfriend in high school. She preferred to keep her life simple and avoid the boy scene. She never realized the problems this caused for her in the background. Ellie never tied herself to a boy, and many girls were always worried their boy was secretly dating Ellie. If these girls had taken the time to know Ellie, they would have known that Ellie didn't want that sort of drama. She had a saying in high school, "Drama is as drama does." And she wanted less drama and more fun.

Ellie was a country club girl. She drove a Lexus, ate at the club, and wore designer clothes. There is another side of her that not many people see. Her other side usually came out late at night or on vacation. Ellie had a love of country music and the stories told in the songs. She loved to dance crazy, jump around and sing–or should I say shout–a song off-key. People missed that she didn't wear much makeup and was just naturally beautiful. They didn't get to see all the years we went camping together, and her favorite part was sleeping on the dock by the lake under the stars. Ellie loves the finer things in life but also admires the simple things. As much as Ellie was a girl from the country club, she always felt the pull of country life.

Ever since we were young, our families would make a trip to an East Coast beach every year. Our parents preferred the busyness of Myrtle Beach, South Carolina, with the high-rise hotels, mini-golf courses at every corner, and crowds on the streets and beaches. Once, when Ellie and I were on our annual family beach vacation, we sat on the fishing pier as the sun was going down and talked about our dreams.

"Alice, what do you think our husbands will look like?" asked Ellie.

"Hahaha! You are crazy, Ellie. I don't even have a boyfriend. How can I think of a husband?" I laughed.

"Maybe you can't say what he will look like, but what would he *be* like? I think about it all the time! I don't care what he looks like, but I want someone that wants to live outside the city. Maybe on a farm or something like that." Ellie pondered some more. "It could even be some place at the coast? There are all these little towns. Remember when we went to Ocracoke? And how simple life looked there?"

"Do you really think you could live somewhere like that? I mean, we grew up in a country club with Target across the street and restaurants everywhere. What would you do if you needed something? I mean, there are no stores around," I commented.

Ellie explained, "Simple. I just want something simple. I don't know why, but I love the idea of just having my husband and family—dinners at home with friends. The kids are running in the backyard and the biggest worry is if the boys will track mud into the house. It just seems sooo much better than running to the country club, dance lessons, cheer practice, and all those crazy things our parents did for us. All I really wanted was to have time with them and not the crazy cheerleading coach. You know...I might feel different later on, but it seems simple right now."

"I think for me…I can't imagine living in a small town. I like good food and being able to go shopping. I can't even think about having to drive for an hour to get to the store. You always do your own thing, though, so it doesn't surprise me. BUT," I insisted, "you can't go live somewhere that I don't want to because then we wouldn't be neighbors! Hahaha!"

"Someday, we will go our separate ways, but we will always be like sisters. I can't see boys or distance coming between us. Love you, girl!" Ellie reminded me.

After that conversation, I knew we would always stay in touch, but our paths would diverge sometime in the future. I would never have guessed at the adventure Ellie's life would become.

2

A Little Bit City

Bodhi Salter's house growing up was just under 1,500 square feet. It had one bathroom and three bedrooms—a small kitchen and a living room just big enough to fit a recliner and couch. Bodhi always felt lucky because he only had one sibling, a sister Beth, and didn't share a room. Off the back of the house was a large deck. A tin roof covered the deck that overlooked Bogue Sound from the shore of Salter Path. This town bore his family's name and was founded by his ancestors more than 150 years ago.

The Salters were a fishing family. Not like the folks from Raleigh that come to the North Carolina coast to fish for fun. His family earned their living by working on the water. The folks in town knew Bodhi's dad as Freddie, although his formal name was Frederick. Freddie inherited a shrimp boat from his dad. The old shrimp boat spewed out black smoke as its diesel engine chugged along. The nets dragged the bottom of Bogue and Pamlico sounds, pulling up Carolina green shrimp that grow bigger throughout the summer. One perfect fall, he and his dad brought in fifty bushels of shrimp in one night. At $28 per bushel, this was enough money for the family to live for months.

Those who earn their living on the water are known as watermen. And if you grow up in a family of watermen, you begin learning the trade early. At eight years old, Bodhi spent his time cleaning the shrimp boat after school. By the time he was ten, he knew how to mend a shrimp net. At twelve, he was going out shrimping as often as he could with his father to work the nets. Bodhi had begun to see his future as another generation of watermen working to keep tradition and family going.

Bodhi loved his family. His sister Beth was three and three-quarters years younger than him. Girls and boys in Salter Path were one and the same. While girls might play with dolls in the evenings, they ran with all the other kids during the day. The Salter Path children spent the summer days playing in the sounds and on the beaches. They always seemed to be "lightly salted" from playing in the saltwater. Their dark tans and a community full of family allowed the kids to run free. There was no getting away with anything because an aunt, uncle, or cousin was always watching. Generations of living in the Path meant that the Salters, Willards, Joneses, and Snows were all now related in one way or another.

Despite these family ties, memories ran long. In a place where hurricanes destroy homes overnight, relationships have long histories that stand the test of time. The Snows built boats for a living. They didn't make the high-end yachts of Jarrett Bay but rather the working boats that earned a living for the people of Carteret County. They built shrimping boats, charter boats, skiffs for clamming, and flat bottom boats for tending crab pots in the shallow Bogue Sound water.

In December 2000, the Snows began building a shrimp boat for Bodhi Salter's grandfather, Jerry. Jerry planned to finish his fishing career on this boat and turn the craft over to Bodhi's father to continue the tradition. In the meantime, Bodhi's father would fish the *Lady B*.

The Salter family would have two boats working the waters of North Carolina.

The new boat looked beautiful. It seemed like a new luxury car compared to the old boat. The winches were fast, the motor was quiet, the crew quarters were comfortable, and the nets did not smell of rotting seafood. The fresh white paint and twin diesel engines made the new boat the pride of the fleet. Jerry bought the boat with cash, a lifetime of fishing revenues saved for this purchase. Jerry named it *Legacy*.

In the late fall of 2001, when young Bodhi was just ten years old, his grandfather, Jerry, and Uncle Nathan headed out on the *Legacy* to make one last late-season shrimp run in the Pamlico Sounds. That evening a storm blew in from the north, stronger than expected, but nothing unusual for seasoned watermen who have spent a lifetime on the water. The wind and waves pounded the one-year-old boat throughout the night. At 3:21 a.m., the Coast Guard Station at Fort Fisher received a call on the UHF Radio from the *Legacy*. She was taking on water, and the hull had a large crack. The Coast Guard dispatched a helicopter out of Elizabeth City, North Carolina, to search for the vessel on the Pamlico Sound. At 4:39 a.m. on November thirteenth, the Coast Guard helicopter located the *Legacy* and approached to assist. At 4:42 a.m., the lights flickered on the *Legacy*, and shortly after that, she burst into flames. The fire and waves took the lives of all hands on deck.

The loss of watermen impacts an entire community. The close-knit fabric of Salter Path meant that most of the townspeople lost a family member. The Coast Guard recovered the bodies of the men from the sound. The townfolk laid them to rest in the cemetery next to the Methodist Church.

The Coast Guard investigates all commercial boating accidents. In the investigation, marine salvage workers lifted the *Legacy's* remains from the bottom of the sound. After six months, the Coast Guard could not definitively say what caused the hull to be breached. It was unclear whether the boat struck an object in the water or if there was a defect in the building of the boat. A lightning strike compromised the fuel system and created diesel mist that eventually was ignited by an unknown source, causing the fire.

This news was difficult for the Salter Path community. The Snows had built the boat that led to the death of family and community members. The town constantly rumbled over what the Snows should do to make it up to the Salters. Many thought they should build them a new boat. Others believed that the Snows had no fault and that Jerry Salter had captained his craft into a dangerous storm, and he alone was to blame. The controversy raged in the underground, creating fractures in the town of Salter Path.

The Snows' boat building facility was located just across from the public beach access. People parked at the beach access would wander over to the facility from time to time. These gatherings happened on the weekends when the boatyard was closed. It was an easy place for youths to do a bit of underage drinking or partake in weed smoking. The boat yard workers would find the evidence on Monday morning in the form of empty beer cans and a few roaches. The trash was usually not much of a concern for the Snow family. They knew this was just something that comes with living at the beach.

One spring morning at 5:37 a.m. in 2002, a call came into the Salter Path Fire Department. A fire had broken out at the Snows' boatyard. Units from Salter Path, Emerald Isle, and Atlantic Beach responded, trying to extinguish the fire. Crews battled the blaze for six hours, preventing it from spreading to the Grand Villas Motel across the street. As the fire raged and the town came to see what was happening, Susan Snow began screaming that her husband, Tom Snow, and owner of Snow Boatyard, was nowhere to be found. Later that day, they found Tom's remains burned in the boatyard.

As the town came to grips with losing one of its main businesses and a longtime resident, Tom Snow, the investigation would show that the fire started when solvents used in boat manufacturing ignited. The fire led to the destruction of the facility and the death of Mr. Snow as he tried to save his business.

When the town came out to mourn Tom's passing, rumors began to swirl that the fire might not have been an accident. The feud between the Salters and Snows was an undercurrent since the *Legacy* went down in the Pamlico. Many felt that Bodhi's dad blamed the Snows for a poorly made boat that led to his father's death and the loss of the family nest egg. The Snows benefited from that nest egg and were never willing to admit any fault, insisting that the *Legacy* must have hit something like a floating tree flushed out of a river into the sound by the fall storms. Rumors pointed to Freddie as the one who started the fire at Snow Boatyard to get back at them for building a faulty boat.

What happened over the next year and into 2003 was just short of an all-out feud between the Salters and Snows. Families drew lines, and the town became divided. The Joneses and Salters aligned together against the Snows and Willards. On Friday and Saturday nights, the people in the town would gather at Frank and Clara's, a local beach bar where the drinks come in plastic cups, and bartenders serve beers only in cans. It could be a fun place, but a fight would break out more often than not.

Those fights became more and more frequent between the two sides of the feud. Snows and Salters, Joneses and Snows, Willards and Salters, drawing lines in the sand—letting frustrations and accusations boil over. The small and peaceful town of Salter Path was like a mother trying to restrain a temper tantrum toddler.

The tensions ran so high that longtime residents began to move away. Bodhi's Aunt Kristy picked up and left for a more peaceful existence in Raleigh. The world turned upside down in Salter Path, with friendships and families strained.

One summer night in June of 2003, Bodhi decided to sneak out of the house to chase ghost crabs on the beach with his cousins. Throughout the night, Bodhi and his cousins bagged thirty-four ghost crabs. They would save these crabs and sell them to vacationers at the public beach access the next day. They would put them in small wooden boxes and sell them for $10 each to kids making their way to the beach.

At 1:21 a.m. on June 6, 2003, a call would again come into the Salter Path Fire Department. There was a house fire at Freddie Salter's house. The family was said to be home at the time.

As the house burned, the sirens called the boys from the beach. Young Bodhi broke over the dunes in a full-out sprint; he dropped to his knees. Tears burst into his eyes as he saw his home in flames. He tried to stand and go to his house, but he could not walk as his legs seemed to turn to jelly. He watched from across the street as the firefighters struggled to save his home. There was no hope, and the house burned to the ground before he could even grasp what was happening.

Young Bodhi, curly dark brown hair just touching his shoulders and soft brown eyes, had everything he knew turned into smoke that night. Over the next day, they would confirm that Bodhi's father, mother, and sister all died in the fire. The fire began in the stairwell and progressed rapidly. The family may not have even had the chance to wake before the smoke overcame them. There were few remains to mourn, making the loss even more painful for Bodhi. In a night, Bodhi had become an orphan. He had no mother, father, or siblings at twelve years old.

The feud in Salter Path seemed to have taken a turn. It had moved into what seemed to be a murder of nearly an entire family. Retaliation against Freddie Salter seemed to be almost complete. There was never any hard evidence of arson, just rumors that pushed tensions in the town higher. Now, the stories turned to the Snow family. That they had started the fire at the Salter's house, taking the lives of three, including young, sweet Beth. Even with help from the State Bureau of Investigation, investigations by Salter Path Police could never pinpoint a cause for the fire. The house burned too hot and fast to have any evidence remaining. The Salter Path feud had taken the lives of five Salters, one Snow, and left Bodhi an orphan. These events would take Bodhi from a rural coastal community to the suburbs of Raleigh.

3

Easterly's

Aunt Kristy had moved away not long before the fire at her brother's house. The fire killed not only her brother, Freddie, but also her sister-in-law and beautiful young niece. She landed in the small town of Garner, North Carolina. Garner was situated just outside of Raleigh. It served as a bedroom community for the city. Single, with an easy-going beach upbringing and a tan, fit beach body, it wasn't long before she had connected with Bill Easterly, a jeweler in Garner. Bill Easterly's jewelry store was a staple of Garner. A family-owned business, with Bill having deep roots in the community. Everyone flocked to Bill's store for anniversary gifts, engagement rings, and "I'm sorry" gifts. Bill had created a nice business, and when Kristy Salter walked through the door looking for a job, it was easy for him to see that a young and attractive woman with a low country accent could do well selling jewelry. He gave her a job, and she performed amazingly, selling more than anyone else in her first three months. Her easy way with customers made them feel good about spending more than they should.

It was only a matter of time, and all who saw them knew that Kristy and Bill would become an item before they did. Bill's happy outlook and Kristy's carefree beach attitude made them a natural couple. Within the year, Bill asked Kristy to marry him. Bill and Kristy set the wedding date for November of 2005. A lengthy engagement, but there was no rush in the easy life of Garner.

"Hello, this Kristy," she said, answering the phone.

"Ms. Salter? This is Detective Natchez from the State Bureau of Investigation."

"How can I help you, Detective?" Kristy questioned.

"Ma'am, I am sorry that I have to call you with this news. Last night there was a fire at Freddie's, your brother's house," he stammered.

"What?"

Detective Natchez struggled to stay professional, "Freddie's house caught on fire. It was fast-moving. The fire department was there quickly." The detective lost his train of thought. He had planned what to say, but the words didn't come. Finally, he uttered, "Ma'am, they died. Freddie, Nathalie, and Beth. They were lost in the fire. All of them, but Bodhi. He was not at home. He is alive."

Confused, Kristy asked, "Wait, what are you saying? Are you saying they are dead? Everyone but Bodhi? This doesn't make sense? Why? How?"

"We don't know how the fire started. All we know is that it was fast moving, and they never had a chance. I am sorry," he finished. "I do need to ask you a question. Would you be willing, or um, can you take in Bodhi? If not, he will become a ward of the state and go to a foster home."

"What? Yes, of course. He's my blood. He isn't going to any fucking foster home!" Kristy exclaimed.

"Yes, of course, that's what I thought. Can you come to Salter Path to pick him up? He is staying with Beatrice Jones," the detective said.

"I am on my way," Kristy confirmed.

Bodhi came to Garner in the back seat of Bill Easterly's Tahoe. He sat silent. Kristy was kind and gentle. Bodhi was still in shock. He would have to return in a few days to lay his family to rest. At age twelve, thrown into a world alone. Finally, Bodhi said, "What happens next?"

Kristy fumbled for words, "You are coming to live with us, Bodhi. We will always be here for you."

"What happens to all my friends? Will I see them?" Bodhi inquired.

"They can come and visit whenever they want. You will see we have enough room for everyone at the house," Kristy tried to assure him. The truth was Kristy left Salter Path knowing things were getting out of hand, and she wasn't entirely sure it was safe for Bodhi to return. It ran through her head that the fire was not an accident but an intentional act of revenge. Kristy knew there was a more sinister motive behind the fire.

When Bodhi got to Bill Easterly's house, he was surprised to find a large home just on the outskirts of Raleigh. There was some land that might offer a chance to get away, but he didn't know any of the neighbors and couldn't wrap his head around living in the middle of a bunch of strangers.

In the years that followed, Bodhi would only return to Salter Path once more. The trip back was to attend a ceremony laying his family to rest. For Bodhi, this all happened in a fog. At just twelve years old, he was old enough to remember but not understand how these events would change his life.

4

Talent

Ellie didn't know her talent. Everyone figured her talent was simple. She was beautiful. For a girl, this can become her defining characteristic. It wasn't in her smile or her kind words for Ellie, but her talent was in her ability never to give up. You might call it grit. Many people saw her move through life easily, but she had her struggles growing up. Ellie always had to try. She wasn't afraid of hard work. She knew her talent was her willingness to take on the things others avoided.

"Ellie, what do you think about college? Where do you want to go?" I asked her.

"Ugh. Alabama! They have the best college football. But you know, my parents don't want me that far away. I will probably end up somewhere in-state," she responded to Alice.

"I want someplace small where I can get to know everyone. Our big high school killed me. I just want a few people to be close to."

"I know you better than my favorite song. You would die in a small college. You will probably just chase your boyfriend wherever he goes," Ellie responded.

"I know you are probably right. My mom says to do the best for *me* and not for *we*," I whined.

"Parents are so cringy. They always think they are funny. It just makes me want to do the opposite. If I can't go to Alabama, I want to go to NC State. That's where I really want to go, but I probably won't get accepted," Ellie let me in on her desire.

"You will get in! Who wouldn't want Ellie Painter?" I told her.

I was wrong, and Ellie was right. She did get into Alabama, but her parents didn't want her twelve hours away. Also, Ellie didn't get into NC State. She would take a path through Meredith College to NC State. In four years, she would graduate using all her academic talents. Ellie had the whole college experience living at her sorority and learning all the liquors that go into an East Village trashcan.

Ellie still waded in the shallow end of the relationship pool. Her friends could not understand why she did not have a boyfriend–beautiful, fun, and football loving–what else could a college boy ask for?

"I can't understand why you don't have a boyfriend?" I asked her one night in our junior year of college.

Ellie responded, "I only want to be serious with someone I can be serious with. I want to keep my love for those who deserve it. I get too close and want to save my heartbreak for when it is worth it."

"I never knew that about you. I guess there is always something to learn about someone," I told her.

If you did not know Ellie's story, you would imagine she glided through life. She is like a duck, smooth and polished on top but paddling fiercely underwater. Ellie would never give up. She would dig in and start working when she decided on a task. Not much could discourage her from figuring something out. In college, this meant many late nights studying hard. She would graduate from NC State in the spring of 2017.

Ellie and I grew a bit apart during college. I ended up going to Appalachian State in the mountains of North Carolina. For me, I enjoyed the change to the small city, getting away from the hustle and bustle of Raleigh. The beautiful mountains and skiing in the winter were a change from country club life. Ellie and I stayed in touch, and whenever we were on break, we were neighbors in the country club once again.

In my senior year of college, I thought I had found the man of my dreams. We dated for most of the year, and I had the idea that I would hear the question that every girl one day hopes to hear. I was heartbroken when heading into graduation week, my college beau told me he got a job in Georgia and would move there after school. I waited for the next question, but it never came. It was a soft breakup. He gave me the sign that this was his decision, and I wasn't a part of it. Within a few weeks, he would make it official. I would be heartbroken.

The only one I could turn to was Ellie. After graduation, we were home, and we spent most of those weeks watching Hallmark movies and poking at job applications online. This period was that lull in our lives when you are unsure of the direction, and everything feels like it could turn for the better or the worst.

After a week or so, Ellie finally announced that we were getting out of the house.

"Alice. A friend of mine is having a birthday party for a college friend. We are going. We need a change of scenery," Ellie said.

"I am not sure I am up for it. I mean, after the breakup, I am still just, blah."

"Alice Grace, this is exactly why we are going to the party. You need to get beyond the blah," Ellie directed me. Ellie and I got out of our pajamas and got ready for the party.

5

Trashcan

I typed the address of the party into my phone. I decided to drive, and I had my reasons.

"Are you sure we should go? I am still not ready to see people," I said to Ellie.

"Alice, you can't hide forever. Next week, you have that job interview, and you need to get your mind in the right state. You don't want to be blah during the interview," Ellie encouraged me.

"I know. I just got into a funk. I need to get in the right state of mind for some fun." I concentrated on changing my thoughts.

"So, Amanda was someone that I hung out with in college. We weren't super good friends, but we always had fun together. Her brother just broke up with his girlfriend a few weeks ago, and he has been in the dumps. She just decided she wanted to move away. Sound familiar?" Ellie questioned me.

"Ellie! Hell no! You are not trying to set me up with this guy. All I need is a rebound or to be a rebound! I am turning this car around!" I said like a mother scolding a child.

"Alice. Stop it. This party isn't a setup. There will be a bunch of people, and we are all just going to hang out. It will be fun. I heard that the house is out in the country, and they have a fire pit and stuff to do. We needed to get out of the house." Ellie had made up her mind, and there was no changing it.

"Okay, but if this becomes a setup, you can uber home," I told Ellie.

As we pulled into the driveway, the sun was just beginning its evening show. The house was white with a large front porch. You could see it had once been an estate house for the upper class of Garner. Large oak trees in the yard and circle driveway brought you right to the front door. The sign in the yard read, "Easterly Farms." I found the sign a bit funny because it was not much of a farm other than a barn in the back, a tractor under a shed, and what looked like a few acres of soybeans behind the house. By Raleigh standards, any land that was more than an acre with a garden might be called a farm. It was nice and just a little bit country.

"Hey, Amanda!" Ellie said while hugging a pretty dark-haired girl our age.

"Ellie! How have you been? I know it has only been a few weeks, but it seems like forever since we graduated! What have you been up to?" Amanda inquired.

"You know the usual. I am looking for a job, filling out application after application. Hopefully, something will come through soon. Do you remember my friend, Alice?"

"Hi. Thank you for the invite. It's good to see you again," I said to Amanda.

"Alice, good to see you again. I know it's been a while. C'mon Alice, I want to introduce you to my brother." Amanda took me by the arm and started pulling me away, leaving Ellie by herself on the porch.

"Ellie! No!" I said, half-laughing because Ellie knew I needed this for many reasons, including having some fun and flirting with a boy. I needed back the confidence I used to have.

As Amanda and I disappeared into the house to find Amanda's

brother, Bodhi Salter walked out the door and onto the porch with two red solo cups in his hands, where Ellie was standing alone.

"Hello, I'm Bodhi," he said to Ellie.

Little do most men know that it isn't what they say to a girl but how they say it. Bodhi sounded casual and confident. Not arrogant, not wanting anything, just welcoming and firm in his tone. Ellie blushed. She didn't even know why. A *boy* saying hello was nothing new. Something in the way he said hello; she knew this was something different.

Ellie pulled herself together and said, "Hi. I'm Ellie. How do you know Brian?"

"Brian and I went to college together at High Point University. We graduated a few years ago, and he has a job in Raleigh. So we still hang out a bit. How about you?" Bodhi asked Ellie.

"I only know Brian a little bit. His sister and I went to college together, and we're good friends. We graduated this year. Brian came to hang out a few times, and Amanda thought it would be fun to get together to celebrate his birthday."

Ellie realized her mistake. She had pushed the conversation into a dead end and was panicking that Bodhi might just walk on by. She didn't know that Bodhi was headed to the backyard with a drink in hand for another girl. But when he saw Ellie, he stopped in his tracks. He was frozen like a deer in headlights, struggling to make words come out of his mouth. His heart rate was finally coming down. He was sweating, but luckily it was June in North Carolina, and the heat and humidity meant that the sweat wasn't a bit out of place.

Ellie jumped in, "Where can I get a drink?"

"Well, you can have this one." Bodhi extended the drink to her.

Ellie paused. An awkward moment with a strange boy, randomly holding an extra drink. "What is it?"

"Oh, yeah. Sorry, I should have asked. It's a trashcan, but we have everything inside," Bodhi said, unsure.

"Are you kidding? What do you have?" Ellie asked.

"A trashcan," Bodhi stated.

"Uhhhh…... These are my favorites," Ellie said, taking the drink from Bodhi. "I think East Village knows me as the trash girl." Ellie heard that awkward statement coming from her mouth.

"Trash girl?" Bodhi sounded concerned.

"Oh. Yeah, it is just what I always ordered when I was there. Probably too many on some nights," Ellie tried to laugh it off.

Bodhi, getting his wits about him, said, "Can I show you around? The drinks and food are inside, and there is a corn hole and fire pit out back."

Bodhi and Ellie walked into the house of Bill Easterly and his Aunt Kristy. Bodhi had grown up and now stood just slightly more than six feet tall. He had broad shoulders and rugged facial features, slightly softened as if Norman Rockwell had painted his face.

Throughout the years, Bodhi had tried to process what had happened in his childhood. He never fully digested the events but had become well-adjusted in his new setting. His aunt never took him back to Salter Path. She felt it would be too painful, and the feud continued to simmer. Instead, Aunt Kristy built a life for Bodhi. She married Bill, but they never had children of their own. They raised Bodhi as their own. Bill's successful business allowed him to provide a good life in Garner. Bodhi grew up on the Easterly Farm, where he had some freedoms like in Salter Path. He rode dirt bikes, played in the woods, built forts, and befriended neighborhood kids. In high school, Bodhi would play lacrosse and wrestle. He was a good athlete but also a good student. When it came time to go to college, he decided on High Point University, where he continued to play lacrosse while studying data sciences. If you didn't know Bodhi's story, you would never think he had a tragic childhood.

"So, Bodhi, where did you grow up?" Ellie asked him.

"Right here. This farm is my childhood home," Bodhi always said this because explaining everything else was more than most cared to hear.

"Really? This place is so neat. I mean, it's like you are in the country and the city at the same time," Ellie stated.

"Yes. It is family land. My dad inherited it from his parents. They used to own half of Garner. Different family members sold off the original farm bit by bit when the price was right. This old farmhouse is the last part of the homestead that we own, but I think the best part," Bodhi explained about the family legacy.

"So, it's Bodhi Easterly?" Ellie is trying to dig a bit deeper.

"Uh, well, no. My last name is Salter."

"So, is Bill your stepdad, then?" Ellie asked.

"Yes. Let's just keep at that. Bill adopted me, but I kept my family name. And he was a great dad to me," Bodhi cut the conversation off.

Ellie sensed more to the story but knew it was not the time to hear it. She let it go and changed the conversation.

"You said there are corn hole boards out back? Let's see if you are any good," Ellie poked. "I will get Alice and Brian. Meet us out back!"

The sun was now melting into the horizon over the soybean field. The lightning bugs were getting ready for their show, and the humidity became palpable as the sun's warmth went away and the coolness of the evening set in.

The two couples finished their first game of corn hole, and Ellie joked to Bodhi, "Well, I think you could practice on these boards some more because Brian kicked your butt!" Ellie was finishing her trashcan, and Bodhi noticed that.

"Let me get us another drink. I will meet you at the bonfire." Bodhi told Ellie.

"Okay," was all that Ellie said as she watched Bodhi walk away. I

23

could see the glow on her face as she looked his way.

When Bodhi was out of earshot, I headed straight for Ellie. "C'mon. Let's go to the bathroom," I said, grabbing her by the arm.

"Well?" I asked Ellie.

"Well, what?" Ellie said with a smile.

I knew something was up here. I could see Ellie was different. She had changed in the few hours since we arrived at the party. She seemed softer, with a glow about her.

"Ellie, we have been friends since forever. And I know! I can see it. What did he say to you?" I asked her.

"Nothing. It isn't what Bodhi said; it is how he said it. I can't describe it. It feels like I am going to float away." Ellie heard the cliché coming from her mouth. "Oh, gosh. That sounds childish. I only met him a few hours ago. Why do I feel like this?"

"So what does he do for a living?" I questioned Ellie.

"I have no idea. I haven't even asked! Hahaha!" Ellie realized how different the conversation with Bodhi was. It wasn't about formalities. It was a conversation of the heart. It didn't matter the content because there was emotion and connection. Ellie never believed in love at first sight, but this made her think there was such a thing.

Ellie and I headed to the fire. Brian and Bodhi were waiting there for us. I had not had the chance to mention Brian to Ellie. Ellie always put others first, and this was not like her. This boy was something different for Ellie. As for Brian, if he played his cards correctly, there might be a kiss for him this evening.

"Another trashcan? Trash girl?" Bodhi joked.

"Dork. Yes, trashcan, please," Ellie told him.

He handed her the drink, and they went to sit on a bench near the fire.

"I have to tell you something, Ellie, because I have enjoyed our time tonight," Bodhi started to explain. The tone in his voice made Ellie's stomach sink. How could things go from so high to so low with one sentence?

"Okay," said Ellie.

"I like to have a cigarette now and then when I drink," Bodhi stated.

Ellie paused. She thought to herself, *This was big news? This secret was the 'Oh shit! he is a fake' moment.* Ellie was relieved this was the reason her stomach sank. He smoked cigarettes when he drank. Ellie then had to admit something back.

"I have something to tell you. I smoke when I drink, too," Ellie revealed that flaw as well.

Bodhi and Ellie laughed. And then Bodhi reached into his pocket to pull out a pack of Marlboro Lights. He offered Ellie a cigarette which she took. Bodhi reached into his other pocket and pulled out a BIC lighter covered in rhinestones.

Ellie looked at the lighter. "Well, I did not expect you to have a rhinestone-covered lighter. Where in the world did you get that?"

Bodhi smiled and laughed under his breath. "It's my Aunt Kristy's lighter. She gets these covers from Bill's sister that lives in Texas. You can't find them out east. They handmake them putting the rhinestones on one by one."

Ellie took the lighter from Bodhi and examined it. "It is kind of nice," she said. Then she lit her cigarette.

The new couple sat and stared at the bonfire. That night they would share their first kiss. It was easy, natural, and unforgettable for Ellie.

6

Patience

Ellie had come to know the history of Bodhi's family. After they had been dating for a few months, Bodhi decided he needed to share his past hurt with Ellie. She needed to understand who she loved.

"Ellie, I think it's time I tell you about my family. Not the Easterlys or my aunt, but my mom and dad," Bodhi started. "I am an orphan. I don't like to tell many people because I had a good childhood in a loving home. And people feel sorry for me if I tell them, and they shouldn't," Bodhi paused.

"Okay," was all Ellie could muster.

"There is a town in eastern North Carolina along the coast named Salter Path. This town is where I lived until I was twelve years old. My ancestors named it." Bodhi reached into his pocket and pulled out a few pieces of worn and folded newspapers.

Bodhi laid out three articles clipped from the *Tideland News*. The first headline read "*Legacy* Lost: Search Underway for Survivors." There was a picture of a large shrimp boat with a family standing in front of it. The caption under the photo read, "The *Legacy* christened in Salter Path, North Carolina. Commissioned by the Salter family to be built at Snow Boatyard. She was the largest boat ever built at

Snow's and believed to be lost in an early winter storm." In the picture was a young Bodhi standing next to his mother, holding his young sister, Beth. His dad, grandfather, grandmother, and Aunt Kristy were also in the picture.

The second article read, "Local Business Destroyed in Fire." The image in this article showed Snow Boatyard in flames. The caption read, "The Snow Boatyard was destroyed in an early morning fire. The local boat builder was surrounded by controversy since the loss of the *Legacy*." The final article headlined, "House Fire takes the Life of Three. Only Son Survives." The picture shows Freddie Salter's house reduced to ashes the morning after the fire.

"What does this all mean?" Ellie looked puzzled and worried.

Bodhi began, "These are the facts that I know. My grandfather and father were watermen. They made a living by shrimping. My grandfather saved his whole life to purchase a new shrimp boat for my dad, Freddie. It was going to be his legacy to the family. The local boat builder was the Snow family and longtime friends." Bodhi took a pause and drank from a water bottle. His voice was beginning to break. "My grandfather died on the boat in the Pamlico Sound when the hull cracked, and the boat sank. Some people blamed the Snows for building a boat they should not have. They had never built a boat that large, and most think it was irresponsible of them. A couple of years later, the Snow Boatyard burned to the ground. No one is sure why, but the Snows blamed the Salters, and the police never determined a cause. Then about a year later, I snuck out of the house to run around on the beach with my cousins. When I heard the sirens, it was too late, and my parent's house was already almost burned to the ground. My parents and baby sister died in the fire."

"Oh, my God. Bodhi, I don't know what to say," Ellie tried to console Bodhi.

"There is nothing to say. My Aunt Kristy left Salter Path earlier in the year. She took me in and eventually adopted me. When she and Bill married, he adopted me. Since my family's memorial, I have never been back to Salter Path."

"How did the fire at your parent's house start?" Ellie asked.

"I don't think they ever figured it out. I asked my aunt, and she said the investigation just showed the house burned very fast. They couldn't tell how it started. I always figured it was just an old dry house, and once the fire started, it went fast," he explained.

"I can't even imagine. How did you move on?" Ellie tried to sympathize.

"Honestly. I haven't ever really had anyone to talk to about it. My aunt and Bill always believed that talking about it just made it worse. I just tried to imagine it as a bad dream. It happened, but it didn't truly affect you. I was onto a new life almost immediately after the fire. My aunt was there for me to make sure I had everything I needed."

"I won't even…I can't even," Ellie stammered.

"It's fine. Now and then, when I was young, it would get to me. I would wonder what it would be like to have a little sister. I wonder if I would still be in Salter Path as a waterman working on a shrimp boat. Now that I am older, I see it as walking down a path. You get far enough along, and you don't have the energy to turn around, so you keep going to see where the path ends. I sometimes think about going back. I know that I still have family there. I just don't know how they would feel about me coming back."

"Well, maybe one day, you will be ready to go back. And you should know that I will be there with you to support you. I love you, Bodhi Salter," Ellie affirmed her commitment to Bodhi.

——————

There are times in our life when we have to have patience. Maybe you remember that week leading up to Christmas as a child. You knew that Santa Claus would fill Christmas morning with gifts and dreams, and waiting for that day was torture. Waiting, in a way, also makes things better. Things need to happen in time, and at the right time, and at the right place. Often we do not see that, and we lose patience.

Since their first meeting on the Easterly Farm, Bodhi and Ellie had become inseparable. They spent all their time together. They were both doing well in their careers, working for bio-pharmaceutical companies located in the Research Triangle Park.

In September of 2019, the couple traveled to the mountains of North Carolina. After a hike to the top of the highest peak east of the Mississippi River, Mount Mitchell, Bodhi got down on one knee to ask the biggest question of his life.

"Ellie, will you marry me?"

Ellie fell onto him. Hugging him and knocking him over, crying, and shouting "YES!"

This "yes" would start the planning of a wedding for the fall of 2021.

When they walked down the mountain as an engaged couple, Ellie already had half the wedding planned. First, she had to call her parents and tell them the news. Ellie was deathly nervous. She didn't know why; her parents loved Bodhi. Could it be that this was one more step away from them and into adulthood? Bodhi reminded her that her parents already knew the plan. A couple of weeks ago, he had stopped by their house to ask her dad for her hand in marriage. Ellie's parents even helped with the proposal plans by reserving a bed and breakfast in Boone for them.

With the call to her parents out of the way, Ellie laid out her plan to Bodhi.

"I want to get married at the farm," Ellie insisted.

"Where would we do that, and do you think your country club friends would want to come to the farm for a wedding?" Bodhi questioned.

"Everyone gets married at the country club. If we get married at the farm, it will be our wedding. It will be our style, not a cookie-cutter country club wedding. I think everyone will have fun!" Ellie exclaimed.

Bodhi thought for a moment. "You know, we could put up a big tent overlooking the fields in the back. We could have a bonfire in the fire pit like the first night we met; heck, I might even make you a trashcan!"

"Hahaha, I haven't had a trashcan in a while...but one hundred percent I am having one on our wedding night!" Ellie laughed.

Ellie and Bodhi finalized the wedding plans. They would have an outdoor fall wedding to escape the summer heat. Everyone would be encouraged to come in a country-western theme. There would be boots, jeans, and sundresses. There would be a sit-down five-course meal under the tent with appetizers beforehand and a wedding cake for dessert. They would have a bonfire in the fire pit, dancing, and corn hole. The marriage would be a time to celebrate in a city/country mix of styles that had come to define Ellie and Bodhi's relationship. The wedding will be like nothing their friends had been to before and they would never forget it.

Ellie and Bodhi had to be patient waiting for the big day as their engagement would be appropriately long, with the wedding date two years in the future from their engagement. During this engagement, Bodhi and Ellie would grow ever closer. Ellie felt a bit embarrassed that she loved to tell people Bodhi was her fiancé. For some reason, this seemed like such a special time where two people are so committed, but not fully. It can either push a couple apart or bring them closer together. For Ellie, she could feel the pressure of the engagement bringing her and Bodhi closer together.

Ellie and Bodhi would spend their engagement refining plans for the wedding, traveling, looking at houses, and talking about the future. The time between engagement and marriage was magical for them as their careers took off, and their dreams seemed to be lining up.

As the wedding approached, it was time to start deciding on the guest list. There were apparent inclusions, close friends, neighbors who were important in their life, and family. Ellie began to make her list of aunts, uncles, and cousins. Then, her stomach dropped. It occurred to her that Bodhi only had Aunt Kristy and Bill Easterly. All of his other family were either dead or estranged. Bodhi had not talked to anyone in Salter Path for more than a dozen years. Ellie knew she needed to encourage Bodhi to connect with his family.

"Ummm, Bodhi, do you have a minute?" Ellie asked.

Bodhi looked up from a video game he was trying to defeat. "What's up, honey?"

"I was working on the wedding invites, and we still have room for about ten or fifteen more people. I was wondering if you might think about reaching out to your friends and family in Salter Path to see if any of them would like to come?" Ellie asked.

Bodhi was not aware Ellie had already decided he needed to connect with his hometown. She had thought about it and knew he needed to get more closure on his past. And she now believed she had found her way to push the issue.

"I thought about that, honestly, you know it is something that was, I mean, *is* my past. But what should I do, just send them invitations?" Bodhi asked Ellie sharply.

"I'll tell you what, we have some time in May. We can take a couple of weeks of vacation and rent a place in Salter Path. You can spend some time there and try to connect with friends and family. What do you think?" Ellie proposed.

Bodhi smiled, "I think I can do it with you by my side. I think I am ready. Let's plan on it."

7

Beach Town

In the time after Freddie's Salter's house burned down, things changed in the island feud. For a time, everyone took a breath, and it seemed like people might go about their way, putting the past behind them. However, in reality, the feud moved to more of a *cold* feud. There was an extensive investigation around the fire. The fire started near the bottom of the stairs blocking any exit. Investigators assumed that the smoke got to the family in the small house so quickly that they never even woke up. The only firm conclusions were that the fire burned very hot, and not much was left to analyze.

In town, the chief of police, Chief JJ Burns, took a lot of grief from the Salters and Joneses over not finding precisely *who* started the fire. On the other side of the town, the Snows and Willards believed that this was an accident, and the chief needed to find out *how* it started. Chief Burns did not pay much mind to the feud going on in town. He believed that it was more important for everyone to keep these tragic events quiet. The townfolks' paychecks depend on people coming to the beach in the summers, renting homes, and eating at restaurants. The chief knew that if they heard of a feud that led to the death of six, including an arson killing nearly an entire family, the vacationers might go elsewhere. He took the path of keeping things quiet and would not pass judgment.

Others in town did not care much for the folks from Raleigh. To many locals, vacationers were like palmettos bugs that came out during summer. The Salters, Willards, Snows, and Joneses could all do without the Raleigh visitors. They would prefer the squatter's simpler life, and while they were happy to take the money from the vacationers, they could get along without them just as well. They also did not much like the police. The vacationers brought the police to the Path because they caused trouble. No vacationers, no need for police. The Pathers could handle justice themselves. At least, that was their opinion.

Despite this tension, Chief Burns got along with the Pathers just fine. For the most part, he stayed out of their way. Chief Burns earned his title as chief. He came to Salter Path in 1986. At the time, he was the junior officer on the force. The police department was small—just five officers and a front desk worker. The officers took shifts making sure at least one officer was on duty all the time. At night, the lone officer would get back up from the neighboring towns of Atlantic Beach and Emerald Isle. During the day, two officers worked patrolling the beaches, tiny roads, and a short strand of state highway that made up the town. There usually was not much going on in their section of the island. The occasional speeder, someone who had too much to drink at Frank and Clara's bar, fishing hooks stuck in hands—these were what an officer in Salter Path expected during a shift. The main point was to be present and be there "just in case."

In June of 1995, things took a turn for the bizarre in Salter Path. Developers from the north built a few condominiums in Salter Path over the years. At one of them, The Summerwinds, a man barricaded himself in one of the units. He let the police and others know that he was armed and did not want to speak with anyone. At that time,

Officer JJ Burns was on duty and was the first to arrive on the scene. Officer Burns was calm and collected. He called for backup, and while his fellow officers and the SWAT team from the Carteret County Sheriff's department showed up, Officer Burns established communication with the man in the condo. After speaking with him for about thirty minutes, Officer Burns negotiated for the man to come out. The price for the man surrendering? Officer Burns needed to get a large shrimp burger, all the way, with slaw and hot sauce from the Big Tree Drive-in. When the shrimp burger arrived, the man had agreed to come out of the condo. It was early morning, and other officers had to go to Darrel Willard's house in Salter Path to wake him up and fire up the fryers. Within twenty minutes, a hot fresh shrimp burger was on the way. The man came out without a scuffle, collected his shrimp burger, and got into the back of Officer Burn's patrol car. After that incident, Officer Burns became known for his reasonable way, and in 1998 the town selected him as the chief of police.

In 2003, when Freddie Salter's house burned, Chief Burns was forty-six years old with a mustache and an increasing waistline of a small-town police chief. The night of the fire, Chief Burns was sleeping at home when his phone rang.

"Chief, sorry to wake you, but there is a major house fire in the Path," Officer Blakely said. Officer Blakely was new to the force, on the job just a little less than a year after leaving the police academy, and was pulling the night shift.

"Is the fire department on the scene?" the chief asked.

"Yes, when they got there, it was already pretty involved and..." Blakely stopped.

"And what?" demanded the chief.

"It's at Freddie Salter's house," Blakely stated.

"Shit. This isn't good. How is Freddie?"

"Chief, we can't find him, his wife, or their baby girl. Their boy,

34

Bodhi, was on the beach at the time, and he said they were all home," Blakely tried to describe the problem. The chief already knew this could put the town into turmoil.

"Damn it! I will be right there. Call the SBI, let them know we will probably need their help." The chief hung up, got dressed, and headed to Freddie's house.

When Chief Burns got to the scene, there were five fire trucks from all over the island. The crews contained the fire to the single house, preventing it from spreading to nearby structures.

"Watch the scene, Blakely. Make sure no one takes anything off the site. As soon as this dies down, we need to tape it off. I want eyes on this scene until we can get in here to look things over," the chief directed Blakely.

The fire crews stayed on fire watch for the next twelve hours, ensuring that a fire did not pop back up. At six p.m. on June 7, 2003, the remains of the Salter home were turned over to the chief, the Carteret County Coroner, and the State Bureau of Investigation. They identified the remains of three people as Freddie and Nathalie Salter, and their eight-year-old daughter, Beth.

Detective Steve Natchez from the State Bureau of Investigation arrived earlier in the day to help with the investigation. He knew he would be there for a while, so he booked a room at the Grand Villa Motel. Salter Path was small enough that from the porch of his motel room, he could see the Snow Boatyard and the burned remains of the Salter house.

The morning of June eighth, Detective Natchez headed over to the Salter Path Police Department. The station was located in the center of town, but the town was small enough that *everything* was found in the center. Across the street from the police department was a small convenience store and gas station called Save-a-Stop. The sign above the store was hand-painted in red with capital letters about two feet tall. You could read it from ten miles away, but the island was less than half a mile wide at that point. Detective Natchez stopped by the Save-a-Stop to grab a cup of coffee.

As he walked up to the door, there were two wooden benches on either side of the front door. A group of men sat there drinking their morning coffee and smoking cigarettes. As Detective Natchez pulled in, the men all stopped and looked at the government-issued sedan. Natchez opened the door of the car and headed toward the store. All the men stopped talking, and as Natchez passed by, he said, "Good morning." No one responded.

"Is that it?" Eric, the owner of Save-a-Stop asked Natchez.

"Yes. Just the coffee," Natchez said.

"Are you in town because of the fire?" Eric asked.

"Yes. I am here from the SBI. Chief Burns called us in to help with the investigation," Natchez explained.

"Hmmm. Good luck. I am not giving advice, but remember, squatters settled this place. They don't care much for outsiders," Eric advised.

Natchez grabbed his coffee and headed to the police station as he thought about what Eric had said.

Chief Burns already had a whiteboard standing on a wobbly tripod. Burns was diagramming the relationships and history of the town over the past few years. Meanwhile, other investigators searched for clues in the ashes of the Salter's house.

"Natchez. Good to see you. I see you found Save-a-Stop," Burns said to Natchez.

"The coffee is not half bad, but those folks on the benches are an unfriendly bunch."

Burns stopped writing and turned to Natchez, "They know, or at least they think they know, who did this."

"Why do you say that?" Natchez asked.

"Look at this town. We have about two hundred and fifty full-time residents, and most of them are somehow related: cousins, uncles, aunts, second cousins, third cousins. They have been here for more than a hundred years and have gotten along fine without police for most of that time. They don't like the idea of a detective from Raleigh coming down to 'fix' their problem. They know, and let me try to explain what I know…" Burns turned to the whiteboard and began writing; Natchez grabbed a chair and kicked up his feet.

"Go ahead…." Natchez took out his notepad.

Chief Burns took the next one and half hours explaining the history of Salter Path and the feud that erupted in 2001 after the sinking of the *Legacy*. He explained the death of Tom Snow following the loss of Jerry Salter and Nathan Jones. The fire at the Snow Boatyard and how there was never a reason for it to start, but the solvents stored in an outside shed were where it began. He explained the alignment in town between the Salters and Joneses against the Snows and Willards. How most of the time, the feud played out in bar fights and petty property disputes. Each faction tried to have their side take over the local government to harass the other side. For this reason, whenever someone from one family moved away, many in the family felt like they were giving up and abandoning their family.

"Where should we start?" Natchez asked Chief Burns. Even though he was much more the experienced investigator, he knew to defer to local knowledge.

"I got two of my officers going door to door throughout the town asking questions. By the end of the week, we should be able to get through the town. The Snows are obvious concerns. I might try Susan Snow, Tom Snow's widow. She is the matriarch of the Snows," Burns said.

"I will start with Susan Snow then. I have some questions for her," Natchez said.

"Good luck," Burns tried to be encouraging.

Natchez made his way out of the police station front door and into the bright sunshine. It was June in North Carolina, and the summer heat had started. On the way to the car, Natchez made an executive decision to lose the tie. He knew it was standard SBI attire, but the heat, humidity, and town made him feel like he needed to get rid of it. He plunked down in his car seat, started it, and rolled down his windows. The town was so small the car's AC would not have time to get going, so keeping the windows down was the only way to get some relief. Natchez made a right onto Salter Path Road and headed the half-mile past his hotel and to the home of Susan Snow.

There was an old boat with "Captain Little Man" written on the side in the front yard. It was a wooden skiff handmade in Salter Path by the Snows. It was one of the first boats made by Tom Snow. Susan liked to keep it in the yard to remind her of him. Natchez walked around the corner of the boat and up onto the side porch. He began to knock and noticed the doorbell. He reached down to ring it. Moments later, the inside door swung open, and a blast of cool air came out through the screen.

"Can I help you?" Susan asked Natchez.

"Ma'am, I am Detective Natchez from SBI. I am here in town to help look into the fire from the other night. Could I ask you some questions?" Natchez tried to be as polite and southern as he knew to be.

"I see. A Salter's place burns down, and you look right at the Snows. Do you think we are that dumb? Don't they teach you anything in Raleigh? Like I—*we*—did something," Susan snapped.

"No. That's not it. We are going to everyone's door in town to ask questions. Ma'am, just a few minutes?" Natchez tried to reason with her.

"What fucking good are you? When our place burned down and

my Tom was killed, y'all couldn't make sense out of anything. You couldn't find a turd in an outhouse," Susan was venting her sorrow on Natchez.

"Ma'am, I heard about your loss from Chief Burns. I am very sorry, but I just have a few questions," Natchez said, trying to negotiate.

"Good day, Detective. I hope you have better luck finding something out in this case," Susan said, slamming the door.

Natchez paused, turned, and walked back to the edge of the porch. He thought to himself, *What the fuck is this place? I have been here less than twenty-four hours, and I am already getting shut down?*

8

Evidence

The following day Natchez headed back to Save-a-Stop. He had a plan this time. He got up extra early and headed over for his coffee. This time the benches in front of Save-a-Stop were empty. Natchez headed inside to grab his coffee, a copy of the *Tideland News*, and a pack of cigarettes. He rarely smoked, but he figured it would come in handy to help him fit in. He sat down on one of the benches in front of Save-a-Stop. He opened his copy of the newspaper, lit a cigarette, and waited.

Natchez began reading about the new fishing regulations that threatened the flounder fishing industry, the Emerald Island Town plan to stop driving on the beach during the winter, and the story of the week, the house fire in Salter Path that took the life of three, including a child. The news article didn't have much detail beyond the facts. Small town newspapers rarely had investigative staff and typically tried to stick to the obvious "who, what, where, when, why." But this article had a picture of a young boy, identified as Bodhi Salter, the remaining survivor of the Salter family. *Shit. Has anyone talked to that boy?*

Natchez's "bench fishing" would have to wait for another day. He got up and headed across the street to the police station. When he pushed open the door, Chief Burns greeted him, "Good morning, Detective. You are up early."

"Yes. I am trying to get an angle into what happens around town. Figured I would stake out Save-a-Stop and then realized you didn't mention questioning Bodhi Salter, the boy," Natchez stated.

"Oh, yeah. We haven't talked to him. The fire tore him up. He is staying with his great-aunt Beatrice," Burns explained.

"Well, let me swing by and see if I can talk to him," Natchez replied.

"Sounds good. It might make the family feel better if they know the SBI is here," Burns commented.

Natchez walked out of the station and looked across the street. The men had started gathering on the benches. He missed his chance to get into the local routine today, but tomorrow would be another chance.

Beatrice Jones was the sister of Jerry Salter. Jerry Salter had died two years ago on the *Legacy* along with Beatrice's husband, Nathan. Beatrice had become Bodhi's de facto grandmother after the passing of her brother's wife. Jerry's wife, Josephine, or Jo for short, had passed away the year before from a sudden heart attack suffered while tending her garden. The death of Jo left Bodhi with his Nana B, as he called her, her daughter Aunt Maureen, or Moe, his cousin Needley, and his Aunty Kristy, sister of his father, Freddie. Aunt Kristy was his closest surviving blood relative.

Beatrice's house was on the sound. In the back was a dock for the shrimp boats to pull up. Her brother Jerry and her husband Nathan would pull their craft to the pier after long nights shrimping in the sounds. Beatrice would always keep a share of the shrimp to sell to the vacationers. Sitting in her living room, she'd watch soap operas while peeling and deveining shrimp. Nana B would package them into one-pound bags and sell them out of the back door. She would admit they weren't exactly one pound if you asked her, but the vacationers didn't care. They loved the idea of supporting a small local business. She still sold shrimp out of the back door, but now the shrimp were given to her by other Salter Path shrimpers. They felt the need to help the waterman widow, and donating some shrimp to sell was the least they could do. Beatrice's house still had the "Fresh Shrimp" sign her husband painted on the side of Salter Path Road. He painted a scallop on it so, "it looked like a Shell Gas Station sign."

Natchez knocked on the screen door.

"Come in. We have mediums for nine dollars, large for ten, and jumbo for twelve. We also have some bay scallops for sixteen dollars," Beatrice told Natchez the shrimp prices, thinking it was a vacationer looking for some dinner.

"Ma'am, those prices sound good, and I might be back for some shrimp later, but I am Detective Natchez from the SBI."

"Oh, I am sorry. I just thought you were looking for shrimp. I am guessing you want to talk about the fire?" Beatrice asked.

Natchez smiled a little inside. Finally, someone interested in his help. "Yes, I am sorry for your loss. We are trying to piece together the events of that evening. Is Bodhi around?"

Beatrice paused, "Yes. But can I talk with you first?"

"Yes, go ahead, ma'am," Natchez said.

"Mister, I mean Officer Natchez, I love Bodhi deeply. He is like my grandson, but I am an old woman. I can't take care of him. I mean, I could watch him for a while, but not forever. Has someone reached out to his aunt? She might be better suited to take care of him," Beatrice explained.

"I am not sure. I will get a hold of social services to see what they say," Natchez told her.

"Thank you. Bodhi is around back on the dock. Let me take you back there. You can imagine he is still quite upset."

Bodhi was sitting slumped over. His feet were hanging off the dock where his grandfather's shrimp boat should be. This boy had more thrown at him than most adults could handle. Overnight he became an orphan and lost his home. This loss would be a test for any human being.

The sun was hot, and Bodhi was sweating through his shirt. All of his clothes burned in the fire, and he was still wearing the same shorts and T-shirt as the night of the fire. Natchez was appalled. How could they not have gotten him some clean clothes and shoes?

"Bodhi, hi, I am Detective Natchez. Can I sit down?" Natchez quietly asked Bodhi.

Bodhi looked up and shrugged his shoulders. Natchez slowly sat down next to Bodhi.

"Bodhi, I know this is a hard time right now. Can you tell me about what you remember?" Natchez did not know precisely how to ask.

"The flames. It was hot. I couldn't see anything," Bodhi said, still not wholly making sense of what happened.

"What else? What happened before the fire?" Natchez inquired softly.

Bodhi looked out onto the water and said, "Me and Needley went to catch some ghost crabs. I wanted some money for a new fishing rod. So we went to catch crabs."

"How about the day before?" Natchez asked.

"I can't remember. I just remember the crabs, then sirens, and the fire. It was so hot." Tears began to build in his eyes. "It was so hot."

Natchez reached out, put an arm around the boy, and pulled him close. He felt that the boy just needed a hug more than anything at the moment. He also knew there was no valuable information to find with the boy.

Natchez stopped by to see Beatrice as he headed to his car. "Ma'am, anything you want to tell me about the fire?"

"I wish I could help. I go to bed at nine-thirty every night. I didn't see anything until the sirens woke me up. Can you try to reach Bodhi's aunt? I haven't talked to her since she left," Beatrice said.

"Since she left?" Natchez asked.

"Yes. Bodhi's aunt left some months ago to move up to Raleigh."

"Any reason why she left?" Natchez inquired.

"Do you know about the disagreements between the families?" Beatrice asked Natchez.

"I heard some things. They said it had to do with your husband and brother."

"Yes, well, she said she didn't feel safe or welcome here anymore and just wanted to get out and be done with this place. It hurt us all. We hate it when a Pather leaves the Path." Beatrice looked down, shaking her head.

"I will try to find her and see if she can help with Bodhi. Maybe it would be good for him to get away for a while. Thank you for your time, Miss Beatrice." Natchez turned and headed to his car. He turned back and asked, "Miss Beatrice, I forgot to ask, what is her name?"

"Kristen, I mean Kristy Salter," Beatrice shouted.

That same day SBI agents in Raleigh would track down Kristy Salter's new address and phone number. Detective Natchez took it upon himself to tell Kristy and ask about her taking in Bodhi. That day she would make the two-and-a-half-hour drive to pick up Bodhi. On the way back to Raleigh, they would stop at the Neuse River Sports Shop to buy Bodhi new clothes and shoes.

9

Stories

Save-a-Stop opened at 5:30 a.m. Coffee was ready by 5:45 a.m., and customers started trickling in at about six. Natchez set his alarm for 5:30 and decided to go for his morning run and stop by Save-a-Stop on his way back to the motel. By seven, Natchez was sitting on the bench in front of Save-a-Stop, reading the *Tideland News*, drinking coffee, and waiting for the Pathers to show up.

The first rusted pickup truck turned into the gas station at about seven-thirty. The light blue truck looked twenty years old and probably hadn't traveled off the island in fifteen years. A short, stocky man with a ball cap pulled over thinning gray hair stepped out of the truck and headed into the store, not saying a word to Natchez.

A few minutes later, he came out of the store. The man's tanned and weathered face suggests a life spent on the water working in the sun. He had a cup of coffee in his hand and sat on the bench next to Natchez. This action surprised Natchez as he thought it would take many days before someone would stop to talk.

"You Natchez?" the man asks.

"Yes. How did you know?"

"There are a lot of people that visit this town, but only a few that

45

belong here. You don't, and we know it," the man says.

"What's your name?" Natchez asks.

"They call me 'Jean Man' because I wear jeans on the beach."

"I am just here trying to find out what happened with the fire, and then I will be on my way. Can you help me?"

"Natchez. You gotta understand. No one is talking to anyone that isn't us. Old Burns is as close as they come, and he will never get us to talk. We handle things the way we handle things. You can stay a week, a month, or the rest of your life, you ain't gonna learn nothin'."

"Are you related to the Salters?" Natchez asks.

"We are all related. You gotta understand that you might fight with your wife at home, and no one minds you. You can yell and scream and throw shit; no cops show up. Well, we are all family, and Salter Path is our home. So if you see us yellin' and screamin' and throwin' shit, you best just go on your way. We don't want to be messin' with those Raleigh folk. I mean no disrespect. I am just tryin' to save ya some time. The rules here aren't the same as Raleigh," the man said, and then he stood up, got into his truck, and drove off.

Natchez's head was spinning. What just happened? He thought he was here to help, but they did not want it. It came to him that the locals had sent Jean Man to tell him to buzz off. Natchez sat and thought about his next steps. Where to go from here? He headed back to his motel to shower and get dressed for his day.

About an hour later, Natchez rolled his car into the police department parking lot. He got out and went in to see Chief Burns.

"Burns, good morning, what's the good word?" Natchez asked.

"I heard you got to meet Jean Man," the chief remarked.

"What? How did you hear that already?" Natchez was surprised.

"It's a small town. Word travels fast. Eric let me know when I stopped for my coffee."

"Who is this guy 'Jean Man'?"

"He is one of the Willard family. He grew up down here and dropped out of school in the tenth grade. He spends his time doing odd jobs fixing things for the people in the trailer park. He is harmless. I picked him up a couple of times for fighting at Frank and Clara's, but nothing more than simple scuffles. The folks appreciate the help he gives them during the hurricanes and off-season. His real name is Jake, but everyone calls him Jean Man." The chief got up from his desk and headed to the file cabinet.

Natchez tried to make sense of his interaction with Jean Man. "He seemed like he had something to say. He made it clear I am not wanted, but I am welcomed here. It was a strange way that he put it. 'Please stay, but don't expect to get what you want.'"

"Natchez, I hate to say it, but he is probably right. When the Snow Boatyard burned, the SBI agent spent about a month here trying to find something out. He got nowhere. By the time he left, he had gained about ten pounds from eating shrimp burgers, and everyone talked to him like a friend, but no one would tell him anything he wanted to know. He just packed it in." The chief was trying to give Natchez some advice.

Natchez changed the subject to the fire he was there to investigate, "So, what did your guys turn up about the Salter fire?"

"As expected, nothing. No one knows anything. The fire just started, and the investigators have not found anything. And I think we should write this up as an accidental fire." The chief was ready to move on to the summer. The high vacation season was coming, and the town didn't need the bad press.

"That's it? It seems like there are motives; shouldn't we look deeper?" Natchez questioned.

That was the last question Natchez got to ask. In two days, he would be submitting his report in Raleigh. In his report, Natchez would state there seemed to be many grievances in town, but there was no physical evidence to support foul play at the fire scene.

10

Dog Island

The Bogue Banks that make up a part of the Southern Outer Banks run primarily east to west. If you go north from Salter Path and a little west into Bogue Sound, you will find an area on the maps known as Dog Island. At one point in time, this was a small piece of land not much bigger than a soccer field that rose just a foot or two above the high tide. In 1943, the United States Army Air Corps used this tiny strip of land as a bombing target. The bombing left the island full of round craters created by the impacting bombs. The bombing continued until 1955, when the military decided to stop using the site as a target because of the growing population on the nearby island.

The Salter Path squatters remember those days of the war when the large explosions in their backyard awakened them nightly. After the bombing stopped and the military gave up their claim to the island, Dog Island became a gathering spot for the locals. They would pack up their boats with lunch and family, and make their way out to the sandy island. In fact, at low tide, you could walk the three-fourths of a mile to the island with the water rarely rising above your waist.

Sometime in the 1970s, a group of men from Salter Path decided to build a fish house on Dog Island. The Pathers used the local law that allowed the construction of fish processing facilities on the water to construct a small building on Dog Island. This old law became a loophole for the locals to create a small cabin on Dog Island called the fish house. The reality was the fish house was a getaway for the Pathers. On Dog Island, the fish house was a place to get out of the sun and store items. Keeping various sundries in the fish house, the Pathers didn't need to transport them to and from Salter Path. It also became a place where youth retreated beyond parents' watchful eyes.

The fish house became a place of fun and relaxation for residents of Salter Path. It was nearby but also far away. It was a place where they could gather as a community and work to build a location where everyone could get a break from the day-to-day life of the Path.

In the fall of 1996, Hurricane Fran struck North Carolina. The hurricane cut a path of destruction and flooding from Wilmington through Raleigh. The massive storm left entire towns in eastern North Carolina underwater. Major storms were nothing new for the folks in Salter Path. They knew that every so often, a hurricane would destroy their community. The townspeople understood you don't build structures to resist storms; you build structures that are easy to rebuild. After the storm surge subsided, there was much to rebuild and clean up in the town. Most residences were put back together in the weeks and months that followed, and life returned to normal.

The fish house on Dog Island did not survive Hurricane Fran, and its destruction was not a surprise to the people of Salter Path. The Pathers constructed the fish house to withstand a nor'easter during the winter, but not a major hurricane. Hurricane Fran was stronger than most hurricanes and took out the fish house and the top of Dog Island, making the island a sandbar that would disappear at high tide. The pilings for the fish house stayed, but the original structure was long gone, likely swept into the Atlantic Ocean by the storm surge and waves.

Perhaps the loss of the fish house was the start of the problems for the town; with a place for everyone to gather washed away by the storm, the issues in town were evermore the focus. After the hurricane, with the loss of Dog Island, there was not a lot of interest in rebuilding the fish house.

In 2000, some of the Salter Path residents began rebuilding the fish house. Since the 1970s, many building regulations have changed in North Carolina. The changes did not deter the hardy group of settlers that had lived on the island for generations. A group of residents ventured to Dog Island and began driving new pilings into the soft sand bottom. By the time local officials noticed the construction going on in the sound, the residents had constructed a new fish house. When state officials tried to take down the structure, the local residents could prove that this was not a new structure but simply a rehabilitation of an existing building. After much back and forth, the state officials agreed that this was a heritage building and it could stay, but could not be expanded. No one is exactly sure who built the new fish house, but it seemed that each of the families of Salter Path contributed to its construction.

The fish house once again became a place of connection for the town. While the feuding factions mostly avoided each other, they found a common purpose in preserving their heritage.

The kids of Salter Path grew up spanning the island from the beach to the sound. When kids on the mainland learned to ride bikes, the kids of Salter Path learned to drive boats and read the shallow waters of Bogue Sound. They threw cast nets for bait and set up a Carolina rig to catch redfish in the marshes along the banks. They also spent time heading out to the fish house. For the kids of Salter Path, the fish house became analogous to a treehouse for a kid from the suburbs.

"Want to go to the fish house?" Needley Jones, or Ley for short, asked DJ Willard. Ley was the son of Maureen Jones and cousin to

Bodhi Salter. Ley had just turned eleven and was looking to use his new cast net in the shallows of Dog Island. Darrel Willard, Jr., or DJ, was the son of Darrel Willard, the owner of the Big Tree Drive-in.

DJ paused for a minute, "I need to go ask my dad. He might need me at the drive-in."

"Okay, go check. I will get my boat ready," Ley told DJ. As DJ ran off to see if he was free for the afternoon, Ley went down behind his Nana B's house to check on his boat. Ley got his first boat the year prior when he turned ten. Since he could remember, Ley had been on the water driving boats and had been the captain of everything from a shrimping boat to a kayak. Now, he had a small Jon boat with a 9.9 horsepower two-stroke Evinrude hanging off the back. He kept it on an old boat lift behind his nana's house.

As Ley lowered the boat to the water, his mother Maureen leaned out the back door – Ley and his mom moved in with his Nana B when their grandfather died on the *Legacy* – and called to him, "Where you goin' with that boat?"

"DJ is coming over. We are heading to Dog Island to try out my new cast net. Is that okay?" Ley yelled to his mother.

"That's fine, but make sure you are home before the ball drops," Maureen reminded her son to be home before the sun went down.

Ley continued to lower the dark green boat to the water. He jumped in, checked for gas, and then grabbed his blue bucket with a cast net inside and a fishing pole. With gas and a cast net on the boat, he waited for DJ. In a few minutes, DJ came running around the corner of Nana's house with a fishing pole in hand. Almost falling before he got to the boat, all he said was, "Let's gooooo!"

Ley pulled the cord on the outboard, and it sputtered to life. DJ pushed them away from the dock, and off they went toward Dog Island. As they rounded Homer's Point, the fish house and Dog Island came into sight. DJ yelled over the wind, and water slapped against the boat, "No one is there! We have the place to ourselves!" DJ pointed out that no boats were anchored at the island or tied up to the fish house. This feeling was freedom for the boys, and they relished the chance to do as they might.

The fish house was a small cabin hovering above the water on a set of nine wooden piers. It had a small porch in the front, about twelve feet long by four feet wide. The cabin itself was essentially an eight by twelve foot shed painted dark green, similar in color to Ley's boat. There was a white door and a tin roof. On each side were two small windows, and the interior was simple wood stud walls. For the boys, it was a perfect escape. They were the kings of Dog Island.

They pulled up, and DJ grabbed a pier of the fish house as Ley cut the motor. Ley ran up and threw a rope around the piling, and they tied off the boat. They climbed up onto the porch throwing the blue bucket and fishing poles up before them. They ran inside to see if there was anything in there. "Jackpot!" yelled Ley. DJ looked through the door. Someone had left three beers in a brown paper bag. This offering was a tradition: never leave the fish house empty. There was always something to be found in the fish house. The items left in the small cabin were an omen to the watermen, reminding them that the sea would provide. DJ and Ley would trade the beers for Cheerwine Ley's mom had packed.

They cracked open the first beer and threw the other two into the cooler. Beer was not their favorite find. It was bitter and tasted even worse when warm, but it was "freedom" to sneak a few. The best discovery was when someone left a bottle of white zinfandel wine. It was sweet like grape juice and could be drunk warm. That usually only showed up after some of the older kids spent the day at the fish house.

The boys sat on the edge of the dock with their feet hanging over, dangling a couple of feet above the water. "I wish Bodhi could be here," DJ said to Ley.

Ley paused for a second, thinking about Bodhi, "Yeah. I can't believe he has gone to Raleigh. I wonder when he will come back?"

"I heard his aunt isn't coming back and that they are gone."

"I heard that too. She kind of just left us here in the Path. You know those kind aren't always welcomed back," Ley stated.

"Yeah, but Bodhi didn't have any choice. He had to go where someone could take care of him," DJ explained to Ley.

"You are right. It is not Bodhi's fault. Kids don't get to make all the choices they want." Ley agreed with DJ, "We should not hold his moving away against him."

"Let's make a promise. If Bodhi ever comes back, he will still be a Pather. Not like the others that leave, he can still be one of us, an owner in the fish house." DJ and Ley made that promise to each other and would never forget it.

Ley and DJ would make many trips to Dog Island in the years that followed. They would see the fish house damaged by hurricanes and then slowly repaired by the people from Salter Path. The fish house would become symbolic of the way people live along the coast. Things get destroyed, and you just put them back together. Trying to resist the forces of nature was futile. The feud in town was a force of nature. It became something that everyone lived with and could not avoid. No one spoke of the Salter's house fire, or at least not in public, but everyone remembered that horrible day. There were rumors about what happened, but no one seemed to have a strong interest in putting all the pieces together. The feud between the families continued, but it seemed the prices paid were significant enough to keep the open hostilities at bay.

11

Butterflies

For longer than anyone in Salter Path could remember, the men in town would fish the fall mullet run. The arrival of the yellow butterflies marks the start of the season. Every fall, these small insects migrate from the north to the south to winter in Florida. Along with them comes the sea mullet. Also known as whiting, these fish were one time called the "chicken of the sea." They were what fueled the establishment of Salter Path, as watermen pulled huge nets full of fish from the water along the beach. The fishermen ported their catch to the sound over a path for shipment by boat to fish processing houses. Workers at the processing houses barreled the fish and shipped them to northern cities.

Over time, the demand in the north for whiting waned. This drop in demand, combined with large commercial fishing vessels targeting the fish offshore, significantly reduced the viability of the fishery. Despite this, the tradition of fall fishing continued. Stop net fishing is unique to Salter Path. The method involves using large stop nets. The nets loaded in flat-bottom skiffs are pulled to the beach by old red International Harvester tractors. In the fall, the winds along the North Carolina coast come out of the north. Due to the east/west orientation of the island, the wind blows over the island, leaving the nearshore water devoid of waves.

The tractors can then back the skiffs into the water, launching the boats. The fishermen then anchor one end of the long stop net on the shore. The small flat-bottom boats run the net out perpendicular to the beach and then parallel to it, a pattern that forms a corral designed to gather fish. Heavy anchors hold the nets in place. These are called "stop nets" because they extend from the shore, stopping the schooling fish from moving along the beach.

The fishermen wait along the shore, watching for a school of mullet to fill the corral. Once the school is spotted, the skiff tows a strike net out with one end tied to a tractor. The boat makes a large loop bringing the far end back to shore. Eventually, the other end of the net is connected to a tractor, which then hauls the net and fish from the ocean. As the fish are pulled from the water, nearly every able-bodied man in Salter Path comes out to pull fish from the nets and throw them into the back of pickup trucks. The day's catches are too small to support the entire town, but it always provides a little extra money before the Christmas holiday.

DJ and Ley have been helping with the mullet run since they could walk. As kids, they would head to the beach with the other men and pull fish from the nets, carrying them one at a time to pickup trucks. By the end of the day, fish slime and sand covered the boys. They remember when Bodhi was there with them. Three boys, learning the ways of the community. Bodhi left a long time ago, and now DJ and Ley are grown men.

Both Ley and DJ stayed in Salter Path. They now drive the skiff and do the heavy work of moving anchors in and out of the boat. Working the boat is typically the role of the younger men in the prime of fitness. The anchors holding the nets weigh fifty pounds each. They have twenty feet of chain attached to them, making the total weight of the chain and anchor almost 100 pounds. As the men in the boat heaved the anchor and chain over the gunnel, they had to move their feet quickly to avoid getting caught in the bite of the rode as it spooled over. If the rode pulled you over in its tangle, you would have to free yourself. With the stop net floating free in the water, the chances of rescuers getting tangled in the net were just too high. For that reason, the men working the skiff always have a sharp knife strapped to their hip, within easy reach.

After the mullet run, most vacationers headed home and then the locals exclusively inhabited Salter Path. When fishing was slow and tourists were scarce at the turn of the season, families began focusing on getting through the winter. The Pathers spent this time mending fishing nets and repairing boats. A few folks left town to head to Florida to work as deckhands on fishing boats for the winter. The town went into a near hibernation until March.

Ley was now twenty-seven years old. He grew up to be what some people would describe as a mountain of a man. Ley was all of six feet five inches tall and weighed 280 pounds. He went to West Carteret High School, where he played football. Ley received a scholarship to play offensive line from several division one schools, including NC State, East Carolina, Auburn, Clemson, Georgia Tech, the Citadel, and others. He planned to go to NC State but decided at the last minute to stay in Salter Path to help his mother make ends meet.

At eighteen years old, Ley began working as a deckhand on the head boat called the *Carolina Princess*. He would work the rail pulling fish off hooks and dropping buckets of bait for tourists hoping to hook a grouper. The *Carolina Princess* was a 140-foot long steel boat designed to carry about 100 fishermen lowering lines onto live bottoms in the deep Atlantic Ocean. Many of the young men from Carteret County had their first job working as a deckhand on the *Carolina Princess*.

If you wanted to become a boat captain, you needed to have

hundreds of hours on the water just to qualify. Working on a head boat made it easy to get your hours up and prepare for your Coast Guard certification. Ley quickly learned that you got a lot of time on the water but not much money. A deckhand started out earning tips from the customers on the boat. A typical day on the water might bring anywhere from twenty dollars on slow days to a hundred on a day with good fishing and fair weather.

Ley soon became one of the crew leads on the *Carolina Princess*. He was able to secure a permanent deckhand position, which meant he now received a minimum wage hourly rate in addition to his tips. The new job meant Ley stayed after the charter to maintain the boat and learn about its systems. After a year and a half, Ley had a chance to join one of the shrimp boats working out of Salter Path. The boat was named the *Lady B*. It was Freddie Salter's old boat and previously the boat of his father, Jerry Salter. The *Lady B* was handed down to Freddie when Jerry built the *Legacy*. The old tired *Lady B* could still raise shrimp from the bottom of the sound. The Salters replaced the diesel engine several times during her lifetime. The nets were worn but still serviceable. In a good year, a waterman working the *Lady B* could expect to earn about $25,000. These earnings were enough to put food on the table but not much else. For that reason, watermen like Ley also needed to work the charter boats or have another job to make ends meet.

Ley grew a reputation around town as a hard worker. His massive frame made him the choice for heavy work. If Ley had a motto, it was, "Work hard, Play Harder." When the wind blew and the captains secured the boats in their berths, you could find Ley at Frank and Clara's sitting at the corner of the bar. Ley liked the corner because he could see everyone who walked through the door. Ley was a sight to see when he had fun. His happy but quiet personality changed as he drank. Ley's voice and sense of humor grew to be a size that fit his body. Joking and talking loudly, Ley created what was like the center of a mosh pit at a rock concert. He was well-liked in town.

The path to adulthood for DJ was filled with twists and turns. If you were to describe DJ's appearance, you would call him wiry. Thin-bodied and with a hard, awkward appearance. He got his first tattoo when he was sixteen at a shop in Jacksonville, North Carolina, just across the street from the marine base. He convinced the artist that he was a marine by shaving his head. The artist likely knew he was underage but also wanted the money. The tattoo read "PATHER" in script letters and was located just under his heart.

DJ struggled to finish high school and probably graduated because the teachers didn't want to see him back in class the following year. He lived in a small trailer behind the Big Tree Drive-in. If anyone asked him what he did for a living, he would tell them he owned the Big Tree Drive-in.

The Big Tree Drive-in gained fame when a reporter from New York traveling on vacation to Salter Path in the 1980s stopped in for a shrimp burger. The shrimp burger was a creation by Darrel Willard, senior. He used local small shrimp, deep-fried on a hamburger bun, with homemade slaw and hot sauce. The reporter was a food writer and declared this the best shrimp burger in eastern North Carolina. Soon, tourists from the north flocked to the restaurant making the Big Tree Drive-in one of the most profitable businesses in Salter Path. Darrel loved his son and wanted him to one day take over the drive-in. As DJ grew older, it seemed less and less likely that would happen. DJ worked in the kitchen at the Drive-in but showed little interest in learning the business. He was happy to live in a small trailer, make an "allowance" from his dad and hang out with his old friend Ley from childhood. By his mid-twenties, DJ's tattoos covered his arms, chest, and face. He had this idea that he wanted twenty-six tattoos by the time he turned twenty-six. He achieved this goal, including a yellow butterfly, symbolic of fall fishing in eastern North Carolina. If you asked DJ about his long-term plan, it was simple. He was going to inherit the Drive-in and live in the Path, always a Pather.

If Ley's spirit animal were an ox, DJ's would be a spider monkey. They were opposites in many ways but bonded together through childhood and place. At Frank and Clara's, DJ liked to start trouble with the tourists that came into the bar. He did this knowing Ley and the other Pathers would have his back. Most of the time, it amounted to nothing other than curse words and posturing. Whenever a group of young marines was in the bar, it always made for an eventful evening. DJ would start by playing pool, and the marines would join in the game. After a few games, DJ would bet the men a round of drinks on the next game. When DJ would lose, he would buy them two dollar Natural Lites, and when he would win, he would insist on a shot of whiskey. The marines would catch on to this, and words would be exchanged. When things were ready to boil over, Ley would stand up and calm the situation. A few times, the marines no longer took kindly to the setup, and they would end up in a fistfight with the Pathers. Chief Burns would break up the brawl, sending the marines back to Camp Lejeune and the Pathers home.

Ley lived in the spare bedroom of his grandmother Beatrice's house. One night, Ley sat on the back porch looking over the Bogue Sound. The water was choppy with white caps as far as one could see. It was early spring, and the island was trying to shake off the Northeast blows of the winter. Ley's phone began to vibrate.

"Hello."

"Hey, what are you up to?" DJ asked Ley.

"With this fuckin' wind? Nothing. Just taking care of some crap that I really don't wanna do. What are you doin'?" Ley hoped DJ was looking to get out of the house.

"About the same here. We closed the Drive-in until Thursday. No business, and I am just sitting in my trailer. Why don't you come over?" DJ suggested to Ley.

"Sounds good. I will be there in a few minutes. I am gonna grab some Natties from Save-a-Stop."

Ley got up from the porch and put on his Xtratufs, and grabbed his wallet. He walked through Freddie Salter's old house's backyard, and then to Save-a-Stop. More than fifteen years later, the Pathers had not rebuilt the Salter's house. The lot lay vacant, but Ley still went over and mowed the yard every couple of weeks. The house's foundation was still there, but nothing else, other than small trees and shrubs that had grown up. Ley walked across the street through the Big Tree Drive-in parking lot, then behind the building and opened the door to DJ's trailer.

"Yo, fagot. Where have you been?" DJ chided Ley.

"I told you, I need to grab some Nattie," he said, holding up a twelve-pack of Natural Lite beer.

DJ was sitting on his couch with a bong in front of him. He was pulling out some weed from a small decorative box and packing it into the bowl of the bong. They turned on the PlayStation, cracked a beer, and fired up the bong.

"Where are you working this year?" DJ asked Ley.

"Gonna run the boat again this year. I might be getting the boat for myself. I would need a mate. Do you know anyone?" Ley asked.

DJ took a draw on the bong. Held his breath and leaned back on the couch. He exhaled, letting out a plume of smoke. "There is that Bobby kid. He has been hanging around. I think he needs some work," DJ said.

"Yeah, that's right. He's young. I think he works hard. I need to get a hold of him." Ley reached over for the bong and took a hit. "Last night for me. I gotta take that drug test in April. I need to clean to keep my captain's license. You workin' at the Drive-in this year?"

"Ley, what do you mean? I own it. I don't work there," DJ insisted.

"DJ, bulllshiittt. I know the truth. One day you might, but your daddy still owns it. No disrespect, I was just asking. I thought you might want to get on the boat with me for a summer."

"Workin' on a boat ain't my thing. I might fill in if ya' need someone, but count me out."

"Gotcha'. I will reach out to that Bobby kid. Let's see how he does. I might need you, but it sounds like you would rather be a fryer jockey for the summer," Ley goaded DJ.

"Fuck you," DJ laughed. They turned to the TV, started up the PlayStation, and dove into Call of Duty.

The wind blew as DJ and Ley played their game and smoked pot inside the trailer. The late winter was a quiet time in Salter Path. With the tourists gone and the chores done, only the boat builders had steady work to complete boats for the summer. Very soon, the weather would start to warm. As February gave way to March, Salter Path would come to life. Watermen would go back to fishing, and the tourists would begin traveling to the Path.

12

Highway 70

Spring had come to eastern North Carolina, and the trees were in full leaf. Highway 70 ran east from Raleigh through Garner and New Bern, ending in Morehead City. The highway, lined with azaleas flowering in pinks, reds, and whites, welcomed the start of the tourist season for the coastal towns of North Carolina. When making the trip to the coast, it is nearly required to stop at King's Barbeque in Kinston.

Eastern North Carolina claims to be the home of pork barbeque in the United States. When early German settlers came to North Carolina, they brought the tradition of slow-roasting pigs over an open fire. Barbeque is a noun that identifies pork pulled from a pig after roasting on an open fire. At the time, the immigrants believed tomatoes to be poisonous and avoided using the vegetable in food. The eastern North Carolina barbeque sauce uses vinegar with seasonings and hot peppers added for flavor. King's Barbeque had been in operation serving traditional eastern North Carolina barbeque for more than forty years.

Ellie and Bodhi pulled into the King's Barbeque parking lot in Kinston. Ellie stepped down out of Bodhi's white F150 wearing cut-off shorts and a printed Piggly Wiggly T-shirt. Her blonde hair was pulled into a ponytail and teased through the back of her Calcutta baseball cap. She had gone and purchased the outfit just for the trip to Salter Path. The small coastal town fashion, she hoped, would help her fit in.

"What's this place?" Ellie asked Bodhi.

"We used to stop here when I was a kid, and we had to go to Raleigh for something. It's a buffet barbeque place. All country food," Bodhi explained the menu. "If you want just the buffet, it's one price. If you want to go to the salad bar, too, then, it is another two dollars. You find these places all over the east, but this is like the original."

"Oh, lord! This place sounds goooood... I can't say it is a smart stop before I wear a bikini, but it sounds good," Ellie said.

Bodhi and Ellie headed inside. An older lady with short gray hair and a slight stoop walked them to their table. She asked, "Tea?" and both Ellie and Bodhi replied, "Yes, please." The response meant they would get sweet iced tea. You would need to be explicit to tell the folks "unsweet" if you did not want sugar. The making of sweet tea was something Ellie had not mastered yet. Her mother had tried to teach her, but the tea still was not like her mom's. King's had real tea. The trick was to get the tea flavor without overpowering it with the sugar's sweetness. The waitress brought two plastic cups filled with ice and tea and set them on the table.

"Y'all doin' the buffet?" she inquired.

"Yes for me. Ellie?" Bodhi responded.

"I will do it as well," Ellie told the waitress.

"One trip or unlimited?" the waitress asked.

"One trip for me with a salad bar," Ellie told her.

Bodhi added, "Unlimited for me, no salad bar. Thanks."

"Go ahead and help yourself. Plates are at the buffet," the waitress said and then turned and walked away.

Country food filled the buffet - green beans and bacon, mashed potatoes and brown gravy, fried okra, stewed potatoes, pinto beans and ham, fried chicken, and of course, barbeque both pulled and chopped. Bodhi and Ellie dove in, and they filled their plates with food. The stop at King's reminded Ellie she was traveling into a different world compared to the country club. Salt, pepper, butter, and sugar were the only flavorings needed. Add a little bit of vinegar, and the tartness on the pork somehow worked together. The acidity of the barbeque sauce and sweetness of the tea somehow fit the people and towns of the low country.

After getting their fill and more at King's, Bodhi and Ellie headed down the street to do some shopping. The Neuse River ran from the Raleigh area toward the coast through Kinston. During the Civil War, Kinston was a site of several battles, and the Confederate army built an ironclad warship in Kinston to patrol the waters of the Neuse. The ship was launched late in the war and never saw action or left the area of Kinston along the Neuse River. Eventually, it was scuttled on a muddy swallow in the river and burned to the waterline. Not far from the banks of the Neuse River, the Neuse River Sports Shop provided everything outdoors for use in Kinston and the surrounding area.

The Neuse River Sports Shop has a folksy way about it. The log cabin exterior and the fish painted in the parking lot were giveaways to what you will find inside the building. Flannels, baseball caps, a Christmas shop, aisles of rods and reels, tree stands, and a large selection of firearms, all serviced by friendly locals with deep eastern North Carolina drawls. Ellie brimmed with excitement as she jumped out of the truck and headed to the doors. While she was born and raised in a country club, the idea of being connected to the country was something that all North Carolina kids held close to their hearts. This longing for rural life makes them different from kids growing up in the Northeast country clubs who clamored to be a part of the big city.

"I want to get something for the beach," Ellie said to Bodhi as she headed straight for the T-shirt section.

"Wow, it's been years since I have been here. Amazing, it is like nothing has changed at King's or here." Bodhi walked in wide-eyed as memories of his childhood came back. He could remember stopping at the Neuse after leaving Salter Path. Aunt Kristy brought him here on the way to Raleigh after his house and family burned. Bodhi had no clothes, and Aunt Kristy let him pick out new shirts, pants, and shoes.

Ellie took Bodhi by the hand and pulled him along. "Look at this. These are only ten dollars!" Ellie said as she pulled a T-shirt off the shelf. She held up a light pink shirt with a print of a fish and duck. The words 'Neuse River Sports' were intertwined into the design. "I like this one. You should get one, too, Bodhi."

Bodhi paused as emotions started to fill his heart. He was worried that this trip would be more complicated than he expected. "Gosh. Yes, I guess I should. I can remember when we stopped here. Kristy picked me up to come to Raleigh. She let me pick out five of these shirts and two hoodies." He looked around and picked up a light brown hoodie sweatshirt with traditional 'Neuse River Sports' printed in sunset colors. "This one. This sweatshirt is the one I had. It was my favorite. I wore it until it fell apart. I am going to get it."

Before they'd packed the car to leave Raleigh, Ellie considered what this trip could be like for Bodhi. She anticipated he would be emotional, but he was never an overly emotional guy. In her mind, it would hit him when he got to Salter Path, but she was not ready for the look on his face as he started to relive those days in 2003. "You should get that. That will look good on you." She took the hoodie from his hand and held it up to him, "you should get a hat, too," suggesting another item to try to snap Bodhi out of his train of thought.

"They do have good hats," Bodhi said as he headed over to the wall of hats. He selected a gray hat with blue and green lettering with 'NEUSE' in big letters with small letters spelling out 'River Sports Shop' below.

Ellie perused the sale racks while Bodhi headed to the fishing and tackle section. So many years had gone by since he had fished in the saltwater. Bodhi went bass fishing around Raleigh and Garner now and then with friends, but had not tried to catch a redfish for more than fifteen years. He picked up a black and red Penn rod and reel combo. As a kid, he'd always wanted one of these. Penn made some of the best fishing rods and reels around. The people in Salter Path did not usually have the money for this quality of gear. Now, he was making plenty of money in his job, and the $180 was something he could afford. He grabbed it. He knew many things may have changed since he'd last been to Salter Path, but the fish would still be there. He picked up some braided fishing line, swivels, hooks, red beads, egg sinkers, and mono-filament leader. This tackle was everything he needed to make a Carolina rig to chase a redfish.

"Hun, you got what you want?" Bodhi asked Ellie.

She was now pushing a shopping cart filled with clothes, hats, and shoes. "Yes, I think I got everything."

"Shit, it looks like you did get *everything*. Leave some stuff for everyone else," Bodhi joked with Ellie.

All she said was, "Stop!"

They checked out and loaded up the truck with all of Ellie's finds. Bodhi placed his new rod and reel in the truck bed. Buying that rod and reel on his own, heading back to Salter Path, he felt that maybe things would be okay. If not, he had his fishing gear now to retreat to the water.

They headed east on Highway 70. The first sight of saltwater came from the overpass in New Bern where the saltwater mixed with the freshwater of the Neuse and Trent Rivers.

"Look!" Bodhi exclaims and points at the water. He surprised himself at how much he felt connected to the water. The water from this area flowed to the Pamlico Sound, where his grandfather and great-uncle died twenty years ago. At the time, he did not appreciate the connection between this water and his family.

Along the New Bern waterfront, recreational boaters tied up their boats in a small harbor. Bodhi and Ellie drove past a sign for Tyron Palace. Then, they passed a roadside marker indicating New Bern as 'The Home of Pepsi'. New Bern was the first capital of North Carolina, founded in 1710, and it became a wealthy area after the Revolutionary War. North Carolinians eventually moved the capital to Raleigh, and New Bern stagnated, becoming a quaint, small, coastal city.

"Oh, wow. Is that the ocean?" Ellie asked Bodhi.

"Well, no, not exactly. It is the river, but it goes directly to the sound and the ocean. The water is brackish here," Bodhi explained to Ellie as the river disappeared under the bridge.

For the next thirty minutes, they rode along Highway 70. They passed Marine Corps Air Station at Cherry Point. Then Havelock, where many small apartments housing enlisted marines lined the highway. Next through Newport with the shops and stores for the people of Morehead City and the surrounding areas. Finally, Bodhi slowed his truck and made a right-hand turn onto the Atlantic Beach Bridge.

The high-rise bridge was the first fixed bridge onto Roosevelt Island, leaving Morehead City and landing in Atlantic Beach. It replaced an old swing bridge that had to open every hour to allow boats and barges that traveled along the Intracoastal Waterway to pass by. The F150 climbed the steep incline of the bridge, reaching nearly 100 feet above the water. To the left, were cranes of the North Carolina Port at Morehead City. Ships crossed the ocean to deliver containers full of goods for the cities of the southeast. There were also specialized vessels docking at the port. These ships brought pieces of enormous wind turbines—the future of wind energy—along the Eastern Seaboard. There were even ships from high-tech companies using giant nets to catch rockets falling from the sky after launch. Just past the port, the U.S. Coast Guard Station was nestled inside the Beaufort Inlet. This station was one of the first coast guard stations in the United States established after the sinking of the *Chrissie Wright* in 1886.

Going up the channel from the Beaufort Inlet, there is Beaufort, a waterfront village and the historical home of Blackbeard. His flagship, the *Queen Anne's Revenge*, sank just outside the Beaufort Inlet. Closer to the bridge, in the shadows of the port cranes, was the Morehead City waterfront.

Small port city bars and restaurants lined the waterfront. Morehead City was the home to 'Big Rock Landing' and the Big Rock Blue Marlin Tournament. In just over a week, large sportfishing boats would come from all over the East Coast to participate in the sportfishing tournament. The tournament attracts some of the best sportfishing teams in the world. Over the years, the stakes grew exponentially. Now, the winning fish could bring more than $1.5 million in prize money.

From the right of the bridge, they gazed down the Bogue Sound, which stretched more than twenty miles long and two and a half miles wide. The mainland and Roosevelt Island created the sound's boundaries. On this clear day, from the top of the bridge, they could see nearly every small town along the stretch of the island, including Salter Path.

13

Anxiety

The high quartz content of the sand made the beaches shimmer, like crystals in the bright Carolina sun. This phenomenon led to the Roosevelt Island beaches gaining the Crystal Coast name. Tourists came from everywhere in the Northeast to visit the Crystal Coast. Turtle-topped minivans with license plates from Pennsylvania, New York, Connecticut, and Massachusetts filled the roads in the summer. As they traveled down Highway 70 and over the high-rise bridge to the island, they experienced excitement, wonder, anticipation, and most of all, relief. As you leave the mainland and enter the peaceful island life, your worries are left behind. This feeling is what most people experience as they climb the long sloping bridge and rise to see the salty sound waters spread out below them.

"What's wrong?" Ellie was looking at Bodhi from the passenger seat. His face was white as a ghost, and he could not catch his breath. "Bodhi, are you okay? What's wrong?"

"Don't know. I can't catch my breath. My heart is pounding." Bodhi stared straight ahead, focusing on the bridge.

Ellie got nervous as Bodhi drifted left and right on the bridge. A mistake on the bridge could send the truck plummeting 100 feet into the water below. She reached over to steady the truck's wheel, but Bodhi pushed it away.

"I am okay. Just let me get to the bottom of the bridge," Bodhi assured Ellie.

Bodhi got to the bottom of the bridge, seeing the Crystal Coast for the first time in more than fifteen years. He pulled the truck off the road into the parking lot of a bait and tackle store called Chasin' Tails. He put the vehicle in park and grabbed his chest.

"Baby! What is wrong?! I am calling 911," Ellie said as she took out her phone.

"No. No. I gotta get out of the truck. I will be fine," Bodhi insisted as he gasped for breath.

"You are not fine! What is wrong!" Ellie was in a panic as Bodhi got out of the truck and walked toward the water, clenching his chest. "What are you doing! Stop!" Ellie yelled.

Bodhi walked his way over the edge of the old causeway bridge and sat down on the edge. His face twisted in anguish as he stared at the water. Ellie was right behind; she got down behind him and wrapped her arms around him. She had never seen him like this before, and it scared her. She did not know what to do, so she hugged him.

"A panic attack. It is a panic attack," Bodhi said softly to Ellie.

He took a deep breath and started, "I used to get them when I was younger. When I left Salter Path, I used to wake up at night screaming with nightmares. It was always the same. I saw the fire starting at my house, and I was on the beach. I would try to run to wake up my parents and get my sister. The faster and harder I ran, the deeper I would sink in the sand. It was like this whole island was quicksand pulling me under as I ran. I would wake up yelling, 'No! No!' and my Aunt Kristy would be there. She would calm me down, and I would go back to sleep."

Ellie wrapped her arms around him tighter, pulling him close and putting her face into the nape of his neck.

"The nightmares stopped when I was about fourteen or fifteen, but they became panic attacks. I would just be sitting in class, and out of nowhere, for no reason, I would feel like I was dying. It was terrifying, but the doctors said nothing was wrong with me. I hardly get them anymore. I don't think I have had one since we have been together," Bodhi trailed off. He told Ellie about a part of him he did not share with anyone. She was the love of his life, but he was just trying to put this all behind him. When he met her, he knew for the first time, since the fire, that he would be okay.

"Honey. It is okay. It will be okay. I understand. I don't understand. I can't even imagine," Ellie fumbled her words.

"Ellie, I don't expect you to understand. I just know that I need you, and I need to close this part of my life before we start a new one."

"Bodhi, you are…" Ellie started.

"Ellie, hush. You don't have to say anything. I love you, and I know you love me. You will help me through this," Bodhi confided in his bride-to-be.

"How are you feeling?"

Bodhi turned to Ellie, still holding him, and gave her a deep kiss. "I am good," Bodhi smiled, and the two of them sat looking at the water for a moment.

"Fucking beautiful place, isn't it?" Bodhi asked Ellie.

She just grabbed him by the cheeks, looked in his eyes, and smiled. "Yes, I love it." She confirmed his feelings.

They walked back to the truck hand in hand. Bodhi gained strength from Ellie leaning on his shoulder. Bodhi opened the door for Ellie and walked around to his side of the truck. When he opened the door, Ellie was there with the armrest up riding 'bitch'. She smiled; he smiled because she had not done that since the first few months of dating.

The F150 pulled out of the parking lot and made the turn onto Highway 58, heading toward Salter Path. Bodhi slipped his hand between Ellie's legs, and she leaned into him. They drove past the Beach Tavern and the Food Lion. They got caught at the stoplight by the North Carolina Aquarium at Pine Knolls Shore, and it seemed to take forever.

About ten miles down the island, they entered into a thirty-five mile per hour zone. A small sign welcomed everyone to Salter Path—Home of the Shrimp Festival. They passed by the Snow Boatyard, which the Snows had rebuilt after the fire, and turned into the Grand Villa Motel parking lot, where they had booked a room for the week.

Ellie stayed in the truck while Bodhi went into the office. The Grand Villa Motel was one of the first motels on the Crystal Coast, a 1950s roadside motor lodge transported to the beach. The motel was purchased in 2017 by a family from Raleigh who wanted to retire at the beach and used their nest eggs to buy the rundown motel. The Gentellis were originally from the Pittsburgh area and had made their money in Raleigh, investing in small businesses. They owned hair salons, a plumbing supply house, and even a dumpster business. They sold them all and purchased Grand Villa Motel with the hope of creating a boutique travel lodge that would attract the wave of young professionals looking for a real beach experience from yesteryear. They invested a good bit of money into the property. They refurbished the pool and added a small cocktail bar with a frozen drink machine. They made high-class cocktails in a low-class motel. This vibe was just the sort of hip thing the young professional sought out. The rooms were small, clean, and adequate, with well-appointed retro fixtures with comfortable beds, Keurig coffee makers, and mini-bar fridges. The Gentillis made a good living with their new investment and loved welcoming people to Salter Path.

Bodhi walked into the office. A small bell rang when he opened the door. Danny Gentilli got up from the back office. He was expecting a few check-ins today and one he was more curious about than the others.

"Good afternoon. Can I help you?" Danny asked Bodhi.

"Hi. I am Bodhi Salter. I am checking in."

"Bodhi Salter, any relation?" Danny asked to be polite, but he had heard about the fire. He knew who Bodhi was.

"Yes, sir. I lived here until I was twelve," Bodhi responded.

"Well, welcome back. What brings you here?" Danny was probably the first in town to know Bodhi was planning to make a return.

"I am here for a little vacation and hope to see some friends and family," Bodhi said, getting a little agitated by this outsider asking about his business. He had not been in the Path for years, but he still felt like he was a Pather, and the outsiders did not need to know their business.

"Credit card?" Danny asked.

Bodhi pulled his wallet out and handed over his card. Danny took it and ran it through the machine.

"This is just for incidentals. The room is paid for already. There is a mini-bar in the room, and we have a cocktail bar by the pool. You can charge things to your room, and it will go on the card," Danny explained. "The pool bar is open from noon to eight p.m. every day. We have towels for the beach by the pool. Please do not use the room towels for the beach."

"Thanks." Bodhi grabbed the keys from the desk. They read room 121.

They drove the truck around the corner, and Ellie grabbed the key. As soon as the truck stopped, she jumped out and turned to Bodhi and said, "C'mon."

Ellie went to the door with Bodhi close behind. He came up behind her and slid his hand around her waist. She pushed back into him as she inserted the key into the lock. The door popped open, and she grabbed his wrist, turning to face him and pulling him into her.

She pulled his shirt over his head and ran her hands down his body. His arms fell behind her, pulling her up to kiss her deeply. She felt herself melt into his arms. He felt the world fall away. She was the only thing he cared for, the only thing he wanted. He lifted her, carrying her to the bed and laying her softly on her back. He starts running his lips against her skin, feeling the heat and friction between the two of them. Gently, he began kissing her from the waist, working his way up. She could feel the warmth of his breath, and her mind filled with the white heat of passion.

For him, it was the release of fear and loving fully. For Ellie, it was the assurance that he trusted her with his deepest feelings.

14

Morning

The air conditioner hummed, pumping cold air into the small motel room. Bodhi and Ellie's clothes covered the light gray wood floors. The shades were pulled tight, but with the window facing east, a ray of light snuck through a small gap and fell on Bodhi's face. The bright sun in his eye woke him up. Ellie was still sleeping soundly next to him. Her blonde hair flowed onto the white pillowcase. Bodhi slowly opened his eyes and rolled onto his back, trying not to wake Ellie.

Bodhi thought to himself, "What should I do?" He did not have a plan when he came here, and Ellie never asked. He could just hang around for a few days and see if he ran into anyone he knew, or he could knock on the door of someone he knew.

He lay there for about thirty minutes, thinking about his options. It seemed like he should get on with it and see what happens. He decided it was something he needed to do on his own. He figured if he went to someone's house and was pushed away, then he could just bring a coffee to Ellie, and they could go to the beach. She would never know his hometown rejected him.

Bodhi quietly slid out of bed, slipped on his shorts, T-shirt, and NRSS hat. He picked up his flip-flops and quietly opened the door.

Salter Path was small enough that you did not have to have a car to get around. Bodhi decided to walk. He stopped by the office to pick up a cup of coffee. The advantage of new motel owners was high-end coffee in the office. He filled a paper cup with a dark roast Columbian coffee, added two creams and two sugars, stirred, and put a lid on it.

"Good morning," Danny said.

"Mornin'," Bodhi responded.

"You are up early. Did you sleep okay?" Danny inquired, worrying that something was not right with the room.

"Room was great. The bed was comfortable. I slept so well that I woke up early," Bodhi tried to assure him that all was fine.

"Good to hear. I noticed your wife is here with you. Do you need another key?" Danny asked Bodhi.

"Well, yes, that would be good. I forgot to ask for one yesterday," Bodhi felt a twinge of oddness that Danny had watched them so closely. He shrugged it off as it was a small motel, and perhaps it was something Danny had just noticed.

"Here you go," Danny said, handing over the key. "So you know, the pool opens at ten a.m., and the cocktail bar opens at noon. Hope you stop by."

Bodhi again could not connect if this was a hospitable person or if there was more to this. Maybe it was just those awkward northerners trying to be southern. Whatever it was, he did not pay it much attention. "Thanks. We will see you around," Bodhi turned and walked out of the office with the key and coffee in hand.

It was a workday in Salter Path because every summer day was a workday. Bodhi remembered this from when he was younger. The motel was still. Cars parked in front of rooms showed how many people were there. It was still early in the vacation season, and vacationers occupied about half of the rooms. The types and sizes of cars—luxury SUVs and electric vehicles—indicated the Gentillis strategy seemed to be working. The vehicles were the hallmark of the young professional as opposed to the turtle-topped minivans of family vacations. Across the street from the motel were the main residential areas for permanent Salter Path citizens.

The permanent residents were still mostly Salters, Willards, Joneses, and Snows. A few other families had moved into the town, but not many. The island was already stirring. Residents had pickup trucks of various ages parked in their driveways. The more successful residents owned the newer trucks. Old or new, various items were strewn in the beds showing the town used their trucks for work. A few older model sedans indicated where the retired residents lived with their Buick LeSabres parked in the driveway. Bodhi knew it was not too early to pay a visit to Nana B's house. He headed that way.

He could feel the pit starting to form in his stomach on the walk. He was going to be walking very close to his old house. He had already decided that he would not visit there until he had Ellie by his side. As he walked down Salter Path Road, he could see the red and yellow shell advertising fresh shrimp. That made him smile; Bodhi remembered helping his Uncle Nathan paint that sign. Well, at least he thought he was helping. He was probably only six or seven years old, and he spilled the black paint can (if you look at the sign, you will notice no black paint.) The memory made him smile a bit because his uncle just said, "Well, I guess we just don't have no black for the letters." Bodhi could still see his mark on the town.

He turned down the stone driveway. A shrimp net was spread out over the yard. The house was modest but nicely kept. The side door was open, and an old dog was sleeping on the porch. Bodhi walked up and said to the dog, "Maggie?" The brown dog with gray around her eyes and chin lifted her head. She was a Boykin. Dogs were bred in South Carolina to work in the fields and water. Bodhi could not believe it. When he left seventeen years ago, Maggie was the new puppy of his best friend, Ley. She sniffed his hand and stood up, wagging her tail. After all these years, she recognized his scent.

He stepped up onto the side porch and rang the doorbell. The screen door was the same door people came to purchase Beatrice's fresh-shelled shrimp. In a flash, it occurred to Bodhi that Nana B might not be here. He had so little contact with Salter Path that he was not even sure she was still alive. In a minute, a petite old woman came to the door and said, "Come on in. I got small for nine dollars, medium for ten, and jumbo for twelve. I also have some scallops. What can I get ya?"

Bodhi just stood there, paralyzed outside the door. He immediately knew that it was Nana B. She had aged, but her voice and smile were unforgettable. Nana B turned to him, "Ya gonna come in?"

"Nana B?" Bodhi said.

She was reaching into the freezer, pulling out her packages of shrimp. She stopped and turned to face Bodhi. She pushed up her glasses and looked him straight in the eye. She knew it was him. She tried to smile but could not help the tears of joy coming to her eyes. She began to cry and said, "Bodhi." He walked through the door and hugged her.

"I can't believe it is you. Why are you here? What brought you back?"

"I am here for a vacation. I brought my fiancée to see where I grew up," he paused, wondering if he had grown up.

"Where is she? I want to meet her?" Nana B asked.

"She's still sleeping. You know, Raleigh folk don't wake up early on vacation," Bodhi tried to connect to Salter Path.

"Well, you be sure to bring her over. How are you? What have you been doing?" Nana B had so many questions. Bodhi tried to answer them all. She enjoyed hearing about how he had grown and how well he was doing in Raleigh.

Bodhi finally was able to ask, "How have you been doing?"

"Oh me. I am old. I am getting along watching my soaps, and peeling shrimp. Things are quiet here, and I like it that way. I am the prayer chain leader at the church, and we are making puppets for a kids ministry."

"What about Ley? Is he still around?" Bodhi asked about his childhood friend and cousin.

Nana B smiled and laughed a little, "He is good. He is actually out on the boat now shrimping. He left about eight p.m. to head to the Pamlico. He should be back around lunch. Why don't you come over for lunch with your fiancée? You can surprise Ley. He will be amazed that you are here."

Bodhi did not have to think for a second. "That sounds great. I am going to head back to the motel, and then we will be back around noon."

"Motel? Where are you stayin'?" Nana B could not figure out why a Salter Path boy had to stay in a motel.

"Well, I didn't want to impose on anyone, and that new family has fixed up the motel nicely. I figured it would be easier on everyone," Bodhi responded, but he was thinking that he might not be welcome in town after leaving.

"Well, okay. Come back for lunch," Nana B instructed.

Bodhi gave her another hug, turned, and walked out the door. Maggie sniffed him again and wagged her tail. He reached down and gave her a scratch behind the ear. Maggie looked at him approvingly. He scratched just the right spot. He walked off the porch, up the stone driveway, and toward the motel.

When he got back to the room, Ellie was still asleep. As he opened the door, the sunlight splashed across the bed. Half exposed and spotlighted by sunshine, Ellie's naked body made Bodhi pause as he studied her figure. He closed the door and turned on the light as Ellie began to wake up.

"Where were you?" Ellie asked in a groggy voice.

"I went for a walk to see if my aunt was at home," Bodhi said.

"Oh, good. Was she there?" Ellie was a little disappointed Bodhi had left without her.

"Yes. She was there, and so was Maggie."

"Maggie? Who is she?" Ellie asked.

"Maggie? She is a puppy from when I left; well, she isn't a puppy anymore. She is an old, gray-faced Boykin now. Just as sweet as I remembered her," Bodhi said with a smile.

"Oh…so tell me about your aunt," Ellie wanted to get some background on Bodhi's family.

"Well, I call her Nana B. Her name is Beatrice, and she was the sister of my grandfather, Jerry. Her husband was with him when the *Legacy* went down. My grandmother died shortly after my grandfather, and Aunt Beatrice was always like a grandmother to me. So, I called her Nana B." Bodhi started to fumble with the Keurig coffee maker. "She still lives in the same house. She is 'the shrimp lady' in town. She sells shrimp out of her backdoor. My best friend Ley is her grandson. I think that makes him my second cousin. He still works on the shrimp boats."

"Did you see him too?" Ellie asked.

"No, he went out last night on the shrimp boat. He is going to be back about noon today. Nana B asked us to come over for lunch to surprise him when he comes back to the dock. Is that okay?"

"I would love that! When should we go? About eleven-thirty? We do not want to be late." Ellie was telling him when she wanted to go.

"We are on island time now. Lunch can be anywhere from noon until two. Let's go a little after noon." Bodhi hinted at the relaxed style of the low country folks.

"Sounds great. What should I wear?" Ellie wanted to make sure she looked the part.

"Nothing too fancy. Shorts and a T-shirt," Bodhi told her.

Ellie reached out her arms and pulled him into the bed. "I can't wait!"

15

Lunch

The *Lady B* chugged along under the Atlantic Beach high-rise bridge. Black smoke from the diesel engine came out of the exhaust. Ley and Bobby had the nets pulled in, and a small flock of seagulls followed behind, smelling the shrimp on the boat and hoping for a handout. Ley was in the wheelhouse while his new deckhand, Bobby, hosed down the deck. They had a good catch for a night's work, bringing in about 600 pounds. They already unloaded the majority at Homer Smith's Seafood in Beaufort, earning $1.75 a pound for the shrimp. After the cost of fuel and an equal share for the boat, the two men would take home $256 for fifteen hours of work. They kept fifty pounds of shrimp for Nana B. She would peel it, devein it, and pack it in freezer bags for sale. The shrimp covered the dock fee for berthing the boat behind her house.

Bogue Sound is a large body of water. It is about fifty square miles of open water. However, Bogue Sound is not deep water. There are shifting sand bars that change from storm to storm. After a strong blow, you have to read the water as you make your way across the sound. Dark and green water is safe; brown and tan water means a sandbar. As you navigate across the sound, you have to gauge your

SALTER'S PATH

bearings by landmarks. If you want to navigate at night, you need to know how the lights look along the shore. The water towers are good markers, the lights on the high-rise bridge in Atlantic Beach, the marina in Salter Path, and the few houses always have their lights on with odd colors. Ley knew these waters like his backyard. He knew where the sandbars were, the cuts to cross out of the Intracoastal Waterway, and how long to run in one direction before making a turn. His twists and turns seemed erratic for those unfamiliar with the water, but he was following a channel across the sound. Shrimp boats like the *Lady B* were designed for shallow water, but they still needed two to three feet of water to pass safely.

Ley turned the boat to the left at the NC State University Marine Sciences building. Every time he saw the building, it reminded him of the other path in life that he could have taken, playing football and going to NC State for a college education. He could have gone anywhere, but he knew captaining a boat on the Bogue Sound was where he wanted to be. About 500 yards across the channel, Ley made a right-hand turn and pointed the *Lady B* down the middle of the sound. He kept an eye out for the duck blinds and random pilings scattered throughout the sound. He turned the wheel to the right when he got to McGinnis Point, swinging the boat out around the shifting shoals off the point. Off the dock for the State Aquarium, he put the stern to the radio tower on the mainland and pointed the bow at the aquarium dock. About 200 yards off the shore, he turned right into the NC Wildlife Boat Channel. From here, he could follow the buoys to Nana B's dock.

Ellie and Bodhi got to Nana B's house about twelve-fifteen. Maggie was lying on the front porch. Ellie walked up and reached out her hand. Maggie gave it a sniff, stood up, and walked to Bodhi. Ellie and Bodhi scratched her behind her ears, and she stood enjoying the attention and wagging her tail. Bodhi pulled the screened door open and walked into the house.

"Nana B!" Bodhi yelled.

"I will be out in a second," an older woman's voice came from the back room.

Bodhi opened the fridge door and grabbed a pitcher of tea.

"Should you do that? Just go in someone's fridge?" Ellie asked.

"Oh, this is Nana's house. She doesn't care. It feels like home to me, like I never left," Bodhi assured her.

Just then, Nana B came out of the back room dressed in polyester pants and a blouse that she bought at TJ Maxx. She smiled wide, and she walked straight to Ellie.

"You must be Ellie," she said, wrapping her arms around her and hugging her. Ellie was stunned and stood there with her arms at her side being embraced.

"Thank you. Yes, that's me," Ellie stammered.

Nana B turned to Bodhi. "You outdid yourself. She is about the most beautiful thing I have ever seen."

"Nana, stop. I know I am a lucky man. Everyone likes to remind me." Bodhi always felt terrible when people complimented Ellie's looks. He did not want people to think he loved her because she was beautiful. He loved her because of how she made him feel safe and loved.

Nana B was at the stove, turning on a burner. "I talked to Ley a bit ago. He was at the AB bridge. He should be here in about ten minutes," Nana B said.

"That's great, but what ya fixin' for lunch?" Bodhi slipped into a low country accent that he forgot he had.

"Shrimp and grits. I will get it started. You go wait on the dock for Ley," Nana B directed the young couple.

Ellie and Bodhi walked out the back door and onto the dock. They sat down on the dock's edge, and Maggie came walking down and lay next to them. "Hey, old girl," Bodhi said. There was a beautiful Carolina blue sky, and being only late May, it was not too hot. It was the best time to be at the Crystal Coast.

"Look," Ellie said, pointing out over the water. "Is that him?"

Bodhi looked up. "Yes. That's it. The *Lady B*. My dad's old boat. I remember waiting on this dock for him to get home," Bodhi said in a low tone.

Ellie sensed the pain again in his voice. She wondered if this might be harder than she imagined. They sat in silence as the *Lady B* made the turn off McGinnis Point and then by the North Carolina Aquarium. Soon she was in front of them, slowly spinning to back into the berth.

"Who's that? She is a sweet piece of ass," Bobby said to Ley.

"Damned if I know. Probably some tourists," Ley replied.

The boat backed down into the slip, and Bodhi stood up to help with lines. The same way he helped his dad.

"Thanks," Bobby said to Bodhi. Bobby could see that the guy on the dock knew how to handle ropes.

Ley walked out of the wheelhouse. He looked at Ellie first because most men looked at Ellie first, then he glanced at Bodhi. He began to turn away and then turned back with a puzzled look.

"I see Maggie is still around," Bodhi said to Ley.

"Are you fucking kidding me? Bodhi?" Ley wanted to be sure before he said more.

"Not fucking kidding," Bodhi said.

All six foot five of Ley jumped from the boat and grabbed Bodhi, lifting him off the ground. His arms were at his side as Ley squeezed him in a bear hug. It was Bodhi's turn to be hugged. Ley dropped him and grabbed his hand, giving it a shake.

"I never thought I would see your ass again! What are you doing here?"

"Ley, this is Ellie, my fiancée. I wanted to bring her to the Path to meet the people I grew up with," Bodhi told Ley.

"Ellie, sorry for the language. I haven't seen this dick, umm guy, in like fifteen years," Ley said to her.

"Not a problem. These aren't virgin ears. They called me trash girl in college," Ellie did not know why she said that. She tried to recover, "They called me that because I drank trashcans."

Ley looked at Bodhi. "I like this girl. Easy on the eyes, too," Ley said to Bodhi.

"I'm Bobby," Bobby said to Ellie, sticking out his hand.

Bobby was from out of town. He came to Salter Path from Florida looking for a job on a fishing boat. He said he had worked long line fishing in the Gulf of Mexico for some years. He was only twenty years old, and everyone knew he was exaggerating his experience. He always seemed to be wearing the same clothes around town. His uniform was a long sleeve AFTCO fishing with stains on the front, American flag-patterned swim trunks, and short Xtratuf boots. He was pretty tall and thin with long black hair that stuck out from under his worn-out baseball hat. He was quiet and spent most evenings by himself away from the social scene in town. Nothing was odd about him, but nothing was exactly normal. When DJ turned down Ley to be a deckhand, he offered it to Bobby. Bobby turned out to be a competent deckhand. He knew how to keep his feet on a boat and wasn't afraid of doing hard work. Ley found he had to be a bit more detailed on his instructions, but overall he seemed to be working out as a deckhand.

Ellie stuck out her hand, and Bobby took it, holding it a bit longer than was comfortable. Ellie said, "Nice to meet you, Bobby."

"Pleasure is the same," Bobby said, staring at Ellie.

"I'm Bodhi. Ellie's fiancée," Bodhi said to Bobby, breaking off the handshake. Ley watched the whole situation play out. For a second, he was afraid that Bodhi might throw Bobby off the dock by the way he was looking at Ellie.

Dropping Bobby's hand, Bodhi turned to Ley. "Nana B is fixin' lunch for us. Let's not leave her waitin'."

Ley turned to Bobby and instructed him to get the boat put up for the day. Ley jumped in the boat, grabbed the cooler with Nana B's shrimp, and headed to the house. Ley made the fifty pounds of shrimp look like a loaf of bread. He was a big, powerful man.

Bodhi, Ellie, and Ley headed inside. Nana B was setting the table, setting down glasses with ice, and filling them with tea. There was a large pot of cheese grits on the stove and a cast-iron frying pan with shrimp, dry sausage, onions, green peppers, and spices. A wooden spatula rested on the side of the frying pan.

"Surprised?" Nana B asked Ley.

"I could not believe this guy is back in town. I never thought..." Ley paused, "that I would get to see him again. Who else have you seen in town?"

"We just got in last night. I woke up and came over here to see Nana B. We haven't seen anyone except Danny, who runs the motel," Bodhi said.

"Danny seems all right for a mainlander. Maybe a little too much trying to get into Pather's business, but he did some good things for the old motel," Ley said.

Nana B asked Ellie, "Do you like shrimp? I can fix something else if you don't."

"Love them. I have not had fresh shrimp like this," Ellie told Nana B. "Can I help you with anything?"

Nana B was spooning grits onto paper plates, "No, you just enjoy yourself, honey." She spooned the shrimp in the frying pan onto the grits and carried the bending paper plates to the table. Ellie got up from the table and asked Nana B, "Is the tea in the fridge? I will pour it." She opened the refrigerator and took out the plastic tea pitcher.

She poured the sweet brown liquid over the ice in the glasses.

"Let's pray," Ley said, bowing his head and reaching out his hands.

Ellie paused for a moment. Her family prayed over meals, but not lunch. Usually, a prayer was reserved for special occasions like Christmas or Easter.

"Lord, thank you for this food you provided to us. Thank you for bringing me home safe from another trip on Your great ocean. You are the one, the powerful, and the provider. Please make Bodhi and Ellie's visit to Salter Path fulfilling and joyful. In Jesus's name, we pray. Amen," Ley finished the prayer and immediately lifted his fork and dug into the shrimp and grits.

"Amazing. These are sooo good," Ellie said to Nana B. Ellie truly meant it. She had never had shrimp this fresh, and the texture and taste were more like lobster than the mealy frozen shrimp people in Raleigh were used to eating.

They finished lunch and cleaned up the table. Ley turned to Bodhi and said, "Beer?"

"Sure. You want one, Ellie?" Bodhi asked.

"Sounds good," Ellie responded.

The three of them grabbed some beer and headed outside. Nana B was in the house watching her soap operas and working on peeling the shrimp Ley just brought back. They sat on the back porch, looking out at the sound. They could see the boats coming and going from Jones Marina. It hosted mostly temporary residents' boats, folks who did not live in Salter Path full time but spent most of the summer on the island. The waves on the sound were lapping against the sea wall. Ellie and Bodhi swung on the porch swing, and Ley sat on a chair across from them.

"How long are you in town?" Ley asked Bodhi.

"We rented the place for a week. We are supposed to check out Friday. We can stay longer if we want. After the pandemic, our work is remote. We can work whenever we want," Bodhi said.

"That's good. You will be here for the Big Rock Tournament, then," Ley reminded Bodhi about the tournament.

The week-long Big Rock Blue Marlin Tournament takes place every June. As kids, Ley, DJ, and Bodhi would spend the week on the docks around Morehead City, watching the fishing coming to the weigh station. It was always an exciting way to start the summer.

"That's right. It will just be starting when we are getting ready to leave. Maybe we will extend for a few more days to see some fish," Bodhi said to Ellie.

"So we are going to stay to look at fish?" Ellie asked Bodhi.

"There is the Captain's Party, too. I can get y'all tickets. It's a lot of fun," Ley tried to help Bodhi's cause.

"Oh, a party? That could be fun. What is this tournament?" Ellie asked the guys.

"It is the blue marlin tournament. People come from all over the East Coast. The biggest fish will win over a million dollars. It is a rich person's sport, and it's fun to hobnob with these folks. Last year Michael Jordan brought his boat to fish." Ley gave his best sales pitch.

"All right, you win. We can stay for a few extra days," Ellie consented.

"I will get you tickets for the Captain's Party," Ley said to Bodhi.

"I will take Ellie shopping for the party," Bodhi smiled, and Ellie stuck her tongue out.

Ley chuckled a bit, "Y'all have fun. I have to turn in soon. Back on the water for me tonight. Calm weather for the next few days. We are looking at storms after that."

Ellie and Bodhi bid goodbye to Nana B, and Ley checked on the boat before he went to sleep. Nana B greeted a customer looking for fresh shrimp at the back door as Ellie and Bodhi walked up the driveway. It was late afternoon, and the young couple headed back to the motel for time alone.

16

Trailer Life

Bodhi walked through the motel door with two cups of coffee from the office. Ellie was sitting up in bed wearing a T-shirt. The news played on the television. There was a storm forming in the tropics. Hurricane season did not start until June first, and it sounded like this storm would be there for opening day. The television reporter said the storm might not even come close to the United States. It was still too early to tell.

"I thought we should go to the Big Tree for lunch today," Bodhi said. "We could then go to the beach or stay by the pool."

"What is the Big Tree?"

"It's a drive-in. They are kind of a thing down here. There is the Big Tree on the island, and El's on the mainland. El's has good burgers and dogs, but Big Tree has the best shrimp burger."

"That sounds fine. I think I want to go to the beach today," Ellie said.

Bodhi got into bed with Ellie. They sipped their coffee and stared at their phones. They were enjoying being connected and isolated in the small motel room. It was good to be away from the regular grind of everyday life. Planning a wedding consumed much of their relationship energy, and being away from it all allowed them to connect. Ellie leaned into Bodhi, and he kissed her on the head.

————-

Ellie was getting dressed, putting on a bikini, and pulling a cover-up over it. Bodhi was enjoying watching. He loved her for who she was, and it was a bonus to admire her body. Bodhi pulled on his swimming trunks, flip-flops, T-shirt, and bucket hat. Ready for the day, they headed to the Big Tree for some lunch.

DJ was working at the Big Tree today. Bodhi had thought about calling him the previous night but decided Ellie meeting Ley and Nana B was enough for one day. DJ's typical workstation was with the fryers. His father, Darrel, ran the window taking orders and money. Today Darrel was fishing offshore doing a few practice runs for the Big Rock Tournament, so today, DJ sat in the window taking orders and money.

It was still early in the season, but the Big Tree was so busy that Officer Blakely stood on the road directing traffic. He waved Bodhi's truck into the parking lot. Bodhi parked the truck under a live oak that stretched its crooked limbs over the lot. Ellie stepped out of the truck wearing a white lace cover-up to hide her bikini. Her beauty was such that the men in the parking lot could not help but notice her. Ellie and Bodhi stood in front of the menu, trying to decide on lunch. It would be fried pickles, two shrimp burgers with slaw and hot sauce, and a Coke.

"What can I get you?" DJ said.

"One large shrimp burger all the way, one regular shrimp burger all the way, fried pickles, and a large Coke," Bodhi said.

"Name?"

"Bodhi."

DJ paused. He looked out the window at the man in front of him.

"Salter?" DJ asked.

"Yes. DJ?" Bodhi said.

"Holy shit! What the hell are you doing here? It has been forever!"

"Wow. I forgot that your dad owned this place. I guess you are running it now. We are in town for some vacation and to catch-up with old friends. I was going to call you last night, but things ran late for us," Bodhi said.

"I can't believe you are here. How long have you been here?"

"We got in a couple of nights ago and went over to see Nana B and Ley yesterday. I told him not to tell you. I wanted to surprise you, but I didn't plan on it being here."

"Look, lunch is on me. You have to come by tonight to hang out. Who is with you?" DJ asked.

"My fiancée, Ellie."

Ellie poked her head around Bodhi and said, "Hey."

"Good to meet you. Can y'all come by tonight? Maybe around eight?" DJ asked.

Bodhi turned to Ellie for her approval. "Yeah, that works. Where do you live?"

"In the park, G-fifteen," DJ said, pointing over his shoulder in the direction of his trailer.

"See you then," Bodhi said, getting out of the way as the line was building behind him.

Bodhi and Ellie got their food and popped the tailgate on the truck. They sat eating their shrimp burgers and fried pickles, sharing a Coke and watching Officer Blakely directing customers into the parking lot. The fried pickles were unlike any Ellie had had before today. They were hand-breaded quarter spears. They were the perfect mixture of pickle and breading. Some things were just better at the beach.

———-

Bodhi's truck pulled into the beach access parking lot. They lifted the beach chairs, cooler, and beach bag out of the truck bed. They walked down a long boardwalk path that snaked through the low

93

maritime forest growing on the island. As they approached the beach, the boardwalk rose to go over the dune. At the top, Ellie saw the Crystal Coast for the first time. The light blue water washed up onto the sparkling sand. Bodhi stopped dead in his tracks as Ellie walked on in front of him.

She was halfway down the steps to the beach when she noticed he was not behind her. At the top of the steps, Bodhi was frozen, with his face turning in a twisted way. "Honey. You okay?" Ellie asked and walked back up the steps.

"It's the first time. This spot is where I was when we heard sirens," Bodhi pointed off to the right. "Ley and I were chasing crabs with flashlights and nets. It was almost time to head back. We had a bunch of crabs, and we're going to try to sell them on the beach as pets. We heard the sirens at the fire station. You could see the fire trucks pull out and start to drive toward us. When they stopped, you could see the smoke lit up by their flashing lights. It was right over the dune in the direction of my house."

Ellie did not know what to say. She just reached out and pulled him close. They held each other. Then, with a deep breath, Bodhi said, "It will be all right."

She was feeling helpless, and Ellie loved the way Bodhi was aware. It made her feel better that she did not have to be the solution to Bodhi's past, but she hoped she would be.

Bodhi finally walked down the steps onto the beach, following Ellie. They picked out a place just below the high tideline on the hard sand. Bodhi flipped open the beach chairs while Ellie took towels from the beach bag. They spread the towels over the chairs. Ellie liked to put a towel on her chair; she said it made her feel cooler. Bodhi pulled two cold beers from the cooler as they sat on the beach, and Ellie pulled two Neuse River Sports Shop koozies from the beach bag.

The panic that overcame Bodhi had subsided. He leaned back in his chair and took a deep breath. He closed his eyes and tilted his head back, feeling the sun across his face. "It feels good. It feels like home," Bodhi said.

"What do you mean?"

"Have you ever heard that if you learn a language when you are young, it will always be easier to learn when you are older?" Bodhi said.

"Yes. You might not even have an accent, people say."

"It is like that for me. I have not been here in seventeen years, but my body remembers this place," Bodhi explained.

Ellie leaned her chair back, thinking about what Bodhi said. He looked up and down the beach, taking in the sights and sounds. The tide was low, and the waves broke on a sandbar off the beach. Kids ran in the surf, throwing skimboards down and jumping on for a short ride. College kids drank beer and laughed. Everyone enjoyed their own experience of the beach. Ellie and Bodhi spent the rest of the afternoon relaxing before returning to the motel.

———

When they got to DJ's trailer a little after eight p.m., DJ was sitting on the deck with a beer in hand. DJ's trailer was a 1973 Flamingo mobile home, single-wide, painted light gray. The trailer park had about 100 trailers, all nestled underneath large live oaks. The park was a mix of part-time and full-time residents. Most of the trailers had well-mowed grass, flowers, and palm trees in the front yard. DJ's trailer had a large covered deck outside the front door, with a TV and bar on the deck. Bodhi and Ellie came walking up carrying a cooler full of beer and a bottle of white wine.

"Welcome! Glad you made it," said DJ.

"Would not miss it. I like the deck. How long have you lived here?" Bodhi asked.

"Oh. I am getting ready to pay my sixth lot rent. Let me show you the place," DJ said.

Ellie had never been in a mobile home before and did not know what to expect. She believed people living in mobile homes did so because they were desperate. She could not recall anyone she knew who lived in one. She walked into the trailer behind DJ. It had the unmistakable decorating touches of a bachelor: a large television, game consoles, and a well-used bong in the corner. The floorplan was simple, with a kitchen, living room, two bedrooms, and a bathroom. Ellie felt the hominess of the trailer. It *was* a home, just smaller.

DJ grabbed a wine glass out of the cupboard. He handed it to Ellie and said, "Do you need a corkscrew for the wine?"

Ellie twisted the top on the bottle, "Nope."

"My kind of girl," DJ said. "I invited a few people over. They should be here soon."

"Anyone I know?" Bodhi asked.

"A few people from the Path. You will probably remember Jill, Abby, and Landon. Ley and Bobby are going to come by, too," DJ said.

"Wow, it has been a while since I heard those names. How are they doing?"

"You know—life in the Path. Everyone has a job. We take care of each other and make sure everyone has what they need. Jill works at Dollar General. Abby is a waitress at Amos Mosquito's. Her name there is 'Bubbles'. Landon works at the boatyard."

Bodhi's mind jumped at the word 'boatyard'. He knew the boatyard was a reference to the Snow Boatyard they rebuilt after the fire. "It will be good to see them again," Bodhi commented.

Just then, a well-worn pickup truck turned into the yard. It had dents on the side, and the sun had faded the roof and hood. Jill, Abby, and Landon rolled out of the cab. They were drunk from a day on the beach.

"Shots! DJ, shots!" yelled one of the women.

"OOOHHH, shit! Here we go!" DJ said as he disappeared into the trailer.

Between DJ, Jill, Abby, and Landon, Ellie saw more tattoos than she had ever seen in her life. The group was ready to have a good time, and DJ's was the place to be in Salter Path that night.

"Damn, Bodhi, how are you? Good to have you back," Landon said.

"I am good. It is good to be back. It has been too long."

"Look at you, Bodhi Salter. You grew up," Jill said.

Bodhi was familiar with people commenting on Ellie's attractiveness, but Ellie was not used to hearing women comment on her man. Something inside her twitched. She did not like the idea of others finding him attractive. He was hers.

"This is Ellie. My fiancée," Bodhi said.

"I am Jill and this is Abby."

"Nice to meet you. How do you know Bodhi?"

"Bodhi was my first kiss," Jill said.

"You didn't tell me that," Ellie said to Bodhi.

"Come on, Jill. You lead with that? We were eight years old," Bodhi said.

"I just want you to remember that I was your first," Jill said.

Ellie did not like this conversation. In Raleigh, you did not talk about these things. She knew it was childhood silliness, but it felt like Jill was directly attacking her relationship. Ellie responded, "Bodhi, remember I am going to be your last."

"Jill, stop bugging them," Ley said, walking into the yard.

"I will bug you, then. Where have you been?" Jill asked.

"Just got up a bit ago. We were on the water last night. Decided to take the day off and come see this guy." He grabbed Bodhi by the shoulders. Bodhi was a big person, but when Ley stood next to him, he looked small.

Bobby walked a few steps behind Ley. Ellie noticed he had the same clothes on from a few days ago when he got off the boat. He had a twelve-pack of light beer in his hand and a cigarette hanging from his mouth. He walked in, sat down at the table, and opened a beer.

"Hey, Bobby," Bodhi said.

"Hey."

"Can I bum a smoke?"

"Sure. They're Camel Lights," Bobby said.

"Beggars can't be choosers."

Ellie noticed Bodhi lighting up. They smoked the first night they were together but had not smoked in about a year. Ellie was happy to kick that habit. DJ walked out of the trailer door with tiny red plastic cups the size of shot glasses and a bottle of ice-cold Creek Water whiskey. A local whiskey at 100 proof, it delivered a good time.

DJ poured out eight shots and yelled, "Listen up! Grab a shot." He raised his plastic cup. "Welcome back, Bodhi. Some said you would never be back, but that won me fifty bucks. Cheers!"

DJ poured another round of shots. Ley took a turn, "To Ellie, we always said Bodhi was a lucky son-of-bitch, and now we know he is!"

Two shots down, a few beers, and the party was getting rolling. The Bluetooth speaker was belting out a mix of country and rap. Jill and Abby danced, trying to get Ley to join in with them. The conversation got louder as everyone got drunker. Bobby got up from the table and walked over to Bodhi.

"Wanna smoke?" Bobby asked Bodhi.

"Sure, I will get you a pack tomorrow," Bodhi said.

"Nah, I mean weed. DJ has some inside."

"What are y'all talking about?" DJ questioned Bobby.

"Going to grab a toke," Bobby said.

"Well shit, c'mon," DJ said, opening the trailer door.

Ellie was starting to relax a bit. Maybe it was the shots or the fact that Jill would not leave her alone. She was jealous Jill knew Bodhi before her, but they were just kids. Ellie realized Jill was testing her to see if she would go bitch mode or could take a joke. Ellie could go bitch mode, but she could also take a joke. Landon, Ley, and the girls were huddling around the bar talking about concerts they wanted to go to that summer.

Inside the trailer, DJ pulled out his bong and packed it with some of his finest. They passed it around, inhaling deeply before exhaling slowly. Bodhi had not smoked pot since he was in college. The combination of pot and alcohol put Bodhi into a proper stupor. He somehow made it outside and walked over to the bar. Ellie looked at him, and he just smiled.

"Are you okay?" Ellie asked.

"Fine. Why?" Bodhi replied.

"Well, you look baked," Ellie said.

"Maybe. I went inside with Bobby and DJ," Bodhi said.

"Oh, shit. You are going to be good for nothing the rest of the night," Ellie could see it in his eyes. She knew that look from years ago. A few nights in Salter Path and her fiancée was drinking, smoking, and *smoking*. All she could think was that this was college Bodhi and not the one she knew. She didn't approve but didn't disapprove either.

A few hours went by, and Bodhi started to come out of his daze. Everyone had plenty to drink, and Landon led the group in volume.

Landon yelled at Bodhi out of nowhere, "So what finally gave you the balls to come back?"

"What the hell is wrong with you?" Bodhi replied.

"You know that half this town thinks your family are cowards, a bunch of chicken shits. Do you think you can just show back up?" Landon said.

"You gotta problem with me? Let's go settle it. You got a problem with my family? You go fuck yourself!" Bodhi yelled.

"Go back, Raleigh boy. We don't need you around here. Take that fake bitch with you, too!" Landon said.

Everyone stopped talking. The music coming from the speaker pierced the night. Everyone focused on Landon and Bodhi.

Ley was sitting at the bar. He stood up and said, "Landon. What the hell? Get outta here. You're drunk, and you don't need to be talking shit because if you gotta problem with them, you gotta problem with me."

"You just can't come back and figure everyone will forget. We know what his family did. Screw y'all, if you want to hang out with him, then fuck you." Landon walked to his truck.

"You're an ass, but I am not letting you kill someone. Give your keys and walk," Ley said.

"Screw you. Try to take them from me."

"You know, I will take them from you. Give 'em."

Landon stood staring Ley in the eyes, contemplating his options. He threw the keys at him and walked out of the yard.

"Sorry, about that. I didn't…" DJ said.

"Hey. It's okay. That shit was crazy. You couldn't have known Landon would do that," Bodhi said.

Jill, Abby, and Ellie just stared at them. Everything happened so fast that Ellie did not even realize what was happening until it was over. She went to Bodhi. Bodhi's face was still flush with the rush of adrenaline. Ellie reached out to try to calm him down. "What was that?" she asked.

"Old stuff. Landon works for the Snows. He probably hears shit from them all the time," DJ said.

"Don't listen to that idiot," Jill said, reassuringly.

Bodhi stood frozen as his blood pressure started to return to normal. "It's okay. I heard of this kind of stuff, but I thought it was over. I guess not."

The group tried to forget the incident with more shots, wine, and beer. All that did was open up the conversation more.

"Have you been to the old house yet?" Ley asked Bodhi.

"No, I haven't felt like it yet."

"You know it's yours," DJ stated.

"What do you mean?" Bodhi asked.

"When your folks passed away. They owned that house outright. Since you were the only one left, it became yours," DJ explained.

Bodhi had never thought about what happened to the land. He knew the house was gone, but he figured someone else owned the land. "I never thought about that. I guess you are right. Who has been paying the taxes and stuff?" Bodhi asked.

"Well, the Salters and Joneses have been covering it. It isn't much, but we thought you might come back one day and didn't want it taken by the county," Ley said. "I go down and mow the lot every few weeks in the summer to keep it up."

"Is anything left from the house?" Bodhi asked.

"Not much. You can make out the foundation, but there is nothing else to speak of," Ley said.

"I got to go and see it," Bodhi said.

"Tomorrow. You need to do this," Ellie told him.

17

Home

The coolness of the tile floor felt good. Bodhi lay on the bathroom floor in the motel with his head between the toilet and tub. He had pulled a towel over himself and tried to sleep. He still had his shirt on from the night before, but his shorts were gone. Bodhi was sure that someone was standing on his head, holding it to the floor. He felt the crushing pain of a massive hangover.

"Bluhhh, Bluhhh, oh God, Bluhhh," uttered Bodhi yacking into the toilet. "El, you there?"

"Yesss. What?"

"Can I get some water and ibuprofen?"

"Yes. Get me some, too," Ellie told him, not feeling much better than Bodhi. "What time is it?"

"Eight-thirty. Here take these," Bodhi said, crawling into bed with Ellie.

Bang, bang, bang. A man's voice yelled, "Housekeeping!" Bang, bang, bang. The keys rattled as the man started to unlock the door. Bodhi jumped out of bed, hustling to secure the door.

"No, thank you! We are fine," Bodhi yelled, but the door cracked open.

"Oh. Sorry, I will come back," said Danny, taking a quick peek into the room. He could see Ellie in bed and Bodhi standing in his underwear with a blank look.

"That's okay; you don't have to come back," Bodhi said.

"No problem. Have a good day," Danny said, closing the door.

"Ellie, it's one-thirty. We need to get up."

"Are you kidding? That was a night last night. Trailer parties are rough. You almost got in a fight last night. I have never seen you like that."

"Don't remind me. Landon just came out of nowhere and attacked me. I just reacted. When you grow up here, you know that if you leave, you are not welcome back. I thought it might be different for me. I guess that feud is still alive, or Landon is nuts."

"I am glad Ley was there. He probably stopped the cops from showing up. I guess we won't be hanging out with Landon while we are here."

"No, I don't think so. Let's get some food. I am still hungover as shit. Maybe some grease will make me feel better." Bodhi walked into the bathroom. "I need to shave my tongue. It feels like it's covered with fur."

The sun's brightness stung Bodhi's hungover eyes as he pulled the shades open. He put on his sunglasses as fast as he could. They got in the truck and headed to Atlantic Beach to find a burger. Bodhi remembered a small tavern they would go to on special occasions when he was young. He hoped it was still there.

"What do you think about what Ley said last night?" Ellie asked.

"About what? He said a lot of things," Bodhi responded, still foggy from the night of drinking.

"How your parents left you the property, and everyone has been keeping it up for you."

"I didn't do a lot of thinking last night," he said with sarcasm. "I never really thought about what happened to the property. I was a kid and figured it went away, that the bank or whoever took it. Thinking about it, though, this property was squatters' land. The families own all the land around here. The banks didn't own anything."

"So, you think you might own it?" Ellie still was trying to understand how Bodhi never knew about this.

"I don't know. I said we would go there today. Afterward, we can head to the police station. They might know something."

"What about the town hall? Wouldn't that be better?" Ellie asked.

"Remember, this is a small town. Town hall is only open on Monday, and today is Wednesday."

They found the small tavern. The inside was decorated as Bodhi remembered. The floor was red-orange linoleum with brown-legged bar stools with black vinyl seats. Smoking had not been allowed inside for more than ten years, but the white ceiling was stained light tan from cigarette smoke. The interior was so out of date; it was like a retro bar you would find in Raleigh. This bar was not a place designed to draw tourists in for food and drink. It was a place where the waterman, boat builders, landscapers, maids, waiters, and waitresses came to get away from the tourists.

Bodhi and Ellie sat at a table near the bar. They ordered burgers, fries, and water from a middle-aged waitress who was too heavy for the tight T-shirt she was wearing. Ellie was surprised by how cheerful she was for someone waiting tables in a bar at three p.m. on a Wednesday. Ellie imagined there was something she did not understand about people from the low country

"When we finish, let's head to the old house," Bodhi said to Ellie.

"Are you ready for that? Last night was hard. Should we wait another day or two?" Ellie asked.

Bodhi sat silently. He picked up a fry to eat, trying to buy some time while gathering his thoughts. When Bodhi's mind drifted to thinking about his childhood home, it made him feel hollow. All feelings went away. He could not feel the love of his family nor any other emotion toward them. He found it better not to talk about it. He knew that he needed to say something. He could not keep pushing this into his past, hoping that someday there would be enough distance that he could forget.

"No. I am not ready. I just have to do it," Bodhi said, gazing at his water. Ellie reached across the table to touch Bodhi on the arm. Her touch brought him back, and he felt the void inside him fill.

They finished their meal, paid the bill, and walked to the truck. Bodhi said, "Can you drive?" He could feel his heart racing already.

"Yes," Ellie said.

The ride to Salter Path was silent. Bodhi looked out the window. Ellie tried to find a radio station, knowing this was not the time for conversation. Bodhi was taking deep, deliberate breaths. That emptiness he felt was complete. It was like riding on a roller coaster and your stomach dropping. Only now, that feeling moved up to his lungs, heart, arms, and down to his feet. Bodhi felt his consciousness being pushed from his body and tried to keep his mind and body as one entity. The ride took about twenty minutes, but Bodhi had lost the perspective of time.

They came to the thirty-five mile per hour zone that marked the start of Salter Path. Bodhi was staring straight ahead. His lips were moving as if he was chewing on taffy. Ellie asked, "Are you all right?" As Bodhi struggled with his return to Salter Path, she had asked this many times over the last few days.

"I will be okay," Bodhi responded, letting Ellie know he was not all right.

They turned right at Hoffman Sound Road. At an intersection with an unnamed road, Bodhi pointed to a mostly vacant lot on the corner one row back from the sound. "It is right here."

The grass was about ankle-high on the property. It was more a collection of low-growing weeds than grass. The outside edge of the property had small rocks about the size of bowling balls placed at six-foot intervals. These rocks were to prevent unwanted people from driving onto the property. About halfway to the back of the lot were taller weeds and short, scraggly shrubs. They could make out a house's foundation made of cinderblocks stacked two or three high behind the weeds and shrubs. If someone drove by unknowingly, it looked like another abandoned lot on the island. This vacant lot was, in fact, the final resting place of Bodhi Salter's family.

Bodhi sat in the truck, looking at the old house foundation. Ellie reached across and put her hand on his back. This time Bodhi did not notice her touch. A flood of memories came back. He remembered running over the dune and falling in the soft sand. He remembered how every time he tried to get up, he fell—the nightmare feeling of sinking slowly into a pit of quicksand. The harder he tried to move, the worse the situation became. Nana B grabbed him as he attempted to cross the street. The look of panic and fear in her eyes. She pulled him down the road, water spraying from hoses and washing across the street. The red and white lights were flashing in the sky against the smoke. The smell of burning wood and plastic set itself deep into his nose. He screamed, "Where is my mom? Mom! Mom! Mom!" Nana B took him farther away from the fire. He was waiting for his family to walk through the door of her house. The sun was coming up, and the police arrived at Nana B's house. Nana B's impossible words, "I didn't think this could happen. Your mom, dad, and sister died in the fire last night." This moment was the first time he felt the emptiness he now knows so well.

Bodhi's shoulders start to move up and down. Then Ellie could hear the sobs. She felt his pain, and he began to cry. He wept as a grown man with the pain of a young boy. The weeping was visceral

- a weeping rooted in the depth of humanness. The intensity of the pain when the soul senses the fabric of life torn apart.

Bodhi took deep breaths saying, "God, please." He began to come back from his sorrow. He noticed Ellie with her arms wrapped tightly around him, holding him upright. He wished he was stronger, but he wasn't in the moment.

She could feel his consciousness coming back into his body. Bodhi saw Ellie crying. He said, "Honey, it's okay. I will be all right." He opened the truck door and felt the rush of humid, warm air from outside come over him. He noticed he was sweating from the ordeal. He stepped out of the truck with Ellie following behind.

"This is it. This spot is where I grew up," Bodhi said. There was no response from Ellie. She just took his hand, hoping it would help him with this pain. "I never told you, but there are no graves. The fire cremated them that night. We had a memorial service, but there were few remains. Someone, I think my Aunt Kristy, decided to cast them over the sound. This place is the last place I saw my family." Bodhi started walking toward the cinder block foundation.

Bodhi got to the edge of the foundation and stopped. "I have never been in my house since that day." A few small oak trees had started growing in the former burnt areas, but there were still patches of barren ground where the fire had sterilized the soil under the house, making it impossible for new life to grow. In some spaces, life had only recently begun encroaching on the land. Bodhi stepped over the foundation wall and into his house. "Here was where the living room was. It ran all the way to the back," Bodhi said, pointing to the back of the foundation. "The stairs were here by the front door. The kitchen was back there." He could recall the basics of the layout. "Our bedrooms were all upstairs. It wasn't very big, but it seemed big enough back then."

Ellie noticed that Bodhi had started to stitch together other memories. The pain of fire interwoven with memories of childhood. Tears were in his eyes, brought there by the confluence of joy and sorrow. He sat down on the foundation wall. "We would put the Christmas tree in the front window. My parents would make us stay upstairs until they went downstairs and made their coffee. Beth and I would strain to see what was under the tree from the top of the stairs. My dad would yell, 'Ho, Ho, Ho!' That was our signal to run down the stairs." Ellie could see he was reliving this in his mind.

"That sounds like a wonderful memory to have," Ellie said.

"I think back to that time. We had everything we needed. Then my grandfather died on the boat. My dad wasn't as happy. He was still a great dad, but he lost the goofy dad side. He was more serious. I loved them all so much. Mom was always there for us kids. Dad would go out to shrimp, and she would be mom and dad. She would cook and work odd jobs for extra cash. She was the most beautiful woman in town back then," he sighed. "Beth was amazing. She was always following us boys around." He paused. "I knew that Beth and I were going to be best friends. She was that person you met, and you can't wait to know better. She just had to grow up and become the person she was going to…" Bodhi's words trailed off as he tried to comprehend the woman he didn't get to know.

Ellie asked, "How did you deal with this growing up?"

"It happened so fast. Before I knew it, I was in Raleigh with Aunt Kristy. I was upset for a while, wondering how this could happen to me? Aunt Kristy just kept me busy trying to start over in Raleigh." Bodhi thought for a moment. "She is a Salter. They are used to rebuilding after a tragedy. When your house gets destroyed by a hurricane, you just rebuild and move on. Life goes on."

"How did it happen? How did the fire start?" Ellie asked.

"It was an accident, I guess. I never really heard any different. I just figured something electrical or something. It didn't seem to matter."

Bodhi had repeated the idea of an accident so many times in his mind when asked; he repeated the thought without thinking.

"Did you ask Kristy?" Ellie was trying to be aware of Bodhi's mood.

"Of course. She said, 'Does it matter? It is what it is' and would move on. She was my parent then, and if she didn't care, why should I? Knowing wouldn't change anything, so why try to know the details." Bodhi was trying to justify why he hadn't tried to find out more.

"Are you curious about how it happened?"

"In the back of my mind, I think about it from time to time. I was not ready to ask the question. Coming here and seeing the old house again makes me think I should know how the fire started." Bodhi was trying to be honest with his feelings. He knew that this had come up more and more as he was getting older. His thoughts changed from, "How can this happen to me?" to "How did this happen?"

Bodhi walked around inside the foundation perimeter. He was looking for something that might have survived the fire. Nothing from his childhood remained other than the cinder block foundation and a few pipes. He grabbed one of the pipes, twisting and bending it, trying to break it free. A two-foot-long piece of iron pipe broke off.

"This is all I could get. I need something to have with me back in Raleigh," Bodhi said, taking Ellie by the hand and heading to the truck. "Let's go see the Chief and see if he can tell us about the property and the fire."

The police station was almost across the street from the old house, but they drove anyway. The sun was starting to get low in the west, and the mirrored window on the door to the station reflected the sun into the young couple's eyes. They moved toward the door, trying to shield the sun from their eyes. They pulled the door open, and the sun now beamed into the hallway of the station.

"Can I help you?" A man's voice came from the desk to the right.

With his eyes still adjusting to the relative darkness inside, Bodhi said, "Hi, I had some questions about the old Salter house that burned down."

"Okay, who and who are you?" the man asked.

"Bodhi Salter. My parents, uh, I, I used to live there with my parents."

"Bodhi, I am Chief Burns. What do you mean you used to live there?"

"I grew up there with my parents until the fire, and then I moved away."

The chief looked closely at Bodhi. He remembered that night; everyone in town remembered that night. He tilted his head and took his reading glass off his nose. "I will be damned. You are Bodhi. I remember you from when you were little. I can see your father's...I, it's good to see you." Chief Burns could see Bodhi's father in his face but realized that it might not be the right thing to say.

"Chief Burns, it *is* you." Bodhi smiled a bit and said, "I didn't know if you would still be the chief. I still remember when you took us kids home to our parents after we climbed on top of the bathroom by the beach access."

"Ha, yes. The life of a small-town cop. Chasing ten-year-olds off of shithouse roofs," Chief Burns said. "How can I help you?"

"We have been in town a few nights, and I was talking with Needley Jones. He said that the old house might be in my name. I wanted to see if that was true and if I needed to pay any taxes or anything." Bodhi could not help but call it the old house even though there was no house anymore.

Ellie whispered to Bodhi, "Who is Needley?"

"Ley. His legal name is Needley."

Ellie nodded her head in understanding. Everyone in the low country seemed to have a nickname. She wondered for a second if Bodhi was Bodhi's real name.

Chief Burns turned to his computer and put his reading glasses on again. "Let me see here…" He poked away at the keyboard. "The county database lists Bodhi Aaron Salter as the owner." He kept looking at the record. "Taxes are paid. No liens against the property."

"Well, I guess Ley was right," Bodhi said. "What are the taxes a year? Can you see that?"

"Hold on. I gotta go to another page." Chief Burns was clicking and typing on the computer. "Looks like the taxes are one hundred and ninety-eight dollars."

"A month?" Bodhi asked.

"Ha. This is Salter Path, and you are on the squatter's side. That's a hundred and ninety-eight dollars a year. You know the town takes care of the locals," Chief Burns said.

"Who has been paying it all these years? Can you see that?" Ellie asked the chief.

"I can't tell that. Best to ask around. It was probably someone in town."

"Thanks, Chief. I never knew I owned this property. Glad I came here to find out," Bodhi said.

"No problem. It sounds like you are going to be a taxpayer now. Can I help you with anything else?" the chief offered.

"I gotta ask. What do you know about the fire? How did it start?" Bodhi asked.

Ellie looked directly at Bodhi's face checking his emotion.

The chief drew in a deep breath. "That's a tough one. I wasn't chief long when the fire happened. We did an investigation but could never find anything. We even called the State Bureau of Investigation from Raleigh. I don't think he got very far. Hold on." Chief Burns turned to an old Rolodex. He fumbled through the cards stopping at the letter S. He pulled out a card. "State Bureau of Investigation, Detective Steve Natchez. He was the investigator. He might know something." He handed over the card to Bodhi. "See if that number still works. Maybe

111

there is an answer there."

Bodhi took the card. "Thanks. I might give him a call. I will see you around, Chief. We will be here for another week or so."

"Good to see you, Bodhi. You take care. Let me know if you need anything. Welcome home."

18

Retirement

Thirty-seven years is a long time. People can live entire lives in thirty-seven years. Married, kids, divorced and married again - more kids and heartbreaks, one lifetime in thirty-seven years.

Steve Natchez had spent thirty-seven years of his life in law enforcement. He started in the Raleigh Police Department and became an SBI detective at the age of thirty-two. He had a long career serving the people of North Carolina.

The Raleigh SBI office assigned Detective Natchez to eastern North Carolina. He spent a career running the roads from Rocky Mount to Kill Devil Hills. He covered every type of case throughout his career, from a missing horse to homicide. In 2007, the population of eastern North Carolina had grown enough to warrant a field office in Jacksonville. It was natural for Detective Natchez to become the head of the new field office. He relished moving to the coast and the place he had spent so many days in his life. He decided to buy a house in one of the few small towns he had not run a case during his career.

Swansboro was the site of the first steamboat built in North Carolina and the home of a pirate ship known as the *Snapdragon*. Swansboro had always been the little sister to Beaufort about twenty miles away, and the village made for a perfect low-key place for an SBI detective to call home. A few blocks from the White Oak River in downtown Swansboro, Detective Natchez bought a three-bedroom, one-and-a-half bath house built in the 1890s. The house had a historical plaque tacked to the side of the house on the front porch. He knew this would be his retirement house when he'd moved there fourteen years earlier. He was turning sixty-five in July and finally to retirement age. In a few more months, he would complete the journey he started in law enforcement. The house he picked was modest and historic.

Every morning Detective Natchez would walk to Sweet Edventures. The restaurant served double duty in town as a coffee shop in the morning and a dessert bar at night. Sweet Edventures had the only good cup of coffee in town. Natchez often got a piece of chocolate cake to go with his morning coffee, and the morning treat was an indulgence he didn't need but wanted. It was Friday morning, and Natchez was already thinking about the weekend. He ordered his coffee from Ed, the owner of Sweet Edventures.

"Good morning, Detective," Ed said.

"Morning, Ed. You got plans for the weekend?" Natchez asked.

"I am planning to see you. Come by this weekend. We are going to have a band Saturday night. It should be fun."

"I will probably stop by for a bit. Molly and I need to get out and about more. That pandemic was a bitch. I am ready to be normal again," Natchez said.

"I hear you. We were lucky to survive. The business has turned the corner now, and we should make it."

"That's good to hear. I don't know what I would do without this place," Natchez said. "I have to get to the office. Can you make the cake to-go today?"

"Of course, no problem," Ed said as he pulled a large slice of German chocolate cake from the display case and placed it in a paper to-go container.

"Have a great day. Say hello to Jess. We will try to stop by tomorrow night," Natchez said. He was walking toward the door, and his phone rang. He stopped, took a swig of his coffee, and looked at his phone. He tapped the screen and raised it to his ear. "Hello?"

"Hello. Can I talk to Detective Natchez?" Bodhi asked.

"This is him," Natchez responded.

"Hi, my name is Bodhi Salter. Chief Burns from the Salter Path Police gave me your number. I was calling about a house fire from back in 2004."

"What can I help you with?"

"I don't know if you remember, but there was a fire in Salter Path years ago. Chief Burns said that you investigated the fire." Bodhi asked.

Natchez stopped; he never forgot that fire. It had been in the back of his mind for a long time. He knew something wasn't right about the fire. He never got anywhere with the investigation. "I remember the case. Can I ask how you are involved?"

"I used to live in the house. I was the one that survived."

It came back to Natchez. The son had survived that fire. He never talked to the boy because he was too heartbroken. The boy was not home at the time, but he might have known something. Natchez remembered calling the boy's aunt in Raleigh to come to pick him up. This child misbehaved and survived. "Bodhi? You probably don't remember me. I was there after the fire. I helped you to get to your aunt's house in Raleigh. How can I help you?"

"Sorry, Detective, I don't remember much from that time. I am just trying to find out how the fire started. Do you have any information on that?" Bodhi said.

"I'll tell you what. Can you meet tomorrow for coffee?" Natchez asked.

"Well, no, I am in Salter Path. I can't make it back to Raleigh," Bodhi said.

"Oh, I should have said, I am in Swansboro. Could you meet in Swansboro?" Natchez asked.

"Yes. That works for me. What time?" Bodhi asked.

"Let's say nine at Sweet Ed's. Does that work?"

"That works. I will see you then," Bodhi said.

Natchez headed to his car, thinking about the Salter house fire. The fire was one case that never sat right with him. He knew there was more to what happened that night, and he also remembered the investigative dead end. He needed to refresh his memory on the case and planned to pull the file for the meeting the following day.

———

The next morning, Bodhi left for Swansboro at quarter after eight. Ellie decided to sleep in, get her coffee and go for a walk on the beach. She figured Bodhi would be back before noon, and they might spend the day at the beach. DJ had the day off and planned to meet them there.

Bodhi drove toward Swansboro, passing the old house and Save-a-Stop. Out front on the benches were a few men from Salter Path. He saw Ley, DJ's dad Darrel, Landon, Bobby, Jean Man, and Officer Blakely. They were having coffee and smoking cigarettes.

Bodhi crossed the bridge leaving Emerald Isle. You could see Swansboro to the left and the many small uninhabited islands that filled the western end of Bogue Sound from high on the bridge. A few boats gently made their way through the shallow waters looking for flounder and redfish. Over the bridge, Bodhi made a left-hand turn onto Highway 24. The brick building that housed Sweet Ed's was part of the historic downtown in Swansboro. Early settlers founded the town hundreds of years ago, and the streets were not wide enough for two cars to pass each other. It was still early enough that Bodhi found a spot to park his truck only a block from Sweet Ed's.

Bodhi walked into Sweet Ed's. "Good morning. Could I get a coffee with two creams and two sugars?"

"Sure. It will be one dollar and eighty-five cents," the clerk said, reaching for a paper cup.

"Do you know Steve Natchez? He works for the SBI," Bodhi asked.

"Yes. He comes in for coffee almost every day," the clerk said.

"Has he been in today? I am supposed to meet him here."

"He is in the back. He told me someone was coming to meet him. He is waiting for you."

"Thanks." Bodhi tipped the clerk and walked toward the back of the restaurant. A man was sitting at a table sipping his coffee and reading the Tideland News. Along the wall was a long bench seat covered in burgundy velvet. The restaurant was a mix of a bistro coffee shop and a 1920s speakeasy. Dimly lit with the sun beaming through the large glass window front, the interior was more dramatic than anything along the coast. There was a pleasant smell in the air, a mix of coffee, confectioneries baking, and fine cocktails still lingering from last night.

Natchez had aged since he first investigated the fire at the Salter house. He was forty-eight then and peaking in his career. Now, he was about to turn sixty-five and had planned his retirement. He was still fit at sixty-five, running ten miles every week, worked out, and made sure he ran the Emerald Isle Half Marathon every spring. It was his only way to offset the calories from the large piece of chocolate cake that sat on the table in front of him. His hair had grayed now, with it being more gray than black. As he sat there, you could have easily convinced anyone that he was the owner of a cigar company from Cuba, exiled under Castro and building an empire of cigars in the United States. He had a quiet and robust air about him.

"Detective Natchez?" Bodhi asked.

"Bodhi, thanks for coming. It has been a long time since I last spoke to you," Natchez said, standing up to shake Bodhi's hand.

Bodhi paused and then extended his hand. The pandemic was finally ending, and people were starting to shake hands and go around without masks. Bodhi extended his hand, "Sorry, I do not remember meeting you. Thank you for taking the time."

"You probably do not remember. It was shortly after the fire, and we spoke out near the water. I helped get you to your aunt's house. It was long ago, and you were going through a lot. It is great to see you grown up." Natchez had felt for the boy. He had also been through a lot in his childhood. Natchez's family came from Cuba as refugees. They crossed the sea to America on a raft. His father drowned in the middle of the night when a wave overturned their raft during the trip. His father was separated from the group in the chaos and darkness and was never seen again. Natchez knew the emptiness one feels when they suddenly lose a parent, but he could never comprehend what happened to Bodhi.

"Oh. I remember someone coming and talking to me by the water. I didn't realize it was you. I should thank you. It was good to have someone looking out for me back then," Bodhi said.

"I am glad I was able to be there for you. After you called, I went and pulled the case file. What can I tell you about it?" Natchez asked Bodhi.

"I appreciate that. I just came back to Salter Path this week. I found out that the property where the old house was is actually in my name. I went and visited the other day and realized I never heard how the fire started. I have asked my family, but they always just say it was an accident."

"That's a good question. I have that same question. I came to Salter Path to do the investigation. I worked with Chief Burns. He is a nice guy and was helpful, but he kind of wanted to get the investigation wrapped up before the tourists came to town. I never found out much. I could not get anyone to talk in town. They let me know that I was an outsider and the locals would handle whatever the problem was in town. I made my report in Raleigh. We never closed the case. It just went cold. There was no physical evidence at the scene, and everyone just clammed up."

"So, all you could come up with was it was an accident?"

"No. We were never able to determine what happened. It might have been an accident, or it might have been arson. Do you remember the Snow Boatyard that burned a couple of years earlier?" Natchez asked.

"I remember that fire. Tom Snow died in that fire, right?"

"Yes, he left his house to try to put it out but got trapped inside. We think that may have been arson. That fire had started near the chemicals they use for making fiberglass. It seems like someone started it. I wondered if the fire at your house was related," Natchez speculated.

"What does that mean?" Bodhi asked.

"Well, it could mean a few things. First, was there someone around that was starting fires? Arsonists tend to start more than one fire. They have patterns and usually target specific areas that they know. So, it could have been a bad actor that was in town. Or, I understand there were rumors about a feud going on in town. I also wondered if that had something to do with it. It is unusual to have two major structure fires in a small town over a relatively short period. It was just a hunch. I was never able to get anywhere."

Bodhi leaned back in his chair and took a sip of his coffee. "That's… that's interesting. Could it have been an accident?"

"Well, yes, of course. There is always a chance. It was strange because the fire seemed to start near the bottom of the steps by the front door. The kitchen is in the back. That is where most accidental fires start. You know, someone leaves the oven on or a burner, something falls on the stove, and a fire starts. At the bottom of the steps, in the middle of the night, would be odd. Would you be willing to try to answer some questions for me?"

Bodhi began to feel uneasy. He always let the fire be an accident in his mind. It was easier to believe that a bad thing had just happened. It is harder to imagine that someone wanted to harm him and his family. "What kind of questions? I am not sure what I know that you don't," Bodhi responded.

"I never got to hear your story about that night and what happened."

"What can I tell you?" Bodhi asked.

"Tell me about the day leading up to the fire," Natchez instructed Bodhi.

"It was a long time ago." Bodhi paused to collect his thoughts. "It was a regular day. Ley, DJ, and I played most of the day. We took some kayaks out on the sound and swam for a while. We had lunch at Nana B's. I remember we had to get out of the house because she was having company that night, and we could not stay. We went to the beach and rode our skimboards for a while. I went home for dinner, and Ley went back to Nana B's. That is where he lived. After dinner, Ley came by and asked if I wanted to go ghost crab hunting that night. I asked, and my mother said no. She said I had to help mend shrimp nets the next day, and I couldn't be out late. So, Ley and I decided to sneak out." Bodhi stopped. He could feel the emptiness of his loss building again, but he wanted to stay strong for Natchez. "I told Ley to wait outside, and I would be out around eleven. My family usually went to bed at about ten-thirty. A little after eleven, I got out of bed, and all the lights were out. I could hear my dad snoring. I remember that because it was my sign to go. I walked down the stairs and out the front door."

"When you left, did you lock the door?" Natchez asked.

"No, I didn't have a key and needed to get back in bed before the sun came up."

"Had you done this before? Sneak out, I mean."

"It was not the first time. We would sneak out and run around town. Steal some beers from a dad's cooler and drink them on the beach. Maybe fish for sharks. Things that boys do in Salter Path," Bodhi said with a grin.

"Did you always leave the door unlocked?" Natchez was pressing this question.

"Most people in town left their doors unlocked. Only some of us locked doors at night. My mom always worried about drunk tourists, so we locked our doors. Most others don't."

"Do you remember anything else? Any other details? Anything, even the smallest thing."

"Nothing right now. The only other thing was Ley said he had to go out his bedroom window because there were still people at his house."

"Do you know who was at his house?" Natchez asked.

"No. I just know there was a party that the adults were having or something like that. I don't know if it was a party or dinner or what. There were a bunch of people there."

"Can you remember anything unusual leading up to the day of the fire?" Natchez was pressing.

"Sorry. I would have to think about it. It was a long time ago, and I never thought much about what happened before the fire that day."

"I understand. I am retiring in a couple of months, and it would be good to get to the bottom of this case, but I need more information."

"From what you have told me so far, you do not know much more than I do. It could have just been an accident, right?" Bodhi was trying to figure out the status of the investigation.

"In an investigation, you have to keep all options open until all options are closed, but one. It could be an accident or something else."

121

Natchez tried not to alarm Bodhi. "You said this is the first time you have been back since the fire, correct?"

"I came back for my family's memorial service, but I have not been here since I was a kid."

"Why didn't you come back?"

"Growing up, my aunt always said that everyone was crazy down here and that I should not have anything to do with this town. She said it was best to move on and build a new life elsewhere. She would tell stories about our ancestors and how a hurricane destroyed their Diamond City homes. She would say they knew when to stop fighting and move on to build again. She said that is what I needed to do. That made sense to me. It is also a place of loss for me, so I never had a lot of desire to come back."

"Why now? What changed?"

"That's easy. I got engaged about a year or so ago. The wedding is this fall. When we started putting the guest list together, I realized there was no family on my side except for my Aunt Kristy. My fiancée, Ellie, convinced me we should come back to see if we could reconnect."

"You said you have been here for a few days now. Have you been able to reconnect with anyone?" Natchez asked.

"Yes, my old friends Ley and DJ. We went to Nana B's for lunch one day. Also, some of the other town rats. The regular folks."

"Have you felt welcomed? Any trouble?" Natchez was probing for something, but Bodhi wasn't sure what he was trying to accomplish.

"For the most part, yes, everyone has been great. The other night a guy named Landon flew off the handle at me. He was talking about why I came back, and I was an outsider now. That my family is shit around town, and why would I want to be here," Bodhi said in a matter-of-fact voice. "It did not bug me much. I figured that there might be some people that would not be happy to see me."

Natchez stared at Bodhi, trying to make sense of people blaming an orphan for the problems in town. "A couple of things, first, make sure you and your fiancée are safe."

Bodhi cut off Natchez, "What do you mean safe? Is there a reason I should not feel safe?"

"I am not trying to alarm you. We have to keep an open mind, though. It seems like someone started that fire. We do not know why, but you are the only one that survived."

"Wait, what? Are you saying you think it wasn't an accident? That someone did this on purpose?" Bodhi's mind was spinning.

"I just want you to keep your eyes open in this. Make sure you are aware of your surroundings. I want to get to the bottom of this, but I need help."

"Help from who?"

"I need your help. I was never able to get anyone to talk to me. The locals just closed me out and made it clear that I would not hear anything from anyone in town. That made me think that there must be something to learn. I need someone that can get inside and help me find out what went on that night. Do you think you could do that?" Natchez had been working the conversation to this point. He knew this might be his only chance. He needed to get Bodhi on his side and for him to want to see the truth.

"I can try. I am only here until after the Big Rock starts. Then I need to get back to Raleigh, but I can see what I can find out," Bodhi replied. "Where should I start?"

"That's a good question. You said DJ and Ley have been good to you. I would start there. See what they can tell you. Maybe they know who has information. When you hear something that might be interesting, give me a call, and we can talk through it. I am going to stay in the background. Chances are, whoever did this feels safe after all this time. They figure that they got away with it. You coming back and asking questions might make them nervous, so, as I said, be aware of things happening around you," Natchez provided Bodhi with guidance.

"We are going to the beach today with DJ. Some other friends might join. I will start to see what they remember about that night and if they have heard anything."

"Great. Give me a call if you hear anything. Day or night is fine. Don't forget to get a refill for your drive back to Salter Path," Natchez instructed, standing up and giving the impression of a parent reminding his kids to be safe and work hard.

"Will do. Thanks for the meeting, and I will be in touch with updates," Bodhi replied.

On the truck ride back to Salter Path, Bodhi started replaying the few things that made him uncomfortable since he came back to town. The way Dan Gentilli seemed to be watching him closely. The outburst by Landon. The way Bobby looked at Ellie. All of these people were either a kid when the fire happened or not even living in town. He could not think of anything that made him feel in danger. He would pay closer attention, and maybe this would change when he tried to talk to the town's older residents. He now hoped he might get answers to questions that had lingered in his mind for years.

19

Feuds

Bodhi rolled down the windows as he drove down the island. The early June air poured into the cab of the truck. As the heat of the day built, the smell of salt and humidity reminded him of his childhood. The Crystal Coast was awake for the day. Families were standing along the road, waiting to cross from sound to the beach - mothers with children by the hand and fathers with overloaded beach carts filled with chairs, umbrellas, coolers, bags, and beach toys. They only had one week to soak in as much sand and salt as possible. By this point in the week, their sunburns from earlier were starting to peel and fade into tanned skin. They went about their vacations, oblivious to the people that lived in these towns. They knew nothing about the feud that started twenty years ago, the boatyard that burned, and the family that died, leaving an orphan son.

Bodhi reflected on what Natchez had said. To be aware and try to find out what he could. He figured that talking with DJ and Ley would be easy. They seemed to pick up where they left off as friends. Others around town might be more difficult to talk to, but he would take it step-by-step.

Ellie was already awake and packing for the beach when Bodhi got back. "Hurry up! Where have you been? You said you were going for coffee, and it's almost noon by now," Ellie said to Bodhi.

"I went to Swansboro to meet with the detective from the SBI. Remember?" Bodhi said.

"Yes, that's right, I forgot you were meeting him. How was it? Did he know anything?" Ellie inquired as she continued to pack.

Bodhi sat on the bed and said, "He did not have too much information. He told me about the investigation. I forgot, but he talked to me the day after the fire. He was the one that helped me get to Raleigh." Bodhi kicked off his flip-flops and started searching for his swimming trunks. "He said he ran into a dead end during the investigation. They never officially closed the case. They never determined what caused the fire."

"You are kidding. What does that mean?" Ellie thought the fire was an accident.

"It means that it may have been an accident or someone might have started it. Remember I told you about the boatyard fire," Bodhi said.

"Yes."

"The detective, Natchez, said they could be related. I might be an arsonist that was in town or something else." Bodhi left this open-ended. He knew that if he said too much about the feud, Ellie might want to go.

"What else did he say?" Ellie inquired.

"He said to let him know if we can find out anything about what happened. He could never get anyone in town to talk, but he believes there is more to this case than an accident," Bodhi said.

"So, we are supposed to be detectives now?" Ellie asked, pursing her face.

"Ha. No, Natchez just said while we are here on vacation, if we hear anything, to let him know, and he would follow up to see if it goes anywhere. He is looking for some tips on the case, that's all," Bodhi said. He neglected to tell Ellie about Natchez's warning to be safe. Bodhi knew that after the Landon incident from the other night, she might want to leave immediately.

"I got it. He wants us to ask around and see what people are talking about." Ellie enjoyed a bit of gossip. "Com'on let's get to the beach. I am ready for some sun."

The young couple made the short drive to the beach access. The routine from the other day was repeated with Bodhi lugging chairs and a cooler while Ellie walked ahead with her beach bag. This time Bodhi wasn't thinking about the night of the fire as they headed to the beach. He watched Ellie's beautiful figure make its way to the beach over the boardwalk and through the maritime forest. The sunlight splashed through the treetops like hundreds of spotlights shining on the boardwalk. The light rolled over Ellie's straw beach hat and then down her back. Bodhi followed the sunbeams down her back, over her backside, along her legs until the light hit the boardwalk. He would do this over and over, memorizing this moment and just how beautiful she was. They emerged from the forest coolness and into the bright beach sun.

The tide was out, and they dropped their cooler and beach bag in the dry sand above the tideline. Bodhi's phone rang, "Hello?"

"Hey, where are you guys? I am just getting here," DJ said over the phone.

"Come down the beach access, and we are a little to the left. We are going to put our chairs near the water," Bodhi said to DJ.

"What's the surf like? I was going to bring my board if it looked good," DJ said.

"Looks good to me, but I never learned to surf," Bodhi said.

"Well, shit, it's about time to learn," DJ hung up the phone.

The waves rolled up and washed into the sand as Ellie and Bodhi parked themselves firmly in their chairs. Cold drinks in their hands, they were settling in to enjoy another day in the sun.

"YO!!! BOOODHI! What's up?" DJ was yelling as he walked down the beach surfboard under his arm.

He had his shirt off, and you could see tattoos covering his arms, chest, and back. Ellie did not even want to think about how many there were and how long it took to get them all. There must have been at least twenty-five different pieces of art. DJ was thin but athletic in a skateboarder/surfer kind of way.

"Hey DJ! Good to see you. You brought your board," Bodhi said.

"Yeah. You are going to learn to surf today. Ellie, are you going to surf?" DJ asked.

"I don't even know if Bodhi's going to surf. You teach him today, and you can teach me later in the week. Deal?" Ellie wanted to learn to surf, but she didn't want to show up Bodhi by learning first. Also, she knew that women should go first, but men loved to go first, and she let Bodhi have some fun.

"That's a deal," DJ said to Ellie. "Bodhi, get your ass up, and let's go!"

"Don't we need another board?" Bodhi asked.

"Nah. We can use mine today. After you learn to love this, you can buy your own. Follow me." DJ ran and threw his surfboard out in front of him into crashing waves. He jumped on top and began paddling for the sand bar. "Bodhi, meet me on the sand bar!"

Bodhi took off his hat and sunglasses and jumped into the surf. He began swimming to the sand bar. Nearshore, it was shallow, but there was a drop-off before reaching the sandbar. This part of the surf was the most dangerous. This area is where rip currents formed as the water pushed by the waves onto the beach tried to make its way back out to the ocean. Before long, Bodhi was in water over his head. He could feel the calmness of the deep water, and the waves stopped breaking. It was easy to panic at this point. You could no longer feel the bottom; the waves breaking on the shore became quiet. You could not yet see the sandbar. You were in an area in between the safety of the beach and sandbar. Bodhi began to swim hard for the sandbar, and then he heard what his father always said to him, "It's a dance with the ocean, not a fight." Watermen learned that you have to learn to move with the force of the wind and waves. It never relents and isn't caring; you need to work with it, not against it. Bodhi stopped swimming. Ellie noticed this and stood up from her chair, thinking something was wrong. Bodhi just floated. Breathing deeply, letting waves move him from side to side. He then rolled over and began swimming lazily to the sandbar. Ellie sat down when she finally saw Bodhi stand up on the sandbar.

"Good swim?" DJ asked.

"Yeah. I forgot how far it is to get out here. How are we going to do this?" Bodhi asked.

"This is easy. I will show you how. You paddle out just beyond the breakers. Wait for bigger waves. You have to start paddling early. When you start dropping into the trough, paddle hard; when you start to rise on the crest, the board will start surfing. Get to your knees the first few times. Then, try to pop up on your feet. When you get to your feet, stand up! Don't lean over. You will never get your balance. Watch!" DJ started paddling out along a rip. Going through the cut made it easier to get past the waves.

DJ turned his board looking for a wave. He let a few waves go. Then DJ turned the nose of the board toward the shore and started paddling. He caught the wave and popped up. He cut the board to the left and right, climbing to the top of the wave before burying the board's nose down the wave. He looked at home on the board. It was an extension of him, and he moved it with ease. He rode the board to about ten feet from Bodhi and stepped off gracefully.

"Got it? It's easy, just relax. It's a dance, not a fight," DJ reminded Bodhi of the local wisdom.

"Okay, I got it. Let me give this a go," Bodhi leashed the board to his ankle and began paddling out past the breakers.

Bodhi's first try failed miserably. He started paddling late and not hard enough. The wave broke over him and flipped him upside down. He felt the tug of the board on his ankle as the wave washed it toward the beach. He gathered it in and started again.

"Earlier! Hard! You have to paddle your ass off!!!" DJ yelled.

Bodhi's second try was better. He still didn't catch the wave. He bobbed up to the top of the wave and then fell back down the trough. He was able to spin the board and paddle back out to try again. This time he began paddling like mad. He fell deep into the trough and disappeared. He felt the back of the board starting to go up and then slide, picking up speed. The board pushed to the top of the water as the speed built. Bodhi stopped paddling as the wave pushed him toward shore. He popped onto his knees and looked up. He was heading straight for DJ. DJ dove down into the water, and he went right over him. He rode the board into the drop off beyond the sandbar, and the wave died out. Bodhi couldn't help but smile.

"That was awesome!" Bodhi yelled to DJ.

"You gotta learn to steer it! You fucking ran me over!" DJ said.

"You are all right! Quit bitching!"

Bodhi paddled out to catch a wave. After a few more rides on his knees, he popped up onto his feet. A few more attempts and he could catch a wave and ride on his feet. Bodhi looked around for DJ. Bodhi thought, "Where the hell did he go?" He looked toward the beach and saw DJ sitting in his beach chair, drinking his beer, and talking with his fiancée.

"Looks like he is hooked," DJ said to Ellie.

"Yep, he didn't even notice you were swimming to shore," Ellie said.

"Once you catch the surfing bug, you are always looking for the next wave," DJ said.

"I have a feeling we are going to buy surfboards tomorrow. I am surprised Bodhi didn't learn when he was younger," Ellie commented.

"Surfing wasn't a thing when we were young. Boards were so expensive our families couldn't afford them. Surfing was for the rich kids that lived in big houses. We had boogie boards and skimboards. I saved up for my first board working in the kitchen at the Big Tree. It was a big deal when I was sixteen," DJ told Ellie.

Ellie never thought about not having money for a surfboard. They were not cheap, but any kid she grew up with that wanted one had one. Ellie was coming to realize the differences between how she grew up and how Bodhi's family lived. She had all the material things she wanted, but Bodhi had all that he needed.

"How long have you been surfing?" Ellie asked DJ.

"I started when I was fourteen. We used to go and borrow surfboards from vacation houses that left them outside. We always returned them when we were done. I don't think the people ever missed them," DJ told Ellie. "You know, we respect the vacationers and part-timers, but this is our town, and if it is here, we can use it if we need it. You know what I mean?"

Ellie didn't know what he meant. He was talking about just taking people's things because they were "in his town." It was odd to think of a mentality where people bought the property but never owned the property. The squatters believed everything was theirs in the town, including the possessions. Ellie said, "Yeah. I get it. It's different from where I grew up, but I get it."

"What have you guys been doing the last couple of days?" DJ asked Ellie.

"Well, we went by Bodhi's old house. It was not easy," Ellie said.

"I wondered if he would go over there. That had to be hard for him."

"He didn't say much. It was hard on him. He doesn't even know how the fire started," Ellie started to fish for information.

DJ paused, "Did he tell you about the other shit that happened before?"

Ellie had heard about it but decided to let DJ fill in his details. She said, "He showed me some news clippings but never said much more. What shit was there?"

"Crazy stuff. I mean, you know, some people in town are even pissed that I had you come over the other night. I am a Willard, and we stick with the Snows. But when we were kids, before we knew about this stuff, we hung out all the time. Back then, Ley and I made a promise out at the fish house; if Bodhi came back, we would treat him as if he never left. Others don't feel like that," DJ said.

"What do you mean by you stick with Snows?" Ellie used her charm to get DJ to talk. She wasn't flirting, but she also knew men had difficulty saying 'no' to her. This power is an advantage of being beautiful. Ellie can manipulate men with ease.

"You know. We don't like the Salters and Joneses. This crap all started when someone burned down the Snow Boatyard. They think it was a Jones or Salter," DJ gave his view of when the feud started.

"Why would they do that? It sounds extreme?" Ellie asked.

"The Snows built a boat. When it sank in a storm, Bodhi's grandpa and uncle died. You probably know that from the news articles. They should have never been out there in that boat. It was late season, and everyone knows those nor'easter blow in out of nowhere. A bad mistake that cost them their lives. It happens when you work on the water. The Salters and Jones think the boat was bad, but any boat would have sunk." DJ gave his thoughts.

"Are storms bad in the winter? Hard to believe they could be. It's so nice here," Ellie said.

"Those nor'easters can be as bad as hurricanes. The difference is that hurricanes come slow like a turtle. You know, for days, a nor'easter can blow up in twelve hours. Catch you with your pants down," DJ tried to explain weather predictions. "Like, did you see that hurricane out in the Atlantic? It is still more than a week off the coast, but people are already talking about it. We know it is coming."

"So, people think someone burned down the boatyard because a boat sank? Why wouldn't they just sue them or something?" Ellie asked.

"Haha. We don't have money down here. Hell, my dad is one of the richest people in town. We do good down here, but in Raleigh or somewhere else, we would just get by. You don't sue people. There is nothing to sue for. You settle scores. That's justice. I think…" DJ caught himself and stopped. He was getting pissed off thinking about the Salters and Jones. He felt they started this whole thing when they burned the boatyard but didn't want Ellie to be caught in the middle. "Never mind what I think, I am glad Bodhi came back, at least for a visit."

Bodhi came paddling in from the water. He picked up the board, put it under his arm, and walked up the sand toward Ellie and DJ. Ellie looked at him. She studied his wet hair hanging over his eyes, the smile on his face, and the beads of water running down his chest. She was beautiful, and she had a very handsome man to match. Their connection happened on many levels, and Ellie was grateful that one of them was physical.

"You telling my secrets DJ?" Bodhi joked with DJ.

"Nah. I was just telling Ellie how I used to borrow surfboards from houses before I bought one. Are you ready to buy one?" DJ asked.

"Hell yes. That was great. Ellie, you are learning tomorrow. We gotta go get some boards." Bodhi was oblivious to the conversation Ellie and DJ had.

"Go down to AB Surf Shop. They are more expensive than other places, but they have good boards," DJ instructed.

DJ and Bodhi took turns surfing the break beyond the sandbar for the next few hours. As the tide came up, the break went away. They spent the rest of the afternoon sitting in their chairs with DJ and Bodhi draining beers from the cooler and Ellie emptying seltzers.

In the evening on the beach, there is a time when the sunburnt vacationers return to their rentals. They go to their rented residences, clean up, and scramble off to dinner at one of Atlantic Beach or Morehead City restaurants. The sun is low in the sky, and the heat of the day is gone. The only ones left on the beach are the locals, that will eventually head home to grab a bite to eat. This moment is the best time at the beach, and most miss it, but that makes it special.

"DJ, I have been trying to remember the night of the fire. I know Ley and I went to the beach to catch ghost crabs, but I can't remember where you were? Why didn't you come with us?" Bodhi asked.

"That night was crazy. I still remember it. You guys told me you were going out. I started to sneak out. I thought my dad was in bed and pretended to get up to go to the bathroom. When I walked into the living room, my dad was sitting in the dark, looking out the front window. He scared this shit out of me. He said, 'Where are you going?' I told him I was getting some water, went to the kitchen, grabbed some water, and went to bed. I don't know why he was there, but I didn't dare try to sneak out after that." DJ got a look of dread on his face as he recalled that night. "I didn't even know anything happened until the next morning."

"What do you think he was doing looking out the window?" Bodhi asked.

"The hell if I know. It has made me wonder. All you see is the road, the parking lot at the restaurant, your Nana B's house, and the Snow's Boat Yard. I am not sure what he was doing," DJ said.

"Did you ever ask him? Maybe he saw something?" Bodhi asked.

"Yeah, I asked, but not until years later when I started to understand what happened. My dad just said he was thinking about the business,"

DJ said. "I just left it. He didn't want to say what he was doing."

Bodhi wondered if Darrel might be involved. Why would he have been sitting in the living room in the dark? Was DJ's dad keeping a lookout on the road, ensuring no one came down while others were starting the fire? Or was he just 'thinking' as he said? Was it just a coincidence? Whatever it was, he suspected that Darrel had something to add to this, and he needed to talk with him.

"I guess he just had something on his mind that night," Ellie chimed in, trying to move to another topic.

The three stayed on the beach for a while longer. The beer and seltzers had finally run out. They packed up their beach gear and walked up the path to the parking lot. As DJ put his surfboard into the back of his truck, Bodhi and Ellie knocked the sand off their feet and chairs.

"DJ, thanks for the surfing lessons. Now you have to teach Ellie," Bodhi said.

Ellie said, "We are going to get boards tomorrow. Can you teach me tomorrow if the surf is up?"

"I got to work, but I already taught Bodhi my tricks. He should be able to teach you," DJ said.

"All right, but if she doesn't learn, you need to come back and teach her," Bodhi said.

"You got it, buddy." DJ grabbed Bodhi's hand and pulled him in for a hug. "Good to see you, glad you're back."

20

Bliss

It was dark in the parking lot, and Bodhi's truck sat parked in front of his and Ellie's motel room. With her babies following, an opossum made its way across the parking lot after a night of forging in the sea oats for crabs. The creatures would find their way to an oak tree nearby and climb up to sleep for the day. They are nocturnal animals with unblinking eyes, pink noses, and gray-white fur. The tails are nude, and the mother carries newborns in a pouch under her belly. These babies are too big to be in the pouch and are quite cute. They have that awkward toddler look to them with heads too big and eyes that always look surprised. When God created them, it was probably a last-minute addition, with the platypus to follow. These creatures of the night grow up to look like their mother. Unfortunately, this is the reverse story of the ugly duckling. The awkward toddler becomes a slow-minded, discolored rat with hair missing in various places. If confronted, after a brief fight, they will play dead.

The sky begins to glow in the east as the sun gets ready to push over the horizon. There is a quietness to the island. The silence is not imagined. There is a time when everything seems to stand still, when the opossums go to sleep in the trees, and the squirrels have not awoken. A few people may have been artificially brought from their rest by alarms to enjoy this quiet time on the island.

Bodhi and Ellie lay fast asleep in their motel. The wall-mounted air conditioner rattled along, pushing cold air through the room. They were naked and wrapped together, arms and legs intertwined, making it difficult to know where each of their bodies began or stopped. Bodhi rolled out of bed and walked to the bathroom.

"Honey, can you get me some water?" Ellie asked.

"Yeah, how are you feeling?"

"Uuuuh. Not bad. Get me some ibuprofen too. Those last few drinks last night almost did me in," Ellie said, rubbing her head.

Bodhi handed her the water and pain reliever. He took two ibuprofen as well and washed them down while drinking an entire bottle of water. "It's still early. Seven-thirty. Let's sleep some more and then spend the day together having some fun," Bodhi said, crawling into bed, pulling Ellie in close to spoon her into him.

A few hours later, Ellie woke up with Bodhi's hands moving gently along her curves. She pretended to sleep for a bit more as she enjoyed his touch on her skin. Then Ellie rolled over to face him, putting her leg over his waist. She put her hands on the side of his face and kissed him. He wrapped his arms around her, hugging her to press her body close to him. He ran his hand through her hair and then down her back and over her buttocks. She could feel her heart beating faster and her breathing becoming deeper. Bodhi's kissing grew more intense, and Ellie submitted to him.

They lay in bed for a bit longer, enjoying their closeness. The lovemaking made the pair feel even more connected. It was a way to speak to each other that no one else had access to use. A private space only they share. A unique world that only they understood. Whenever they went to this place, they felt their connection even more thoroughly.

"What are we going to do today?" Ellie asked.

"Well, I thought we could go to AB Surf Shop and get a couple of new surfboards. We can head over to the waterfront in Morehead and watch the boats ride by for a while."

"That sounds good. Maybe we can do some more shopping, too?"

"Haha. That's fine. We can walk around. The boats are starting to come in for the Big Rock. There could be some celebrities there. Ooouu…I need to take you to the Big Rock store."

"Well, let's get going." Ellie rolled out of bed and started getting ready for the day.

Ellie had on a ball cap, T-shirt, cut-off jeans, and sneakers. Bodhi mirrored Ellie with a ball cap and T-shirt, but swapped the cut-offs for swim trunks. They climbed into Bodhi's truck, wearing designer sunglasses. Ellie's outfit made her feel like a Pather, simple and straightforward. Together they were a beautiful couple, dressed the part of the country club-raised kids, pretending to be down east country, complete with a pickup truck. The truck with no dents, designer sunglasses, and soft hands showed they did not work with their hands for a living.

As they made their way to the surf shop, Ellie asked, "What do you think about what DJ said?"

"About his dad?"

"Yeah, the way he was sitting up looking out this window."

Bodhi took in a slow breath. "I am not sure what to make of it. It sounds odd that he would be sitting there. It sounded like it surprised DJ. So, he probably didn't do it all the time. We snuck out at night more than I care to admit."

"It sounds like he was watching, waiting for something to happen. Do you think you should call Natchez?" Ellie asked.

"Not yet. I don't have anything—just a guy sitting in his living room. He could have been doing anything."

"I know, but still. DJ thought it was odd; maybe there is something to it."

"Maybe there is. I want to talk to Darrel first, then maybe I call Natchez," Bodhi said as they pulled into the surf shop.

AB Surf Shop was a fixture on the Crystal Coast. It was one of the first surf shops in eastern North Carolina and stood the test of time. It evolved into a combination of boutique and surf shop. You can buy a longboard and sex wax on one side of the shop, and high-end clothes and shoes on the other side.

Ellie stepped out of the truck. "Get a picture of me under the sign!" she instructed Bodhi.

"Okay. Come over to this side. The light is better." Bodhi knew that Ellie still felt that youthful connection to social media. She enjoyed giving a level of exposure to her life. He saw it as a way to mark happy points along life's path, and Bodhi did not mind playing the role of photographer.

"Got it. I took like ten. There should be a good one," Bodhi said.

"Let me see." Ellie thumbed through the picture. "I love it. These are so good."

They walked into the shop, and Ellie went straight for the Southern Tide merchandise and Bodhi to the surfboards. Ellie started looking through beach cover-ups, high-priced T-shirts, and colorful sundresses. She pulled the items from the rack one at a time, carefully studying them and considering them. She evaluated each piece thinking about the colors, her skin tone, and the break in the waist. Ellie returned something to the rack and collected other items over her arm. She was transfixed by the name brands, colors, and warm lighting of the shop. Shopping was more than acquiring things for Ellie. It was exploring the possibilities of who she was, shaping the way she communicated to the world, and the thrill of finding the perfect item for the ideal price.

Bodhi was near the surfboards. Admittedly, he knew little about surfing and had only caught his first wave yesterday. He began looking through the boards. There were shortboards, longboards, fish boards, and funboards. They were different lengths, had various fins, and the tails and noses were all different. Some boards curved more, and some were flatter. He fumbled through the boards, trying to make sense of them.

"Can I help you?" a mop-haired teenage boy in an AB Surf Shop T-shirt asked him.

"Yeah. What can you tell me about the surfboards?"

"Are you looking to buy or rent?" the boy asked.

"Buy. I just started surfing yesterday, and I think I am hooked," Bodhi replied.

"Awesome. What kind of board did you use?" the teen asked.

"I don't know. How could I tell?"

"Was the nose round or pointed?"

"It was a point," Bodhi said.

"And the tail? One point or two?" The teen asked.

"Two. It made a v shape in the back."

"Fish," the teen said.

"No, I haven't fished in a while, but why does fishing matter?" Bodhi said, looking puzzled.

"No. You had a fish board—the ones with the point for the nose and fishtail. They are pretty common around here. They work well in the surf we have most of the time," the teen continued, "Was the board taller than you?"

"Yeah, about six or eight inches, maybe more," Bodhi said.

"Okay, probably a seven-foot fish." The teen reached into the stack of boards and pulled out a seven-foot fish board with four fins. "This is about what it sounds like you had. It is a good board. You can do a lot with it. It's good for surfing big waves and smaller waves. If you are looking to buy, this is on sale now. It's a good deal."

"Perfect. That's what it looked like. I will take it, but I need another," Bodhi said.

"Okay. Why two?"

"For my fiancée, she's over there shopping." Bodhi gestured toward the other side of the shop.

"Has she surfed?"

"No. I am hoping to teach her today or tomorrow. What would be good for her?"

"Tomorrow. The surf is shit today. Tomorrow it should be good after three. There should be three to five footers at ten seconds. It should be good." The teen got lost for a minute, thinking about surfing the next day.

"Sounds good."

"This one. It is called a funboard or Malibu board. Some people like to start people off on longboards, but they feel like riding a log once you get the hang of it. These are still easy to learn. Is that your fiancée?" The teen tilted his head in Ellie's direction as she headed to the dressing room with a pile of clothes over her arm.

"Yes. That's her, and it looks like she found something."

"This will be a good board. She is light, so this will be like a longboard for her. Easy to paddle as well. Take this to the register, and I can help you get these out to your car. Tell them that E helped you."

Bodhi took the two slips of paper from the boy and started wandering the store, waiting for Ellie. A few minutes later, she emerged with a look on her face like she was trying to solve a puzzle.

"Did you find anything?" Bodhi asked.

"Yeah. I have these two cover-ups and a few other things. I am not sure what to keep, though," Ellie said.

"Don't worry about it. Get it all. We are on vacation. We have good jobs. We should enjoy it a little," Bodhi encouraged her.

"Really? Yeah, I guess you are right. This shopping trip might be my last with *my* money before it is our money," Ellie exercised her independence and smiled at Bodhi. What Ellie didn't know was that Bodhi had committed to buying almost $1,500 in surfboards.

The floppy-haired teen was waiting by the door to help Bodhi. He was pleasant and helpful, telling Bodhi how to care for the boards and telling him, "If you ever wanted another board, come back. I work most evenings when the surf is not up. "

Ellie looked at the boards and looked at Bodhi. "I know why you told me to get everything."

They got in the truck and headed over to Morehead City for some drinks and lunch. The waterfront was already buzzing with the Big Rock fleet. Last year, *Catch-23* was an entry to the tournament. This sportfisher was the boat of Michael Jordan, and he made an appearance at the tournament weighing a blue marlin. The rumor was he'd be back, bringing friends to charter other boats along the waterfront.

The sportfishing boats had a unique design created in North Carolina. The Carolina flare was the design of these larger forty- to eighty-foot boats where the bow flares out, allowing the bow to be a sharp V to cut the waves off the Carolina coast. Morehead City was uniquely positioned along the eastern coast. If you looked at the East Coast of the United States, you would see that North Carolina stuck out like an elbow pushing its way into the Atlantic Ocean. The Gulf Stream brought a warm water current north along the Eastern Seaboard. Morehead City was the closest major port to the Gulf Stream along the East Coast. This location allowed fishermen to head out and chase mahi-mahi, wahoo, sailfish, white marlins, and blue marlins from Morehead City. The king of the gamefish was the blue marlin. The largest weighed more than 1,000 pounds and are known as Grandeurs. These were the fish the crews would be chasing in the tournament.

Captains backed their boats in along the waterfront. They had names like *Energizer*, *Reel Country*, *Sensation*, and *Carolina Girl*. Mates on the boats fold up the outriggers, extending forty feet into the air, looking like a tangle of antennas and wires. Twenty-five-thousand-dollar teak fighting chairs filled the cockpits of the boats with glints of sun shimmering from their polished surfaces. This sport was for the wealthy, where the essential equipment cost hundreds of thousands of dollars. The top teams in the sport came to Morehead City for the tournament and had outfits costing more than fifteen million. Ellie and Bodhi walked by these pieces of fishing elitism, admiring the boat builders' craft and the boats' beautiful lines impressing a forceful grace onto the water.

"Let's try this place. It looks like they have outside seating upstairs," Ellie said, pulling the door open to Jack's.

They climbed the stairs and secured a seat on the waterfront deck. From the second floor overlooking the water and Sugarloaf Island, they could watch the boats passing through the no-wake zone in the harbor. Larger sport fishing boats, small skiffs, center consoles, and pontoon boats filled with people enjoying the water and sun. Beyond Sugarloaf, they could see the Coast Guard station and, to the left, the Morehead City Port with its large cranes to unload ocean-going cargo ships.

"I love this. The salt air and boats are going by slowly. It is like the world moving in a beautiful slow motion," Bodhi said.

Ellie took Bodhi's hand. "I love you. I love that you see beauty in simple things."

"I love you too, babe. Don't you love this view?" he asked.

"Yes. Of course, but being here with you, seeing where you grew up, means a lot to me. I feel like I am learning about who you are." Ellie replied.

"I understand that. I am a different person than when I left here. Coming back has felt like going to see an old friend. The place and the people, I guess it is just imprinted somewhere in your mind."

"I can sense it. I know some of this has been hard, but I can tell you missed this place when we are alone or away from what pushed you away."

"I didn't even know that I did, but when I got here, I *felt* this place," Bodhi said. "Then, I have that property. What should we do with it?"

Ellie paused before she started, "What do you think?"

"I don't know. It's probably worth twenty or thirty thousand dollars. We could sell it and use it for a honeymoon or help pay for the wedding?" Bodhi said.

"I don't think you should make that decision now. It should be easy to sell that property, and we can do it later if we need to," Ellie said. "You should just take your time with this."

"You are right. We don't need to do anything now. Hell, I don't even know what happened there. I want to see what I can figure out before we leave."

"C'mon. Let's get a selfie," Ellie said, taking out her phone and pulling Bodhi in close. She snapped the picture—two beautiful young people in the sun with the background of boats and nature intermingled in quiet harmony. They sipped on cold micro-brew beers from a local brewery and ate brick-oven flatbread pizzas with prosciutto and asiago cheese.

After lunch, they headed to the boutiques located along the waterfront. Ellie enjoyed searching for that perfect thing to remember the day. Bodhi was simply in love. Even after their time together, he could still be transfixed by just merely watching her and being with her. Ellie was oblivious to how Bodhi looked at her. She had grown accustomed to it but never took his companionship for granted.

She finally narrowed in on a Christmas ornament made from local seashells.

"Look at this. Isn't it cute?" Ellie asked as she picked up a Santa Claus fashioned from oyster shells.

"Is that made from shells?" Bodhi asked.

"Yes. It says here that a local craftsman makes them. I think this is perfect. We should always get an ornament when we travel. Then, when we put them on the Christmas tree, we can remember the trip," Ellie said, feeling very satisfied with her decision.

"I like that. It will be something we can come back to every year," Bodhi said.

They searched through the ornaments and decided on a snowman made from three sand dollars found on the Crystal Coast. The snowman had a red scarf, a small orange 'carrot' for a nose, and a little black pipe. Each ornament was handmade, and no two of them were the same—a perfect reminder of how everyone experiences the same thing in different ways.

"Let's go in here. I need to find something for the Big Rock party," Ellie said, walking into a store that had various types of dresses in the window.

"I'll tell you what, I will stay out here on the bench and watch the boats. If you need me to give an opinion, text me. Here is my credit card; get what you need for the party." Bodhi handed her his credit card and took a seat on the bench strategically placed in front of the store for boyfriends and husbands to sit and wait comfortably.

Ellie emerged from the store with a shoebox and a dress on a hanger covered in an opaque white bag.

"What did you get?" Bodhi asked.

Ellie gave a half-smile, batted her eyes, and said slowly, "You are just going to have to wait to see me in it." As much as Ellie was grounded and pragmatic, she wasn't naïve about the power her looks could have on men, and she especially knew how Bodhi liked her to look.

"Well, okay, if that's the game. Count me in. Let me carry that for you." Bodhi took the garment bag from Ellie and held it over his shoulder. With his other hand, he took Ellie's.

Down the street, past most of the boats, and across from the Big Rock Landing was the Big Rock store. The Big Rock Tournament was a non-profit that donated hundreds of thousands of dollars every year to the local community. The Big Rock store leveraged the tournament's popularity and sold an assortment of branded merchandise. There were hats, T-shirts, fishing shirts, hoodies, buckets, bumper stickers, belts, dog leashes, dog collars, flags, and just about every nautical trinket you could imagine with the Big Rock logo. The store was well laid out and had the feel of a high-end boutique rather than a beach T-shirt shop. Lovely hardwood floors, proper lighting, and custom shelving made a positive impression on the customers.

As they walked toward the store, Ellie turned to Bodhi, "Is this a fishing store?"

"I don't think so. It did not exist when I was little, but I want to see what it is like. I could use another hat or a T-shirt."

"Okay, let's go check it out," Ellie said, holding Bodhi's hand and walking close to him.

Ellie walked up the steps and into the store. It was a perfect blend of high society and low country. The style and feel of the place fit Ellie perfectly. She grew up in the country club but was drawn to the quieter, simple life of the country. This store blended these two worlds. Ellie started shuffling through the racks as Bodhi examined the shelf full of hats.

After about a half-hour, Ellie proclaimed, "I'm ready." She had an armful of shirts, hats, and other items, "Perfect to take home to my parents. I got some things for Bill and Kristy, too."

"Ellie, I don't know if that's a good idea," Bodhi said.

"Huh?"

"I mean, yes, get something for your parents, but I didn't tell Kristy or Bill we came down here. She never had an interest in coming back here."

Ellie looked at Bodhi with a confused look. "Why didn't you tell her?"

"She always told me not to come back. She said it would not be good for me. I am grown now, so I didn't feel like I had to get her permission, but I also don't want to disrespect her," Bodhi explained.

"Let me get this, and if we don't want to give it to her, I can keep or give it to Alice or my parents, okay?" Ellie wanted to push Bodhi into telling Kristy about the trip and what he found out about owning the land in Salter Path.

"Yeah, that's fine." Bodhi had a hard time saying no to Ellie.

"If the Big Rock dinner is like the store, I think it is going to be fun," Ellie said.

Ellie and Bodhi headed back to Salter Path. Ellie moved to the center seat of the truck and leaned into Bodhi. She loved their day together. It was a simple day of shopping and lunch, but spending time away and alone, exploring new places, made her feel ever closer to Bodhi. On this trip, she saw a side of him that most women never see of their men. Bodhi was reliving childhood experiences that shook him to his core as he tried to comprehend his life.

"What do you want to do tonight?" Bodhi asked Ellie.

"Let's call the caterer and just stay in," Ellie said, referring to their name for getting takeout.

"That sounds perfect."

When they arrived at the motel, Danny was standing at the office door. He waved them down. Bodhi stopped the truck and rolled down the window.

"Well, did you enjoy your day?" Danny asked the couple.

"We had a good day," Bodhi said.

"Looks like you got some nice boards in the back. Planning on surfing?" Danny asked.

"Yeah, I think tomorrow. I heard the surf is going to be good," Bodhi said.

"Yeah, it should be. I just wanted to tell you that Maureen Jones came around today looking for you. She was knocking on your door. I told her that you were out. I figured you might want to know. Oh, don't forget the pool bar is still open for a few more hours," Danny said.

"Thanks for letting us know. Maybe we will come to grab a drink at the bar."

Bodhi pulled away from the office as he rolled up the window. "Who is Maureen?" Ellie asked Bodhi.

"She's Ley's mom. I wonder what she wanted."

"Just stopping by to say hi?"

"Probably not. I wasn't her favorite, if I remember correctly. She blamed me for the trouble Ley got into. We can swing by tomorrow to see what she wants. Maybe she has forgiven me for Ley getting in trouble." Bodhi smiled, thinking back to his youthful shenanigans. "Let's grab a drink at the pool and take it to the room. I am getting tired of Danny pushing his drinks. Let's give it a shot and see how it is."

They took the surfboards and Ellie's shopping scores into the hotel. They grabbed a drink at the bar and then locked themselves in the motel room for the night. The only break they took was to get the food from the UberEats driver at the door. It was a day of bliss in their relationship. Their lives and memories now intermingled more completely.

21

Family

You cannot comprehend the ties that bind you to people and places. Our DNA guides who we are and how we perceive the world. If you have ever observed a family from the outside, you can see common threads that extend beyond learned behaviors.

After the fire, the closest blood relative to Bodhi was his Aunt Kristy. While Bodhi lived in the Path, his father's sister, Aunt Kristy, was there for all the birthday parties, Thanksgivings, and Christmases. She treated Bodhi and his sister, Beth, to ice cream and miniature golf. She played with them like she was a kid herself. Bodhi felt his connection to Kristy, and when he moved to Raleigh after the fire, she made him feel at home.

Bodhi always felt there was an uneasiness to his life in Raleigh that he could not put his finger on. When he returned to Salter Path, that uneasiness ebbed and flowed. At times, it was at the forefront, and he was utterly at peace at other times. Salter Path was the place he felt in his soul. Bodhi's last memory of Salter Path was terrible beyond comprehension; he could sense that the island had affected his DNA.

Ellie was getting ready for the day. They planned to visit Maureen to discover why she came by, then head to the beach where Bodhi would give Ellie surfing lessons. Bodhi stepped out of the motel room door and onto the small porch in front of his truck. He pulled out his phone and started dialing.

"Hello, Bodhi?" Kristy said, answering the phone.

"Hey, Kristy. How are you?" Bodhi replied.

"What's going on?" Kristy asked.

"Ellie and I went away for a vacation. We are trying to get some time together before the wedding. It's been crazy with the planning and work. And during the pandemic, we felt so cooped up. You know?"

"Well, that's good. I think everything is pretty much set at the farm. Bill has been painting and getting everything ready, but it should be fine. He is funny. He still has months but is worrying about getting everything done," Kristy said.

"Tell him not to worry. We are going to be outside most of the time. He doesn't have to wear himself out getting things ready."

"Where did you go for vacation?" Kristy asked.

"Well, we decided to go to Salter Path. I thought it would be good for Ellie to see where I grew up." Bodhi said, trying to put the choice of location on Ellie.

There was a pause. Then, Bodhi could hear an exhale on the phone. "That's a hell of a place to go to get away."

"Well, I thought it would be good to see some people here, ya know?"

"You know how I feel about that place. I haven't been back since you came to Raleigh. There are a bunch of snakes in that town."

"I know. But, it has been good. I got to see Ley and DJ. I think it is good for me to try to get some closure on the fire before I get married."

"Ha. You ain't gonna get closure. That place protects itself. Whatever you might be thinking you are going to find, I wouldn't count on it."

Bodhi knew Kristy would disapprove of him being there, but he also felt like he needed to tell her. "It was hard, as well. There have been some times when I wondered why I came back. I did find out a few things."

Kristy paused again before she spoke. "What did you find out?"

"I still own the property where the old house was. Since I was the only one left, the property went to me. Some of the people in town paid the taxes in my name, so it's still in my name." Bodhi waited for a reply from Kristy, but none came. He continued, "I also talked to the SBI detective who investigated the fire. He lives down here now."

"Oh, really, what did he have to say?" Kristy asked.

"Nothing, really. He told me that he ran into a dead end in the investigation. He said it is still an open case. He told me to call him if I find anything out while I am in town."

"Have you found anything?" Kristy asked.

"Nothing much so far. Nothing to call Natchez, the detective, about. The only thing was I talked with DJ. I wondered why he didn't sneak out with us the night of the fire. He said his dad was sitting in the living room looking out the window. Seems weird, doesn't it?"

Kristy thought carefully before speaking, "What could he have seen? He can see the boatyard and Nana B's, not much more. Did you talk to DJ's dad to see what he was doing?"

"Not yet. I hope to catch up with him soon," Bodhi said.

"You know, he is one of them. Snows and Willards are a bunch you can't trust. Be careful. He will probably lie to you," Kristy warned.

"Yeah, I know. I haven't run into much of that yet, but some of that bullshit is still around. If I hear anything, I will let you know."

"Bodhi, be careful down there. There is a reason why I pulled you away. You gotta be smart. Don't just trust what everyone tells you."

"I know, Kristy. I will be careful. Love you. See you when we get back."

"Be careful and love you," Kristy said and hung up the phone.

Bodhi took a minute to think. He went to his truck and pulled out a pack of cigarettes he had bought the other day. He lit one and leaned against the grill of his truck. He wondered if she knew more about what happened but did not want to say. He finished his smoke and went back into the room.

Ellie smelled Bodhi. "Did you smoke?"

"Yes. Sorry, something about the salt air and being here makes me want to smoke. I just called Kristy."

"Okay, but when we get back to Raleigh, no more." She looked at Bodhi disapprovingly. "What did Kristy say?"

"Not much. She said that everything is ready for the wedding. She did sound a little off when I told her I talked to Natchez."

"What do you mean?"

"She just told me to be careful and let her know if I hear anything. It seemed like she knew something I didn't," Bodhi said.

"Do you think she would tell you everything she knows about the fire?"

"I am not sure. You know, sometimes people will keep something secret to protect you. It must be something that she thinks I do not need to know."

"I know. That is probably why she never brought you back. She might have felt like it would bring too many questions." Ellie took Bodhi by the shoulders and looked him in the eyes. "You have to be prepared. If you dig into what happened with the fire, you might find out things you don't want to know."

"It just feels like I need to know how that fire started and if someone is to blame or was it just an accident."

"I will be here for you. Let's see what we can find," Ellie said, turning and walking out the door.

Bodhi grabbed his hat and sunglasses, walked out, and locked the door. Then said, "Where are we going?"

"To Maureen's, let's see why she came by to see us," Ellie replied.

The truck made a crunching and popping sound as it drove over the small rocks of Nana B's driveway. Ley, Ley's mother Maureen, and Nana B shared the house on the sound. Everyone in town understood Ley and Maureen would take over the place when Nana B passed. Their payment was to care for their mother/grandmother in her later years. The truck rolled to a halt, and Maggie lifted her head off the porch. The old dog recognized the truck, and she began wagging her tail.

"Hey, old girl," Bodhi said to Maggie as he scratched her on the head, and then he knocked on the screened side door.

"Bodhi. I can't believe it is you!" Maureen said.

"Aunt Maureen, it has been a long time. How are you doing?" Bodhi responded.

"You know, living in the Path, getting by. All is good here. Come in," she said, motioning the pair inside. "Who is this with you?"

"Sorry, this is Ellie. My fiancée. We came down so I could show her where I grew up," Bodhi responded.

Ellie spoke to Maureen, "Nice to meet you. Bodhi said you are Ley's mom. He seems like a nice guy and a good friend to Bodhi."

"Yeah. That boy is good to others, but he gave me a run around when he was little. He and Bodhi used to run around this town gettin' into all sorts of trouble," she said, laughing under her breath.

"It's hard for me to imagine those boys being little. They did have a good time the other night," Ellie said.

"Yes. Ley works hard, but he can have a good time, too," Maureen said, pulling a cigarette from a plastic container. "Mind if I smoke?"

Ellie looked at the plastic container, not knowing if it was a cigarette or a joint. "No, that's fine," Ellie said.

Maureen noticed Ellie looking at the container. "I roll my own cigarettes. It is a lot cheaper. I can almost roll an entire carton for the price of a pack. You get around those taxes and all," Maureen said as she lit her cigarette. She took a drag. "Grab yourself some tea from the fridge, and let's sit and talk."

Bodhi went to the fridge, grabbed the sweet tea, and filled two glasses with ice. "Aunt Maureen, do you want some tea?"

"That would be good," Maureen said.

Bodhi filled another glass with ice and poured the tea. "I heard you came by the motel the other day. I figured we would stop by," Bodhi started.

"Well, I heard you were in town, and you had not been by to see me. I wanted to make sure you weren't gonna sneak back to Raleigh without saying hello."

"No. Not the case at all. We have been busy enjoying the beach and doing some touristy things. Ellie has never been here before, and it has been ages since I have been here."

"Well, that's good. It can take a bit of time to get your bearings again after being gone for so long. Is it how you remember?" Maureen asked.

"It's funny. A lot of things I remember and haven't changed much, and then some things I don't recall," Bodhi said.

"What don't you remember?" Maureen asked.

"I always thought the town was bigger. I guess when you are a little kid, this place is plenty big enough. Also, it seemed like Morehead was so far away. Now, I drive that same distance every day in Raleigh on my way to work," Bodhi said.

"Haha. Yes, like going back to your elementary school and seeing how small the desks were. Things haven't changed, but you have," Maureen said.

"Yeah. That might be true. It does feel good to come back. I get an idea of what an animal feels like after being set free from the animal rescue. They tend to forget what it is like to be free, but it comes right back after a few steps."

"Good that you are back. How long do you plan to say?"

"Until after the Big Rock Captain's Party. DJ and Ley were going to get us tickets," Ellie said, trying to be part of the conversation.

"That's a big deal around here. Good that you will be able to see it. Be careful though; that open bar will catch up to ya," Maureen warned Ellie.

"Based on the other night, I will probably need to keep Bodhi, Ley, and DJ under control," Ellie said.

"Good luck with that. The boys usually cut loose that night. It is a busy week afterward with all the tourists. Ley works down at the weigh station pulling up the blue marlin when they come in. They need some fat asses to pull them big fish up, and he's about the biggest one on the island," Maureen said as if letting Bodhi and Ellie in on a joke about Ley's size.

"I noticed he didn't miss many meals while I was gone," Bodhi said, taking a sip of his tea.

"So, who have you seen since you have been back?" Maureen asked.

"Nana B was first. Where is she, by the way?" Bodhi asked.

"She is at the church doing something with the lady's group. Not sure what. I think they mostly just gossip."

"Good, she has something to do. So, we had lunch here and surprised Ley. I think you were working that day. Then we connected with DJ at the Big Tree. DJ had a party, and Landon, Jill, and Abby showed up. That turned into a shit show," Bodhi ended.

"Why? What happened?" Maureen asked.

"Landon decided to bring up the fire. Said I should go back to Raleigh," Bodhi said. "Ley had to keep us apart."

"That's too bad, Bodhi. You know he works for them, Snows. They probably run their mouths about that whole thing," Maureen said.

"What is going on with that whole thing?" Ellie asked, wanting to see what was happening.

Maureen looked at Ellie. She wasn't family yet and didn't realize there were some things that only family could ask. Maureen thought she seemed nice enough even though her looks made her easy to hate. Maureen decided to answer Ellie's question but directed it to Bodhi, "I can go back and fill you in some. You are grown up now, and we used to keep the kids out of this. You haven't been around, and you should know if you are going to stay around town for any time." Maureen paused, trying to think of where to begin.

"Sounds like I need to hear this," Bodhi said.

"You probably know some of this. There were always some squabbles around town. Families that live together for so long find disagreements. Mostly small stuff, people argue over who gets to put crab pots where and what the price for oysters should be, who was running around with whose wife. Stuff that happens in a lot of places. Overall, small-town stuff that people gossip about." Maureen took a sip of tea. "Your grandpa built a pretty good shrimping business. He worked hard and wanted to have a better life for his son and daughter. He didn't have a lot of education and thought they could make some good money if they could have two boats shrimping. They would have about half the shrimp business on the island."

"That's why he built the *Legacy*?" Ellie chimed into the conversation.

Maureen looked at her, then went back to talking to Bodhi, "Yes, the boat was a key to the future. He was an old-school kind of guy. He saved for that boat and paid cash for it. Never got any insurance on it. They just didn't worry about those things. Everyone in town takes care of everyone." Maureen paused to shake her head. "Well, after the boat sank, your dad was in a bad way. He knew how hard his dad worked to get that boat. He and your mom struggled. He got angry with everyone except you. He had patience for you but not much else. I think he lost three mates on his boat that year from being an ass to them." Maureen wasn't sure if he should tell Bodhi this next thing but decided it was time for him to understand. "Most people around town said your mom was going to leave with you and Beth and head to Cedar Point. They said she even found a place up there."

"I never knew. They never let us kids know. I can't believe it."

"It was hard. Your dad and his dad were close. They worked together and spent a lot of time on the water. You should be easy on him." Maureen took a sip of tea. "Well, just before your mom was going to leave, the Snow's place burned down. And something changed in your dad."

"What do you mean, changed?" Bodhi asked.

"It was like a weight was lifted off him. He started smiling again and joking with people. It was as if an itch was scratched. Your mom decided to stay because he had changed. It was like that fire somehow set things right in his mind."

"What are you saying? Are you saying you think he started the fire?" Bodh asked.

"I am not saying anything. I just know that your dad changed after that. But other things in town changed as well."

"I don't believe he set that fire. It was just an accident, a coincidence." Bodhi realized what people might think of his dad and how it clashed with how he knew him.

"I am not getting into that, Bodhi. They never figured out what happened there. They use a lot of chemicals, and who knows. That's neither here nor there," Maureen said.

Bodhi was breathing heavily, his face turning red at the thought of his dad being an arsonist. Ellie reached her hand over and put it on his leg. Her touch jerked him from the path he was going down. "I just don't believe it. We don't have to argue over it." Bodhi was ready to move on for now.

"After the Snow fire, things started to get crazier. You should ask your Aunt Kristy. Have you ever asked her?" Maureen asked Bodhi.

"She never wanted to talk about it. She always just said to stay away."

"I am not sure what to say. Kristy should probably tell you some of this, but shit started happening around town after the Snow fire. People's tires would get slashed. One morning I went to my car and had two flat tires. You would check your crab pots, and they would be empty. You always had to check your boat over before going out. People would pull wires, and you could have a fire or breakdown. Things went from small-town problems to a full-on feud. At Frank and Clara's, the bar fights got nasty, and a few people ended up in the hospital. One night Darrel got in a fight with Mike. They both fell down the stairs and went to the emergency room. Darrel broke his wrist, and Mike had a big cut on his head. That stuff started happening more." Maureen shook her head.

"I didn't know any of this. Us kids all got along; we didn't know anything," Bodhi said.

"Like I said, we kept the kids out of it. We let y'all have fun and be kids. I am glad you never knew."

"So, I found out that I still own the property where the old house was," Bodhi said.

Maureen nodded her head, "Yeah, we wanted to keep that for you. We figured you might want to come back sometime, and if you wanted to sell it, then it should be your choice."

"It surprised me. We went there. It was hard. I had to do it, though, you know?"

"Yes. Hopefully, it helped," Maureen said.

"I realized that I never knew how the fire started. I contacted the SBI detective that investigated the fire. He lives in Swansboro. His name is Natchez. He said the case is still open technically, but they have no leads."

"Natchez. I don't remember that name. It was a long time ago. Old Chief Burns was around, but he never seemed interested in figuring out the fires."

Bodhi had not come to ask but realized he needed to ask, "What do you know about the fire?"

"Nothing. I know what everyone else does." Maureen seemed to try to cut it short.

"What does everyone else know? I have been away, and I want to get some closure on this," Bodhi said, trying to use sympathy to get information.

"The fire. Well, we were all shocked. It took us by surprise. We knew there was some craziness in town but never thought there could be a fire." Maureen stopped.

"So, you think it wasn't an accident? Do you know something?" Bodhi said, sounding troubled.

"Bodhi. Things in the Path were not normal. The official thought is that it was an accident, but it didn't seem like one to the Joneses and the Salters. We thought it was probably part of the feud…" Maureen stopped.

"It seems like it, but everyone just wants me to believe it was an accident. It doesn't make sense. How does a fire start so fast?" Bodhi asked.

"I know. But it was a long time ago, and things have settled down. Kind of like, each side just staying out of the way of the other." Maureen was trying to encourage Bodhi not to upset the relative peace that had come to the town.

"It was a long time ago, but it seems like yesterday. If we can find out who did this, maybe we can bring an end to this whole thing?" Bodhi said.

"Maybe, but maybe it starts things up again," Maureen replied.

"Did you know that Darrel was up the night of the fire looking out his front window?" Ellie blurted out at Maureen.

Maureen turned to her and said, "Not sure what to make of that.

How did you find that out?"

"DJ told Bodhi." Ellie said, "When DJ tried to sneak out to go catch crabs, he said that his dad was sitting in the living room staring out the window."

"It seems odd to me. We used to sneak out all the time, and DJ's dad was never there. The night of the fire, he is just sitting there. You think he did it? You said he got in a fight with Uncle Mike."

Maureen paused, "Bodhi, be careful what you say in this town. Things get around fast."

"You didn't answer. Do you think Darrel could have done it?" Bodhi asked.

"It could have been anyone, even an accident. We don't know. But you start pointing fingers, and things can go sideways in a hurry," Maureen said to Bodhi while looking at Ellie.

"Yeah, it could have been anyone or anything," Bodhi said. "Ley said you had people over that night. He had to go out the bedroom window because you were still up. Who was there?"

"Not sure why that matters. Everyone was gone long before the fire started."

"I don't know, but did you have someone from off the island or anything out of the ordinary?" Bodhi inquired.

"That was a long time ago. I am not sure I can remember everyone that was there."

"Who do you remember?" Bodhi asked.

"Let me think," Maureen took a breath and paused. "Jake was there. Eric from Save-a-Stop and Mike came, but he left early. Ed and Jess from Swansboro were there, too."

"Wait. Who are Ed and Jess?" Bodhi asked.

"They live in Swansboro. They own a coffee shop and dessert place there," Maureen said.

"I think I met Natchez at that place. Sweet Ed's is what it's called?"

Bodhi responded.

"Yeah. That's it."

"How did you know them?" Ellie asked, feeling left out of the conversation.

"Ley went to school with their kid. We invited them over. It might have been the first time."

"You said Jake was there. Is that Jean Man?" Bodhi asked.

"Yes. Sorry, Jean Man. I wasn't sure if you would remember him."

"What was he doing there? He's a Willard," Bodhi said, knowing how the feud lines were drawn.

"Well, it's a small town. A woman doesn't have a lot of choices."

Bodhi tilted his head back and then sipped his tea. "Got it. Did anything odd happen?"

"Bodhi. Nothing. Enough for now, poor Ellie is sitting here with nothing to say, and I gotta get to work."

Bodhi could sense more to this than Maureen was letting on, but he could not push anymore. He would have to pick this up later. "Yeah. We gotta get to the beach. It's surfing lessons this afternoon."

"That sounds great." Maureen stood up, wanting the conversation to end. Bodhi and Ellie stood up as well, given the cue to leave. "Bodhi, there is a band tonight at Frank and Clara's. You and Ellie should come by. It's usually a good time."

"What time? We will try to come by," Bodhi said without consulting Ellie.

"Band should start around nine. Finally, this stupid COVID is almost gone, and we can dance again."

"Hope to see you there. Give me a hug," Bodhi said, reaching over to hug his aunt.

"It was good seeing you, Bodhi. Just be careful if you start poking around," Maureen said softly to Bodhi.

Bodhi and Ellie walked out, stopping to pet Maggie again on their way to the truck.

"What do you think?" Ellie asked Bodhi.

"I think there is something she isn't telling me."

"I listened, and I think you are right. I think you should call Natchez," Ellie said.

"Tomorrow. I will call him tomorrow. Let's see if something turns up tonight."

Ellie tilted her head and looked at him, locking his eyes. She smiled and said, "Now you have to do something for me."

"What?"

"Teach me to surf, you crazy man!" Ellie said, laughing, trying to break the tension.

"Hahaha! Let's do it!"

22

Island Fun

Life on an island takes on a different vibe than life on the mainland. Salter Path was two miles out into the ocean, and the warm waters and sea breeze protected the island from occasional rain showers that pop up along the mainland. The sea cools the salt air in the summer. In the fall, the ocean warms the island. It creates a microclimate that can feel like paradise. Bodhi had been back home for just about a week, and his skin had taken on island life. He had a bronzed look of a man who had spent most of the summer in the sun.

"Oh my gosh!" Ellie said as Bodhi started to change into his swimming trunks.

"What?" Bodhi said.

"Your bum is white! I didn't realize how tanned you are!" Ellie said to Bodhi as she hit him on the backside.

"Stop! Yes, I can get a tan. I have always been able to. As a kid, I would be so dark by the end of the summer."

"I like it." Ellie turned Bodhi around so she could kiss him.

He kissed her back and started to run his hands over her body. His breath fell softly on her neck. She felt a chill run over her body.

"Not now," she said. "Later, you have to teach me to surf."

"C'mon. You can't do that to me," Bodhi pleaded.

"I can, and I am. You need to wait," Ellie smiled as she said it, knowing she had her man wrapped.

"Okay. Fine. But I am not forgetting," Bodhi said, blowing a kiss to Ellie as she headed into the bathroom to change.

They loaded the surfboards into the truck. It was about three in the afternoon. This time was when E—the kid from the surf shop—said the surf should be up. The sun was still high in the sky at three, but the day's heat was starting to relent. They parked the truck and walked to the beach down the boardwalk through the maritime forest. This time Ellie followed behind Bodhi. She watched the light flicker over his broad shoulders and tan back as he made his way toward the beach. Ellie enjoyed the sight of her man with a surfboard under his arm, looking more boyish than she had ever seen him. Ellie enjoyed seeing Bodhi's youthful side.

The wind was coming out of the north, blowing over the island. That meant the wind was nearly calm on the beach. The tropical storm out in the ocean just turned into a hurricane. Hurricane Adrian was a bit ahead of the dates planned by the weathermen. The storm was still some 300 miles away from Salter Path, but its power was undeniable. Already there were waves generated by the storm, creating almost perfect 4 – 5 foot swells. The surfing conditions were ideal, and the Crystal Coast had beautiful blue-green water punctuated by white breaking waves rolling onto the beach.

Bodhi stopped at the top of the boardwalk to take in the view. A small path wasui8 tramped through the sea oats that led you onto the soft shimmering sand of the Crystal Coast. Ellie walked up to Bodhi and stopped beside him.

"Wow. Is this North Carolina? I can't believe this is right here in our state. This place is like paradise," Ellie said.

"These days, you never want to leave this place. Let's go. I got to do some teaching," Bodhi said, smacking Ellie's behind and running to the beach.

"I am going to get you!" Ellie said, chasing Bodhi down the steps and onto the beach.

Bodhi jumped into the water between breaking waves, and Ellie followed in unison. Bodhi began paddling and turned to Ellie, saying, "Follow me. Just paddle through the waves. Keep your head down if you think they will go over your head."

They paddled out to no-man's-land between the shore break and the sandbar break. Bodhi stopped, and Ellie floated alongside.

"Okay. See that over there." Bodhi pointed to a flat area in the waves with seafoam being drawn out into the ocean.

"Yeah. That foam, kinda going out to the ocean," Ellie said.

"That's the riptide. It will pull you out to the ocean. It is an advantage when paddling out. Find the riptide and ride it out past the break," Bodhi said.

"Okay. Then what?" Ellie said.

"Meet me out there, and I will give you the next step," Bodhi said, dropping belly down onto his board and paddling away. Ellie followed.

Out past the breakers, Bodhi sat up on his board, waiting for Ellie.

"Okay, take a break. Enjoy it for a minute," Bodhi said to Ellie.

She sat up and looked around. The sound of waves breaking had changed. The breaking waves pushed the noise toward the shore. Ellie turned her head to the vast open ocean. There was complete silence which was eerie and peaceful at the same time.

The silence is a reminder of the vastness of the ocean. There was nothing for thousands of miles. The sea was a space more extensive than anyone could comprehend. Ellie could hear the waves crashing onto the beach behind her as she stared at the ocean. The noise of the breaking waves reminded her she was at the edge of two worlds.

"This is amazing. Like living at the edge of peace," Ellie said.

Bodhi paddled up next to her. He reached for her hand and looked out over the sea. They bobbed together in the water. "I sometimes feel like that is where I am living. Peace is out there. I have to be strong enough to conquer it," he said.

Ellie gazed at Bodhi. Small water droplets ran down his chest, and the sun glinted off his smooth, tanned skin. "I am here for you. I know you are strong enough. We will do this together." Ellie squeezed his hand tightly.

Bodhi felt the confidence build in him, knowing he had his mate there. "Okay. Now, we need to do some surfing. Here is what you have to do. You see the waves. They come in sets. There will be five to seven waves, each one getting a little bigger and then starting over. You get the timing?"

"Yes, I get it," Ellie responded.

"When you get near the end of the set, pick a wave and turn the board toward the shore. Then start paddling as hard as you can. Start early. You will feel yourself drop into the bottom of the wave. Keep paddling hard! Then, you will rise up and start to feel the board gain speed. Keep paddling. When the wave pushes the board, pop onto your knees and ride it in."

"Okay. So basically, paddling your ass off until the wave pushes you," Ellie summarized the lesson.

"Uh. Yeah. That's about it."

"Got it," Ellie said, turning her board toward the shore and starting to paddle like crazy.

Bodhi smiled. She was just better at some things than him. He loved that she was a true partner. Ellie paddled hard as her board picked up speed. She popped up onto her knees and then onto her feet!

"Go, Ellie!!!" Bodhi yelled. She got it on her first try. She was a surfer. Bodhi grabbed a wave and followed her into no-man's-land.

166

"How was it?" Bodhi asked.

"Amazing. Like flying from one world into the next."

"I know, c'mon!" Bodhi said, starting to paddle back out. Ellie followed, and they surfed for the next few hours. Taking breaks beyond the breakers to talk, kiss, and connect. They had found another tie that bound them together.

With the surfboards back in the truck, Ellie and Bodhi headed back to the motel. The truck pulled into the motel parking lot, and Danny was outside the office to greet them.

"Hey! How was your day?" Danny asked.

"It was good. Is the bar at the pool still open?" Ellie replied, trying to cut off Danny's sales pitch.

"Yeah, it is. We would love for you to come by."

Bodhi turned to Ellie and said, "Let's get a drink and then get ready for dinner."

"Danny, we will be over. Make us something special!" Ellie yelled to him as they pulled away, heading toward their room.

Ellie and Bodhi gathered their drinks from the bar. A mint margarita for Ellie was a combination of margarita and mint julep. And a raspberry bourbon smash for Bodhi with whiskey, freshly crushed raspberries, and a splash of soda. They headed to the room to get ready for their evening.

The evening led Bodhi and Ellie to Amos Mosquitos for dinner. The restaurant in Atlantic Beach blended a generous portion of southern fusion cooking with a unique southern swamp atmosphere that fits perfectly in the low country of North Carolina. The restaurant received its name based on a knock-knock joke, and the feeling in the establishment was fun, but the food was seriously delicious. All the wait staff had "restaurant names" chosen to represent their character, much like picking a spirit animal, so you could be waited on by Peaches, Buttercup, Stargazer, or Bubbles. Bodhi and Ellie were seated when Abby, wearing her waitress uniform with the name tag "Bubbles" pinned above her heart, walked by.

"Well, look at y'all!" Abby said to the couple. "You two are looking good. Glad you came by."

"Abby! I was hoping you would be here," Ellie said. "Are you going to be our server?"

"Shug', this is Buttercup's table, but let me switch with her. There is another couple over there, and they look like big tippers. She will be happy to switch.".

Abby walked away, looking for Buttercup. The brief conversation was more than Abby had spoken to them the other night at DJ's. Ellie thought she might have been overwhelmed by Jill and Landon. They were both big personalities.

"Awww. I am so happy we saw Abby here," Ellie said to Bodhi.

"Yes. She seems sweet. She did not say much the other night, but a lot was going on," Bodhi replied.

"Agreed. I like her. We need to see if she is coming to Frank and Clara's after work."

"Let's ask her."

Abby returned to the table and said, "Buttercup was happy. She said that the other couple has the Vineyard Vines look, and y'all have the twenty-something Raleigh look." She chuckled a bit as she said it.

Ellie wondered what exactly that meant but was also taken aback by the idea that the wait staff sizes up their tip when you walk through the door. "Well, we are the twenty-something Raleigh couple," Ellie said, trying to be in on the joke.

"What can I get you to drink?" Abby asked.

"I'll have Amos Mojito," Bodhi said.

"Skeeterita, please," Ellie responded.

"Good choices. Let me get you a bread bucket," Abby said, walking away briskly.

"Bread bucket?"

Bodhi just shrugged his shoulders. "When I was a kid, we could never afford to eat at a place like this. It has been around for a good long time, but this is the first time I have been here."

A few minutes later, Abby was back with a tin bucket with a white cloth napkin inside, wrapping an assortment of cornbread, dinner rolls, and peppery crackers. "Try those crackers in there. You can't get them anywhere else. Here are your drinks. I'll be back in a few to grab your dinner orders."

The cornbread was just how it should be—a little sweet with a moist crumbling texture. The dinner rolls were there to please the folks who expected dinner rolls. The pepper crackers were a fantastic delight. Crispy with a Cajun and black pepper taste. A smear of butter on top made them a unique experience.

"Okay, what can I get ya?" Abby asked.

Bodhi and Ellie had already discussed their order, so Bodhi ordered for both of them. "We are going to do some sharing. Can we get an order of fried pickles, shrimp and grits, and the southern fried pork chop?"

"You bet. Anything else?" Abby asked. Bodhi and Ellie shook their heads, and Abby hurried off to the kitchen to drop the order.

When Abby returned with their meals, they looked fantastic. The fried pickles came as the appetizer and perfectly set up the southern meal.

"Are you going to the band at Frank and Clara's tonight?" Ellie asked.

"I sure am. Are y'all?"

"Yes, we will probably go there after here. When will you be there?" Ellie asked, hoping to have another woman to hang out with at the bar.

"I should be there at about nine-thirty or ten. I don't have to close

169

up tonight. One good thing about this place is we take turns closing. Jill should be there when you get there."

Bodhi had already dug into the shrimp and grits and was not paying attention to Ellie and Abby. "Did you hear that, Bodhi?" Ellie asked.

"Sorry. No, what?"

Abby and Ellie laughed. "I guess he likes it," Abby said.

"See you tonight. It should be fun!" Ellie looked forward to having some female conversation.

Bodhi and Ellie finished their meal and tipped Bubbles generously. They hoped they tipped more than the Vineyard Vines couple. They said goodbye to Abby and drove halfway down the island to Frank and Clara's. The band was ready to start soon, and Ellie wondered who she might meet from Bodhi's past this night.

Frank and Clara's owners built the bar on the second floor above the restaurant. The upstairs was open when the downstairs was closed, and a crowd circulated on the second-floor porch. It still seemed odd to Bodhi and Ellie to see crowds. The pandemic had pushed people into their homes for more than a year, and finally, they were able to get back to normal after President Trump's vaccine was widely distributed. Ellie and Bodhi parked the truck at the motel and walked the quarter-mile to Frank and Clara's. Leaving the car behind meant they could enjoy the evening without worrying about getting back to the motel.

Frank and Clara's was a two-story cinder block structure with a slanted wooden roof. The bottom floor restaurant served a particular type of broiled seafood platter. The locals did not care for this as it drowned out the fresh fish's flavor, but the tourists somehow found it a unique draw. Outside there was a set of stairs to a second-floor porch. The porch was covered with a roof, creating a perch overlooking the ocean across the street. As Ellie and Bodhi walked up the steps, he did not recognize anyone on the porch. They were probably part-time residents and vacationers looking for a night out. He pulled the door open for Ellie, and she walked into the time warp beach bar.

It had an open space with a high ceiling. An old pool table filled the corner to the right, and a makeshift dance floor to the left. Frank had constructed a plywood bar with a black Formica top and gray indoor/outdoor carpet wrapping the rail. The establishment was a favorite spot for the locals as it was designed for fun and not to impress. There was plenty of cold beer and music, and you could get a mixed drink, but not a cocktail.

The second-floor bar was like walking into a setting from a science fiction movie. There were characters throughout the bar in a clash of styles and cultures, like the retirees dancing to the eighties music playing from the sound system as the band set up. A group of preppy college boys pretended to be pool sharks near the pool table while their heavily made-up girlfriends sipped red-colored drinks through stirring straws and talked amongst themselves. At one end of the bar, near the television, was a group of middle-aged couples. The men focused on the television while the women laughed at one another and took turns dancing with the retired men on the dance floor. At the other end of the bar, a group of men wearing baseball caps, T-shirts, and worn-out shorts slumped against the bar rail. The women in the group intermingled, drinking beer and wrapping their arms around the men's necks, pulling them close and giving them playful kisses on the cheek. Everyone was enjoying their own experience of Frank and Clara's.

Bodhi forgot how Ellie could change a room. Her blonde hair and long legs distracted the men as if they had a sixth sense that a beautiful woman had walked into the room. When the women in the room saw her, they immediately looked at their men hoping they weren't gawking at her. When that happened in Raleigh, it was no big deal. When that happened in Salter Path, the women started shooting daggers at Ellie. As Ellie and Bodhi made their way across the room, everyone wondered which group they would join. Ellie and Bodhi recognized a familiar face wearing a baseball cap. DJ was standing at the corner of the bar talking to Jill and drinking a Creek and Coke.

"DJ! DJ!" Bodhi yelled, trying to get his attention.

DJ thought he heard his name over the music and turned to see Bodhi with his arm in the air. "Yo! Bodhi!" DJ waved back.

Bodhi got two beers. He and Ellie headed to the corner of the bar where DJ was standing. "DJ! Good to see you!" Bodhi said, giving DJ a bro-hug.

"Bodhi. You teach her to surf?" DJ asked, gesturing to Ellie.

"Ha. She is a natural. She picked it up like nothing. Better than me after two rides."

"I can see that. Good to see you, Ellie," DJ said, kissing Ellie on the cheek.

"Good to see you! What have you been doing?" Ellie asked DJ.

"Working, smoking, and trying to surf. Have you met Alex?" DJ turned to a man in his early thirties but looking like he was in his forties. His hairline was receding before it should. He did not have a beard but was not clean-shaven. Alex was the quintessential townie who never left his hometown and never intended to see more than his part of the world.

"No. I haven't," Ellie said.

DJ knew every man in that bar wanted to meet Ellie. He also knew no one had a chance. In Salter Path, knowing her was like knowing a celebrity. The woman Alex was talking to before DJ introduced Ellie tilted her head and pursed her lips when she saw Ellie.

"Nice to meet you. You are not from around here, are you?" Alex asked Ellie.

"No. I am a friend of DJ's. I am in town for vacation," Ellie said innocently.

Alex started turning his body away from the woman he was talking to and moving toward Ellie. DJ chimed in, "Do you remember that Salter kid that lost his family in the fire?"

"Yeah. Years ago. Why?" Alex asked.

"This is his fiancée," DJ said.

"Hey. Bodhi," Bodhi said as he extended his hand to Alex. "You're Alex, right?"

"Yeah. This is your girl?" Alex asked, nodding his head at Ellie.

"Only one I can handle," Bodhi said with a smile.

"I hear ya. I remember you from when you were a kid," Alex said to Bodhi.

"Yeah. It's been a hot minute since I came back. You were one of the cool teenagers back then."

"Huh. Yeah, I guess. That was what, fifteen years ago?" Alex asked.

"A little more, but about that," Bodhi said, knowing it was seventeen years ago.

"You're a Salter then," Alex Snow said to Bodhi bluntly.

"I can't hide that. Especially in this town," Bodhi replied.

Alex thought about how to handle having a Salter right there in front of him. DJ seemed to like him, but he couldn't understand why. "You haven't been back. You know it's been a long time, but people ain't forgot what happened." Alex felt he needed to set the record straight.

"Well, you know I ain't forgotten either. Around here, it seems like people should have let it go," Bodhi said.

"That's why you came back. To see if you could just walk back into this town." Alex was smirking and nodding his head. "Well, let me give you…"

DJ stepped in, "Alex. Relax. He hasn't been here. He doesn't know anything. It is like we are still kids. He didn't grow up here. Just chill; he doesn't want trouble."

Alex stopped and moved his head to the side as if cracking his neck. He looked at DJ. "Yeah. I didn't think of it that way. I should give you a break. You are just a kid in this town. Tell you what, how about a shot? Fireball, okay?" Alex decided he couldn't hold a kid responsible for things that happened. "Three, no four Fireballs!" Alex yelled at the bartender.

The bartender was a middle-aged blonde woman with her hair pulled up in a ponytail. She was wearing a white tank top and jean shorts. She was a little on the heavy side for the shorts and tank top, but she had worn that outfit for many years, and it seemed to work for her. She splashed the shots into plastic shot glasses, and Alex handed them around. One to Ellie and Bodhi each, and one more to DJ. He kept the last for himself.

"Let's toast. To kids that get to live without worry," Alex said, raising his glass.

Bodhi looked Alex in the eye and raised his glass. He knew that Alex was trying to rub it in that he had left the Path. He just said, "Cheers!"

About then, Ellie noticed a familiar face sitting at the far end of the bar. Bobby sat on a stool hunched over with a hoodie and baseball cap. He had canned light beer in front of him and his phone in his hand. He was scrolling through something with his thumb. The light of the screen gave an eerie glow to his face. Ellie let herself gaze a bit too long, and apparently, Bobby felt it. He turned to look her way, and he caught her eye. She felt a shiver of panic go over her. She did not know why and then turned away.

"Bodhi, there is Bobby at the end of the bar. Is Ley here?" Ellie asked Bodhi.

"He said he would be here, but I have not seen him yet. Where's Bobby at?" Bodhi asked.

"Down there," she swayed her head in Bobby's direction. "He is sitting by himself."

"Yeah, well, he isn't from around here. He does not fit in with the townies or the others. He should be all right. I am sure Ley will take care of him when he gets here," Bodhi said.

"He is kind of quiet. You think he is all right?" Ellie asked.

"Yes, he should be fine. Nothing wrong with quiet," Bodhi said.

Ellie knew there was nothing wrong with being quiet. She was worried there was something more than him just "being quiet." He seemed to lurk on the perimeter of the town. Not an insider and not an outsider, like the wolf that can't find a pack. There was something that made it seem as though he was stalking something. Ellie decided to let it go for now.

"So, Alex is a Snow?" Ellie asked Bodhi.

"Yes, he is the nephew of Tom. He was the one who died in the Snow Boatyard fire," Bodhi said.

"Do you think he knows anything about the fire?" Ellie asked.

"Ellie, I think everyone around here knows something about the fire. I am not sure if they will tell me."

"Well, can I try? I have some other tricks." She gave Bodhi a sly smile.

"If you want, take it easy on these guys. They aren't used to your superpowers," Bodhi said with a bit of sarcasm.

"Okay, let me see if I can find out something tonight," Ellie said.

Just about then, Ley walked in the door. He filled the frame of the door as he stepped through. The tourists paused as he added another character to the sci-fi bar. Ley looked around to see who was there but knew his tribe would be at the corner of the bar.

"Bodhi!" Ley shouted.

Bodhi heard the boom of Ley's voice and turned in the direction of it. "Ley! Good to see you. Come on, let me buy you a beer." Bodhi turned to the bartender, "Two Miller Lites."

"Thanks. When did y'all get here?" Ley asked.

"About half an hour ago. Where have you been?" Bodhi asked.

"We just got back off the boat. I had to grab a shower and comb my hair." Ley smiled and lifted his hat showing his slicked-back hair being held in place by his hat.

"Your boy Bobby has been here since we got here. Was he out with you?" Bodhi asked.

Ley nodded his head. "Yeah. I wouldn't get too close to him. He probably didn't shower. You might get a whiff of day-old shrimp."

"Is that boy all right?" Bodhi asked Ley.

"He is quiet. He works hard. I can't complain about him. He does everything he needs to and stays out of the way. He just doesn't like to talk to people he doesn't know." Ley said as he took a swig of his beer. "I will tell you, though. At two a.m. on the boat in the middle of sounds, you start him talking, and he will go all night. Not a bad kid, just a little different."

"I can see that. Bobby is probably good on the boat," Bodhi said.

"Where is Ellie?" Ley asked.

Bodhi realized he had lost track of her when Ley showed up. He spun his head around and saw her sitting at a table talking with Jill. Abby was walking toward the table with three plastic cups filled with a blue liquid in her hands and a Red Bull can sticking out of the top. Ley looked in the same direction as Bodhi to see the three girls laughing as Abby tried to manage the drinks.

"Looks like they're having fun. Time for a shot," Ley said to Bodhi.

"Oh no. Trashcans," Bodhi said, knowing when Ellie broke out the trashcans, it was going to be a party.

"What? No shot?" Ley said.

"Shit, yeah, I need a shot. The girls are into the trashcans," Bodhi said.

"Oh, shit fire! Gonna be a night!" Ley said.

The band started playing at about nine-thirty. Love Tribe blended

176

the best music from the eighties to the present. The front man wore skin-tight leather pants and had a receding hairline with long, mousy brown curly locks flowing down the back of his head. He was the quintessential 1980s throwback. By nine-thirty-one, they had the entire bar dancing, singing, laughing, and smiling, reliving by gone days.

Ellie walked out to the second-story deck off the front of the bar. Compared to the inside's stale beer and liquor atmosphere, the cool air felt refreshing as she opened the door. She had just enough trashcans to make her feel free from the constraints of her country club upbringing. Standing on the porch was an assortment of folks getting a break from the music and grabbing a smoke. Alex leaned against the front railing, looking over the edge down at the lawn below. There were two couples on the grass trying to play a game of cornhole but not succeeding. Ellie saw her chance to pry into what Alex might know about the fire.

"Hey, Alex!" Ellie said.

"Look at you. How many of those trashcans have you had?" Alex asked.

"Just enough for me to wanna talk to you," Ellie said, knowing she could bend him with the veiled flirtation.

"Well. What you got to say?" Alex asked.

"Tell me about growing up here. What was it like?" Ellie asked.

"Well, that's a good question. Most of us that grow up here stay here. Your boy is different. He is one that left." Alex started defending his hometown.

"I know he left. That's not what I care about. What was it like growing up with the sound and sand? This beautiful place," Ellie was trying to get him to think back.

Alex pulled out another smoke. He offered one to Ellie and she took it. Why not? Bodhi was smoking. Why shouldn't she?

"Thanks. It's been a while since I had a cigarette, but why not. Good to have one every now and then, isn't it?" Ellie said rhetorically.

"Going back to old habits can be a comfort." Alex took a drag on his cigarette. "What do you wanna know about me growing up?"

Ellie had him where she wanted. A man with a big ego falling for her pretty face. He could not wait to talk about himself. She just had to work it in the right direction. "Well, what did you do for fun?"

"We were boys. We did a lot of running around. You know, doing stupid kid things. We fished and rode boats. We would go out to the fish house and look for beer that people would leave. We stole beers from coolers. Maybe I smoked a little pot. Small town kind of stuff," Alex said.

"Did all the kids hang out together? I mean, did you know Bodhi?" Ellie wanted to remind Alex that she was taken.

"I was a few years older than him. So, we kind of had different circles, but I remember him. He was a cool little guy back then. Of course, everyone knew him after what happened."

"You mean the fire?" Ellie left the question open as to which fire.

"Yeah. There was a lot of talk around here back then. I was like fourteen or fifteen, and we heard lots of rumors. You know the adults think kids don't listen."

"Like, what were they saying?" Ellie took a drag of her cigarette and tilted her head. She knew how to use her body language to communicate a message. She made Alex think he had a chance if only he said what she wanted to hear.

Alex found himself staring at Ellie. He knew what he would say next might cause problems, but he could not help but for it to come out of his mouth. "They said that Bodhi's dad started that fire at my uncle's boatyard. They were saying that someone needed to even the score."

"Oh. Wow. Oh. That's crazy. I don't know what to say. What do you think?" His statement caught Ellie off guard.

"What I think doesn't matter much. I can say that not everyone thinks that anymore. Some people think other things." Alex stopped, wondering if he shared too much with an outsider.

"What other things?" Ellie asked.

Alex smiled. He shook his head, trying to come out of Ellie's spell. "All I will tell you is you need to ask Kristy. She probably knows as much as anyone. Ellie, you are a nice girl. I will give you some advice. Don't be asking questions that you don't want to know the answer to." Alex flicked the butt of his cigarette at the two couples playing cornhole below but missed them and walked back into the bar.

Ellie took the last drag on her cigarette and dropped the butt off the deck, watching its orange tip shed sparks as it spiraled to the ground. Her head was spinning in the same way. Now she understood why Landon yelled at them. He thought Bodhi's father killed Tom Snow in the boatyard and burned it down. Did he burn it down? She didn't know. If Kristy knew something, then why didn't she tell Bodhi? Did someone come to get revenge on Bodhi's dad? If they wanted to kill the whole family, then what about Bodhi? Would they still be after Bodhi? Is that why Kristy took him to Raleigh? There were too many questions. Ellie turned to go inside.

"Hey," Bobby said.

Ellie jumped back as Bobby was right behind her. "Bobby. Hey, what's up?"

"I saw you talkin' with Alex."

"Yes. We were just having a cigarette." Ellie tried to figure out why she was explaining this to Bobby.

"Well. That guy, you gotta watch. I am just sayin'. I do a lot of watchin'."

"Well, thanks. I will keep an eye on him."

"You know. I am not from here."

"I heard that." Ellie was feeling a bit uncomfortable with the conversation.

"That means people don't pay attention to me. So, I can keep watchin'."

"That's good, right?" Ellie asked.

"Yeah. I will keep watchin' and let you know if you need to know."

Ellie maneuvered to get by Bobby and started backing to the door. "Thanks, Bobby. Let me know if I need to know something, okay?"

"I will," Bobby said, pulling out a cigarette and lighting it up.

Ellie walked inside, looking for Bodhi. He was on the dance floor with Ley and DJ. They were singing "Sweet Home Alabama" at the top of their lungs and laughing as they did. She was still trying to digest what Alex said and had not even considered the odd encounter with Bobby. She knew all the townies would have their eyes on her, and she couldn't let on what Alex might have said to her. Ellie wanted to pull Bodhi off the dance floor and tell him what she had learned but decided to sit back down with Abby and Jill. She waited for Bodhi to come to her.

"Saw you were talking with Alex on the porch," Jill said to Ellie.

Ellie wondered if everyone stalked everyone in this town. "I bummed a smoke from him. You know how it goes."

"Ahhh. Yeah. Did he hit on you?" Jill asked.

"No. He was just telling me about Bodhi when he was little." Ellie stopped there.

"That's amazing. Alex will hit on a bullfrog if he thinks it's croaking at him," Jill laughed.

"Ha! No, he was fine. I was asking if he knew Bodhi before he left."

"I knew him," Abby butted into the conversation.

Abby was not technically a townie. She wasn't part of one of the four original families. Her family moved to the town when she was little. Her parents bought a house on the beach and worked at the

Marine base in Jacksonville. When they retired, they decided to stay in Salter Path. That meant she was friends with the kids, but the Pathers saw her parents as temporary.

"Really? What do you remember?" Ellie asked.

"I got to tell you. I had a crush on him," Abby confessed. "I am three years younger than him. So, I was friends with Beth, his sister. When we played at her house, I always thought he was soo cool."

Ellie had not even considered that someone would know Beth. She was taken aback. It was like a glimpse into Bodhi's past she did not know. She was learning about an alternative path that Bodhi's life could have taken. Ellie took a long pause, and her mind tried to process this. "Tell me about Beth," Ellie said to Abby.

Abby took a deep breath. "Beth. Well, she was my best friend. We kind of did everything together. We would play with dolls. Then we would go sit on the dock and fish. We would play in the waves on the beach and build sandcastles. It was tough when the….." Abby didn't want to change the mood but was caught in a corner, "…the fire happened. I think I cried for a week."

"That must have been so hard. Were you like nine at the time? I can't even imagine. It must have been terrible," said Ellie.

"It was, but it was also a long time ago now. I miss Beth and wonder, but also I think it made me thankful for everything I have," Abby said. "Does Bodhi ever talk about the fire?"

23

A Step Closer

The Four Corners diner smelled like Belgian waffles and syrup, with a backdrop of coffee. Just off the high-rise bridge into Atlantic Beach, the Four Corners diner had provided breakfast and lunch to locals and vacationers for as long as anyone could remember. Bodhi and Ellie sat in a booth with hardbacks and an orange tabletop. Bodhi's fork clicked against his plate as he ate his eggs. Ellie was eating her omelet as they tried to recover from the night at Frank and Clara's. They drank their coffee and focused on their food.

"What did you think of Frank and Clara's?" Bodhi asked.

"I should ask you the same. I would guess that was your first night there as well," Ellie poked back.

"Yeah. True, but I knew it from my parents and their friends going there. It was about what I figured. Cheap drinks and a fun time. Not too complicated."

"It was good to see Jill and Abby. They were fun to hang out with. No judgment with those two," Ellie said.

"That's good. Glad to hear you connected with them." Bodhi went back to eating.

"Did you find out anything?" Ellie asked.

"About what?"

"About your family and the fire."

"Not too much. I mostly just hung out with Ley and DJ. Did you find out something?"

"Sort of, I talked with Alex."

"You did? What did he say?"

"Nothing specific. I asked him what it was like growing up here and if he knew you. He said you were younger, so he didn't know you well. He also talked about what he heard about your father." Ellie paused.

"What was that?" Bodhi asked while he ate his eggs.

"He said, well, he said…" Ellie stopped as Bodhi looked up from his food, "that your dad was the one that started the fire at Snows' boatyard."

"How do they know that?" Bodhi asked.

"Well, he didn't say that specifically. He said that some of the people in town said that. So, it might not be true, but that's what people think. He hinted that the fire at your house might be some type of revenge."

Bodhi took a deep breath. "Well, damn. That would make sense why some of these folks have been going off on me. They think my dad started all this."

"I am sorry. I didn't want to tell you last night. We were having fun, and I figured it could wait until this morning."

"What else did he say?" Bodhi asked.

"I tried to see if he knew about the fire at your old house. He didn't seem to know much. He just said that Kristy knows something from what he hears."

"You know. Everyone keeps saying that. They treat me like I am a kid. They keep telling me 'to go ask your mom'. It is like they think I can't take it."

"I'm not sure. Maybe there is something else. Have you ever thought that whoever started the fire at the old house might still be in town?"

Ellie asked.

"I always thought it was an accident. I didn't think much about it until I met with the detective." Bodhi took a sip of his coffee as he collected his thoughts. "He said I should be careful. He said that someone in town might still want to settle a score."

"What? Why didn't you tell me?"

"I didn't want you to worry. I wanted you to have a good time. It seems like you have come to the same possibility as the detective, though."

Ellie went quiet and started eating her whole wheat toast. She thought about the night and the interaction with Alex. He was a Snow and must know more. Then she remembered Bobby. "Another thing from last night. I talked to Bobby, or more accurately, Bobby talked to me," Ellie said.

"And?"

"It was weird. Bobby just told me that he was watching."

"What do you think that means?" Bodhi asked.

"He said that he wasn't from Salter Path, so everyone ignores him, but that he watches." Ellie paused, then continued, "It was creepy, but Bobby is kind of creepy."

"Yeah. He has that kid in the shadows vibe to him. Ley says he is an all right kid. I trust Ley."

"You think we should call the detective?"

"It is probably time to see what he thinks."

They finished their breakfast. Ellie got a sweet tea to go, and Bodhi got a coffee with two creams and two sugars. They climbed into the truck and drove back toward Salter Path. They rolled down the windows to take in the salty humid air. The green trees rolled by on the side of the road. There were glimpses of the ocean and the sound. The waves breaking on the shore threw a fine salty water mist. Over the sound, you could see boats buzzing about, making their way to fishing holes and sandbars. The truck emitted a pleasant rumble from its exhaust. A low manly growl told everyone that a truck was coming without being too desperately masculine. The truck rolled into the motel parking lot a little before noon.

"Morning! Did you have a good breakfast?" Danny asked as they passed by.

Bodhi stopped the truck to talk, minding his southern manners. "It was good. I hadn't been to the Four Corners since I was a kid. Same as I remembered."

"Great to hear. Is everything okay, with the room and all?" Danny asked.

"It's good. Everything is great. We couldn't have expected more," Ellie said to Danny.

"Good to hear," Danny said.

Ellie sensed something in Danny. She knew he did not stop all the guests on their way back to the room. He did seem to stop them, though, and she was thinking now it wasn't so that Danny could get a closer look at her bikini. Therefore, she decided to press her instinct. "Do you know anything about the fire at Bodhi's old house?" she asked Danny from the passenger seat.

The question caught Danny off guard. When that happened, he was not in Salter Path and did not expect the question. "What do you mean?" was the only response he could muster.

"You have to have heard the story about Bodhi's family. I was wondering if you knew anything. Maybe someone has told you a rumor or something else." Ellie tried not to sound accusatory.

"I had heard about the fire. When I saw Bodhi's name pop up on the reservation, I wondered if it was the Bodhi I had heard about. I heard that you were taken away by your aunt after the fire." Danny looked at Bodhi. "That you might never come back. There are a few people that said you would, but most thought you never would. They didn't get into any details. I'll tell you what. If you want to find out more, go to the Save-a-Stop for coffee in the morning, Bodhi."

"Danny, thanks. If you think of anything you may have heard about the fires, can you let me know? We are trying to find out what happened." Ellie looked straight into Danny's eyes. Like so many men, Danny could not help but comply with Ellie's request.

"If I think of anything, I will let you all know," Danny said.

They drove to the front of their motel room and parked the truck. Bodhi grabbed a cigarette from the pack he bought the night before and stepped onto the porch of his motel room. He lit the cigarette and pulled out his phone. He scrolled through his contacts until he came to Detective Natchez. He hit the button and put the phone to his ear.

"This is Natchez," the voice came over the phone.

"Detective, Bodhi Salter here. How are you?"

"Bodhi, good to hear from you. Have you got something for me?" Natchez asked.

"I don't have a lot, but we have found out a few things. My friend DJ, I talked to him about the night of the fire. He was supposed to come out with us to the beach, but he never made it. He said when he went to sneak out, his dad was sitting in the living room with the lights off. He was just looking out the front window. I wonder if he saw something?"

"Have you talked to DJ's dad?" Natchez asked.

"Not yet. I haven't come across him, but tomorrow I will try to go and see him at the Save-a-Stop."

"Morning coffee?" Natchez asked, remembering the men who gathered outside.

"Yeah. How did you know?"

"The men in town even gathered there way back when. I never got anywhere with that."

"Also, Ellie, my fiancée, talked to Alex Snow. He is the nephew of Tom Snow, the boatyard owner. Alex told her that the rumor in town was that my dad had started the fire at the boatyard. Alex thinks the fire at my old house was a payback of some sort."

"I don't know about the Snow Boatyard fire. I heard about it and thought it must have something to do with the fire at your house." Natchez confirmed that this made sense.

"There seems to be more to this. I asked my Aunt Maureen about that night of the fire. My friend Ley is her son. He was on the beach with me. Ley said they were having a party. So, I asked her who was there. It was a bunch of people from the town and two others from off the island. Their names were Ed and Jess." Bodhi stopped.

"Ed and Jess? From Swansboro?" Natchez sounded a bit confused.

"Yeah. I guess they own the coffee place we met in."

"I know them. They never mentioned anything about this. I might have to ask them what they know."

"Another thing is everyone ends their conversation by telling me to talk to my Aunt Kristy. It is like she should have told me something, and everyone can't understand why I don't know."

"I'll tell you what. I am going to talk to Ed tomorrow when I get my coffee. Why don't you try to talk to DJ's dad. What is his name?" Natchez asked.

"Darrel," Bodhi responded.

"Okay, you try to talk to Darrel, and I will talk to Ed. Let's see what we can piece together. I will call you tomorrow," Natchez finished.

"All right. Talk to you tomorrow." Bodhi hung up the phone.

Bodhi stood in the shade of the porch looking at the pool across the parking lot. Danny was walking around the pool with a long pole with a screen basket on the end. He scooped leaves from the pool and flicked them over the fence into the garden. Keeping up his pool, Danny looked somehow at peace. Bodhi couldn't help but think

Danny truly enjoyed running this small motel. It must have made him feel like he was connecting generations together—showing the young folk a glimpse into the past and how the beach was before anyone could drive to the island. Bodhi admired how Danny had embraced the simpler life on the island.

As Ellie was getting ready for a day on the boat with Ley, DJ, Jill, and Abby, Bodhi thought about what this place meant to him. He could feel a connection to the town. Even though he was very young when he left, he could still remember the island. He remembered it in a very different way from simply recalling directions. He recognized trees from his childhood. How they still held the same basic form. He could remember how to distinguish between high and low tide from the sound of the waves. He still intuitively knew if it would rain based on the wind and clouds. There were things about Salter Path that living here had ingrained into Bodhi.

A short time later, Ellie and Bodhi emerged from the motel room, ready for the day. Ellie had her hair pulled back, wearing an artificially worn-out baseball cap. She had a colorful cover-up on and was carrying a straw bag filled with towels, sunscreen, and a few snacks for the day. Bodhi brought the cooler, putting it down to make sure the door locked after they walked out. He elected to throw his T-shirt over his shoulders, and Ellie took note of his well-tanned body with muscles flexing as he carried the cooler.

They headed to Nana B's house, where Ley kept his pontoon boat. The pontoon was Ley's party barge. Ley and his friends would pile onto the boat and make their way to the islands and sandbars located throughout the area. Today they were headed for the backside of Carrot Island.

The wind was blowing out of the north, which would make the backside dead-calm flat. The wind and tides formed Carrot Island between the Beaufort waterfront and Shackleford banks. The ancestor of the original families who moved to Salter Path likely spent time on those same beaches as the island would have been in plain sight of Diamond City. Carrot Island had its population of wild horses known as Carrot Island ponies. These horses intermixed with the horses on the Shackleford Banks by swimming between the islands. Carrot Island was also the home of the Rachel Carson Nature Preserve. It was a small island, only a couple of hundred yards wide but a couple of miles in length. The pure sand along the backside of the island was washed over with the tide from Beaufort Inlet, keeping the water crystal clear throughout the year.

"Ley! What's up? Are you ready?" Bodhi yelled as he got out of his truck.

"Let's go! We have been waiting for you!" Ley said.

Ley was standing by the wheel of the boat. Jill and Abby had staked out a spot near the front of the boat lounging on the long couch-type seats. DJ was standing up, leaning on a seat back next to Ley. He waved to Bodhi and Ellie when they pulled up. Ellie and Bodhi made their way down to the boat. Ellie was widely smiling as she had never been boating on the coast. She had spent time on friends' boats on Falls Lake back in Raleigh, but the idea of riding over the clear blue waters of the beach made the experience very different.

"Sorry. I had a phone call I needed to take before we could go," Bodhi said to Ley.

"No problem. We were just sitting here listening to music and drinking some beer," Ley said as country music came out of the speakers on the boat. "Get in. Let's get this barge moving."

"Hand me that," DJ said to Bodhi, reaching for the cooler.

"How are you, DJ?" Ellie asked.

"Getting by. How are y'all after last night?" DJ asked.

"We went and got breakfast down at the Four Corners. A little bit of grease makes the morning easier." Ellie said, smiling.

189

"All right then, here you go." DJ reached into his cooler and handed Ellie a hard seltzer.

She took it, opened it, and took a long drink. "Thanks. That's just what I needed," she said calmly, knowing that DJ was trying to rattle her.

"I hear ya. C'mon, get on board," DJ said, reaching out his hand to help Ellie step onto the boat.

Bodhi climbed on as well, and Ley fired up the engine. Bodhi and DJ untied the lines from the bow and stern of the boat, while Ellie made her way to the bow and found a place with Jill and Abby. The boat backed off the dock, slowly pointing the stern to the east, then Ley popped it into forward and made a circle directing the bow toward the center of the sound.

The sound was shallow, and the boat moved along a little faster than a walking pace. There was a slight chop on the water that slapped against the pontoons. Ley turned up the radio, and everyone settled in for the cruise to Carrot Island. The sun was shining, and the weather was warm. Being the first day of June, midsummer's high temperatures and humidity had not yet come to the Crystal Coast. Ley turned the boat to the starboard and then laid into the throttle. The boat sped up and began clipping along with the wind blowing through the girls' hair.

Ley maneuvered the boat through the constantly shifting shoals in the sound. These waters were literally Ley's backyard. The crew cut down the middle of the sound, ignoring the marked channel and taking a shortcut to their destination. They went under the high-rise bridge, and Ellie was in awe, seeing the bridge from the water. You only appreciated the bridge's height when you stared up at it from the water. It rose more than seventy feet to allow tall sailing ships to pass.

Suddenly, Ley spun the boat to port and slowed down. Ellie's heart jumped at the abrupt change in direction. She turned around to look at Ley as he raised his arm and pointed straight off the bow.

"Dolphins!" Ley yelled to Ellie.

"Where?" Ellie said just as she saw one, then two, and finally, a third dolphin break the surface to grab a breath of air. "Oh! Look at them! Bodhi, give me my phone."

Bodhi dug through the bag they brought and handed the phone to Ellie. She immediately started trying to capture pictures of the dolphins as they surfaced.

"Why are they here?" Ellie asked.

"Hahaha! Ellie, this is their home," Bodhi said. He recalled seeing the dolphins many times as a kid. He still marveled at how they moved through the water. These creatures moved with intelligence. They hunted together to catch fish, cared for their young, and lived in communities. The watermen knew the dolphin by your boat was a good omen.

"I know that. I guess it is just so amazing to see them right here. They are not afraid of us at all!"

"We are visiting them. The dolphins have control of this situation, and we just get to watch," said DJ.

They spent a few more minutes watching the pod move along as they tried to locate lunch. They even spotted a pup about half the size of the adults. Ellie stood on the front of the boat, trying to film the mammals as they went about their business, but the videos couldn't capture the true magic of the encounter.

Ley engaged the engine and circled the boat back to the east. They passed a few boats breaking through their wakes. They slowed down to cruise through the no-wake zone and the Morehead City waterfront. The waterfront was where Bodhi and Ellie had lunch a few days ago. Many of the charter boats were out to sea on charters for the day, but a few remained in port. Tied with their stern to the dock, the boats' bows poked into the channel at the passing pontoon. The sterns of the boats were covered in teak wood, harkening back to the days of wooden boats. The view of the boats from the bow made them look more like space-aged creations designed to slice through the waves. The lines on the boat were aggressively feminine. There was strength and beauty in the design of the boat. Ellie connected with these beautiful sportfishing boats. They used their beauty and structure to conquer the much stronger ocean. Braving the vast expanse time and time again, and always coming out on top.

"There it is, the *Catch-23*," Abby said to Jill.

"Is that MJ's boat?" Ellie asked.

"Yes. This year is MJ's second year fishing the Big Rock. I guess he had a good time last year," Jill said to Ellie.

"That boat is amazing. How big is it?" Ellie asked.

"Eighty-foot Viking. Custom made for him," Ley responded.

"Why did he name it *Catch-23*?" Jill asked.

The eighty-foot Viking was custom made and custom painted. It bore the same pattern on the hull to match MJ's favorite trademark shoes, and it coincidentally matched the paint job on his private jet. The design was similar to that of a blue and gray reptile print.

"He built that boat to be fast. He said he didn't want anyone to be able to catch him on the water. So, I guess it's a challenge to 'catch twenty-three,'" Ley said.

The crew on board the pontoon stared at the boats as they passed by. It was not every day a celebrity made themselves known at the dock in Morehead City. However, more than people could imagine, many stars passed through secretly as they moved around on their large motor yachts.

They cruised by the State Port at Morehead City with large cranes that unloaded ships. People moved around on the docks unloading from a large cargo ship. These ships even made MJ's eighty-foot boat look small. Soon, Ley laid into the throttle again, and the pontoon made its way to Carrot Island.

As they turned toward Beaufort, Ley began to turn the boat back and forth, following a path through the sandy shoals only known to him. These were the same shoals Blackbeard mastered to find a safe harbor from the British navy. DJ got up from his seat and grabbed an anchor from under it. He handed the anchor to Bodhi.

"This will go off the front," DJ said as he grabbed another anchor for the stern of the boat.

"Got it," Bodhi said and went to the bow of the boat. He had not set an anchor in many years, but he assumed not much had changed in anchoring. Ley turned the craft toward Carrot island without slowing down. Bodhi wondered if he saw the large landmass rapidly approaching. About thirty yards from the beach, Ley turned the engine off and pressed a button to lift the motor out of the water. The pontoon boat glided up to the beach and gently slid about three or four feet onto the sand. Tying the anchor line to the front boat cleat, Bodhi jumped off the boat's bow and set the anchor into the sand. DJ had already dropped the stern anchor and paid out the line as they approached the beach. The boys had tied off the boat, and the day on Carrot Island started.

24

Sand Dollars

If you looked down from above, you would see the pontoon tied off just on the other side of Carrot Island from the Beaufort waterfront. Even though this was less than a quarter-mile away, you would be in what looked like a tropical paradise. The clear blue water and white sand created a world unto itself. Bodhi remembered this from his childhood, but the scenery took Ellie to another place in her mind. It was as if she had escaped from eastern North Carolina and was now on an exotic beach. Ley, DJ, Jill, and Abby had been to this spot so many times in their lives that the magic had worn off. They still appreciated the beauty, but it would be like a beautiful person looking in the mirror every day. Those people only see the pimples and flaws and forget about the big picture.

Ellie, in her paisley-patterned bikini, jumped off the front of the pontoon onto the island. Her mind was wondering what she might find on this island. She found a type of mystical experience exploring beautiful places. Though the others had experienced this place before, she appreciated that each person experienced things in their own way. The sand was soft and powdery. It "squeaked" as she walked across it and made a yipping sound when she scuffed her feet. Ellie took out her phone and began taking pictures. She was not certain exactly why, but she was pretty sure she wanted to try to capture the awe she felt.

"Beautiful, isn't it?" Bodhi asked Ellie.

"I cannot believe this place is right here in North Carolina. It's right here," Ellie said. "Growing up, I went to the coast, but we never got to see a place like this."

"We used to come to this place as a kid. I remember my parents sitting on the beach as we ran around on the island, playing in the water and chasing fiddler crabs. Come on, follow me."

Bodhi walked up the short beach to the high ground. There was a small path that he walked down. When he was young, he, Ley, and DJ would wander down this path to find an adventure. He wondered if things would still be the same. As he walked down the path with Ellie following along, he could see that the large tidal pool in the island's center was empty. This island was nothing more than a large sandbar that somehow persisted long enough to grow trees and grass. The center sat low enough that the tide would flood in and out twice a day. When the water came in, fish would swarm into the shallows in search of an easy meal. When the tide would run out, there would be a sizable sandy flat covered with creatures that thrived on the things water leaves behind. Fiddler crabs, hermit crabs, and various birds, including the Eastern Willet, combed the wet sandy flat looking for items to eat.

"Oh, wow!" Ellie exclaimed when she saw the large flat crawling with life. "What are all those things?"

"When we were little, they were pets," Bodhi said. "We would spend the day looking for the biggest hermit crab we could find. Our parents would only let us bring one home, and we could only keep it for a week before returning it to the sound. So, we always tried to find the biggest one to take home."

"I can't believe there is that much life existing right below the water.

It is like the island itself is alive!" Ellie said.

"I never thought of it that way, but that is probably a good description. This place and the things that live here are so closely tied to one another. It is like they are one living thing. If the island gets damaged in a hurricane, then the animals suffer as well."

In the back of Bodhi's mind were the morning weather reports. The hurricane off the coast was starting to make its move. Still about four or five days out, the storm started its turn to the north. The turn was happening so that the storm would likely brush the coast of Florida before making its way toward North Carolina. The next couple of days would likely determine what Bodhi and Ellie would do to prepare.

Ellie and Bodhi explored the flats as Bodhi picked up a hermit crab. These crabs did not grow a shell of their own. Instead, they scavenged old shells from welks and conchs, making them their homes. "Hold out your hand," Bodhi said to Ellie.

Ellie extended her hand flat out. "Why? What are you going to do?"

"Hold still. Very still." Bodhi placed the hermit crab on the palm of Ellie's hand. The crab had retreated to safety inside the welk shell.

"No. Stop. What's it going to do?" Ellie pleaded.

"Just wait," Bodhi said.

The hermit crab slowly grew the courage to check out the surroundings. Ellie could feel a tickle in her palm as the crab extended a leg to examine the surroundings. Then another leg came out, and next, an eye poked out of the shell. Soon, all the legs were tickling and exploring the palm of Ellie's hand. She laughed as the crab made his way off her hand and started to go up her arm. Bodhi picked the crab up by the shell, releasing Ellie from her frozen position. The crab disappeared into his shell, and Bodhi set him back on the ground.

"That was amazing! He was so cute. I can't believe those crabs are just walking around here."

"It's an amazing place. I forgot how amazing it is. I guess growing up, it is just your backyard, but coming back after being gone so long, it seems all new again."

Ellie and Bodhi wandered back to the pontoon, where the gang floated in the water. They were bobbing on cheap blow-up pool toys they likely bought from the Dollar General. They had a donut-themed inner-tube float that was keeping the cooler in place.

"Come on. Join us!" Jill waved to Ellie and Bodhi as they emerged from the island's center.

Bodhi jumped into the water and swam out to the group. He grabbed a beer for himself and a hard seltzer for Ellie. Ellie followed more cautiously, wading out to the group. On her way, she got a white swan float from the pontoon and took to floating on it as she sipped her seltzer. The group listened to music and joked, having fun in the clear, shallow water.

"DJ, look." Ley pointed to a white boat making its way through the inlet toward the group.

"Looks like my dad's boat. I told him we were going to be out here," DJ said.

A few minutes later, the twenty-four-foot *Grady White* slowly approached them. The boat slowed and spun around. DJ and Ley waded out to help guide the boat up the island shore. DJ's father Darrel was at the helm, and a group of others gathered in the boat's cockpit. They anchored the bow and set the stern anchor firmly in the sand on the beach. Darrel was the only person Bodhi recognized on the boat. The others were friends of Darrel he had met through the Big Tree. The group piled off the boat and lugged beach chairs and coolers to the beach.

"Hey, Mr. Darrel," Ley said.

"How are you, Ley? Y'all been here awhile?" Darrel asked.

"Not too long. Maybe a couple of hours. Have you been out fishing?"

Ley asked.

"We went and trolled for Spanish mackerel off the beach for a while. Caught a few, but it was slow," Darrel said. "Who is that with you?"

"DJ didn't tell you?" Ley questioned. "That's Bodhi Salter and his fiancée."

"Nah. He didn't mention that. What is he doing back?" Darrel asked.

"Well. Bodhi is getting married and wanted to bring the girl down to see where he grew up," Ley said.

"A tough place to come to for him," Darrel said as a matter of fact.

Darrel poked around on the boat for a while, organizing fishing tackle. He stowed away the fishing gear and fiddled with something sitting on the seat. Eventually, he made his way off the boat to join the group on the beach. The pontoon crew continued floating in the water, drinking and listening to music.

Ellie pulled Bodhi aside and said, "That's DJ's dad. You need to try to talk to him."

"I will. I just don't want to make it obvious. I need to wait for the right time."

Ellie felt frustrated. She thought he should just ask Darrel what he knew about the fire. "Just go talk to him."

"Trust me on this. It's a small town, and we are not from around here. Darrel will not be able to resist finding out what I am doing here."

Almost as if on cue, Darrel stood up from his beach chair. It was a bit of a struggle. Darrel was the opposite of his son in physical appearance. While DJ looked like a spider monkey in build and movement, Darrel was more like a potbellied pig with a large belly and sparse hair. He got to his feet with a beer in hand and started walking to the pontoon crew still floating in the water.

"Ley said you are Bodhi Salter. Do you remember me?" Darrel

asked Bodhi.

"I do, Mr. Darrel. It has been a long time. Good to see you," Bodhi said. "Oh, this is Ellie, my fiancée."

"Ellie, good to meet you. What are you doing with a guy like this?" Darrel asked.

Ellie didn't know exactly how to take that remark. She stumbled on her words. "Good to meet you, Darrel."

"What brought you back to Salter Path, Bodhi?"

"I thought I would show Ellie where I grew up."

Darrel paused, thinking about his following words. "That had to be tough. You know, with the house being gone and all."

"Well, not exactly the house. I meant the town," Bodhi said, not realizing Darrel was going directly at him, trying to tell him to go away.

"Oh. Yeah. I know what you mean. What do you think of it?" Darrel asked Ellie.

"It's been a great visit. I was surprised to learn that Bodhi still owns the land where the old house was." Ellie was sharp with her words realizing the game Darrel was playing.

"I am not sure who would want that property. I mean, with all that happened there," Darrel said.

Because Ellie realized Darrel was not pulling any punches, she was happy to spar with words in the polite southern way. "I know the town isn't much, but the island is nice. Bodhi tells me about all the great stories from when he was growing up here. He was friends with your son, DJ, right?"

Darrel did not expect such a beautiful woman to have such a sharp wit. He was not sure how to respond to the question. "Yeah. DJ's my boy. I guess he and Bodhi were friends a long time ago."

"DJ has been good to us since we got here. He even had a little party over at his place. He taught Bodhi how to surf. We appreciate his

199

hospitality."

Bodhi was just standing there, seeing Ellie take control of the conversation. She was the one who could get people to talk. Ellie would leave the grocery store and somehow know the life story of the checkout clerk. She had weathered Darrel's attempt at intimidation and now put him in the position to accept a compliment.

"That's good of him. He didn't mention you were back, Bodhi." Darrel tried to turn the conversation away from Ellie and back onto Bodhi's appearance in town.

"It has been a long time. About seventeen years since I have been in the Path. It still feels like home to me."

Darrel thought about that for a second before he spoke. "How's your Aunt Kristy?" he inquired.

"She is doing fine. Thanks for asking."

"Does she know you are down here?"

Bodhi thought that was an odd question. He was a grown man, and he could go where he wanted. Why would Darrel wish to know this? "Yes. I talked to her the other day."

"That's good. How long do y'all plan on staying?"

"We are staying through the week. Bodhi is taking me to the Big Rock dinner." Ellie made herself part of the conversation again.

"You will enjoy that. It should be a good time," Darrel said with a bit of distance in his voice.

"You know the other thing. You asked why we came down. I think Bodhi is also trying to figure out just what happened the night of the fire." Ellie cut to the chase.

"You talking about the Snow's fire or the fire at Bodhi's house?" Darrel asked.

Ellie knew Darrel understood which fire, but she decided to be direct with him. "The one at Bodhi's house. He never really found out what happened."

"I think they said it was an accident. Didn't his aunt tell him that?"

"We heard that, but it doesn't make sense. Why would that fire spread so fast at the bottom of the stairs?" Ellie challenged Darrel.

"You got me there. I don't know about house fires."

Bodhi spoke up, "I was talking with DJ. He was supposed to be out with Ley and me that night. He said you were up looking out the window when he went to sneak out."

"I don't remember that."

"DJ did. Can you think of why you might have been up looking out the window in the dark?" Bodhi asked.

"If you are thinking I know something or did something, I can tell you right now you are asking the wrong questions. There are many other people in town, and you probably know that the Snows are no friends of the Salters. Why don't you bother them with these questions?"

"I'm not accusing anyone of anything. I'm just trying to find out what might have happened. I was young when I left, but I understand that this town has its own memory."

"I'll tell you what. You were a kid. You didn't have much to do with all that happened. I am going to give you some help here. Go by and talk to my sister Susan Snow. I will tell her that you will stop by," Darrel said. "Oh, you should talk to your aunt as well. She might know something."

"Well, I appreciate that, Mr. Darrel. I will try to stop by tomorrow. Does she live in the same place?" Bodhi asked.

"Not many changes in town, Bodhi. She is still in the same place," Darrel said, ending the conversation.

Darrel waded out to the pontoon crew floating in the water as Bodhi and Ellie grabbed another drink from the pontoon.

As Darrel went out of earshot, Ellie turned to Bodhi. "What do you think about what Darrel said?"

"Not now, they might not be able to hear, but they are watching." Bodhi raised his eyes toward Darrel's friends on the beach, who spectated the exchange. "Let's go for a swim. I want to show you something."

Bodhi started swimming out toward a small sandbar that had emerged as the tide went down. Ellie dove in behind him with her long hair flowing down her back. They had to swim about 100 yards to get to the sandbar. The water was refreshingly cool as the day was starting to get hot. The sandbar was only inches above the water and made of pure sand. Bodhi made it there first, stepping up onto the sandbar. The afternoon sun made his water and tanned body seem to sparkle. Ellie came up out of the water and went straight to Bodhi to give him a long kiss. They were a perfect couple embracing and kissing. From the beach, it looked as though they were standing on the water, a miracle happening right before everyone's eyes.

"I want to show you something. Sit down." Bodhi sat down in shallow water. Ellie surprised him by sitting down right in front of him so he could wrap his arms around her. "Umm. This position is nice," Bodhi said as he kissed her on the back of the neck.

"What do you want to show me?" Ellie asked.

Bodhi's mind had switched from what he planned to show her to tasting the salt on her skin. "I forgot."

"C'mon. Save it for later. Why are we sitting here?".

"Watch." Bodhi started to dig his hands into the sand gently. He poked around for a second and then pulled up two handfuls of sand. He began washing away the sand, and there in his hands were three sand dollars. These were not the ones you find in the gift store at the beach. Those bleach-white sand dollars were dead. These gray-brown sand dollars were alive and covered in fine fur.

"What? Are you kidding me? How did you know they were there?" Ellie asked.

"Just dig your hands into the sand very gently. You will feel them. They are everywhere out here. They call this sand dollar island," Bodhi said.

Ellie dug her hands into the sand. She brought up a handful of sand and moved them back and forth in the water, revealing a sand dollar. "Eww. He is peeing on me," she said as her hand began to turn brown.

"Hahaha. Yeah. Don't worry. They do that. It is like a natural self-tanner. It will go away in a little bit."

Ellie was amazed again by the natural beauty and magic of this place. There was this whole world above and below the island. She could not help but see the contrast between Raleigh and city life with this place of natural beauty.

"I love you, and I love this place. You have shown me a whole part of the world I never thought I would know. Thank you for bringing me here."

"I'm glad we came here. I needed this, and without you, I don't know if I ever would have had the confidence. I love you."

They sat there for a good long time, enjoying each other's touch. The water slowly moved lower as the tide retreated. Soon the couple was sitting on dry sand. They stared toward the Beaufort Inlet and watched the boats. The sea was calm, and boats moved at a smooth and steady pace. Folks from the city might sit and watch ducks swimming on a pond; people from the coast watch boats. You could not help but wonder where each craft might be going.

"What do you think about what Darrel said?" Ellie asked Bodhi.

"I think I need to talk to Susan."

"Yes. I just think Darrel was lying. I have had my share of men lie to me over the years."

"Lying about what?" Bodhi did not pick up on what Ellie sensed.

"When he said he didn't remember sitting in the living room. He remembered that. It was a practiced answer he gave us."

"So, you think he knows something?" Bodhi asked.

"I think he knows more than he is telling us."

They swam back to the island but now could walk a good part of the way as the tide was out. They could see the pontoon crew loading up and getting ready to leave. By the time they got back to the island, everyone was on the boat.

"Bodhi, grab the front anchor," Ley said.

Bodhi pulled the anchor up, winding in the rode. He set anchor on the deck with a thump and then pushed the boat off the sand. Ley gave the boat some throttle, and the boat began backing away under its power. Bodhi jumped on the boat, and they were on their way back to Salter Path.

25

Leads

Bodhi walked through the door carrying two cups of coffee from the office. Ellie was sitting up on the bed wearing one of Bodhi's T-shirts. She had her hair pulled back and was looking at her phone.

"Thanks, honey. How was Danny?" Ellie asked.

"The usual. Pushing the drinks at the pool. We should probably support his cause today."

"I think we should call Natchez. Give him an update."

"I was thinking the same thing. Hold on." Bodhi took out his phone and began dialing. He set the phone on the bed between them.

"Natchez. Is this Bodhi?" Natchez answered.

"Detective. Good morning. It's Bodhi, and I have you on speaker. My fiancée, Ellie, is here. We have been asking some questions around town. I thought I would give you an update."

"Did you go by the Save-a-Stop this morning?" Natchez asked.

"Shit. No, I slept in. We did get to talk to Darrel. We ran into him on an island. Ellie did a lot of the talking, so I wanted her to be in on the conversation."

"Nice to meet you, Detective," Ellie said.

"Nice to meet you. Thanks for helping Bodhi with this. I know it is

205

probably not easy for him."

"I am glad I can be here for him."

"So, what did you learn from Darrel?" Natchez asked.

"We didn't learn too much. He did want to talk about the fire, though. We were on an island, and he came up to us. He started talking. He gave us the same old 'you aren't welcome around here' that we have heard before," Ellie said.

"The people down that way aren't always welcoming," Natchez said.

"You just have to break the ice with them. Once you get past that, they let you in on a lot," Ellie said.

"What did Darrel let you in on?"

"He was very territorial about the whole thing. Bodhi asked him about him sitting in the window. You know about that, right?" Ellie asked.

"Yes."

"He said he didn't remember sitting in the window, but you could tell he was lying. He wouldn't admit to anything, but he said we should talk to Susan Snow."

"I tried that years ago. Susan was my first stop. It was a dead end for me. Maybe you will have better luck."

Bodhi joined in, "Darrel said he would call over to Susan and let her know I was coming by. He felt like she had something to say."

"That's good. Maybe there is something we can work with there."

"What do you think about Darrel lying about looking out the window?" Ellie asked. "I know he was lying because you could tell he practiced his answer."

"I have conducted a lot of investigations over the years. People lying is the one thing you can count on most of the time. Sometimes it's to protect someone else, but most of the time it's to protect themselves."

"So you think Darrel has something to do with it?" Bodhi asked.

"I am not sure yet. We have to figure out if there is someone else he might want to lie for. If we can't figure that out, he is probably protecting himself."

"How do we do that?" Ellie asked.

"Well, I need to tell you something. Could you meet me at the Trading Post in Emerald Isle? Maybe around lunch?" Natchez loved the fried chicken at the Trading Post, and he had not been there in a while. He figured if he had to break some news, he should have a good lunch.

"We can do that. Should Ellie come?" Bodhi asked.

"Yes, I think so. She is part of this now."

"Okay, see about twelve-thirty, then?" Bodhi said.

"See you then."

Ellie and Bodhi finished their coffee and lay in bed. It was already late morning, and there wasn't much point in doing something before lunch. They both picked up their phones and began killing time. Ellie pushed through social media posts while Bodhi looked up "how to tell if someone is lying." He clicked and read article after article. There were things about eyes, how their stories never changed, a liar might touch their face, but it never got to what Ellie sensed. She knew the story did not fit. That is the number one way to tell if someone is lying. Bodhi knew everyone in town remembered precisely where they were and what they were doing the night of the fire. It was one of the biggest things to happen to Salter Path, and there was no way DJ and Darrel remembered that night so differently.

Ellie and Bodhi made their way to the Trading Post. It was about a twenty-minute ride to the restaurant. The restaurant had weathered the pandemic by taking advantage of its large backyard. They put tables everywhere and kept the lights on, making it to another summer. Not all businesses were lucky enough. The building was bright beachy green on the outside. The white and blue "Trading Post" sign popped against the green of the building. It specialized in southern coastal food. When Bodhi and Ellie walked in, Natchez was sitting at a table with a sweet tea. Natchez first noticed Ellie walking into the room. It took him a minute to realize Bodhi was walking behind her.

Natchez stood up from the table. "You must be Ellie?"

Ellie extended her hand, "Nice to meet you in person, Detective."

"The pleasure is mine. I got us a table," Natchez said. "Bodhi, good to see you. Are you doing okay?"

"I am doing good. How about yourself?" Bodhi asked.

"Well, getting closer to retirement. In fact, they have taken most things away from me. So, I have some time to spend on this."

"You are a short-timer, I guess. I am sure you will find plenty of things to do," Bodhi assured him.

"I am not worried one bit about that. I have missed enough over the years that I am more worried about running out of time than things to do."

"What's good here?" Ellie asked.

"Their fried chicken is about as good as you can find. Most other things are good, too."

Ellie looked over the menu. She loved fried chicken, but it didn't go well with a bikini. "What are you getting, Bodhi?"

"The chicken and waffles. It seems about right since I didn't get breakfast. How about you?"

She thought for a moment. "The Southern Soul Roll and the spinach salad. I have to try that roll. Collard greens and country ham in an egg roll. I am intrigued."

The waitress came by to take their order. She was a college student from East Carolina University, ECU, and lived at her parent's place on the island for the summer. They said she could stay as long as she got a job. She had been a waitress for only two weeks but seemed to enjoy serving.

While they waited for the food, Bodhi, Ellie, and Natchez made small talk. They told Natchez about their jobs back in Raleigh and their plans for the wedding. Natchez told them about the boat he planned to buy after retiring. He also sought their opinion on whether he should get a dog after he retires. His wife thought it was a good idea to keep him busy, but he believed it was so he had something to distract him. Soon, the food came, and they began to eat.

"How's the food?" Natchez asked.

"Couldn't be better. So, why did you want to meet?" Bodhi finally asked.

"I thought I should tell you in person what I found out when I talked to Ed and Jess," Natchez said.

"I was guessing that it had to do with that. What did you learn?" Bodhi asked as Ellie listened.

"They were there at Beatrice's the night of the fire. They confirmed that. They were having a party with some friends. They had gotten to know Maureen from their kids going to school together." Natchez took a bite of his fried chicken, then he continued, "That was only, maybe, the second or third time they had been to Salter Path. It was not long after they had moved to North Carolina. They were trying to make friends."

"Do they know anything about the fire?" Ellie asked.

Natchez dabbed a napkin on his face and pushed the plate away, indicating he had enough to eat. "Not exactly. They said that after that night, Maureen wouldn't return their calls. They would see them at school, and the Salter Path people were always nice but never asked them back." Natchez took a sip of his tea. "They have always wondered if maybe they saw something that night that they weren't supposed to. That was the only reason they had for getting the cold shoulder."

"That makes sense. Maybe, they know something, but they don't know it is important," Bodhi said.

"Do you have any idea what they might know?" Ellie asked.

"We went through the whole night as they could remember it. Nothing stood out as different or new. Except there was one thing." Natchez stopped and looked at Bodhi. "Have you talked to your Aunt Kristy about the fire?"

Bodhi smiled and shook his head. "Everyone asks me that. When I start talking about the fire or ask questions, everyone ends with 'ask your aunt'. Why are you asking?"

"Well, Bodhi, it turns out that your Aunt Kristy was at Beatrice's that night," Natchez said.

"That couldn't be. Kristy moved to Raleigh like a month before. She would have been in Raleigh."

"I went through the people Ed and Jess remembered at the party. I talked to them separately. They both listed the same people at the party. It included your Aunt Kristy. They also said they remembered her name from reading the newspapers." Natchez paused. "Bodhi, she was in Salter Path the night of the fire."

"I'm not sure how that is important. She probably just came down for the party. Maybe she just wanted to see some friends. I imagine she didn't know anyone in Raleigh yet. Why would it be important?" Bodhi was struggling to digest this information. He could not understand why his aunt never mentioned this.

"When you talked to her about the fire, what did she have to say?" Natchez asked.

"She always said it was an accident. She wouldn't say much more. I guess she must have gone home that night. So, she probably only knew what you were able to find out."

"What do you think about asking her about it directly?" Natchez asked.

Bodhi paused, thinking about this new information and what it could mean. "I need to do that. She could remember something from that night."

"When should we talk to her?" Ellie asked Natchez.

"I think the sooner, the better. Do you think we can try to get her on the phone after lunch?" Natchez suggested.

"Uh, sure, we can do that." Bodhi was still trying to make sense of this.

Thankfully, Bodhi had already eaten most of his lunch before Natchez shared his information about his aunt because he now felt sick to his stomach. The group got the check, and Ellie offered to pay, tipping the waitress well. They walked out the back door into the large backyard of the trading post. The seating area was empty as the afternoon lunch business was dying down. They found an open table under a big oak tree. Bodhi took out his phone and dialed Kristy's number. He put it on the speakerphone and set it on the table.

"Hello," Kristy said.

"Hey, Kristy. It's Bodhi. How are you?"

"I am good. Is everything all right?" Kristy must have been able to hear the tension in his voice.

"Yeah. Everything is fine. Ellie and I were just finishing up lunch at the Trading Post."

"I hope the food was good. The Trading Post always had the best fried chicken."

"Actually, one of my friends said it was really good," Bodhi said.

"Who is that? Your friend?" Kristy asked.

"Natchez, the SBI detective, joined us for lunch."

Kristy paused for a moment, "Oh, well, I am sure he is a nice person. I can still remember when he called to ask me if you could come live with me. Why did you all have lunch together?" Kristy's heart beat a bit faster, knowing Bodhi and Ellie were talking with the detective.

"He had something he wanted me to ask you. He said you were at Nana B's party the night of the fire. Is that true?" Bodhi asked.

There was a long pause. "Where are you, again?" Kristy asked.

"I am in Emerald Isle at the Trading Post," Bodhi responded.

"When are you coming home?"

"After the Big Rock dinner. Why?"

"Okay. I am going to come down there and get this straightened out. I will call when I get to town."

"When will you be here?" Bodhi asked.

"Tomorrow. I need to finish up something at work, and then I will be down."

"Okay, call me when you get into town," Bodhi said.

Kristy hung up the phone. Bodhi looked up from his phone at Ellie and Natchez standing over him, listening.

"I guess we are going to get this straightened out," Bodhi said.

26

Growing Up

Jerry and Josephine (Jo) Salter were the fifth generation of Salters living in the Path. Their families settled in Salter Path before the squatters had moved from Diamond City. They raised two children in the Path. Their oldest was Freddie Salter, who was born in 1969 at Carteret General Hospital. The hospital was nearly new at the time, having opened in 1967. Six years later, in 1975, Jerry and Jo would welcome their baby girl Kristy to the world at the same hospital.

Freddie adored his little sister. He was six years old and remembered his mother walking through the door with Kristy wrapped in a pink blanket. They set up a crib in an alcove off the hallway. They strung a curtain across the opening to make a small nursery. Jo did her best to make use of the limited space in their tiny house. Money was tight before Kristy arrived, and Jo knew things would just be tighter with the new arrival. She didn't know how, but she believed things would work out.

After Kristy came home, Jerry embraced the idea of having a daughter. He was a waterman and scraped together a living. Jerry worked as a mate on a shrimp boat and made just enough money to support Jo and Freddie. Jo did some odd jobs to add to the family income, but Jerry felt the weight of a new mouth to feed. Jerry wanted a better life for his family, and all he knew was how to fish.

Jerry got a job in the winter working at the Snow Boatyard. At that time, the Snows mostly built smaller skiffs and coastal boats the watermen used. Jerry saved half his winter earnings every year, scraping together a small nest egg. He learned the art of boat building and helped the Snow Boatyard become known for well-built working boats that would last for years.

Jo loved her family and her hardworking husband. Jerry would always take Freddie with him wherever he went, and even made a few trips on the shrimp boat Jerry worked. He taught Freddie how to mend nets, set anchors, handle the ropes on a boat, and read the water. He spent days with Freddie teaching him to fish and how to drive the small family skiff.

Jo was left to care for Kristy. Kristy was not a planned baby, and Jo referred to Kristy as "a blessing." Jo felt that way but was never sure Jerry agreed. Kristy was constantly by Jo's side. Outside the family, people thought Kristy was just insecure and never wanted to leave her mother. What they could not understand was how Jerry had come to treat Kristy.

A son needs his father to teach him to be strong, honest, and a person of his word. A daughter needs a father to understand men can be strong, honest, and a person of their word. Jerry took the obligation to his son seriously. However, Jerry never thought he should have a role in raising his daughter other than providing for her.

Kristy did not understand what was missing as she grew up. Her mother was always there for her. She would be home when she returned from school. She would teach her how to cook and make her do her chores around the house. Her mother would take her to the store and would never leave her with her dad. Kristy did not know what a father should be as a child, so she believed that fathers did not interact with daughters.

Jerry was strict. He had rules about the house. When to be home, what to do on Saturday, and how to behave in church. He enforced the rules with Kristy with an iron fist. She never got any wiggle room in following the rules. If she did not pay attention in church, she would be grounded in her room for the rest of Sunday. If she forgot to make her bed, she would also have to make her parent's bed for a week. These rules seemed to be applied disproportionately to her. Freddie being older and a boy was allowed his mistakes. He might chew gum in church, and Jerry would say, "At least he is quiet." He might track sand from the beach through the house, and Jerry would ask Jo why she let Freddie do that. As Kristy grew older, she sensed something was missing in her relationship with her father.

Kristy could still remember the day they bought the shrimp boat. She was in the fifth grade. It was October and a school day. They were eating breakfast, and her father told Freddie he did not need to go to school that day. He needed to come with him to bring the boat back to the dock in Salter Path.

Jerry had taken the nest egg and invested it in a boat of his own. He knew that the only way to improve their lifestyle was to own a boat. It was a used boat, but it was well equipped. The engine had a top-end rebuild the year before and should be reliable for years to come. The nets were well mended, and the entire rig was ready to go to work. Jerry named her *Lady B* after his sister. It was considered bad luck in Salter Path to name your boat after your love because it was said you would soon lose both. Thus, Jerry decided to pay homage to his sister Beatrice.

When the new boat arrived, Freddie's time in school started to decrease dramatically. Jerry would allow him to skip school to go fishing on the boat with him. By Freddie's senior year, he had dropped out of high school and was the first mate on the *Lady B*. Freddie had tied his future to fishing with his father. Eventually, Jo would make Freddie get his GED, but he never returned to school after working with his father.

Kristy became more detached from her father. As Freddie and Jerry spent long nights working and bonding together on the water, Kristy stayed by her mother's side. As time went on, she noticed she was happier when it was just her and her mother. When her father and Freddie returned from the water, Kristy sensed the tension in the air. She was growing closer to her mother but further from her father.

The turning point in Kristy and her father's relationship came one night when her mother went on an overnight women's church retreat. Kristy, Freddie, and their dad were all at home together. They decided to go to Morehead City to get dinner. Bojangle's was a fried chicken restaurant that dotted North Carolina. Going to any restaurant was a treat for the Salters, who worked hard for every dollar they had. Kristy was looking forward to it. She was in the eighth grade, and her brother had been working on the boat for about a year. They piled into Jerry's pickup truck. Kristy sat between her dad and Freddie as they made their way over the bridge to Morehead City.

Kristy was feeling very special on the way to the restaurant. She was between the two men in her life. Since Freddie left school, he no longer seemed like a brother but more of an uncle who would help look over her. Kristy felt comfort knowing there could be more male figures in her life than just her father. Still, her dad was her dad. She loved him and always hoped he would be there for her when she needed it. She had yet to test that as her mother was always there. For her, she could live in the space where she believed her father was someone who he was not. It was a comfortable place because she never had to know her father.

They pulled into the restaurant and parked the truck in a handicap space right by the front door. Jerry reached above the sun-visor, pulled out a handicap hangtag, and put it over the mirror. They got out of the truck, and Freddie slammed the door. The truck shuddered as if the rusty door might shatter into a thousand pieces. They made their way to the counter, and Jerry ordered first. Next, Freddie picked his meal. He got a three-piece dinner with mashed potatoes and gravy with a Pepsi and two Bo-berry biscuits. It was Kristy's turn. She loved the idea of having someone cook for her. Even if it was a fast-food restaurant, this was still a memorable trip that only happened a few times a year.

"I will have a two-piece meal white, with fries and tea. Can I also get two Bo'berry biscuits?" Kristy said to the worker behind the counter.

"No problem," the worker said.

"What did she order?" Jerry asked the worker.

"A two-piece meal with fries and tea. Also, two Bo'berry biscuits."

"She doesn't need those biscuits. Take them off," Jerry said.

"Dad, Freddie got them. Why can't I?" Kristy asked.

"He works and helps this family. When you make yourself useful, you can get the things you want."

Kristy's mind spun. She could not make out what he meant by that. She was only thirteen years old, and how was she supposed to be "useful?" She did not know what that meant, but she could feel an indifference in her father's voice. She had felt her dad did not take an interest in her, but she never confronted it. She wanted to believe he loved her deeply and that the lack of attention was just the way dads were with daughters. Even though she saw her classmates' dads doing things with their daughters, she ignored the fact that her dad never seemed to have time for her. Her mother would say, "He works hard," and "He is tired." These were the excuses Jo made for Jerry to protect Kristy from reality. Jerry tolerated Kristy. A simple biscuit was all it took for Kristy to realize if he would not do these small things for her, why should she expect him to do the big things?

They finished their dinner and made their way back to Salter Path. After that night, Kristy no longer waited for Dad to come home. She knew her worth to him was not in who she was but in what she could provide. They were never close before that night, and they would grow increasingly distant. When Jo returned home from the church retreat, Kristy did not mention the night at the restaurant. It made no difference anymore. She would focus on her relationship with her mother.

Through Kristy's high school years, the family continued to scrape by, trying to make ends meet. Kristy never understood why she had to shop at the thrift store and why they could not go to Amos Mosquitos for dinner now and then. Homecoming, prom, and the spring fling dance were all events Kristy went to in hand-me-down dresses or thrift store finds. While she tried to make the best of things, her father grew increasingly resentful of her.

Kristy got a job when she was sixteen. She worked a few hours a week at the Save-a-Stop. Kristy would clean the restroom, sweep the floor, and mind the register while the owners ran errands or took a break. She made the minimum wage of $2.75 an hour. After the government took its share, her weekly work would net her between six and ten dollars a week. She saved that money to have something to spend when she wanted to do things with her friends. Shortly after she started work, her friends invited her to the movies. Her father and mother were sitting in the living room watching TV. She came in and asked her mother if she could go to the movie. She had only ever been to a movie once before, when her mother took her as a birthday treat. Her father rarely took an interest in her, so she did not even consider asking him for permission.

"Mom, some friends invited me to go to the movies tonight. Is it okay if I go?" Kristy asked, thinking that the money saved would be well spent at the movies.

Jerry took his gaze from the TV and placed it on Kristy. He furrowed his brow a bit and then asked, "Where are you gonna get the money for that? Some boy taking you?"

"I have the money that I saved," Kristy said.

"Money you saved? From what?" Jerry asked his daughter.

Kristy realized her father didn't know she had a job. He paid so little attention to his daughter; he didn't notice her missing from midweek family dinners as she worked.

"I got a job at the Save-a-Stop."

"How much do you make?" Jerry asked.

"Just minimum wage."

"Well, now that you are working, I guess it's time for you to start paying your share. I tell you what, you need to give me half what you bring home, and you can keep the other half. We need some money for food and bills, not to go to a movie," Jerry proclaimed and turned his attention back to the TV. Jo sat in silence, afraid to cross her husband.

Kristy felt a rush of adrenaline pulse through her veins. She felt a tingle in her skin, and her face turned flush red. This feeling was anger. She felt its power. At that moment, she wanted to scream and throw something at her father. She had worked hard for that money. Her father was just taking it because he could, and she had no choice. Her fists clenched. She stood there frozen. Her anger wanted to drive her forward and attack her dad. Her fear made her want to run out of the house. The two emotions held her frozen for a moment.

"I am going. If you want half my money, you can have it, but I will do what I want with my half." Kristy tried to assert some level of control over the situation.

That night at the movies in the darkness, her anger turned to sadness. When others were crying about the love story they were watching, Kristy was crying about her life. She loved her mother. She also loved her father, but she did not know why. Why should she want to have a relationship with her father when he did not want one with her? She could not understand this, and it only brought sadness and confusion to her.

Jerry and Freddie continued to run the *Lady B*. Any extra money the family could ever scrape together would be put back into fixing something on the boat. There was always something that seemed to be going wrong. The engine needed maintenance, the nets needed repair, a winch went out, and the lines replaced. It was one thing after another.

When Kristy was a senior in high school, Freddie pulled into the driveway with a brand new Ford F150 pickup truck. It had a double cab and a four-wheel drive. At the time, it was the nicest vehicle in Salter Path. Kristy could not help but wonder how he got the money for the truck. She was still working at Save-a-Stop. She now worked most weekends and got a raise to $3.50 an hour. Her father still took half her paycheck each week to help with the bills around the house. She wondered how Freddie could afford a truck and how her father would let him do such a thing.

Kristy found her mom in the kitchen making a pie. She was rolling the crust out thin with a wooden rolling pin. She had put on her apron to try to keep the flour off her clothes, and it looked like a good idea since the apron was dusted in white powder. The windows and screen door were open. It was September, and the summer heat had faded enough that baking and cooking in the kitchen was no longer miserably hot. The window and the screen door on the other side of the house were open, creating a breeze through the kitchen. Kristy wanted to see what her mom knew about the new truck that had just arrived.

"Mom, did you see Freddie's new truck?"

"Yes. It is quite the truck. One of the nicest I have seen," Jo said.

"How did he afford it? I mean, Dad is so tight with money, I can't believe he let Freddie buy that. His other truck was fine," Kristy wondered.

"Well, you know your father. When he decides something, there is not much to say. I guess he didn't see a problem with it."

"I do not think it is right. I have to give half of what I earn to the family, and I don't even have a car. Freddie can go buy a truck? Why doesn't he give more to the family, so we aren't always scrounging for money?" Kristy asked.

"Your father said that he works hard. So, he pays him a regular share from the boat, just like he would pay anyone else. He said that if he didn't, Freddie could just go somewhere else. Then he would have to hire someone anyway."

"That does not seem right. Why do I have to give up my paycheck, but Freddie doesn't?" Kristy insisted.

"That's how your dad sees it," Jo said.

"Well, heck, I want to work on the boat then, and Freddie can go to Save-a-Stop," Kristy said.

"Hahaha! Sweetheart, women don't work on boats. We stay back here and make sure the men have a place to come home to. It's just how it is."

"Well, that is bullshit!" Kristy fumed. She stomped out, slamming the door behind her.

Kristy knew that living this way would not work for her. She could not imagine living her life in a place where the only role for a woman was a housewife. She respected the traditions of the town. The problem was the traditions did not respect her. She was a senior in high school, but she decided to start planning her exit from the town once she graduated.

Freddie's new truck brought a lot of attention around town. All the young women thought the truck meant that he was now making a good living, or at least better than most in town. It was not long

221

until Nathalie came into his life. They began dating, and Freddie and Nathalie were getting married within a few short months. Seven months later, Bodhi was born.

Kristy had planned her exit from town, but things changed with the arrival of her nephew. Nathalie and Freddie had to work hard to start building their new life. Freddie kept working on the boat, and Nathalie took a job at one of the local restaurants to earn extra cash. Kristy became one of Bodhi's evening babysitters. While Freddie was out fishing and Nathalie was waiting tables, Bodhi would come in his car seat to Save-a-Stop. He was a good baby and would generally sit quietly as the evening at the store went by. The owners of Save-a-Stop did not mind that Kristy brought Bodhi. In fact, many of the customers would just stop by to see him. Bodhi was good for business.

Kristy began to think that Bodhi might be the first male in her life who loved her unconditionally. Her father and brother loved her, but that love was conditioned on her doing her part. Bodhi would smile the minute she walked into the room. She was fun Aunt Kristy to Bodhi. The connection she felt to him made life in the Path just bearable.

Kristy was working a lot of hours at Save-a-Stop. With Freddie moving out to another house just around the corner with Nathalie, her time at home was minor. With her father out fishing or helping Freddie do something at his house, it was usually just her and her mother when she was home. She decided to abandon her plans of leaving the Path, at least for now.

Kristy settled into the rhythm of going to work, watching her nephew, hanging out with friends, and gossiping around town. She could sense she was falling into the trap of a guarded life that many women in Salter Path led. Kristy was still giving half her wages to her father for the privilege of living in his house. At this time, she began to think that perhaps life in the Path was not as bad as she made it out to be. Her dreams of leaving and making her way in the world were starting to die down. Like a campfire at the end of the night that still glows warm, the last few flames struggled to hang on, and the warmth was dying down.

Nathalie showed up in Jo's kitchen one morning when Jerry and Freddie were out shrimping. Jo was making waffles in a new waffle maker she had purchased from Roses. Kristy was sitting at the kitchen table drinking her coffee. Jo and Kristy were both surprised by Nathalie's presence. She walked in with Bodhi in tow. He immediately ran into the living room to dig into the toy box Jo and Kristy had filled over the years. He was four years old, and kindergarten was right around the corner for him.

"Nathalie, what brings you over? Were we supposed to watch Bodhi today?" Jo asked.

Nathalie began crying. Jo stopped her waffle making to hug Nathalie and said, "What's wrong? Is everything okay?"

Nathalie sobbed, "I am pregnant."

"Oh! My! Well, that is terrific news! Why are you crying?" Jo asked.

"How are we going to do it? We are just getting by now with me working and Freddie fishing. If I have to quit, I don't know how it will work," Nathalie said through her tears.

Kristy was stunned. She sat there watching this play out in front of her. Kristy exactly knew what this meant. Kristy knew she was a surprise and that her father never accepted her, seeing her as an extra burden. She feared for Nathalie and the new baby. Kristy wondered if Freddie would follow in his father's footsteps.

"We don't worry about things like that. God will provide. You worry about the baby and not those other things," Jo tried to comfort her.

"Have you told Freddie yet?" Kristy asked.

"No. I don't know how to. I am afraid he won't want the baby."

"Well. That you don't need to worry about for sure. He may be grown up, but Freddie is still my boy. And he already made his choice in this matter," Jo said.

"Thank you," Nathalie said.

"When they come back, we will let them sleep, and before they go back out, we will tell him," Jo explained.

"Will you be there too?" Nathalie asked Kristy.

Kristy did not want any part of that conversation, but she also knew she needed to be there. "I will be there."

"Thank you," Nathalie said.

The three women gathered around the table, drinking coffee and talking about the new addition to the family that was on the way. Bodhi sat in a booster seat, eating waffles covered in syrup. A mix of butter and syrup covered his fingers, and he was thoroughly enjoying the sugar rush.

The next day, the three women would go to Freddie and Nathalie's house to sit with Freddie and tell him about Nathalie's state. All he asked was, "Are you going to keep it?" When he heard the answer, he stood up and walked out of the door. Nathalie cried. Kristy and Jo tried to ease her fear and hurt. They bonded together at that moment.

Before they knew it, Elizabeth Jane had arrived. Beth was a healthy and happy baby girl. Freddie and Jerry were fishing on the boat when she was born. Jo and Kristy were by Nathalie's side during the birth, and three women now became four.

Freddie followed in his father's footsteps. He only did what was required of him to provide. He began spending more time with Bodhi, which Nathalie didn't mind as it allowed her to care for Beth. Nathalie did not see that Freddie was using Bodhi to stay away from Beth. He was growing closer to Bodhi at the expense of leaving his daughter.

Kristy still spent time with Bodhi. When Freddie was on the water, she would visit Nathalie, watching Bodhi while Nathalie tended to Beth. The families would carry on somehow making just enough money to put a roof over everyone's head and food on the table. Kristy's thoughts of leaving the Path were no more than warm coals on the campfire.

————————-

The doctor walked into the room. Black pens and a red stethoscope punctuated her white coat. Kristy sat on the examination table. She had changed back into her clothes while the doctor was out of the room analyzing the results. Kristy was nervous. She had been having more painful periods and bleeding and could not understand what had changed.

"Kristy, you have uterine fibroids. There are two types of fibroids. The first kind gives you heavy cycles and some additional pain, but they are mostly harmless. The second type is more serious. They interfere with pregnancy and fertility. It makes it very difficult or impossible to get pregnant. Unfortunately, you have the second kind." The doctor stopped, leaving those last words to drop on Kristy.

As the statement hit her, she suddenly felt double her weight. She tried to process what she had just been told, but it seemed too big to digest. "So, I can't have kids?" was the only question she could ask.

"I am afraid not."

Kristy's mind flashed to all she would miss. She thought of how she considered it practice in caring for Bodhi when he was born. Now, she knew that Bodhi might be the closest thing she ever had to a child of her own.

27

Weather

Bodhi woke up early to head to the Save-a-Stop. He wanted to join in on the conversation over coffee and cigarettes in the parking lot. Everyone in town now knew why he was in town. It was not just to show Ellie his hometown but to understand what had happened to his family. When he pulled into the Save-a-Stop parking lot, no one was out front. He decided to fill up his truck to kill some time. He leaned on his truck as the pump ran. Ley's truck pulled into the parking lot and stopped by the front door.

"Morning, Bodhi," Ley said. "What are y'all up to today?"

"No plans for the day. My Aunt Kristy said she would be down later today."

"Well, when you finish there, grab a cup of coffee and come sit for a bit," Ley said as he walked into the store.

Bodhi finished pumping his gas. He got in his truck and moved it a few feet to pull up in front of the store. He grabbed a large coffee. It was $1.79 for twenty ounces of gas station coffee. If you were desperate, it would do, but Danny's coffee at the Grand Villa was actually good. He now understood why Danny needed to have coffee for his millennial clientele. He tried to drown out the bitter burned coffee taste with cream and sugar, which worked well enough. Bodhi walked out to take a place on the bench with his white Styrofoam coffee cup in his hand.

"You see what's coming?" Ley asked.

"No, I didn't get a chance to check the weather," Bodhi said.

"That hurricane is coming our way," Ley said with a matter of confidence.

"I knew it had a chance, but how are you so certain?" Bodhi asked.

"When you spend as much time as I do on the water and with nature, you can sense the signs of a storm. Those fish and shrimp know long before we do. They change their patterns. We haven't caught shit in the last two days. Maybe it's bad luck, but I think it's that hurricane."

Bodhi had no reason to doubt Ley. The years Bodhi spent in Raleigh, Ley had spent on the water. "When do you think it will be here?" he asked.

"I think we have about three days to get ready. Enjoy the next couple of days because it's going to go downhill fast. Adrian looks like she could be a nasty one. Maybe a cat four when she hits us."

"When was the last time a cat four hit the island?" Bodhi asked.

"Not in our lifetime; some of the old-timers say that was what wiped everyone off of Diamond City."

"What does that mean for the Big Rock?"

"Ask that guy he should know," Ley said, gesturing to Darrel pulling into the parking lot in a late model suburban.

Darrel pulled in slowly and put his SUV into park. He swung his belly out of the vehicle and walked toward Bodhi and Ley.

"Good mornin'," Bodhi said to Darrel.

"Thought you would come to see the men this morning? Finally got away from that woman, huh?" Darrel asked.

"I gotta keep an eye on her, or someone else will," Bodhi said.

Darrel laughed and walked in to get a coffee. He came out a few minutes later with a white Styrofoam cup and lit up a cigarette.

"What do you think of the storm?" Ley asked Darrel.

"Could be a bitch."

"What's it going to do for the Big Rock?" Bodhi asked.

"Well, the board was talking about that. I think we will move the fishing out a week, but probably keep the Captain's Party on Saturday. Everyone will be down here anyway. We are going to have to haul out those boats before the storm."

Bodhi forgot the hardiness of the people in Salter Path. Darrel and Ley had just told him that a massive storm would likely destroy their town and they acted like it would be a few bad days at the beach. Bodhi knew the storm could be powerful enough to cut holes through the island, connecting sound and ocean in places where there was once land. Yet, the down easter's of Salter Path saw it in the bigger picture of just being weather and a change in their plans.

"I guess we will try to stay down here for the Captain's Party, then. We can head back to Raleigh the day after."

"It will be a busy couple of days. A lot of your kind from up in Raleigh will want us to board up places," Ley said to Bodhi. "It's good money, especially when you can't get out there to fish."

"Are you going over to Susan's today?" Darrel asked Bodhi.

"I was planning on it. Later this morning, I thought would be a good time," Bodhi said.

"I talked to her yesterday. She is expecting you to stop by."

"Can you give me an idea of what she might tell me, or don't you know?" Bodhi asked, knowing that Darrel would not want him to think he did not know.

"I will tell you this. She knows more than a lot of people around here. I think you will want to hear what she has to say."

"That's not much, but I will take it," Bodhi said, and before Darrel could respond, in rolled a rusted pickup truck, a balding man with a gray beard behind the wheel. He picked up a dirty red baseball cap and put it on his head. The door popped open, and the hinges squeaked as the door swung. A man in cut-off blue jean shorts stepped out of the truck. It was Jean Man. The same man who stopped at Save-a-Stop to deliver Natchez a message from the town.

"Who's this?" Jean Man said.

"I'm Bodhi," as he extended a hand.

"The fuck? Bodhi Salter?" Jean Man asked.

Bodhi dropped his hand. "Yes, Bodhi Salter."

"What you come back for, boy?"

"I am getting married soon. Figured I would come back to visit before I tie the knot."

"You wanna get married, that's your own trouble. Don't be bringing that shit to town," Jean Man said. "Last time I saw you, you were still shitting green. You have been outta this place. Now you coming back. Shit, don't make sense."

"Don't know what to tell you," Bodhi said.

Jean Man pulled out a pack of Chesterfields. He bumped it three times on his hand and then pulled out a cigarette. He popped open a Zippo lighter and, in one smooth motion, inhaled and lit his cigarette. "I remember when that fire happened. There was this guy snooping around, trying to get into our business. Someone from the state. I told that guy to fuck off, and he left. I guess I need to tell you the same?"

"Jake, chill out. He was a kid when all that went down. He is good," Ley spoke up. Ley never forgot he had pledged that Bodhi would always be a local Pather. He and DJ made that pact as kids, and neither he nor DJ would break it.

"I do not want any trouble around here. This place is where I grew up. It seems like you are the problem, not me," Bodhi said.

"Jake, he is going to talk with Susan today," Darrel said.

Jean Man looked at Darrel and took a drag from his cigarette. "If you think that will settle this, then I will let it be." Jean Man walked into the Save-a-Stop for his coffee.

"Since you don't have plans today, why don't you and Ellie take the skiff out to the fish house?" Ley changed the subject, trying to let Bodhi know he belonged in the town.

"I haven't driven a boat in years. If you are all right with it, it would be good to show Ellie the old shack."

Darrel smoked and sipped his coffee, sitting on the bench with his belly seemingly hanging between his knees. He watched the exchange between two old friends reunited by the ebbs and flow of life.

Ley said, "You are welcome to use her. Just put some gas in it when you get back."

Bodhi popped the plastic top off his Styrofoam coffee cup. He finished the last of the burnt coffee and pitched the cup into a nearby trashcan. He thought he would stop by Danny's office to grab a couple of cups of decent coffee for him and Ellie. "Ley, thanks again for letting us use the boat. Darrel, thanks for letting Susan know we will stop by. I am going to get my day going." Ley and Darrel tipped their cup to Bodhi as he drove off.

Bodhi sat on the bed drinking his coffee as Ellie got ready. She enjoyed being in the Path, where a baseball hat and T-shirt counted as getting ready for your day. Bodhi had not even bothered to give Ellie any details on his interaction with Jean Man. They had been through so many of these exchanges since coming to town they were hardly worth mentioning anymore. In fact, it might be worth telling Ellie if the first time they met a Pather there was *not* an ugly exchange.

They were going to stop by Susan Snow's house. She still lived in the same place as she had for many years. The house was falling into disrepair. After her husband died in the fire, she did not have anyone to care for her home. The Snows had rebuilt the boatyard after the fire, but it was hard for Susan to go there. Tom's younger brother Tony now ran the boatyard. The Snow family generally let Susan do as she pleased. She had given the insurance money over so the family could rebuild the boatyard. In return, Tony made sure that Susan had everything she needed.

Ellie and Bodhi pulled up to Susan's house. The yard was mostly sand, with a few low-growing weeds acting as a substitute for grass. The white paint on the house was bubbled, chipped, and falling off, creating a well-weathered look. The porch was slightly slanted, and when Bodhi stepped on it, he was unsure if it would support him. In the front yard was the *Dixie Queen*. The wooden skiff was one of the first boats built by Tom Snow. The salt air and weather nearly rusted away the trailer holding the boat. Leaves from the nearby live oak trees filled the small skiff. The motor on the back looked like something you would see in a museum. Surprisingly, the transom of the boat was still intact.

Bodhi pulled the screen door open and knocked on the front door. Ellie, a half a step behind him, was nervous about who might answer the door. Bodhi knocked again. You could see some movement through the curtains covering the door window, and then the door handle started to turn.

As the door opened, there was a small elderly woman. She wore a faded red cotton shirt and blue polyester pants with an elastic waistband. Her hair was gray and thinning. It was easy to tell she still went to the beauty parlor to keep a perm, likely first acquired in the 1970s. Her face was pale. The wrinkles and frown lines showed a hard life making a living on the island.

"You must be Bodhi," Susan said.

"Good to see you again, Ms. Susan," Bodhi responded, thinking how much she had aged since he left. "This is my fiancée, Ellie."

"Nice to meet you," Ellie said.

"Darrel called over and said you were going to stop by. Come in, let me get you some tea." Susan said as she walked off into the kitchen. "Go ahead and have a seat."

Bodhi and Ellie looked around the small living room. There was a loveseat with a slipcover placed over it. A small rocker/recliner by the window with an end table next to it. Some books were sitting on the end table and a small lamp. The items in the room were older than Ellie and Bodhi. Even though the room was dated, it was not dirty. Susan still took pride in her home. The only thing that seemed to be from the current century was a 42-inch flat-screen TV. It looked out of place in the room, like a portal between two different worlds. A daytime talk show played on the screen.

Susan returned with three glasses of tea. She handed Ellie and then Bodhi the tea. She turned down the volume on the talk show. This greeting was the warmest reception they had received in the town from anyone on Snow's side of the feud. Susan sat in her rocker-recliner as Ellie and Bodhi sat on the loveseat.

"Darrel said you have been wondering about what happened before you left," Susan said.

"You probably remember that I was young when I moved away. I never knew much about the town."

"There are some things that people have probably forgotten. Probably why Darrel sent you my way. Most people don't remember what happened yesterday, let alone fifteen years ago."

"What is it that you think I should know?" Bodhi asked.

Susan paused as she rocked in her recliner. "Let me start before you can remember. Your grandpa Jerry and my husband were friends. They both grew up here in Salter Path and made their lives here. There was never any bad blood between them for all those years. Jerry saved all that money for all those years to get my husband to build him that boat. Jerry knew this was the biggest boat we ever built, but they felt like it could be the start of something new for Salter Path. We could start building big commercial boats here in Salter Path."

"So, they were friends?" Ellie asked.

"Yes, they were. The two of them were trying to grow Salter Path. They wanted to have a boat building and a fishing village. They could see that the town could be the commercial center of the island as it grew. Then, Jerry's boat sank." Susan looked down at her hands, trying to hold in some emotion.

"What happened after that?" Ellie asked, sensing a woman's softness was needed.

"Tom never was the same. He never had a boat go down like that before. There were defects in boats, but never anything that caused something to sink. I do not think he ever forgave himself for what happened to Jerry."

"I never heard about any of that. I didn't know they were friends," Bodhi said.

"Son, we were all close here in the Path. You know where we come from, and we always have to get along. We have trouble in town, and we need to get things right. After that boat sank, things changed. Your daddy, well, he never seemed to be able to get over your grandpa's passing."

"What do you mean by that?" Ellie asked.

"Sweetheart, you are still young and pretty. I don't know you or your story, but I can guess that you have had it better than most. Sometimes, it doesn't seem like there is a way out of where you are when you lose someone like that. Freddie just seemed to be in that place. He stopped talking to us. He didn't want to have anything to do with any Snows. We felt that tension. What happened then surprised us all. We never thought something like that was coming."

"You mean the fire in the boatyard?" Bodhi said.

Susan took a long pause. She took a drink of her tea and rocked in her chair. "Bodhi, you were still a boy, and thank God we kept you kids out of everything. You do need to know that your dad started that fire," Susan said with a matter-of-fact tone.

Bodhi felt his face turn red, and his breathing became deeper as anger built in him. He knew that might be the case, but he never had anyone tell him to his face. "Why do you say that? How do you know that?"

"It only makes sense. Who else would start a fire at the boatyard? I can't think of any other reason for there to be a fire. It's the only thing that makes sense."

"So, you just 'know' he started the fire? Did someone tell you something, or did you see something?" Ellie asked.

"I just know. I don't need anyone to tell me what I know." Susan said as her demeanor started to turn.

"What if it was an accident? What if it was just a coincidence? Or vandalism?" Ellie asked as Bodhi sat there, stunned by his anger.

"Vandalism? By who? Everyone keeps an eye on everyone. There is no getting by with anything without someone knowing."

"Then, why hasn't someone said something to you about Freddie? Why didn't someone see Freddie if everyone knows everything?" Ellie asked Susan.

"That's not how it is! I know Freddie had to do that. I don't blame him for Tom dying. Tom was hard-headed. He didn't need to go into the fire. I told him not to. I said it was gone. We have insurance. Let it burn. He still went." Susan shook her head. "He never came back. I loved him, but he was always a hard-headed son of bitch, and it finally caught up with him."

Ellie sat in silence, trying to understand the disconnect between the fire, insurance, and Susan holding no grudge.

"Is that how you rebuilt it? With the insurance?" Bodhi asked.

"Yes. Tony was kind. He took over where Tom left off. He built the business back, and he takes care of me. The insurance was enough for us to start over."

Bodhi looked at Ellie. Ellie was staring at Susan. Ellie put the pieces together and wondered why Susan could not see it. "Susan, did you ever think Tony had something to do with the fire?"

"Why would he have something to do with the fire? Tom was his brother, and he had a good job in the boatyard. He was Tom's righthand man," Susan said, ignoring what was in her face.

Ellie was young, but she could also see Susan was happy to believe that Freddie had started the fire. It made her life easier to believe that rather than what might be the truth.

"What about the fire at Bodhi's house?" Ellie asked. Bodhi had turned into a spectator watching the two women engage.

"That's another thing altogether. What do you know about it?" Susan asked Bodhi.

"I was told it was an accident. But since I have been back in the Path, it doesn't seem like that is the case. Darrel seems to know something, and he thinks you do too."

Susan sat rocking in her recliner, looking at Bodhi with a mix of anger and pity. She was trying to decide how she should tell him. "There are stories around town. I can tell you one thing for sure. The Snows and the Willards did not have anything to do with it. I know they say it was us. It wasn't."

"So, it was an accident?" Ellie asked.

"I didn't say that either. I do not think it is my place to say what I hear. Some things are better left unknown. Bodhi, you lived here long enough to know about the sound. There are things below the water that you don't see, but others know they are there. They tell you to stay away, and what would you do?"

"Well, you listen. You stay away," said Bohdi.

"I am telling you. Stay away. Some things are better left under the water."

Bodhi sat looking at Susan, thinking about trying to continue his pursuit or whether to take her advice. He decided to let it be for now. "Well, Miss Susan. I do appreciate your time. We need to be getting on with our day. Thank you for speaking with us and the tea."

"I hope I was able to give you some information and that you can understand how things are," Susan said.

Ellie and Bodhi stood up and walked to the door. The sun outside was bright and high in the sky. They were just getting through the door when Susan called to them, "What are you doing about this storm? You know we got about two days before it hits us."

"Well, I was planning on staying. My Aunt Kristy is coming into town tonight."

"You best find a good place to stay," Susan said.

28

Changes

The days leading up to a hurricane are like no others. The power of the storm churning off the coast pulls all the energy out of the atmosphere. This phenomenon makes the weather warm, tropical, and calm. One may hear about the calm before the storm; they do not realize it truly happens. Those who spend their lives living along the coast realize the calmer it is, the bigger the coming storm. It was uniquely calm today.

The waves on the beach had built into large rollers, created by the hurricane miles away, aggravating the ocean's surface. They came into the beach in Salter Path, slamming into it and pushing the water nearly up to the dunes. Ironically, there was no wind. The doldrum made the sound dead calm flat. It was as if the water did not know what it should do. The weather made it a perfect day to take the skiff to the fish house. Bodhi would get to show Ellie one of his favorite escapes when he was a kid.

"Are you concerned about this storm?" Ellie asked Bodhi.

"Well, yes, of course," Bodhi responded.

"Maybe we should drive back to Raleigh. It might not be safe here on the island."

"I feel like I should stay, or at least let's stay until after the party. We should be able to leave the next day."

"I guess we can stay for the party and then leave the next morning," Ellie paused and then continued, "What happens if it arrives early? Will we be stuck here?"

There was a knock on the motel door. Bodhi walked over to see who it was. He turned to Ellie, "It's Danny." He opened the door.

"Bodhi, how are you doing?" Danny asked with a bit of nervousness in his voice.

"I am doing fine. What's going on?" Bodhi asked.

"I do not want to bring bad news, but Chief Burns stopped by a few minutes ago. He said they are going to evacuate the island. Anyone who isn't a property owner will need to leave the island in the next forty-eight hours. I wanted to give you a heads up."

"Hmm, can property owners stay?" Bodhi asked.

"Yes, if you are a property owner, you can stay, but they want all the visitors off the island."

"Good thing I am a property owner. I want to keep my reservation through the weekend if that is okay with you."

Danny looked confused for a minute and then asked, "Do you own property on the island?"

"I found out I still own my parent's old property. So, I guess staying should not be a problem," Bodhi said.

"Well, then yes, you can stay. I want you to know that we won't have the bar open or the coffee stop. But you are welcome to stay in the room. I am hoping that the weather people come here and stay. They are saying landfall should be right here. It would be good publicity," Danny said.

Ellie could not believe what she was hearing. A major hurricane was bearing down on the town, and Danny was hoping for publicity. She could not yet understand living with the island's beauty and the hurricane's tragedy so closely related.

"Well, I hope it is less than they think. You know the weather people can really build up these things." Bodhi said.

"I guess we'll just wait and see. Thanks again for staying with us. I will check in on you later to see if you need anything." Bodhi closed the door as Danny walked away.

Ellie was looking concerned as she sat on the bed. Bodhi moved close to her and put his hands on her shoulders. "Don't worry. If it looks too bad, we will head back to Raleigh. Think of it as an adventure."

"That type of adventure doesn't sound fun," Ellie said.

"Let's get ready to go on the boat and not worry about it. It's still days away. I do want to give Natchez a ring before we go out. Why don't you get your bathing suit on, and I will give him a call."

"Nope, call him. I want to listen. I am part of this now."

Bodhi took out his phone and scrolled through his old calls until he found Natchez's number. He tapped his phone and then put it on the speaker.

"Natchez here."

"It's Bodhi and Ellie. I wanted to check in with you. Ellie and I went and talked with Susan Snow. We just finished up."

"Did she have anything?" Natchez asked.

Ellie felt like Natchez was a good guy and cared about the case, but sometimes he just cut to the chase too fast. Bodhi described their conversation, "She did not have anything really about the fire at my old house. I do think she knows something about that but doesn't want to say it. She was adamant that the Snows and Willards had nothing to do with it."

"Okay, then what did she have to tell you?" Natchez asked.

Ellie jumped into the conversation, "She told us about the fire at the boatyard. She said that Bodhi's dad did it. I don't think that was the case. She told us that they were able to rebuild because they had insurance on the place. It allowed her husband's brother Tony to start the business over again. I think Tony started the fire so they could rebuild better, and Tom didn't know."

"Explain. Why do you think Tony would have started the fire?"

"Susan said everyone knows everything in town. It's a small town, and you can't get away with anything. When she told us that Bodhi's dad burned the place down, we asked how she knew. She said she just knew, but no one saw anything. Then, she explained how Tony provides for her and gives her everything she needs. That he took over the business after Tom died. Tony probably burned the business without telling Tom, hoping to grow their business with insurance money. He probably never expected that his brother would die," Ellie said.

"That doesn't sound impossible. Insurance fraud isn't an unusual thing, but I would need more information than what you have. It is just speculation now."

"Maybe you can come question Tony? Look into the finances of the business? Something? It might help clear my dad's name," Bodhi asked.

"I want to get to the bottom of this and find out what happened. I will look into the files on the boatyard fire for you and see if there is something to pursue. Let's try to keep the focus on the fire at your house. If we figure out how that fire started, we will learn more about the boatyard fire."

"You are probably right. My Aunt Kristy is going to be down here tonight. She might have something to add."

"Keep me informed," Natchez paused and then continued, "What are you going to do about the storm? Are you going back to Raleigh?"

"I have been talking to everyone here, and most people are staying. So, I think I am going to stay. The motel is built of cinder blocks on high ground. I should be okay."

"Be careful," Natchez said.

"I will, for sure. I will be in touch if I hear anything." Bodhi replied and hung up the phone.

Bodhi and Ellie got ready for the boat. Ellie in her bikini and cover-up and Bodhi in board shorts, a hat, and flip flops. They had a bag of essentials and a cooler. They loaded up the truck and made the short drive down the road to Nana B's.

No one was home at Nana B's where Ley kept the old skiff in the water tied to the dock. It was a white, flat bottom nineteen-foot skiff. The motor on the back was a newer four-stroke Suzuki ninety horsepower. The new engine on the old boat reflected the hardiness of the skiff. It was built long ago by the Snows, who made most of the skiffs in town. That was their specialty until they began building large commercial boats. The boat was plain inside. It was a working boat with a seat in front of the center console and a leaning post behind the steering wheel. The bow of the craft had a large casting platform covered with cushions for pleasure cruising.

They loaded the boat, and Bodhi found the key in a hiding spot under the center console. He fired up the boat. The four-stroke motor purred quietly in the water. Unlike the older two-stroke motors, the four-stroke was efficient and quiet. It had been several years since Bodhi captained a boat, but it returned to him quickly. He remembered the feeling of gently handling the boat on the water—how the water and the boat needed to work together like a boy and his bicycle racing down a hill. There were moments of smoothness and ease followed by a sudden bump before returning to normal. Today, the boat and the water predicted the other's movements. Ellie laid out a towel on the boat's bow where she could lie down and sun herself as Bodhi drove.

"Let's go for a little ride before we go to the fish house," Bodhi said.

"Where to?" Ellie asked.

"We can head toward Swansboro and see how far we get."

Ellie rolled onto her stomach on the boat's bow, propping her head up with her hands so she could look at the water. Bodhi paused to admire her body in the sun and then pushed the throttle forward, lifting the craft onto a plane. It slid over the top of the water, making a clicking, thawping noise as the hull broke over the small waves. The sound was smooth, looking more like a farm pond on the surface than a large body of saltwater.

They sped to the west, following the white poles placed in the water to guide the boater safely across the shallow water. They passed the fish house sitting oddly in the middle of the sound and pushed onward across the water. As they neared the shore on the far side, small islands appeared. These sandbar islands created a barrier between the open sound and the Intracoastal Waterway. Bodhi identified the turning pole and headed straight for it. There was a small break in the island, only about three boat lengths in width. Ellie looked back at Bodhi, wondering if he saw the islands, but he pushed on at full speed. Bodhi cranked the wheel to the starboard at the turning pole and looped around the pole. He then cranked it hard to port and entered the Intracoastal Waterway.

The water spread out in front of the boat like a sheet of glass. It was a perfect day for boating. Ellie and Bodhi made their way past Cannon's Gate, a high-end community with multi-million dollar houses. Then past Goose Creek and a trailer park set along the water. It did not matter who you were or where you were from; the saltwater attracted everyone looking for a place to disconnect and relax.

They cruised under the high-rise bridge connecting the town of Emerald Isle with Cedar Point on the mainland. Up ahead, Bodhi noticed a few boats slowed in the waterway. As he approached, he slowed the boat, then Ellie sat and pointed, "Look! Dolphins!"

There was a pod of dolphins. It is hard to say precisely how many, but there were at least six of them. The dolphins circled the boats, likely curious as to why it had stopped. Bodhi and Ellie watched them as they played in the water. Seemingly, they were having a game of tag with the young ones swimming between the adults tagging them with his nose before shooting off. Even though they saw these marina mammals just the other day; the creatures still held a magical quality for Ellie and Bodhi. It was hard to grasp the dolphins' freedom moving through the water.

Bodhi eased the boat to one of the small uninhabited islands that dotted this part of the sound. The islands were mostly sand, small scrubby trees, and seagrass. During the weekends, people would anchor their boats along the islands to be genuinely on an island of their own. Bodhi slid the bow of the boat onto the sand. He cut the motor and jumped off the bow in one athletic move carrying an anchor that he set in the sand.

"C'mon, let's go explore," Bodhi said.

Ellie climbed off the front of the boat and onto the sand. "What is this place called?"

"We always call it Gecko Island. When we were kids, these islands would be covered with geckos. When we came here, we chased them and tried to bring them back home as pets. One time, DJ decided he was going to bring three of them home. Our parents would never let us, so he decided to hide three of the geckos in his shorts." Bodhi was laughing, and he had to stop to take a breath. "About halfway back to the Path, he got up in the middle of the boat, dancing around. The parents were looking at him like he was crazy. Then he pulled down his pants right there in front of everyone! The three lizards ran out, and the moms started screaming. The dads were laughing so hard they couldn't contain themselves! That was so funny. We called DJ lizard dick for a year."

"Y'all sound like some crazy boys back then. And maybe much hasn't changed," Ellie said.

They walked around the small island, exploring the shallows on the backside. The water was clear, and you could easily see the hermit crabs porting their shells over the bottom. There was also a skate, a stingray-like fish feeding on scallops and clams. They even scared a flounder off the bottom as they walked along. Of course, they went looking for geckos hiding among the small scrubby trees. After about thirty minutes, they boarded the skiff and headed to the fish house.

The fish house had been hanging on since the last hurricane. The townspeople painted the fish house green leaving the door primer white. The Pathers still used it as their hideaway. Kids from the area used the small cabin hovering above the water as their escape from the prying eyes of grownups. They would go to smoke pot and drink beer. As the skiff motored toward the fish house, Bodhi wondered if the tradition of leaving drinks in the fish house persisted.

As they approached, the water got shallow. It was nearly high tide, and there were only about twenty-four inches of water around the fish house. A passing hurricane had long since erased Dog Island, leaving the area around the fish house very shallow. Bodhi slowed the boat and trimmed the motor up to reduce the boat's draft. Ellie stood on the front of the boat, waiting to catch a piling as it came closer. Bodhi could not help but be distracted by Ellie's beautiful curves. The North Carolina summer sun seemed to be just for her skin tone as she radiated beautiful energy.

They tied the boat to the piling. The water was still calm, and the boat drifted without aim, tugging gently on the rope. Bodhi helped Ellie up onto the small porch. He lifted her by the waist, depositing her backside onto the wooden planks. He reached down and into the cooler, pulling out two beers, twisting the top on one bottle, and handing it to Ellie. Bodhi climbed onto the porch as Ellie sat with her feet dangling above the water. She had a contented smile as she brushed back a lock of hair that had fallen in front of her sunglasses. She was enjoying learning about who Bodhi was before he came to Raleigh.

Bodhi had already gone into the fish house, looking for what was left there. He walked out with two warm hard seltzers in his hand. "Look. They still do it," Bodhi said to Ellie.

"They do what?"

"Way back when there was a tradition always to leave something to drink in the fish house. It was how the community connected. As kids, we would come out here hoping someone had left a bottle of wine. It was like a treasure hunt to see what there would be. A bottle of sweet white wine would definitely be our favorite."

"So we need to put something back then?" Ellie asked.

"We will leave a couple of beers. Let me put these in the cooler, and I will grab the beers." Bodhi hopped back down into the skiff. He was happy to find this small tradition persisted. It was one way the community shared and cared for each other. It was comforting for Bodhi to know the community still connected in this way.

"Hand me my towel. I want to lie out here."

Bodhi handed her the beach towel off the boat's bow and then dug a Bluetooth speaker out of the boat bag. He connected his phone and put on country beach music. Ellie sipped her beer, and Bodhi climbed back onto the porch of the fish house. He went back inside to look around at the graffiti scribbled on the walls. The inside was mostly empty. There were a couple of old folding chairs and a small handmade wooden table. An old cooler was under the window, and this was where people left things for the next person to come to the fish house.

It was midweek, and most others were getting ready for the Big Rock Tournament or preparing for the hurricane. The fish house was left to just Bodhi and Ellie. The air was still, but the temperature was manageable, and Ellie was enjoying the hotness of the sun. It was incredibly quiet on the sound, and the music from the speaker carried across the water. Bodhi pulled one of the chairs out from inside the fish house and set it on the porch. He sat down, leaned back, took a large swig of his beer, and gazed back toward Salter Path.

Bodhi thought about his life and his trip back to his hometown. He lived through a twist in his life made right by his aunt. He felt good about how he had handled that. He knew many people would never recover from such a tragedy, and he felt like he had recovered. Coming back to the Path reminded him how different his life would have been if his parents had never died. It would have been simpler and more complicated. He would probably be working on a shrimp boat and have a small home in town or maybe still living with his parents. Weekends and evenings would be spent with his friends drinking and smoking pot. There would not be much worry, but not much more than that. He was surprised he felt so torn about the two paths his life could have gone down. Raleigh and the city pulled him toward more. He could not help but think that more wasn't the answer.

Ellie looked at Bodhi. She could see he was lost in thought, sitting in the chair. "I am thinking the same thing," Ellie said.

"Huh? What do you mean?" Bodhi changed his focus to look at his fiancée.

"Let me guess. You are thinking. What if this is all we need—a skiff and fish house? A small place by the water. What if this is more and Raleigh is less?"

"I wasn't thinking exactly that, but that is pretty much what I was thinking. It is odd because I just feel pressured to live the Raleigh life. What if we moved here and then we hated it? What if we weren't happy being in a small town?" Bodhi asked.

"I don't know. I think we should think about it. How could we make a place like this home?"

"It is my home. I can feel it, but Raleigh feels like a habit I can't break."

They sat and enjoyed the thought of a different direction for their life. One can fear uncertainty or embrace the flow of life and how it brings you to places you never expected. They spent the afternoon in the quiet of the sound and then headed back to Salter Path, making sure to leave two beers in the old cooler in the fish house for the next visitor. As they pulled away from the fish house, Ellie asked, "Do you think this place will make it through the hurricane?"

Bodhi responded, "I hope so. It's part of the town. If it doesn't, we will just have to come and build it back again." He leaned into the boat's throttle, and they were shortly at Nana B's dock.

29

Flotsam and Jetsam

Growing up and building a life in Salter Path was not easy for Kristy. At times, she could not imagine anywhere else anyone would want to live in the world. Then, reality would smack her in the face, that if she stayed in the town, she would be nothing more than a fisherman's wife or girlfriend. She knew there was more beyond the reach of Salter Path, but she also loved her mother, nephew, and niece. The young ones made her feel like there was more to the world than just Salter Path, and although she had not given up that dream of moving on to another life, it was getting harder for her to imagine how it would happen.

Freddie had established himself as the heir to the family business and property in town. Jerry and Freddie worked the boat hard to keep food on the table for the families. Kristy continued to work at the Save-a-Stop. She spent so many hours there that people began to think she owned the place. The truth was she was making just more than minimum wage but liked the owner and the ability to have her niece and nephew come to spend time with her while she worked.

One afternoon, Kristy worked the register when a young mother pulled up to the gas pumps. She began pumping gas with two young ones in the truck's front seat, not much older than Bodhi and Beth. Just about then, Chief Burns pulled up behind the truck and noticed the tags had expired. He decided that since she wasn't from the Path, he would give her a ticket. When he ran the plates on the truck, he discovered that the truck had not been insured or registered for two years.

The young mother was distraught. She was from Clayton, a working-class suburb outside of Raleigh. Chief Burns proceeded to take the plates off the truck and explain that she would need to register it or have it towed, but it could not be driven on the road until then. There was no one in the store, and Kristy watched the entire event unfold.

The young mother came into the store with her two children in tow. She was holding back tears as she entered. She went and got two small cartons of chocolate milk from the coolers in the back and two honey buns. She came to the register and paid for the gas, milk, and treats. She sent her two youngin' to sit on the benches in front of the store and enjoy their snacks. The young mother began to cry.

"Are you okay?" Kristy asked.

"No. I don't know what to do. That is my boyfriend's truck. I am almost out of money, and my kids just wanted to see the ocean. They have never been to the beach." She continued sobbing. "I just want them to see the beach. I had just enough money for gas and lunch, and now I don't know what to do."

"Where are you from?" Kristy asked.

"Clayton. It took us half a tank of gas and three hours to get here. How am I going to get home? I have nowhere to go here," the woman said.

Kristy walked around the counter. She could see that this was a woman who was at her wit's end. She only wanted to give children an experience that others expect. Now, bad paperwork stranded her with two young children on an island with no one to call. Kristy hugged the woman. "It will be all right. You see that right there." Kristy was pointing to the beach access across from Save-a-Stop. "You head up there with your two kids. That's the beach. When you come back, I will have a plate on that truck, and Chief Burns won't bother you. When you get back to Clayton tonight, throw the plate in the trash. Go enjoy your day." Kristy instinctively understood this was a woman ready to break. She had played a life of Jenga and every move she made threatened to bring her world tumbling down.

"Oh my God. Thank you. You can do that?" the woman asked.

"I will make it happen. You go give those youngin' a day at the beach."

The woman composed herself and thanked Kristy again. She walked outside to her sticky-fingered children licking the honey bun sugar off their fingers. "C'mon, grab your stuff. We are going to the beach," she instructed them as they headed across the street.

Kristy got off work at three. She headed over to Beatrice's, where Freddie's truck was parked. She grabbed a screwdriver out of the toolbox in the back and then proceeded to take the license plate off Freddie's truck. She walked back to the Save-a-Stop and attached the plate to the woman's truck. She knew that Chief Burns finished his shift at two p.m. and that the next officer would not pay any attention to a truck driving down the road with a perfectly good license plate on the back.

Kristy never forgot that woman and her desperation to give a memory to her children. She reflected on how her father treated her and never cared to give her that kind of memory.

Kristy still lived with her parents and gave her father half of the money she earned each paycheck. The amount didn't matter; it was a tax at fifty percent of her earnings. One evening Kristy's underlying current of disdain for her father finally came to a head after Jerry called a family meeting.

The family gathered at eight in Jerry and Jo's house in the kitchen. They sat around the kitchen table. It was April, and the humidity was building along the coast. The windows were open, and opossums were climbing the live oaks looking for water bugs. Freddie and Jerry each had a canned Miller Lite in their hands. Jo drank sweet tea. Bodhi and Beth played in the living room with those special toys you only find at grandma's house.

"Nathalie, do you need a beer?" Kristy asked.

"Yes, that sounds good," Nathalie said as Kristy pulled two Miller Lites from the fridge.

All the adults were sitting around the kitchen table. It was in the 2000s, but the table was a holdover from the eighties. It was a faded tan Formica top with fake wood grain. The chairs were wood that probably matched the table before it faded. The light above the table was a faux stained glass. The family sat around the table with the women trying to understand precisely why they were there.

Jerry began to speak. "Freddie and I have something to tell you. You know we have been fishing and have done pretty well the past few years. I have been saving a lot of money. We have some good news." Jerry looked at Freddie.

"Daddy has been able to save enough money that we can buy a second shrimp boat. We are having the Snows build it. I am going to take over the *Nana B*, and dad is going to fish the new boat," Freddie said.

"We are naming the new boat *Legacy*. I will hand it down to Freddie, and then Bodhi can run the *Nana B*," continued Jerry.

Jo and Nathalie started asking questions. How much was the boat? Where did the money come from? How many other deckhands will there be? They were excited at the idea that there would now be two boats to support the family. They were hopefully ending the scraping of money for food and utilities.

Kristy fumed inside. She could not believe her father had just announced this. She had been working and giving money to her father, thinking that this was helping keep the family afloat. Now, she realized she was funding a future for Freddie. That her father saved her money so her brother could prosper was beyond what she had ever imagined. She felt her face becoming hot. Her palms were sweating. She had felt this feeling before, and she knew it was anger.

"Are you fucking kidding me?" Kristy interjected. The family stopped and went silent. The sounds of Bodhi and Beth playing echoed off the linoleum floor.

"What's the matter?" Jo asked her daughter.

"What's the matter? What's the matter? Are you kidding? I have been working for years at the Save-a-Stop, giving half my paycheck to YOU! And now I find out you have been saving the money. That is my money, not yours!" Kristy was breathing heavily.

"Your money? Who the hell do you think puts a roof over your head? Puts food on the table? You could have left anytime, but you wanted to stay and live under my roof. They are my rules. As long as you count on me, what yours is mine. But let me be clear, what's mine is not yours," Jerry said.

"Fuck you! This is fucking bullshit! You have always been up Freddie's ass, and now you screw me over. Take my money and give it to him."

"Honey, he has a family. He needs more than you," Jo said.

"So, he has a family, and now he gets everything? What is there for me?" Kristy asked.

"You will find a good man someday. Then you will get yours," Jo told her.

Kristy realized she could not try to talk sense into this family. Even her mother, who she loved, could not see how unjust this was. Kristy knew that this was the last straw. She wouldn't spend her life waiting for a man to rescue her. She needed to get out. She needed to get even. She walked out and headed for the beach.

Kristy walked down the driveway across the road and to the beach access. Tears were running down her face, and her hands balled into fists. She needed to breathe. She needed to get to the openness of the ocean. She needed to understand just how big the world was by looking at the inky blackness of the sea at night.

Kristy slogged through the sand. The anger and hurt made the sand feel like thick heavy mud around her feet. She needed to get to the beach. She trudged up the dune hearing the waves breaking on the beach. As her head peered over the top of the dune, she saw someone sitting in the moonlight on the beach. She could not believe someone had intruded on her only peace.

Kristy walked to the edge of the water. Looking out at the vast ocean, trying to imagine all the alternative ways life can unfold, she couldn't help but feel the man's gaze on the beach looking at her. She finally turned to look his way.

"Kristy?"

"Yes. Who is it?"

"Darrel. Darrel Willard. What are you doing out here at this time?" Darrel asked.

Kristy walked toward him, knowing he was not a vacationer but a local. Maybe she could find some solace in a fellow Pather. "It's been a tough night. What are you doing out here?" Kristy asked.

"Well, Darrel Junior's mom and I are on the outs. I think we have run it to the end of the track. I am doing some drinking and trying to figure out what's next."

"I get that. I am trying to do the same. Crazy how life will twist you around."

"What's up with you?" Darrel asked.

"You won't believe it." Kristy sat next to Darrel and reached into his cooler to grab a beer. "We met as a family tonight. My daddy is building a new boat."

"Well, what's wrong with that?"

Kristy took a long draw on her beer. "I paid for it. My daddy makes me give half my money to him. He saved that money to build the boat. He is giving it to Freddie."

"So, what do you get?"

"They told me I can get a man. Not sure why that makes it all right."

"Well, what are you going to do?"

"I don't know. I have always wanted to get out of this town, but I never had the courage. Then Bodhi was born, and he gave me a reason to stay here. Now, I don't know. Should I just get a man?" Kristy asked.

"Well, sometimes we ain't what you think. Just ask my wife."

"Does she know you are out here?" '

"I am guessing she doesn't. We just have gotten to where she doesn't care much about what I do. She would probably say it about figures that I am out here with another woman."

"It sounds like you might be looking for another woman soon. Is that where you are headed?"

"I don't think we are headed there. I think we already got there. It is a matter of time before she moves out."

"What would make you say that? Don't you think you can put things back together?" Kristy probed.

Darrel paused. He finished his beer and opened another, thinking about what to tell Kristy. "I am going to tell you something. Can I trust you? I don't want this getting around."

"We have known each other for years. I don't have any reason to go running my mouth around town." Kristy said.

"Well, I found out something a few months ago. I had my head in the sand for a long time, and it's finally clear to me. So, I asked her straight away. I asked if she was cheating on me. I knew it somewhere in the back of my mind, but I never dared to ask," Darrel trailed off.

Kristy sat quietly for a few minutes, waiting for Darrel to continue. He didn't, so she took the initiative. "Did she give you an answer?"

Darrel opened Kristy another beer and said, "Worse." He took a long pull on his beer. "She told me she did, and she thinks DJ isn't mine." He turned to look at Kristy through the darkness to see if she reacted as he handed her the beer.

Kristy stared at the water, thinking about how to respond. "That doesn't matter. If you love him like your own, then he is your own. End of story, in my opinion."

"Kristy, thank you. I needed to hear that. I don't care about that. He is my boy, and I will never think of him differently. I do think I am done with his mom, though."

"I can understand that. How about you? Have you ever cheated?" Kristy asked.

"Shit. She tried to tell me I cheated on her, but I never did. If I am getting blamed for it, maybe I should have done it."

"Well, you are still married. You can still make her dream come true."

Darrel smiled and said, "It's not every day you get to make someone's dream come true."

Kristy leaned into Darrel, and they began to kiss. As she kissed Darrel, Kristy felt the rage that filled her leave her body. It was like breaking free from her father's grip. She was breaking free with Darrel, a married man. She felt like she was finally taking control of her life. She liked the feeling of not being the sister, babysitter, or daughter who couldn't fill a man's role. The kiss was long and deep. She could feel Darrel needed that kiss as bad as she did. He needed to feel wanted and more than just a provider.

The kiss finally ended. Kristy touched the corner of her mouth, instinctively trying to fix the lipstick she wasn't wearing. Darrel took another slug of his beer.

"Sorry." Kristy didn't know why she said that.

"Not sorry. I have wanted to do that for longer than you know, but I was, I mean, I am married. So I never could. When I came to get my coffee at Save-a-Stop in the morning, you were there. I could have stood and talked with you all morning, but I couldn't," Darrel confessed.

"I never knew that. I always thought you were just happily married. I am sorry you were living in that."

Darrel opened another beer. "I will be honest. I thought I was happy, but now I know I wasn't. It was like getting glasses and finally being able to see clearly."

Kristy leaned into Darrel. Darrel put his arm around her. He enjoyed feeling the warmth of a woman pressed against him. Kristy wondered if this was the man she needed to find. Was it just a coincidence that Darrel was on the beach the night she walked out of the house? Or was this meant to be? Darrel seemed like a person put into her life at just the right time. They sat there on the sand, drinking beer and looking at the water. They did not say much more that night, but Kristy knew this was the start of something.

30

Wrath

The waters off North Carolina are known as the Graveyard of the Atlantic. German U-boats prowled these waters during World War II, looking for unsuspecting merchant ships. They would quietly stalk vessels in the coastal water off North Carolina. The U-boat tried to launch a torpedo at the target ship and strike it at the waterline. Ideally, it would hit mid-ship and break the ship's backbone, damaging the keel and sending the ship to the bottom of the sea. The keel provides integrity to the boat and holds it together front to back. A weak keel means a fragile boat. These U-boats intended to sink ships, but American forces sunk many of them off the coast. U-352 was built in Germany and set to service in January of 1942. She and her crew prepared to serve in the Third U-Boat flotilla to stalk the United States Eastern Seaboard water. On April 7, 1942, she left the port of St. Nazaire, heading to her station off the coast of North Carolina. On May ninth, she spotted what she believed to be a merchant ship passing alone not far off the coast from Morehead City, North Carolina. As the U-boat approached and surfaced to fire her torpedoes, she realized she was stalking a U.S. Coast Guard ship. The *Icarus* identified the U-boat and made way to pursue the foreign submarine. Dropping depth charges U-352 was disabled and forced to surface. U-352 eventually sank with thirty-three survivors rescued by the Coast Guard, and fifteen of the crew perishing in the sinking.

————————

Being nice only goes so far. There becomes a point where someone can no longer take the strain others place on them. When someone reaches this point, there are two paths they can choose. The first is to walk away and turn the other cheek. The person goes quietly into the night, walking away from the situation and sometimes simply walking out of someone's life. They have had enough, deciding it is better to rebuild than take it anymore. Rarely, people who choose this path have a book written about them. Kristy was not that person. She chose the other path.

The other path is a path of wrath. The journey is filled with anger and fight. It destroys things in the hopes of building them back in a perfect image. Kristy's family pushed her into a corner. She knew her hard-earned wages were being taken from her and given to someone else. She gave up nights out with friends for long nights working, and that sacrifice was being used to fund her brother's future. In the pit of her stomach, she felt she had to do something about this. She could not just let this happen.

Kristy figured that the boat they were building was hers. As she figured it, her job at the store had paid for the down payment. Fifty thousand dollars which she had earned at a rate of $9.25 an hour since she was sixteen years old. She deserved that boat as much as, if not more, than Freddie. She would not let this rest.

Kristy was unsure how she would get her share of the boat, but she knew that Freddie would not get his. She needed to develop an idea about how to get back at the family for taking her money. Kristy did not know where to turn. She decided to confide in her new lover, Darrel.

Darrel was building a business at the Big Tree. He was known for being level-headed and able to think things through. Kristy needed someone to help her find a way to get what was hers. Kristy headed over to the Big Tree one Monday morning. She knew Darrel prepped for the week of business that day, and she could find him alone in the drive-in.

Kristy went around to the back of the building and knocked. There was no answer. She knocked again and then said, "Darrel, it's me, Kristy. Open up." Moments later, she could hear the deadbolt flip in its casing, and the door opened.

"Well, what brings you here?" Darrel asked.

"Not now. Can I come in? I need to talk."

"Sure. What's on your mind? Is something wrong?" Darrel was worried about the surprise visitor.

"Yes, something is wrong. My dickhead dad is making me work for his son's boat. I gotta do something about that. I just don't know what to do. I thought you could help me figure it out."

"Not sure what you mean by 'do something about it.' Are you thinking of moving out or something?" Darrel did not understand her level of anger.

"No, I mean, yes, I am moving out one day soon. I might go somewhere like Raleigh and start over. Leave these POSes down here. But I cannot just let them have everything, and I get nothing. I want to do *something*," Kristy stressed.

"You mean like something to set the score even? Something like that."

"Yes. Then I can leave, and it will not be a big deal. I will walk away with an even score, not losing. I just can't figure out what to do." Kristy stopped.

Darrel looked at Kristy. She was beautiful, and he wanted to tell her what she wanted to hear. He was almost divorced from his wife and needed to wait just a few more months before it would be final. Kristy had more than adequately filled the gap in female companionship for Darrel. They were making love more than he ever did to any woman. He wanted to keep this going. "Are you thinking of getting revenge?"

"I guess that is what you call it. Maybe I take Freddie's truck and roll it into the sound or cut the nets on the fishing boat, so they have to buy new ones. Something like that."

"Well, it seems like you should just stop that boat from being built. Then you could at least try to get your money back."

"What do you mean? Explain."

"Well, the boat is being built right over there." Darrel pointed across the street toward Snow's boatyard. "They are laying the keel right now. If you go and mess that up, the boat won't be worth a shit. The Snows will have to give the money back to your dad. No boat, no payment," Darrel explained.

"Yes. You are right. If I do something to that boat to stop the Snows from building it, my dad will not have to pay. I can demand my money now that I know he has it." Kristy was excited about the idea of having fifty thousand dollars.

"You have to mess something up big, something that will stop them. They are building it out of fiberglass. I saw a truck here the other day, and they were unloading barrels of fiberglass resin. Maybe you do something to the resin, so there is a flaw in the boat."

"I got it. After dark, I can go in there and pour out resin and replace it with water. It will mess up everything, and the workers will not realize it until it's too late." Kristy did not realize she was confessing a future crime to Darrel.

That night, at about two-thirty a.m., Kristy made her way through the backyards and woods to the Snow Boatyard. She went into the shed in the back that held the chemicals and flammables. She fumbled around in the dark, not exactly sure of what she was doing. She finally found a drum marked 'Resin.' The drum was bigger than she expected. The fifty-five gallons of resin must have weighed almost 400 pounds. She found a barrel dolly that she hooked onto the barrel. She maneuvered the barrel to the floor drain, took off the cap, and tipped the barrel, pouring the resin down the drain. The barrel was heavy even with the dolly, and she lost control, dropping it and letting it empty more than she had planned. Finally, enough material had drained from the barrel, and she could tilt it back onto its end. She found a water hose and refilled the barrel making the resin a nearly useless mixture.

Kristy made her way out of the shed. She carefully looked around before she exited the building, ensuring no one saw her. She made her way back home feeling as though she had struck one for justice.

The next day the Snows would work on the boat soon to be christened the *Legacy*. They had built the wooden keel and were getting ready to mold the boat's bottom around it. Tom Snow would head to the shed to pull out resin to be mixed and applied to the fiberglass matting. The ratio of resin to fiberglass was critical for guaranteeing the boat would have the strength needed to take the punishment of the sea. He did not notice the altered formulation as he sprayed the resin onto the fiberglass. The weak resin would be added to the boat's port side from the keel to the waterline. The defect would go unnoticed by the Snows and the Salters. It only appeared again when it catastrophically failed one night in the Pamlico Sound, taking the lives of Kristy's dad and uncle.

Kristy had hoped her sabotage would halt the build and return her money to her. The outcome of her efforts was not what she expected, but she never thought twice about it. Yes, her uncle did not deserve to go when the boat sank, but that was just an "accident" in her mind. Her father dying as the ship went down was what he deserved for the years of abuse he had inflicted on Kristy. Although she was now without a father, she felt that this was a sign of things turning her way.

31

Scorn

The waves from a hurricane can pound the beaches of the North Carolina coast. There are no rocks or concrete walls to strengthen the shoreline along the Crystal Coast. Instead, dunes of sand were piled twenty to thirty feet high to protect the waves from washing over the island. When a hurricane thrashes the island, the waves and storm surge scour the dunes, cutting away at the sand. The storm destroys the dunes and washes over the island if the storm is too strong. It leaves a scar on the island, opening a new connection between the sound and the ocean. The hurricane can reshape the island and waterways in a few short hours.

When the *Legacy* sank in the Pamlico, Kristy never expected anything to come of it. She was never confident whether her sabotage of the boat build was the reason for the sinking or if it was just bad luck her father and uncle got caught in a strong storm. To her, the intent was never to sink the boat but to destroy it before it was launched.

Kristy knew her chance to get back her hard-earned money was gone. She did not know how to escape Salter Path for a new life. It would now be just her and her mother in the house, and she was the only one earning a steady paycheck. She began to resign herself once again to living out a woman's life in Salter Path.

Kristy could begin to see her future panning out. She would be the daughter of a widow in Salter Path. Kristy would be the good girl taking care of her mother in her old age as her brother lived with his family. She began to sink into the morass of being trapped in taking care of her mother. But, she loved her mother for always being there for her, and she could not imagine abandoning her.

After the *Legacy* sank, Freddie Salter saw his chance for a more prosperous life fade. The money invested in the boat fell to the bottom of the Pamlico Sound. In a short time, he had lost his father, business partner, and the most significant family-owned asset. He needed to recalibrate and begin thinking about providing for his wife and two children.

The family was in disarray after the *Legacy* sank. Kristy knew she may have brought this on herself in the back of her mind, but she would never let this bother her. The only thing that pained her was seeing her mother trying to recover from the loss of her husband.

Jo had always been a strong woman. She helped the family navigate the difficulties of life. Jo patched the holes as they started to form before they pulled the family apart. With the loss of her husband, she now felt all her efforts were for nothing. Jo fell into a deep depression after Jerry's death.

Jo spent her day sitting quietly in the living room. She would stare blankly at the television with her soap operas playing. She was not listening or watching. She was just waiting. She did not know what she was waiting for. Perhaps it was for Jerry and Nathan to return, or for her to join them wherever they were now. Jo was lost and felt the fight to keep going was becoming too much.

"Mom, I am worried about you," Kristy said to Jo as she sat in her chair.

"Why are you worried about me? I will be fine."

"I am worried about you because you are not well. You stay inside all the time and hardly eat anything. It is not good," Kristy responded.

"I know. It's just so hard with your dad gone. We were together for so long. I feel like a part of me is missing."

"Please, you need to try to get out of this. I know it has only been a few months, but you are not getting better. Can you try to at least get outside a few times a day?" Kristy pleaded.

"Why? I am fine here. I have everything I need inside."

"Mom, for me? Can you try? You used to like to garden, and the gardens need attention. Maybe you can try to get outside and take care of the gardens?" Kristy was trying to find some motivation for her mother.

"I can try for you. I will try to get outside and look at the garden. Maybe tomorrow." Jo left her commitment at that.

Kristy worked the early shift the next day at the Save-a-Stop. She was arranging the cigarette packs behind the counter when Chief Burns pulled up outside. He drove into the lot with purpose, stepped out of the car, and headed into the store hurriedly.

"Kristy! You need to lock up; it's your mom. The ambulance is on the way to take her to the hospital!" the chief said.

Kristy dropped the carton of cigarettes she had in her hands and fumbled for the keys to the store, not saying a word. Fear and panic consumed her. She fumbled with the keys as she tried to lock the door. Burns finally took the keys from her hands and told her to get in the car while he locked the door.

They made the short drive to Jo's house. The ambulance had already arrived, and the medics worked on her in the front yard. The lawn was strewn with orange-colored bags that were open with all types of medical equipment protruding from pockets. There was a small machine with wires extending from it and attaching to various points on Jo. As Kristy approached, Freddie came up behind her grabbing her and pulling her back as she cried.

"We have to stay back, let them do their work," Freddie said to Kristy.

"No! No! I can't lose her," Kristy wailed.

A medic yelled, "I am clear, everyone clear!" Then he shocked Jo with her body seemingly jumping off the ground. "I am not getting a pulse," the medic said, "let's do it again." Still no pulse. The medics placed her onto the stretcher. One medic was on the stretcher giving her CPR, as another was providing air with a giant squeeze bulb. They loaded her into the ambulance and sped off toward the Carteret County Hospital.

Kristy slumped in the yard, crying and staring at the spot where her mother lay a few moments ago. There was a small garden rake, a shovel, and her garden cart. She had taken Kristy's advice and went to the garden that morning.

The memorial service for Jo was small. With the feud stirring in town, the funeral of this longtime Pather was very different. Jo was laid to rest next to her husband in the small graveyard near the church. It had only been a little more than a month since the same people had gathered to lay Jerry and Nathan to rest. It was quiet and eerie as the three funerals hung over the small town. The tensions were building as everyone waited to see what would happen between the Salters and Snows.

————————-

Freddie sat at his kitchen table, looking through papers that listed his expenses for the boat. His mother had always taken care of the business side, and now he was trying to learn it. There were expenses for diesel, nets, depreciation, taxes, and a reserved fund at zero after being emptied by the *Legacy*. Freddie wondered how he would make this all work with just one boat operating and the growing needs of his family of four. The *Nana B* was a good fishing boat, but she was old and not fit to support a family of four. Freddie needed to figure out how to make things work, but he was unsure how. This problem weighed heavily on him.

Nathalie walked into the kitchen after coming from the mailbox. She flopped the mail down on the table in front of Freddie. He dropped the papers on the table and began going through the mail. Junk mail, junk mail, bill, North Carolina Farm Bureau Insurance...

Freddie peeled open the envelope and unfolded the letter inside.

Dear Frederick Salter,

I am sorry for your loss. I am writing to inform you that you have been named the only beneficiary of Josephine and Jerry Salter's life insurance policy. The amount of $100,000 will be deposited in a bank of your choosing. Please call (555)302-1663 at your earliest convenience to arrange payment.

Sincerely,

Nicholas Stansky

Claim Adjuster, Farm Bureau Insurance

Freddie read the letter twice. Then said, "Nathalie, come here. You are not going to believe this." He handed Nathalie the letter. She read it and then reread it.

"What does this mean?" Nathalie asked.

"It means that our money problems are solved. We have one hundred thousand dollars. I can get a new boat built!" Freddie could not believe his fortune. It had been nearly nine months since his parents had passed away, and he felt crushed under the pressure of making ends meet. This windfall was a blessing.

There was a knock at the backdoor. Nathalie went to see who was there. She opened the door to find Kristy standing on the deck.

"Hey. I am here to take Bodhi to the beach," Kristy said.

Freddie stared at her blankly, as did Nathalie.

Kristy noticed the odd mood. "What's going on?"

Nathalie looked at Freddie. Freddie started, "I just got word that Mom and Dad had insurance. They left me one hundred thousand dollars."

"What do you mean?" Kristy asked.

"I just got a letter. They had insurance and named me the beneficiary. The policies were worth one hundred thousand," Freddie explained.

Kristy paused, thinking about her following words. "Don't you think half should go to me? I mean, I worked for the *Legacy*, and we don't even have that anymore. It seems like half isn't too much to ask."

Freddie had always gotten his way, and he had already spent the money in his mind. He was not going to give up his windfall. "Mom and Dad only made me the beneficiary. So, the money is mine, but you should get something that is fair."

"Yes, half. That would be fair."

"Well, you don't have mouths to feed like me. I think five thousand should help you. You could go on a very nice vacation with that. You have always wanted to travel."

Kristy could not believe what she was hearing. Her work paid into a boat that sank, her parents were dead, and now her brother was willing to take the money that was more than enough for them both. She exploded.

"Freddie, F-U-C-K-Y-O-U! This crap is the same bullshit that you and the family have always laid on me. I'm not going to take this shit anymore! You are going to fuck up your kids, too. Unless he gets out of here, Bodhi will probably be an uncaring, unforgiving ass just like you and Dad! Take your fucking five thousand and stick it up your ass. Nathalie, why do you put up with this crap? He keeps you in your place. You're not much better than him." Kristy was screaming, spewing the years of pent-up frustration and hate.

Freddie and Nathalie stood in stunned silence. Then Freddie

snapped out of it and into his dad's role. "I have obligations. You need to find a man and move on. Get the hell out of here until you can respect me, and my family." Freddie finished and walked away.

Kristy's mind was spinning and filled with rage. She had deprived Freddie once before by destroying the *Legacy*. It cost the lives of her father, Jerry, and her Uncle Nathan, but they did not care for her anyway. Now, Freddie had taken over where they left off. She couldn't let Bodhi grow up in this environment. Kristy could not let another generation of Neanderthal men hold their thumb on the women in their lives. She slammed the door as she left, determined to figure out a way to get Bodhi out and leave Freddie with nothing.

————-

Kids do what kids do. They like to push the boundaries and find out where the hard line is. A beach is a gathering place for youth where they can be free. In the summer, they came from everywhere. Some came with their parents from the Northeast states. Some lived in nearby towns and made day trips that extended into the night. The public beach access provided a means for locals and vacationers alike to enjoy the Crystal Coast. On any given summer day, there would be a mix of locals and vacationers parking at the beach access as they headed to the beach.

One night a group of young people had spent a long day on the beach. They had been drinking and enjoying themselves throughout the day. The sun had gone over the horizon, and they continued to party on the beach. The evening was warm, and the darkness only made the experience more enjoyable. The group wrapped up their time and walked back to the beach access parking lot across from the Snow Boatyard.

One of the young men standing next to his car asked the group, "Do you wanna smoke?" He looked at the group, and they agreed it was time for smoking. The parking lot was too exposed, with

Officer Blakely traveling the short route around the town. The group went across the street to the boatyard. It was late in the evening and primarily quiet in town.

The youth walked around the back of the main building and found a spot next to a shed. They did not see the "flammables" sign. The alcohol and intoxication of the experience made them oblivious to the danger.

A boy, who was heavier than his confidence suggested, pulled a joint out of nowhere as if conducting a magic trick. Another boy produced a lighter, and the group stood around, passing the joint. They smoked weed and cigarettes in the shadows by the shed.

They finished their party across the street, flicking the roaches and cigarette butts through a crack in the shed door. They stumbled across the street laughing and joking, got into their cars, and went back to where they came from.

The ashes from the butts and roaches retained enough heat to start a rag smoking, then burning. The fire grew, creeping, making its way to the walls of the wooden shed. As the heat grew, the solvent began to heat and spew fumes from the drums. The drums erupted into flames coughing fire out of every crack and crevice in the shed. The fire jumped to the main building climbing the exterior walls and through the gaps in the eves. Within a few minutes of the kids departing, the boatyard was an inferno, consuming all inside, even Tom Snow as he tried to save his business.

The fire would change the tenor of the town. Fingers would point in different directions, and the simmering feud would become a boil. The town would never be the same, and Bodhi would lose his family.

32

Preparation

The late afternoon in the summer makes for an interesting scene at the coast. It was easy to pass by everything and go about your business. If you want to understand the intersection of locals and vacationers, watch the beach in the late afternoon. If you sit near one of the beach entrances, you will see people frantically looking at the skies over their shoulders. They will see the clouds and hear the thunder of the afternoon storms.The bright red, sunburned faces frequently glance back. They will stand up and look, check their phones and sit down. Eventually, they will pack their things and head for the condo. The locals will sit looking at the water, listening to the music, playing corn hole, and laughing. They know the weather, and know the summer thunderstorms get pushed to the mainland by the sea breeze. Those who live their lives on the island know the weather and when to take shelter.

Bodhi and Ellie had made it back to the motel. They brought the skiff back from the fish house, filled it with gas, and tied it up behind Nana B's. They were showering and getting ready for the evening. They planned to meet Kristy for dinner after she arrived.

Ellie was in front of the mirror in the bedroom, drying her hair.

The television was on the local weather forecast, and Ellie caught a glance out of the corner of her eye. She turned off the hairdryer to hear what the weather woman was saying. "Bodhi! Come look at this!" Bodhi walked out of the bathroom. He had shaving cream on half his face and a razor in his hand.

"What, what is it?" Bodhi asked.

"Watch."

The woman on the television described the hurricane churning in the Atlantic Ocean. "The hurricane has strengthened since the last forecast at two p.m.Hurricane hunter aircraft just finished their pass through the storm, and the new data will be fed into the models for the eleven p.m. forecast. Currently, the hurricane is showing peak winds at one hundred and thirty-five miles per hour. That is up from one hundred and seven miles per hour this morning. This hurricane is a powerful storm for this time of year.The current path of the hurricane takes it through Wilmington, North Carolina, just a little over thirty-six hours from now. Be aware that this cone of uncertainty means that this hurricane could directly hit Myrtle Beach, South Carolina, to Cape Lookout, North Carolina. Everyone in these areas needs to prepare and be ready for a major hurricane."

"What does that mean? Do we need to leave? It looks like this storm is going to be bad," Ellie said.

"I am going to talk with Ley and see what he has to say. He will know what we should do."

Ellie was not happy with that answer. She wanted a definitive response from Bodhi about what to do. Ellie felt frustrated, but she knew that safety was just across the bridge. So, she decided to let it go for now, but not for much longer.

"I am guessing the Big Rock dinner is off now?" Ellie asked.

"I heard that the board moved it to tomorrow night. They will postpone the tournament, but they will have the Captain's Party.

Pretty much all the fishing crews are in town anyway, so they are going to do what they can."

"Okay. I think we just need to watch the weather."

Bodhi looked at Ellie and smiled. "I understand. We can pack up and be out of here in twenty minutes. No big deal. In three hours, we could be back in Raleigh."

Ellie smiled back. She could feel that Bodhi was trying to make her feel better, and it was working. She flipped on the hairdryer and went back to fixing her hair.

Bodhi was nervous about Kristy coming. He did not know why. He felt it was strange she decided to come to the beach. Everyone kept pointing to Kristy for information about the fire, and maybe that was unsettling him. She should arrive soon, and they were going to dinner in Morehead City at the Ruddy Duck.

Ellie looked beautiful in a simple white dress. It was the first time since they came to the coast that she went full makeup and hair. Bodhi loved his down east country girl, but his uptown city girl could make hearts skip a beat. She stood at the bathroom door with lights highlighting her from behind. Through the dress, Bodhi could make out the curves of her body.

"What?" Ellie asked.

Bodhi was startled by the sound of her voice. He had been thinking just how lucky he was. He was envisioning their life together and how they fit together in a way that no one else in this world could. Bodhi snapped out of it. "Sorry, nothing. You look amazing."

Ellie walked toward him. She put her arms out and hugged him as he sat on the bed. His face pressed into her chest, and he wrapped his arms around her slender waist. She stood there holding him. She could not help but think about what this trip to the crystal coast had revealed about her future husband. She saw him angry, sad, vulnerable, and happy all in this short time. She was amazed at how much more

273

profound and complex her husband was than she had ever thought.

They held their embrace, each thinking their thoughts until Bodhi's phone began to buzz.

"It's Kristy," Bodhi said as he looked at his phone. "Hello, Kristy?"

"I am here. Where are you? I see your truck," Kristy said.

"Hold on. I will be right out," Bodhi said as he opened the motel room door.

Kristy was parked next to his truck in her BMW. Bill had bought the car for her as an anniversary gift the past year. She loved driving the car, and she was thankful for her city life anytime she went anywhere in it. Kristy turned the car off, opened the door, and stepped out.

"Have you checked in yet?" Bodhi asked as Ellie came to stand in the door behind him.

"Well, hello. Good to see you." Kristy hugged Bodhi. "Ellie, you look beautiful as ever. How has your visit been?"

Ellie considered responding honestly but decided to be practical. "It has been good. We have really enjoyed the beach. Bodhi even taught me how to surf."

"Bodhi surf? How did you learn to surf?" Kristy asked.

"DJ taught me. Ellie learned faster than I did. She definitely is better than me in one day."

"Your vast experience of two days?" Ellie chided Bodhi.

"I am just happy that Bodhi finally learned to surf. He never wanted to do that when he was little," Kristy said.

"That's not true. I was just too little," Bodhi pleaded.

"If that is what you want to believe," Kristy said. "What do we have planned for tonight?"

"I thought the three of us could go to dinner in Morehead?" Bodhi said.

"That sounds good. Let me check-in. Let's meet in thirty minutes."

"That works. We will be by the pool having a drink. Believe it or not, the cocktails they make here are amazing," Ellie said.

"The Path surprises you all the time. See you in about thirty minutes," Kristy said as she started toward the office. Ellie and Bodhi checked the motel door and then made the short walk across the parking lot to the pool for a drink.

Ellie and Bodhi were sitting at the small bar by the pool. The bar was in a shaded corner of the pool deck. The late-day sun cast a shadow over the area where they were sitting. The bar itself looked to be handmade in Salter Path. It had the distinctive island flair assembled of old wood and new nails. Ellie had a martini glass with a purple liquid garnished with a lemon wedge and cherry. Bodhi had a short rocks glass with muddled herbs, lime, and brown whiskey. The humidity of the late day meant that the glasses were drawing moisture out of the air, covering them in condensed water. Ellie held a paper napkin under her glass to stop the condensation from dripping on her lap. Bodhi and Ellie wondered how Danny found the recipes for these drinks, but it likely took a lot of practice or a skilled bartender.

"How are you going to bring up the fire?" Ellie asked.

"I think I am just going to tell her what we found out and ask her about what she was doing in the Path the night of the fire," Bodhi said.

"Should you take another approach? Something more subtle?" Ellie suggested.

"Kristy came down here to tell me something. So, I can ask what she had to say. Better?"

"That isn't more subtle, but you know her best. So, I will follow your lead."

Bodhi's eyes glanced up and focused across the pool deck. Ellie knew it was Kristy coming and she best not continue. Kristy made her way to the bar where they were sitting. "Y'all ready?" Bodhi downed the last of his drink and then finished Ellie's. Kristy said, "Why don't I drive."

The Ruddy Duck was situated "above" the Morehead City water-front. It seemed like you were walking into a ground-level restaurant from the outside. The reality was that the restaurant was in an old fish processing facility built on piers driven into the seafloor. The restaurant focused on local food and fresh ingredients. It blended low country food with a flair that the vacationers from Raleigh had come to expect. The lighting inside was all incandescent bulbs giving a pleasant yellow glow. The bar was the centerpiece of the establishment. A finely crafted bar and bar back with a figurehead of a naked woman from the front of a ship hovering over the patrons. In another world, rough and tumble seafarers would have filled the bar seeking good food and strong drinks after a long sea voyage. Tonight, vacationers bellied up to the crowded bar.

The three of them were seated at a table next to a window. Outside the window, there was nothing other than water. Peering out of the window made you feel like you were on a boat. Kristy, Bodhi, and Ellie made small talk as the waitress took their drink orders. The waitress returned with their drinks a few minutes later. In a slow southern drawl, the waitress asked, "What can I get y'all?"

Bodhi started, "I will have the whole fried flounder." It was a medieval meal where the entire fish was plated, head and all. Kristy had the grilled mahi-mahi sandwich with an extra side of slaw, and Ellie a salad with fried oysters.

Shortly after the food arrived, Bodhi asked, "Kristy, why did you want to come down here? Why couldn't we talk on the phone?"

Kristy was caught in mid-chew. She finished chewing her food, which gave her time to collect her thoughts. On the long drive down, she had been thinking of what she would say. She never came up with anything, and now the time had arrived. She would have to figure it out as the discussion unfolded.

"I wanted to see you in person. You must be going through a lot, and I felt like I needed to be here," Kristy finally said.

Bodhi was at first confused by this. He had the impression she was coming to tell him something. To explain why she was on the island the night of the fire. "There have been ups and downs. I think coming here is helping me to put some closure on this. Is there anything you think I should know?" Bodhi asked.

"About what? What do you think I know?" Kristy asked.

"You know I have been asking about the fire. I have figured out some things, but everyone keeps telling me to talk to you. It seems like they think you know something?"

"Could it be that they want me to tell you there is nothing to know? Could they just want you to stop asking questions?"

"It could be. They could want to move on from the past. I don't think so, though. They have brought it up to me as much as I have brought it up to them." Bodhi took a breath. "Why were you in Salter Path the night of the fire?"

Kristy knew this question was coming. She had thought about this response. "I came down to see friends and go to a party."

"Why didn't you tell me you were here that night?" Bodhi asked.

"I never thought it was important. What difference would it make if I was here?" Kristy asked.

"I have been talking with Natchez, the detective. I, we," Bodhi looked at Ellie and then back at Kristy, "have tried to piece together what happened that night. We have asked a lot of questions. What did you see that night?"

Kristy was not expecting this direct question. "Where? At the party? Nothing unusual. We just had a party and did some drinking."

"Did you drink?" Ellie asked a bit out of turn.

"Yes. I had a few drinks. It was a party; everyone was drinking." She was on the defensive now.

"You had already moved to Raleigh. Where did you stay that night?"

Bodhi asked.

"I drove back to Raleigh. I was just down for the party."

"It must have been late, and that was a long drive. What time did you leave for home?" Ellie asked.

"Well, I stopped along the way and took a nap at a rest stop. You know that one near Kenansville."

"Before you left, did you notice anything unusual? Can you think back then? Any little thing might be important," Bodhi said.

Kristy stared down at her plate, pretending to be thinking hard about that night. "There is nothing that comes to mind. I just left the party and headed home."

"Why does everyone want me to talk to you?" Bodhi insisted.

"Bodhi, I think they might want me to put an end to this. The fire was an accident. That is what they determined. They can probably see your pain and just want it to end."

Ellie could hear that Kristy was not convinced it was an accident. "So, there was nothing unusual about that night? What about Ed and Jessica? They were outsiders, new to the coast. Could they have had something to do with it?" Ellie was hoping to keep the conversation going.

"I do not think so. They were new to the coast and just friends. If you cannot find any explanation, maybe the explanation is that it was an accident."

"I went by the old house. I forgot how small it was. I remembered where the kitchen was, the stairs, and the front door. How would a fire block the stairs? It does not seem to make sense," Bodhi was half talking to himself.

"The house was old. The wood was dry. It could have just spread very fast and blocked the way out. It is an accident because no one knows what happened." Kristy tried to put it to rest.

"What about Darrel? What do you know about him? DJ did not go to the beach because Darrel was sitting, looking out his front window. Like he was waiting for something. Could he have done it? Or does he know who did it?" Bodhi asked.

Kristy's heart bumped in her chest. She was surprised to hear that Darrel was up and looking out the window. "I do not think he would know anything. Would he say something if he did?"

Bodhi responded, "I was young when I left, but I also know that people keep things close and do not want outsiders in their business. So, he might not want to say anything, even if he knows something. What do you know about the fire at the Snow Boatyard?"

"That's a tricky one. Tony Snow took over that boatyard after the fire. I do not know anything for sure, but it seemed strange that he seemed so ready to jump into that business. The Snows insisted he had nothing to do with it. I am not so sure," Kristy said.

"Susan Snow said that my dad started that fire. Do you think he did?" Bodhi asked.

Kristy paused, and silence twisted Bodhi's stomach into a knot; then she started, "We never talked about it. He was mad after Dad died. I do not think he was that kind of mad. I think he also understood when you go to sea, accidents happen. When Tom died in that fire, he never seemed much bothered by it. None of that means anything, though."

Ellie was listening to the exchange. She reached for Bodhi's hand, which was now gripping his leg tightly under the table. She had to coax his hand to relax.

"I just do not believe he would do that," Bodhi stated.

"I do not think so either. We just never discussed it," Kristy said. "This is why we should leave the past in the past."

Bodhi was tired of the conversation and decided to let Kristy have the last word in it. They finished their meals and continued with some small talk. Kristy told stories about growing up in Salter Path and how isolated it was back then. Those days there were no tourists, only a few people with small beach places that were used as fishing shacks. So much had changed since she was little.

They got out of the car at the motel and started to their rooms. Kristy asked, "Are you heading home tomorrow? That storm is barreling down on us here."

"Bodhi wants to stay, but I don't feel comfortable," Ellie said.

"I am going to talk to Ley tomorrow. I wanted to go to the Captain's Party to show Ellie the high side of fishing."

"Let's talk tomorrow to see what our plan should be. I want both of you to be safe," Kristy said.

They said their goodnights. Bodhi and Ellie headed into their room for the night. Kristy made her way across the parking lot toward her room. Halfway across the parking lot, Kristy turned to look back at Bodhi and Ellie's room. She saw the shades drawn and the door closed. Kristy then changed directions and headed out of the motel complex.

She walked between two of the motel buildings. She knew from her time growing up in the Path how to move through the backyards without being seen. There were paths neighbors used between houses and holes in fences that gave the locals the ability to walk where they wanted, especially at night. Kristy wove through sandy paths and ducked under the limb of a live oak that hung low. She emerged not far from the Big Tree Drive-in. She walked up to the backdoor of a house nearby and gently knocked on the door.

A dog started barking inside. It was not a loud "woof," but a little dog "rarf!" She could hear heavy steps making their way to the door. The deadbolt flipped over, and the door opened. Darrel Willard stood in the door frame.

"Good to see you, Kristy. I am glad you came by," Darrel said.

"When you called to tell me Bodhi was asking around, I figured we should talk," Kristy said.

"Come on in. Can I get you something?" Darrel asked.

"What do you have?"

"I got some liquor, white wine, and beer."

"Whiskey on ice?"

"You got it."

Darrel went to the corner cupboard. He bent over, reached down, and pulled out a bottle of brown whiskey. He grabbed two crystal rocks glasses out of the cupboard and dropped two ice cubes in each.

"It's a nice night. Let's sit on the back porch," Darrel suggested. The back porch was covered and big enough for two chairs, a small table, and a grill. It was covered with a tin roof, and the low-growing coastal forest provided privacy for the well-protected backyard.

"Cheers," Kristy said. They touched glasses, and she consumed one finger in the first taste.

"When did you get in town?" Darrel asked.

"Earlier today. I just got back from dinner with Ellie and Bodhi."

"Where did you go?"

"Ruddy Duck's. It was a good place. I had never been there. I remember it when it was the Sanitary."

"Things have changed around here. A lot more business down here now. It's good for my gig."

"I am glad for you. We need to talk about what Bodhi has been up to. What can you tell me?" Kristy asked.

"Why rush? Can't we catch up?"

"Darrel. This visit is not one of those. I did not come here to see you. I came here to try to clean up the mess Bodhi has created. I got everyone down here calling, telling me he is asking a lot of questions. He even reached out to the detective. We can't let him bring up these old things. They are behind us."

"You are right. It has been, what, six months since we last saw each other. I have been waiting to see you again, but you are right. We need to do something about this."

"Tell me, what has been going on?"

"When Bodhi got here, there were the usual things. A few people did not care much for him being back. The women did not kindly take to those long legs he brought with him. They began asking around and stirring things up. I tried to find out what they knew on the beach one day, and they did not know much. They knew I was sitting up that night, but not much else. I sent them over to Susan Snow's to ask about the fire. I knew she would speak her mind about Freddie. That would confuse them," Darrel finished.

"So, they don't know anything, then?"

"I don't think so. I think Bodhi is ready to move on, but that girl keeps pushing him. She came after me on the beach. She would not let up."

"Yeah. Ellie seems sweet at first, but I see her taking Bodhi away from me. She is steering him toward her. At first, I liked her, but Bodhi just lets her have too much influence. He is led around by his nose with her," Kristy said.

"We need to get them off the island. This hurricane should drive them off."

"I'm not so sure. Bodhi seems like he wants to stay. He is building a connection to this place. I can see it."

"It's not so bad, is it? It would give you a reason to come back here more and see me." Darrel reached for Kristy's hand.

"Darrel. Not now. We have bigger things we have to handle." The strain in Kristy's voice was uncharacteristic of her.

"Hold on. They have been here for over a week. Asking questions and haven't gotten anywhere. I don't think we have to worry."

"You might be right. Let's go over it again. Let's make sure there are no loose ends. Okay?" Kristy insisted.

"Okay." Darrel started a story they had gone over many times to make Kristy feel better. "That night, I was waiting for you to leave the party. I didn't see anyone on the road. I kept an eye out, which is why I left the porch light on. All the other houses were quiet. Blakely was on duty that night, but he always sat in his car by the Trade Winds sleeping. So he wouldn't be a problem. You came around to the back door like always. Think now. Was there anyone that saw you?"

"I left the party and headed back up the road. I didn't see any cars. I ducked into the woods and cut through the paths. There was that one dog that barked, but no lights came on. There was no way someone could see me come here," Kristy finished.

"What about how you talked to Ley?" Darrel asked.

"He has never connected that conversation to me, planting the idea in his head to go crabbing. He was so young; I'm not even sure he remembered I was there."

"He had never mentioned anything, even when he talked with Bodhi. I am guessing he just blocked it out," Darrel said.

"I think that is where we could have a problem, but it has been a long time. No reason to think it would change."

"We left at about three-thirty a.m. We went to the Snow Boatyard and got the can of paint thinner," Darrel said.

"Were there cameras there?" Kristy asked.

"Yes. I think so, but the police never looked at those tapes. The footage was probably blurry and that footage is long gone."

"Then, through the backyards. Maureen's dog Maggie barked, but it didn't look like anyone woke up. Then to the house, the front door was open. Paint thinner on the front door and the hall. You threw the lighter in, and it went," Kristy said.

"Yes. That lighter must have disintegrated in the fire. Then, we went our separate ways. Did anyone see you leave? Which way did you go?"

"I went toward Atlantic Beach. Blakely was at the other end of town, so he would not see me."

"When did you get back?"

"A little after eight in the morning. Not unusual for a girl in Raleigh to show up in the morning after a night out. I stopped on an off-ramp to grab a nap."

"That's when the cop knocked on your window?" Darrel asked.

"Yes. He just wanted to see if I was okay. I told him yes and that I had just pulled over because I was tired. There shouldn't be a record of it," Kristy said.

"The only place we have a weakness is Ley and maybe that cop. Ley knows you talked him into sneaking out, but we can probably mess his memory if we need to. That cop probably didn't tell anyone, and those records should be long gone."

Kristy didn't care much for Darrel anymore. He had let himself go and looked nothing like the man she once knew. He also grew bitter when she left to go to Raleigh. They still shared this terrible secret. She needed to see him, sleep with him, keep him obedient, manipulate him as a woman can do. She did not want to lose Bodhi, and if Darrel turned on her, he could destroy everything. Kristy finished her drink.

"We have to keep holding this together. If we can just get Bodhi to drop this, we will be in the clear," Kristy said. "I have to go. I need to get back to the motel. I will call you if I need anything."

Darrel stood up as Kristy stood up. He took her hand and pulled her close. He kissed her. "I love you. Come back, please?"

"We have been over this. I have Bill and a life in Raleigh. I love us the way we are. We just get to have fun. I have to go." She walked off the porch, slipping into the paths and making her way back to the motel.

As Kristy made her way through the trees and shrubs lining the path, she didn't see Bobby.

284

The deckhand had gotten off the boat earlier in the day and went to the Dollar General to buy a six-pack of beer and find a quiet place. That quiet place was in the shade behind the Big Tree next to Darrel Willard's house. He could hear the entire discussion from his spot hidden in the maritime forest. Bobby's nature was to be observant. That night he listened to a secret he knew he must share. He needed to tell Bodhi what he heard. He fell asleep thinking about how he could tell Bodhi that his Aunt Kristy was the one who killed his family.

33

Leaving

There is an element of uncertainty with a hurricane. The Weather Channel plays on this by exciting a large swath of America with impending doom. They are not being dishonest. Hurricanes are just unpredictable. Sometimes they fizzle. The hurricane starts as a mighty storm and then fades with the first encounter with the land. Other times they lurch forward, like a running back shooting through a hole in the line, slamming into the coast with full fury and aggression, destroying homes and lives. They can also sidestep. One minute heading west, then to the north, and then back to the west, before double stepping to the east. This movement is how a hurricane is. For that reason, when the storm comes close, those who know prepare. Those who don't know leave. Leaving is what Ellie wanted to do. She had never experienced a hurricane, and she did not care to see the destruction. Bodhi recalled riding out storms in his parent's house. The walls shook as the wind blew, and everyone in town bonded together through the threat. Bodhi longed for that feeling of connectedness. Since he left the Path, he had not felt that mortal bond to a community.

Hurricane Adrian was wiping the ocean. She had grown in strength and size overnight. The cone of uncertainty narrowed. The Crystal Coast was in the storm's path, and it looked like there was no chance of avoiding a clash with the first hurricane of the year.

The time before a storm is truly calm. Everything falls into slow motion. Work stops. Neighbors help neighbors. A threat to a community fixes people into their roles as members of a group beyond their immediate family. Boards go up to cover windows. Sandbags fill the stoops of doors to hold the floodwaters back. Every loose object is put up or tied down. The wind will carry garbage cans into the sound and throw boats off their trailers. Everyone connects and strengthens the community. The hurricane breaks and binds at the same time.

"Ley. Good morning. How are you doing?" Bodhi said into his phone.

"I am good. What's up?" Ley asked.

"I told Ellie I would check in with you to get your thoughts on the storm. What do you think?" Bodhi asked.

"Looks like we are going to take it on the chin. Prep today. Party tonight. That's what I am thinking," Ley said, talking about the Captain's Party.

"I think I am going to stay here. Maybe I can help out. I am not sure what Ellie is going to do. I am going to try to talk her into staying for the party and then heading home in the morning."

"If you can make that work, it would be good. The party should be double fun with the storm. The only thing better than a Captain's Party is a storm party. This shindig is going to be both combined."

"Sounds like it will be fun. Are you staying on the island for the storm?" Bodhi asked.

"I always do. As a matter of fact, I will probably get a room in the motel. Those cinder block walls keep you safe. We'll have a hurricane party. Talk to Ellie. Then give me a call. I need to run the boat over to Beaufort to get it hauled out. Do you want to go with me? I can't get ahold of Bobby, so I need a mate."

"That would be great. I haven't been on that boat in forever. It would be an honor to ride her to safety. Let me talk to Ellie, and I will get back to you."

"Shit. I need to know. We are leaving at eleven to make our haul-out at one. Your ass better be at the dock."

"Got it, Captain. See you at eleven," Bodhi said, hanging up the phone.

Bodhi needed to tell Ellie that he was in for the hurricane. There was an element of fear in planning to stay for the hurricane, but that fear brought adrenaline that his young mind still sought. Bodhi walked back into the motel room to lay out his plan for the storm, hoping she would approve.

"Ellie?" Bodhi asked.

"Yes?" Ellie said as she rolled over in bed. Wearing one of Bodhi's T-shirts, she was trying to wake up.

"Are you awake? I just got off the phone with Ley."

"I am awake now. What did Ley say?" Ellie responded.

"He is staying on the island. He said the Captain's Party should be good tonight. I think we should go to the party."

Ellie sat up in bed, still trying to shake the grogginess of sleep out of her mind. "When is the hurricane going to be here?"

"The weather people are saying that it will pick up tomorrow in the morning, but not too intense until early afternoon. I thought we could stay, though. Ley said he was staying in the motel. It's built out of concrete, so it's a safe place to stay."

"So you are going to stay in the path of natural disaster on purpose?" Ellie questioned.

"I thought you might stay as well?" Bodhi hoped.

"I don't think I want to stay here through that. I would rather be safe back in Raleigh," Ellie stated. "And, I wish you would come too. I will be worried sick if you are here."

"I know you can't understand why I want to stay. I just feel like I need to experience it. It is like a right of passage for us who grew up here in the Path."

"But you didn't grow up in the path. You grew up in Raleigh," Ellie reminded him.

The jab at Bodhi's childhood made Bodhi want to snap at his wife-to-be, but he claimed himself. "I know what you mean, but coming back and connecting with Ley and DJ reminds me of the childhood I missed here. I know you can't understand. Can I just say it's a man thing? You know, 'Bodhi—Storm Chaser.'"

"You are a grown man. If you want to stay, I can't stop you, but I do not approve."

"I know. It is just one of those things. Me, Ley, and DJ will be together. We will be safe in this place," he said as he thumped on the cinderblock walls. "I'm staying even if you don't want me to."

"How am I going to get home? Should I take your truck?" Ellie asked.

"Kristy should be going back today. Maybe you can ride with her. You all should come to the Captain's Party for a little while and then leave from there. You will only be two hours to Raleigh from there."

"I will talk with Kristy and see what she wants to do. I would like to see what this party is about, but I definitely don't want to be here during the storm."

"Okay. That's fair. Can you try to catch up with her? I am going with Ley to take the boat over to Jarret Bay to haul it out before the storm. We have to leave at eleven to make the appointment," Bodhi explained his plan for the day.

"So, you are going to leave me for the day? That will be fine, I will have the truck, and I was thinking of doing some exploring on my own."

Bodhi knew that "exploring" was a code word for shopping and looking for deals. It made him feel good that she wanted to see more of the area that gave him his earliest childhood memories. "That sounds good. There are lots of places in Beaufort and Morehead that we haven't *explored* yet."

Bodhi crawled into bed with Ellie. They were still young and very much in love. At times, he could not believe that this girl was his. She was everything that he ever imagined he would find in a woman. He pulled off his shirt as he crawled on top of her and straddled her. He stared down, looking at her face.

"What?" she asked.

"You. I love you so much." He leaned over to kiss her as his body enveloped her beneath him. He kissed her lips softly. Then again. Then slowly parting his lips and deeply. He made his way down her cheek and to her neck. She relaxed, giving in to his advances and enjoying the touch of his lips on her soft skin. She began to breathe more deeply, and Bodhi felt the heat of the moment, filling him with bliss. Soon they were naked, wrapped in passion with the morning light peeking through the shades adding a textured light pattern to their tanned bodies. Endorphins pumped through their bodies as they fucked away the tension of their minor disagreement. They then lay in bed with Bodhi napping, spooning Ellie as she quietly thumbed through social media on her phone.

"What time is it?" Bodhi's eyes sprang open, realizing he had fallen back asleep after sex.

"It's ten-thirty. Don't you have to meet Ley at eleven?" Ellie said.

"Yeah. At the boat. I need to get dressed and head over there." Bodhi jumped out of bed, kissing Ellie and squeezing her buttocks.

Bodhi dressed, throwing on the standard island uniform: sneakers, shorts, a faded T-shirt, ball cap, and sunglasses. He almost looked like a local, except his sneakers were $150 Adidas boosts and were practically brand new. They weren't the type of working shoes the waterman preferred for comfort and stability on the boat. He gave Ellie a final kiss and headed out the door.

He turned around abruptly. "I almost forgot." He reached in his pocket, grabbed the keys, and tossed them to her. "I love you. Have fun today and get up with Kristy. Let me know what you decide."

Bodhi made the short walk across the street and down the road to the *Lady B*. He got there just as Ley was walking to the boat. The sun was shining high in the sky, and the breeze picked up and brought thick humid tropical air over the island. For the *Lady B*, the wind had no impact on the sturdy shrimp boat. The *Lady B* had weathered many storms while at sea, but a hurricane can tear piling from the ground setting the boats free. It was too much to risk leaving your means of earning a living tied to wooden poles buried in the sand. They needed to get the boat on the high ground and set it on blocks to be safe from the sea stirred by the hurricane.

"You ready?" Ley asked Bodhi.

"I sure am. It's been years since I rode the *Lady B*," Bodhi said.

"Not much has changed. The old pig still does her thing. I was thinking of painting her this year. You know, a little lipstick on the pig to dress her up a bit."

"If I am around, count me in. It would be me giving back for all y'all that kept that little slice of land for me here."

"Glad you are here," said Ley as he fired up the engine. The diesel coughed a puff of black smoke out the back as the engine came to life. "Grab that line over there. Let's get out of here."

Bodhi pulled the line from the pile, and Ley engaged the drive on the boat. It began to lumber forward. Bodhi wrapped the lines on the deck. He remembered how his dad and grandfather had shown him, keeping neat loops and tucking them under the gunwale to be out of the way of working feet.

"Nice job, Bodhi. Maybe I will hire you as a mate," Ley said.

"Where is Bobby? Why isn't he helping you?" Bodhi asked.

"The fuck if I know. He was supposed to be here, but he didn't answer his phone. I didn't know if you would still be able to handle the lines. You know you haven't done it in a long time. I might have to fire Bobby's drunk ass when we get back."

"Maybe he lost his phone or something. It seems like the kid needs work; maybe you should give him a break. Shit!" Bodhi said.

"What?"

"Speaking of losing your phone. I left my damn phone at the motel."

"So? You are on a boat. It's better without a phone," Ley reminded him.

"Yeah. The thing is, Ellie is thinking of going back with Kristy rather than staying here during the storm. She was supposed to call me and let me know what they decided to do. It might be me going stag to the Captain's Party."

"If you do, watch out. There are more predators in this town looking for fresh meat than you might think."

"I hear ya. I am a taken man now," Bodhi said, standing next to Ley, looking through the salt-caked windshield of the boat.

The diesel engine chugged, pushing the shrimping boat along at a modest clip. Bodhi remembered standing in the wheelhouse with his father as he explained the water, showing him how to read the shallows, where to look for birds and tell if they were chasing fish or shrimp. Bodhi could smell the fresh shrimp splashed on the deck for more years than he had been alive. He wondered how many thousands, maybe millions of dollars in shrimp had gone across the boat's deck. The smell mingled with the diesel exhaust brought back the unique smell he identified with his father. Bodhi paused for a moment, wondering if he might be captaining a shrimp boat had his life taken a different turn. There was something powerfully simple about earning a living doing honest work. He wondered, would he be happier living this life? He shook it from his mind. He could not be happier than he was, but what if you could have both? He liked the idea of trying to have both worlds at the same time.

————————-

Ellie was getting ready to start her day. She had spent the last hour perusing the Internet looking for out-of-the-way shops and boutiques to explore on her day to herself. She was going to clean up and get dressed before venturing out. She figured she could get connected with Kristy a little bit later. Selfishly, she wanted the day to herself and didn't want to contact Kristy until she was off the island. Bodhi and Ellie had been together non-stop for the past week and having a little alone time wasn't a bad thing.

Ellie had begun to grow into the pace of life in the Path. She felt her city life fading, and the timing of her life being driven by the sun, sand, and weather. In Raleigh, you tried to live by a schedule. Places to go. New restaurants. Bigger houses. People seemed to be trying their hardest to build homes where they needed no one else. In the Path, your community wanted to know who you were. For all the questions from the locals when they returned, she could see that they were trying to understand how Bodhi fit into the Path after he had left. She wondered if there could be life for her and Bodhi in the Path away from Raleigh.

Knock, knock, knock. A short pause. Knock, knock, knock.

Ellie was startled by the knocking, snapping her out of her island daydream. She headed to the door wearing only Bodhi's T-shirt. "Who is it?" she asked, looking through the peephole. Standing there was Bobby. He had a dark blue trucker's hat on with his greasy black hair sticking out from underneath, almost touching his chin. His clothes made it look like he had spent the night sleeping in the dirt, which he had done.

"It's Bobby. Ley's friend," Bobby said through the door.

"How can I help you? Is everything okay?" Ellie suddenly connected Bobby with the boat and wondered if there was a problem.

"I need to talk to you. Can you talk?" Bobby asked.

"Bodhi's not here. He is with Ley. Why aren't you with them on the boat?" Ellie asked through the door.

"I needed to talk to you. It's important. So, I stayed back."

"Okay. Hold on. I will come out. Just wait there," Ellie instructed him. Ellie fumbled to find some shorts and pulled them on. She grabbed her phone and looked through the peephole to see where Bobby was. He was leaning against Bodhi's truck staring at his shoes. She opened the door and stepped outside.

"Bobby, good to see you. What can I help you with?" Ellie asked, puzzled as to why he would show up at her door when Bodhi was gone.

"Do you remember the other night when we talked at Frank and Clara's? How I said I hear a lot of things? You know I don't like to talk much, but I like to listen," Bobby explained.

"I remember you saying that you hear things and to be careful. Does it have to do with that?" Ellie asked.

"Well, it isn't exactly what I thought it would be. I heard something and needed to tell you. I didn't know who else to tell, and you seem like you will listen." Bobby stumbled through his thoughts.

"What did you hear? You can tell me whatever. I won't tell anyone." Ellie was trying to get him to spit it out.

"Well, you know how I like to listen. I sometimes just sleep in the woods around here. It's peaceful. No one bothers you, and you can just listen to people. All sorts of things. I just like to hear people talk, and you know, listen." Bobby knew that sleeping in the woods wasn't typically a way to impress someone, and if he lived in the city, he would call it camping.

294

"That's okay, Bobby. I understand, but what did you hear?"

"Last night, I heard something awful, and you need to know. I got some beer at the DG and went back behind the Big Tree. There are a bunch of trees back there and some good spots to sleep deep down under the trees. People can hardly even see you in the day, let alone the night. I was in my spot for the night when I heard someone coming walking through the trees. It scared me because I thought they were coming for me. They walked by and then to the house I was near." Bobby paused.

"And?" Ellie asked.

"Well, it was Kristy, Bodhi's aunt. She went to Mr. Darrel's house. They came out on the back porch and started talking. They were talking about the fire at Bodhi's parent's house. They said they started it. They are nervous that Bodhi is asking questions around town." Bobby stopped and looked at his feet.

"Wait. What? Did you just say you heard Kristy admit to starting the fire? Why would she do that?" Ellie asked.

"She likes Mr. Darrel. They meet together so he will keep the secret. He wanted to meet more, but it didn't seem like she wanted to. They went over the whole thing how they did it. They wanted to make sure they covered their tracks." Bobby stopped.

Ellie was half confused and half stunned. Why would Bobby show up out of nowhere to tell her this? Was it a lie? Why would he lie? Is he crazy? How could Kristy...why would she raise Bodhi after starting the fire? It did not make sense. What would that mean? She had to be sure she exactly understood what Bobby was saying. "Tell me that again. What exactly did you hear?"

Bobby began his slow and thoughtful recounting of the conversation. He talked about how Darrel and Kristy were having an affair and got the solvent cans from the boatyard, how they made their way through the backyards and paths so no one would see them. Bobby explained how Darrel was waiting on Kristy in the window to leave the party and how she left and drove back to Raleigh, stopping at a rest stop along the way where the police knocked on her window as she slept. Bobby gave every detail he could recall.

"Bobby, I don't know what to say. Thank you for telling me this. If you think of anything else, please let me know," Ellie told Bobby.

"If I hear something else, I will come to tell you. I will just knock on the door," Bobby said and walked away in silence.

———-

Kristy rolled over in bed and kissed Darrel. DJ was gone staying with his mother, and Kristy could sneak over to Darrel's house for sex and comfort. Since that night on the beach, they had become more and more involved with each other. Kristy thought that this could be her life in the Path. When Darrel finally divorced his wife, she could move in and become Darrel's new wife. She would be out of her father's house but still be able to see her beloved nephew and niece.

"When is it going to be final?" Kristy asked Darrel about the divorce.

"We have to be separated for a year in North Carolina. It's been ten months. Not much longer."

"Can we tell people about us then? I am getting tired of sneaking around."

"I want to. I think we can tell whoever we want. It's just, you know." Darrel referred to the feud that had blown up after the boatyard fire.

"The bickering between the families? I'm not worried about that. I mean, when people see us together, they will know it is okay to talk to each other again."

Darrel took a long deep breath. He knew that Kristy didn't understand the dynamics of what was happening in the town. "The problem is everyone thinks Freddie started that fire in the boatyard to even the score for the boat sinking. I don't know if they are willing just to let that go."

"We know what caused that boat to sink, but no one knows how that fire started." Kristy looked at Darrel coldly.

Darrel stared back, thinking carefully about his following words. He needed to pick his words carefully. He was falling in love with Kristy and didn't want to be cross with his opinions. "That boat sinking was an accident. That's all that I know. The fire, I guess we don't know what happened."

"That's right. I think us being together could be the best thing for this town," Kristy said.

The day finally came when Darrel was divorced from his wife. Kristy couldn't have been happier. She could finally tell everyone about her plans for the next steps in her life. Kristy went to Freddie's house to tell him and Nathalie about the man she had been dating. She was hopeful that this would be the turning point in bringing the town back together.

"I have to tell you something," Kristy said to Freddie and Nathalie, sitting in their kitchen.

"What is it? Are you okay?" Nathalie asked.

"I am good, more than good. I haven't been better. I found someone. And I think I am in love with him," Kristy blurted it out.

Freddie was bothered by being called in to hear that Kristy had a boyfriend, but Nathalie had been hoping for a long time Kristy would find someone. "Wow! That is great news! I am so happy for you." Nathalie said. "Do we know him? Who is it?"

Freddie was drinking his coffee and looking mildly interested. He read the *Tideland News* and scratched at the egg yolk on his plate. He looked up at his sister. "That's good." He went back to breakfast and the newspaper.

"Yes, you know him. He lives here in the Path. It's Darrel. Darrel Willard."

Freddie stopped, put down his newspaper, and looked Kristy

straight in the eyes. His pupils widened, and his eyes seemed to go black. He was looking through Kristy, and she thought she saw a fire burning in his dark black eyes. "What the fuck are you saying?"

"Freddie, stop. Kristy is…" Nathalie tried to intervene.

"You know that the Willards are on the same damn side as the Snows. How fucking long has this shit been happening?" Freddie shouted at Kristy.

Kristy flinched at the unexpected attack from Freddie. She hoped this would be good news, but Freddie wasn't taking it that way. Kristy recovered from the initial assault and changed her objective. "About two years. He is the only good man in my life!"

"Two damn years? Are you the reason they are getting a divorce?" Freddie asked.

"Hell no. That girl was running around on him. He was just there for me when I needed someone. And Darrel *is* divorced," Kristy said.

"That fucker. I can't believe a Willard is screwing my sister. I am going to beat the shit out of him. I can't believe this!" Freddie shouted.

Nathalie yelled, "Freddie! Don't! You can't! Stop!"

Freddie was already up from the table and thundering to the door. Kristy jumped between him and the threshold, trying to stop Freddie from leaving. "Get out of my way. I can't have a Willard with my sister. I can't believe those scums would do this. After they killed my father with that boat, they now want to take my sister. Out of my way."

"Freddie. You can't. It won't change things. Darrel and I are going to be together." Kristy was pleading now.

Freddie's senses had left him. He was focused on one thing now. It was putting people back on their sides of the feud. He pushed past Kristy and Nathalie and stormed out the door. Freddie's shoulders and arms bulged as he walked toward Darrel's business. Strengthened by years of working on commercial fishing boats, Freddie was no match for a man who spent his days working fryers in a drive-in.

The dust from the crushed rock in the parking lot of the Big Tree kicked behind Freddie's work boots. It was May, and at ten in the morning, people were already waiting for their "World Famous Big Tree Shrimp Burger." Few noticed Freddie walk by and around the back of the drive-in, but Darrel did, as he peered out the food order window. Freddie tried the doorknob. The door was locked. He banged on the door. He banged on the door again. And again. No one came to the door. Inside, Darrel stood on the other side of the door, not knowing but guessing why Freddie was "visiting."

There was a huge cracking sound as the doorframe gave way. Freddie came rushing through the broken door like the backdraft of a fire. He grabbed Darrel before he reacted and dragged him into the sand and dirt behind the restaurant. Darrel tried to fight back and throw Freddie off him. Freddie did not let him up. He hit Darrel in the face. Darrel bucked with all his might flipping Freddie off him. He tried to crawl away, but Freddie still gripped his leg with his hand like a crab claw. He dragged him back as Darrel kicked. People were coming out of the kitchen, and vacationers were walking around behind the drive-in to see the commotion. Darrel kicked at Freddie's arms and face. Freddie clutched Darrel's leg.

Then, out of nowhere, a voice came, "Dad?"

Bodhi and DJ stood side by side, two young boys not understanding why their dads were fighting behind the drive-in. The voice of the boy made the two men stop mid-fight. Grown men brought back from boyhood craziness by two boys.

"Bodhi. What are you doing here?" Freddie asked.

"I came to get DJ. We were going to cast net," Bodhi responded. "Why are you fighting with Mr. Darrel?"

"It's complicated. He did something. That's it." Freddie stopped at that.

Darrel had stood up with blood running down from the corner of his mouth. His eye was beginning to swell already. "You boys go on. Get to what you were doing. We are fine. And you," turning to his employees, "get back to work." Darrel followed everyone back inside.

Freddie stood up. The curious onlookers gawked at him as he tried to compose himself. "What are y'all looking at?" Then he walked past everyone, slightly limping as he headed home.

Kristy had since left Freddie's house and was back in the home she had grown up in. Without her mother, she sat there all alone, wondering what had transpired with Freddie and Darrel. The phone rang on the wall, and she picked it up.

"Hello?" Kristy said.

"I guess you told your brother about us?" Darrel asked rhetorically.

"He didn't take it as I thought. I didn't think…"

Darrel cut her off, "I don't need this, Kristy. I need you, but not that crazy-ass bullshit. I knew this wasn't going to work in the open. We need to do something different. We need a break."

Kristy could not believe what she was hearing. Another man in her life ran over her, using her and leaving her with nothing to show for it. It brought back flashes from her past, and she had to work to suppress them. "We can. We can just go back to how we were. You know, keep everything quiet. We did that for years." Kristy was trying to keep something of value for herself.

"Kristy. It's over. We need to do something different. To go another way."

Kristy heard enough and hung up the phone. In the next couple of weeks, she would pack her things and move to Raleigh. She would try to start over. With her parents gone and Freddie not supporting what she wanted, she needed to start anew, but it wouldn't be that easy.

———

The night of the fire, Kristy had come back to Salter Path to see Darrel. As much as she wanted to get away from that place, Darrel kept calling after she left. She still burned inside with hate for Freddie because he took from her at every turn, from her father's attention to the insurance money, the disapproval of her and Darrel's relationship. She wanted to take from him and decided that it would be that night she would take his house.

Bodhi gave her hope. When she was at one of the worst places in her life, that boy came into this world and gave her a new purpose. She thought that he would be a different man. If Bodhi was hers, she could raise him and make him into what she believed a man should be. If only he was hers.

Her plan was to come to the Path and talk Darrel into helping her burn the house. She figured if anyone was in the place, they would have time to get out. This fire would even the score with her brother. This *accident* would give her peace in moving to Raleigh. As the evening drew on at the party, she worried someone might get hurt. Still, she needed to settle things with her brother.

That night, she convinced Ley to sneak Bodhi out of the house. That would be her chance to start the fire and protect Bodhi from harm. Kristy had cared for Bodhi since he was a baby, and he was the nearest thing she had to a child of her own. She did not believe that the others would get hurt, but she could not risk Bodhi getting hurt.

What transpired after the fire was even more than she had hoped for in her life. She was able to have Bodhi all to herself. Her family was out of the way, and she had been able to shape Bodhi into the man she wanted. Bill Easterly was the husband Darrel could never have been, and she had her boy Bodhi to raise as she wished to. She vowed that no other person would come between her and her son, Bodhi. Wrath was something that made Kristy feel in control for the first time in her life. It was a drug addict finding the fix that they never knew existed. She realized it was a powerful tool she could call on when needed.

34

Staying

"What's going on here, Randy?" Ley talked into the handheld microphone of the VHF radio.

Randy of Jarret Bay squawked back, "We are working on it, Ley. The lift broke down, and we are trying to get it fixed. We are backed up here. I have a lot of boats in front of you."

"What are we looking at? I need to get his boat secured sooner rather than later. Are you going to get me on the high ground today?" Ley asked through the radio.

"They are telling me three-thirty before we are swinging boats again. It might not be until the morning until I can get you out."

"Not sure that's going to work. That storm is going to be on the doorstep by then. Can you get me tonight?" Ley was pleading, knowing his livelihood was floating under his feet.

"Can you hang on the hook? I will try to get you out at about five or so. Would that work?" Randy was trying to take care of the folks who counted on their boats to make a living.

"Roger that. We will drop a hook just north of the haystacks. This wind is starting to pick up out here. So, sooner seems better," Ley replied.

"I hear ya', Ley. We are trying our best. Stay on channel nineteen," Randy said.

"Give us twenty minutes, and we will be there. Standing by on one-nine," Ley said back.

"Are we going to make the Captain's Party?" Bodhi asked.

"We should. Once they get her in the sling, our work is done. We can head back to the Path and be at the party by seven-thirty."

"Okay. I should call Ellie and let her know what is going on. Can I borrow your phone?" Bodhi asked.

"Give her a little time. Don't make her stressed. Let's call her when we know something for sure."

"You are probably right. Ellie was going to do some 'exploring'. I should let her enjoy the day. I will call her later."

———————-

Ellie was sitting in the hotel, still trying to digest what Bobby had just told her. Could it be true that Kristy was the one? It seemed far-fetched, but also, was this why everyone said to talk to Kristy? Did others know but didn't want to say? There were more questions than she could comprehend. It was nearing one o'clock in the afternoon, and she was still trying to decide what to do with this information. She decided that she needed to know for herself before she told Bodhi. If this were true, it would break him. If it was a lie, he might not forgive her for thinking his aunt could have done such a thing. She picked up her phone and called Kristy.

"Kristy? How are you?" Ellie asked.

"I am fine. And you?" Kristy replied.

"Good. Where are you? I was wondering if maybe we could talk? Are you still at the motel?"

"Yes. Let me come by your room. I was getting ready to go out for some lunch."

"Okay, see you in a minute," Ellie responded.

Ellie got off the bed and went to the mirror, pulling her long blonde hair back and tucking it under a baseball cap. She leaned in to look at her skin as a habit most women have in critiquing themselves more than anyone else does. There was a knock at the door. Ellie opened it, and Kristy walked in, taking a seat by the small round table in the window by the door.

"What did you want to talk about? Is everything okay? Where is Bodhi?" Kristy asked.

"Bodhi went with Ley to take to the boat to have it pulled out for the storm. He is fine. I wanted to talk to you about a visitor I had this morning."

"Okay. Was it someone from the Path?"

"He didn't grow up here, but he works with Ley on the boat. His name is Bobby. He is his first mate on the boat."

"I'm not sure I know him, but what did he want?" Kristy asked, a bit confused.

"Well. I had met Bobby when we got down here. Ley brought him to a party at DJ's house. He is a little bit odd but seems harmless. He told me something. Something he said that he heard and needed to tell me. It is crazy, but I just need to talk to you about it." Ellie was rambling a bit.

"Well, just spit it out. What did he say?" Kristy was still not worried about anything, but curious about what Bobby had to share.

"He told me that he likes to sleep in the woods here around the Path. He said he likes it because it is peaceful. He said last night he was in the woods behind Darrel's house. He was drinking by himself. Then he said, um, he said that he saw you and Darrel on the back porch together." Ellie paused.

"Yes. I stopped by to see Darrel. We are old friends." Kristy remembered their conversation and now felt her pulse quicken.

"He also told me that he heard something. He heard that you and

304

Darrel started the fire at Bodhi's parents. That can't be true." Ellie was hoping she was right.

"Why, what else did he say?" Kristy was flat-footed. She never suspected someone was listening in on her conversation with Darrel.

"He said that you talked about the whole night of the fire. How you got the fuel from the boatyard and then poured it inside the front door. He said you went home and were stopped by a policeman when you took a nap on the way home. He had a lot of details, but it doesn't make sense to me. Why would he say that?".

Kristy was staring at Ellie. She felt a burning inside herself as Ellie explained the night of the fire. Ellie looked at the bed and floor, not wanting to make eye contact as she accused Kristy of murder. It was too surreal to be true. Kristy knew it was true, and she knew that Ellie was now a threat to take Bodhi away from her. She would not let that happen.

Kristy stood up slowly. "Ellie, I don't know why he would say something like that. I was at Darrel's last night, but I wouldn't say that. I mean…" Kristy pulled her handgun from her purse and pointed at Ellie. Ellie was still staring at the bed. As her eyes slowly rose to meet the barrel of the gun in her face, she found herself paralyzed.

"What are you doing?"

"Not now. You can't. You won't take Bodhi from me. Get on the ground. Lie on your stomach," Kristy ordered Ellie.

"Kristy. What are you doing? You don't have to do this. Bobby is crazy; he probably didn't know what he heard. You don't…"

Kristy cut off Ellie, "Shut up. Just shut up." Kristy pulled her phone from her pocket and dialed Darrel. "Hey, come to the motel. Room one oh six. We have a problem."

Ellie lay flat on her stomach with Kristy hovering over her, holding the gun. They waited for Darrel to arrive.

Kristy unlocked the door, and Darrel slowly pushed it open and walked into the room. He closed the door behind him and locked it.

"What the hell is going on? What are you doing?" Darrel asked Kristy.

"She knows," Kristy said.

Ellie was crying, trying to hold it in, but squeaks and sobs leaked out through her lips. "I won't say anything. I only heard something. Just say it's not true, and it's not true," Ellie pleaded.

"Shut up!" Kristy yelled at her and then turned to Darrel. "We need to get rid of her and then find that son of bitch, Bobby. Whoever that is," Kristy said to Darrel.

"What? Tell me what this is?" Darrel pleaded with Kristy.

"Bobby was in the woods last night. He heard everything when we were on the porch. He came here and told her, and now she knows, too."

Ellie heard that phrase and realized just how dire her situation was. She now knew the truth. Kristy had just confessed. She also knew she was fighting for her life. Ellie couldn't hope Kristy and Darrel would let her go. She needed to act. Ellie was still sobbing. She opened her eyes, trying to focus on her situation.

As she lay on her stomach, she could see her phone that had fallen under the bed. If only she could reach it. Ellie slowly extended her arm for her phone, hoping Kristy and Darrel were consumed with trying to decide what to do next and miss her stealthy move.

"What can we do with her?" Kristy asked Darrel.

"I don't know. It's the middle of the day. Are you sure she knows anything?" Darrel asked Kristy.

Kristy thought about what had transpired and knew that her actions gave away her guilt. "She knows. It is either her or us. You need to decide right now," Kristy instructed Darrel.

Ellie was still lying on her stomach, but now an arm extended under the bed. She felt the cold glass face of the phone. She pressed her thumb on the small button at the bottom, and the phone glowed under the bed. She needed to dial 911. As she moved her head to look at her phone, Darrel said, "What are you doing?" Then he grabbed her arm, and her phone skidded to the end of the bed.

Kristy picked up the phone and looked at it. "She was trying to call someone. It didn't go through."

"Grab that blanket," Darrel instructed Kristy.

Ellie's instincts kicked in, and she jumped to her feet. She knocked Kristy over as she made her way to the door. Kristy grabbed at her as she fell and slowed her enough for Darrel to force her to the ground. He lay on top of her, smothering her with his heft. Kristy scrambled to grab her gun.

"Get the blanket!" Darrel said as he began choking Ellie from behind. In a few moments, Ellie stopped struggling and went limp. Darrel continued to squeeze until he knew she was done fighting.

———————-

It was 4:13 p.m. Ley and Bodhi were still sitting on the *Lady B,* waiting for their turn at the lift. The radio finally squawked, "Jarret Bay calling the *Lady B."*

Ley picked up the mic and held it to his mouth, "This is the *Lady B.* Go ahead."

"Ley, I got bad news for you. The lift is down again. I am not sure we will get you in tonight. I have been watching the weather, and that storm is pushing faster than we thought. I can't promise you that we can get you on the ground," the radio reported the bad news.

"Randy, give me a number that we will get her out before the wind? Five in ten?" Ley asked.

"Not sure on the number, but that or lower. The parts for the lift will be here in a few hours. They are coming from Wilmington. Then we need to install them. We are looking at one a.m. or later before we start hauling again. It looks like we could be getting wind by that time," the radio shared the facts.

Ley decided that he couldn't risk it. If the storm hit and they got caught on the water, it was likely the end of the *Lady B*. They could make a run back to Salter Path and lash her down for the storm at the dock. It wasn't ideal, but for years that is what they did. "Copy that, Randy. We are going to tie her down at home. If something changes, give me a shout on the radio."

"Copy that, Captain. Best of luck and safe travels."

"Shit. We are going to miss that party. We need to get back and tie her down. Sorry about that, Bodhi," Ley told him.

"I understand we need to do what we need to do. How long until we are back? I want to call Ellie on your phone to let her know," Bodhi said.

"It will take about two hours. We should be back by seven. Tell her seven-thirty to be safe," Ley advised as he unlocked his phone and handed it to Bodhi.

Bodhi took the phone and dialed Ellie's number. It rang and rang. Voice mail, "This is Ellie. Leave me a message at the tone! Thanks!" Bodhi hung up and dialed again. Voice mail. He dialed again, but this time he left a message. "Hey, hun, this is Bodhi. I left my phone at the motel. This number is Ley's phone. We didn't get to pull the boat out because of a problem with the lift. We are heading back to Salter Path but won't be there until late. I'm not sure if you are going back with Kristy, but we won't make it to the party. I wanted to let you know. Just tell me if you are heading back with her. Love you."

"No answer?" Ley asked.

"No. She usually picks up, but I guess she did not recognize the number. She will probably call back when she hears the message."

————-

Ellie's phone began to vibrate. The screen lit up with a 252 area code number. There was no name associated with it. Darrel picked up the phone and stared at it, waiting for it to stop.

"Someone is calling," Darrel said to Kristy.

"Who is it?" Kristy asked.

"Doesn't say, but it's a local number. What should we do?" Darrel asked.

"Don't answer it! Let it go to voice mail. See if they leave a message."

They sat looking at the phone. Shortly the notification popped up, showing a voice mail. Darrel said, "Wait, I know that number. It's Ley's number. Why would he call?"

Kristy took Ellie's hand. She was still groggy from being hit on the head. Kristy pressed Ellie's thumb against the phone and unlocked it. Darrel pulled up the voice mail and hit the speakerphone. They heard Bodhi's message.

Kristy looked at Darrel. "Bodhi thinks she is going home with me. This message is our chance. We can take care of this issue with the storm."

"What do you mean?" Darrel still did not comprehend what Kristy had in mind.

"I will text Bodhi from her phone pretending to be her. I will tell him that she went back to Raleigh with me. When the sun goes down, we take care of this once and for all."

"What do you mean?" Darrel asked.

"Just listen to me." Kristy took the phone from Darrel and began texting Bodhi. "Hey! I know you left your phone. I got the message. I wanted to text and tell you I am going home with Kristy. See you after the storm! Be safe!"

Kristy put the phone down and turned toward Darrel. "We need to take care of this tonight. Do you still take those painkillers for your back?" Kristy asked, knowing that Darrel was addicted to them like so many who started opioids.

"Yes. I still take them. You know that back pain doesn't just go away."

"Here is what we are going to do. We are going to crush up a bunch of those pills. Enough to make her unconscious, but not kill her. Then, when the sun goes down, we will give them to her. We will take her out to the fish house with all her belongings. By the time she wakes up, the storm will be raging. It will be too late. The fish house will get washed away with her in it. When they find her, she will have drugs in her body. They will think she wandered away, telling Bodhi she was leaving."

"What if the storm doesn't come?" Darrel asked.

Kristy turned to the Weather Channel, showing a large category-five hurricane making its way toward Salter Path. "We aren't getting away from that storm. It is only a matter of timing now." Kristy paused for a moment. "I will drive back to Raleigh tonight and plant some of the pills in her house. That way, when they start looking into things, Bodhi will discover that his wife-to-be was a drug addict."

"I don't know if I can do this. It doesn't seem right."

"What the fuck are you saying, Darrel? When we burned that house years ago, there was no turning back. You need to imagine yourself in jail because your ass is going down with me. Grow a fucking backbone. We need to do this. No questions," Kristy stated the strength of her convictions.

"You are right. This is it. We need to do this."

"We also need to find Bobby. Do you know him?" Kristy asked.

"Yes, a bit. He is a new kid around here. He is working as a mate on the *Lady B*. I can probably track him down, but then what?" Darrel asked.

"Try to run him off. If he won't go, we need to do something else."

"Let's take it one step at a time. I will get to him, and then we will see where it goes," Darrel said. "He didn't go to the police, so he probably isn't sure if it is true. I can tell him that he needs to get out of the

Pather's business and find another job."

Kristy was leaning over, checking the ropes that bound Ellie as she lay on the floor of Darrel's spare bedroom. "Okay. She is still out. I need to get her things from the motel. You meet back here after you find Bobby."

Kristy left Darrel's and headed back to the motel. Darrel picked up his phone and dialed DJ. "DJ, I have a question for you. I am trying to get a hold of Bobby. Any idea where I can find him?"

DJ was at home finishing the recovery from a night out. "I haven't seen him in a couple of days. I don't know where he is."

Darrel asked, "Where does he usually stay? I need to ask him something."

"He kind of roams around. No one is sure where he stays, and we don't ask. We think he sleeps under vacation houses when nobody is there. Hell, he could have split town before the hurricane."

"Well, if you hear where he is or see him, let me know. I gotta ask him something."

"What? Why do you need to get a hold of him?" DJ asked.

"Something with the drive-in. I don't want to say anything until I ask him. Just let me know if you see him." Darrel hung up the phone.

He paced the floor, thinking about how to find Bobby. He considered getting in his truck and driving the streets, hoping to bump into him. The island wasn't that big, and he could probably track him down, but he could not leave the woman tied up in his spare bedroom alone. He decided to ask a friend whose job was to keep track of everything going on in town. Darrel took out his phone and dialed Chief Burns.

"Salter Path Police," the chief's emotionless voice answered.

"Chief, this is Darrel. How are you?"

"I'm good. What can I help you with?" Chief Burns asked.

"I'm looking for somebody. I think he has been stealing from the drive-in. I'm not sure yet, but I thought you had seen him around. Do you know that Bobby kid that works for Ley on the *Lady B*?" Darrel inquired.

"I do. Is that who you are looking for?"

"Yes. I wanted to talk to him."

"I don't think you will find him around any time soon. I saw him walking west toward Emerald Isle with a bag of stuff over his shoulder this morning. With the storm coming, I'm guessing he has decided to move on."

Darrel paused, thinking what that meant for his current situation, and it seemed good that Bobby wanted out. "Thanks, Chief, that is good to know. Can you give me a ring if you see him around?"

"Will do. Do you need me to ask him anything?" Chief Burns asked.

Darrel suddenly realized he was talking to the police with a woman tied up in his house. "No, no, that's not necessary. I just had a question for him, and I should be able to handle it. Thanks, though."

"Sure, just trying to help out. Keep safe during the storm," the chief said as he hung up.

Darrel sat in the front room and put his head in his hands. Leaning over his round belly, he could only wonder how he got into this situation. He needed to sidestep this one more time and then be done with Kristy. Darrel wanted Kristy, but it was now clear it was for the wrong reasons. It was quiet in the house. So much so that he could hear the waves pounding the beach.

35

Storm

Hurricane Adrian was not a patient storm. Other storms were akin to being stalked by a turtle. Day after day, those storms stagnated and loitered off the coast, waiting to slowly cut a path across the land. Perhaps because Adrian was an early season storm, it didn't have the patience and was moving ahead of schedule. It was so far ahead that the Big Rock Board of Directors canceled the Captain's Party to ensure everyone could get home safely. The storm prediction was off by at least twelve hours, and it seemed like those who hadn't prepared would pay for their mistake.

As Bodhi and Ley returned to Salter Path, the sun was already hanging low in the sky. The first rain bands from the hurricane were just off the shore. The wind was already blowing a steady twenty-seven knots with gusts to thirty-two. Ley was an experienced captain, and the deteriorating weather could not stop the progress of the *Lady B.*

"We are going to have a time of it when we tie her up, Bodhi!" Ley shouted.

Bodhi stood on the aft deck looking at the building seas and turned to Ley. "You call it, and I'll do it. Just let me know where to be."

"Roger that. We are going to drop the anchor and back her into the slip. That will let the anchor help hold her."

The *Lady B* chugged her way across Bogue Sound. The storm rolled the boat from side to side. The rigging above Bodhi's head banged and clanked. Instinctively, he would look up when there was a metallic clang and crash as if something broke. Bodhi had never been in seas like this, but he trusted Ley's experience.

"Drop the anchor on my mark!" Ley said as he spun *Lady B* around, getting ready to back into the slip. "Mark!"

Bodhi turned a small metal wheel, releasing the grip on the chain and allowing the anchor to plunge into the water. As the chain rode paid out, Ley throttled up the engine. The *Lady B* backed into the slip. "Lock it off!" Ley yelled to Bodhi as he spun the small wheel in the opposite direction securing the anchor.

The chain rode pulled tight. Ley and Bodhi began lashing the lines to the piers that defined the slip. They spent the next thirty minutes adding lines and ensuring the boat could rise and fall with the storm surge, but not float away.

The sun had touched the horizon as Ley and Bodhi cracked open a beer looking at the boat secured in the slip in front of them. The day twisted in a way that they hadn't expected, and without checking the weather, they both knew the storm was coming sooner rather than later.

"I need to get back to the motel and grab my phone. I should see where Ellie is," Bodhi said to Ley.

"C'mon, jump in the truck. I will run you over there." Ley motioned, and they made their way to Ley's pickup.

Bodhi slipped the key into the lock and opened the door. His phone was sitting on the dresser next to the TV. He could see right away that Ellie's things were gone. He looked at the text messages.

"Looks like she went with Kristy back to Raleigh. She should about be home by now." Bodhi was half talking to Ley and half to himself. He began texting her, "Hey. I guess you found my phone. Are you home?" The text popped up green. Bodhi said to Ley, "That's weird. It shows green instead of blue. I wonder if the storm is causing problems with the service."

"Could be. When did Ellie leave?" Ley asked.

"Looks like at about five-thirty or so," Bodhi said, checking the time stamp on his text messages. "Let me call her." The line rang once and went straight to voice mail. "Odd. Her phone must be dead. It went straight to voice mail."

"It must be the storm. I wouldn't worry about it. Grab a jacket, and let's go back to Nana's. We can drink some beers and watch the storm roll in."

"Sure. Why not? I'm here for the storm for sure. I might as well get the full experience."

As they headed back to Nana B's, something didn't sit right with Bodhi. He felt odd that Ellie's phone was dead or the lines were down. His mind warped as he thought perhaps he had jealous fiancée syndrome. He needed to give her some space for a while. *She will be fine*, Bodhi said to himself.

Bodhi and Ley sat on the back porch shielded by the home from the wind coming out of the south. An hour or so later, they turned on the TV to check on the weather.

"Shit. Look at that," Ley said, standing up and looking at the TV with the remote in his hand.

The weather channel showed a large category-four hurricane moving fast straight toward them. The prediction lines put the storm's eye right over Salter Path at about five in the morning.

"This is a crazy one. Let's check those lines, and then we need to get back to the motel," Ley said.

As Ley headed to *Lady B* to make sure he had firmly tied the lines,

315

Bodhi's mind kept wandering to Ellie. He tried to call again, but it went straight to voice mail. It was nearly eleven by now, and the first rain bands from the storm had already moved over the island. Bodhi felt he needed to talk to Ellie before this storm hit. He called Kristy to see if they had made it home.

Kristy was passing through Maysville when her phone rang. She expected the call. "Hello?"

"Hey, are you all home?" Bodhi asked.

"Not sure what you mean? I am home," Kristy said.

"Didn't Ellie, I mean, you didn't take Ellie?" Bodhi asked.

"No. I couldn't get a hold of her, and she wasn't there when I went by your motel room. So, I came home."

"What? No, she texted me and said she went with you." Panic started to creep into Bodhi's mind.

"Bodhi, Ellie wasn't there and didn't answer her phone. So, I came home. Have you checked the motel?" Kristy knew she was not there.

"I was there an hour ago. She wasn't there, but most of her stuff was gone. I am going back to the motel; maybe she came back? I will call you." Bodhi hung up with some urgency.

Bodhi told Ley what was going on with Ellie. They made their way to the motel where Bodhi and Ley planned to ride out the storm. They walked into the office where Ley needed to check-in. They hit the after-hours button, and a few minutes later, a sleepy-looking motel owner came out of a door behind the desk.

"Hey, guys. How are you? Checking in, Ley?" Danny asked.

"Yeah. That storm is coming in early. Question for ya. Did you see Ellie today?" Ley asked.

"Only this morning. She was talking with Bobby. Then Kristy stopped over. Didn't see her after that." Danny was talking and focusing on his computer at the same time.

"Did Ellie leave with Kristy?" Bodhi asked.

316

"I didn't see. I saw Kristy walk that way and figured she was going to see you. How many nights, Ley?" Danny asked.

"Make it two. Just in case. Hurricane special?" Ley was hoping for a cheap rate.

"You got it. Two nights for one. Only for the locals, though." Danny looked at Bodhi. "Sorry."

"So, you didn't see Kristy and Ellie leave together?" Bodhi asked Danny again, confused by the situation.

"I didn't. I was in the back; I just saw Kristy walk to your room. Everything okay?" Danny inquired.

"Not sure. I don't know where Ellie is. She was supposed to go home with Kristy, but Kristy said that Ellie stayed here, but Ellie isn't in the motel room, and most of her stuff is gone."

Danny stared at Bodhi as Ley signed the forms to get his keys. "You mean you can't find her?" Danny asked the clarifying question.

Bodhi did not think of it like that, and a flush fell over his face. "No. I don't know where she is, and her phone is going straight to voice mail."

Danny looked straight into Bodhi's eyes and said, "The storm is coming. You need to find her. Call the police."

Bodhi suddenly felt the urgency of the situation. If she was gone, if something happened, he only had hours to find her before the hurricane's full force battered the island. With the storm's strength, it might be weeks before anyone could help. Bodhi responded simply to Danny, "I will."

— — — — — — — — -

Detective Natchez had spent most of the day securing his property and readying for the storm. He put all of his outdoor furniture and anything not tied down into his shed. He boarded up most of the windows, leaving only two of them open if they needed to escape through them in the storm. He had finally begun to settle down, and he put his nose in his liquor cabinet, trying to select a bourbon to keep him company during the storm.

There was a Bang! Bang! Bang! on the door. It repeated with a sense of urgency even greater. With the storm bearing down, Natchez was surprised by the visitor. Maybe it was a neighbor checking on him?

Natchez went to the door and cracked it open to look out. A skinny kid with long dark hair and a weathered baseball cap stood on his porch. It looked like he was carrying most of his possessions on his back. It flashed through his mind that this could be a homeless person looking for an empty house to ride out the storm. Natchez put his hand on his concealed sidearm in the small of his back and then slowly opened the door.

"Can I help you?" Natchez said.

"Sorry to bother you, I'm looking for a Detective Natchez," Bobby said as he stood on Natchez's front stoop.

"I'm Detective Natchez. Can I ask why you are looking for me?" Natchez still found the visitor to be suspicious.

"Sorry to bother you. But my friends, Bodhi and Ellie, talked about you. I think I have something you need to know."

"Bodhi Salter? You know him?" Natchez asked.

"Yes. I worked down in Salter Path for Bodhi's friend, Ley. I was Ley's mate on the shrimp boat. I heard stuff, and I wanted to tell you."

"What's in your bag?" Natchez asked.

"My stuff. I am leaving. I think I need to get down the road, but I wanted to tell you what I know."

The young man on the steps seemed introvertly intelligent but also a bit uneasy in his skin. "Leave your bag on the steps." Natchez opened the door and waved Bobby inside. "What do you want to tell me?"

Bobby set his bag down and walked into Natchez's house with his head down and slightly hunched over. He stepped onto an oriental rug that covered the old hardwood floors of the small coastal bungalow. Then, he looked up at Natchez and began, "I went by the motel this morning. Ellie was there, and I told her this..." Bobby went on to tell Natchez the story he heard from Kristy and Darrel.

Just as Bobby finished telling Natchez what he'd heard, the phone on the table next to the door began to vibrate. Natchez glanced toward his ringing phone and saw "Bodhi Salter" on the caller ID. Natchez reached down and picked up the phone. "Excuse me. I need to take this."

"Detective Natchez," he said as he answered the phone. He retreated into the kitchen, standing in the archway to keep an eye on Bobby.

"Detective, Bodhi, Bodhi Salter. I think we have a problem. Ellie is missing," Bodhi blurted to Natchez.

Bodhi explained the events of the day and evening. Natchez listened closely. As Bodhi went on, his heart began to race as he stared at Bobby standing slouched inside his front door. Natchez said as little as possible, thinking that Ellie's capturer may be standing in his doorway. "Where are you now?" Natchez asked. "Okay. I will be there shortly. Stay put."

Natchez hung up the phone, slid it into his pocket, and walked toward Bobby. He did not have anything that warranted an arrest, but it was suspicious that Ellie went missing and a young man arrived telling a story about a murder. "Bobby. I just talked with Bodhi. He was hoping we could go back to Salter Path. Will you come with me?"

"Well. I am not sure if they want me back there," Bobby said with a bit of nervousness in his voice.

"You will be with me. You can ride in my car. It would be good to have you there. We could maybe get all this straightened out tonight. You know, before the storm. Then you can head on wherever."

"Well, if I go with you, I should be okay," Bobby said.

"Okay. Let me get my keys. Grab your bag and meet me by the car."

———————-

Bodhi and Ley were sitting on plastic chairs on the small porch outside their motel rooms. Bodhi was nervously drinking a beer, and Ley pulled on a cigarette. The lights from Natchez's car flashed in their eyes. Ley raised his hand to block the headlight, but Bodhi was still unsure what to feel.

"Stay in the car. I will be right back," Natchez said to Bobby, who was sitting in the back seat.

Natchez got out of the car and walked up to Bodhi. He looked around as the storm was getting closer. The wind was swirling, and the trees were bending. You could see flashes of lightning in the distance as another early storm band rolled over the island.

"Detective, good to see you. Do you know something about Ellie?" Bodhi asked.

"When was the last time you saw her?" Natchez asked.

"This morning. Then I headed out on the boat with Ley for the day. I left my phone here, so I didn't talk to her all day."

Natchez checked his surroundings, which was a habit he gained working in a tough part of Durham, North Carolina. "And where was she when you got back?"

"That's the problem. I don't know. Ellie was supposed to go home with Kristy, but she said Ellie didn't ride with her. I don't know where Ellie is."

"Did you see Bobby today?" Natchez asked.

"No. He was supposed to come on the boat with us. Right, Ley?" Bodhi asked, and Ley confirmed. "But he never showed up."

"Can I look in your motel room?" Natchez asked.

"Of course." Bodhi stood up and swung open the door to his motel room.

Natchez looked around. It looked like a standard motel room. He walked into the bathroom and noted a flatiron sitting next to the sink.

320

Other than that, there were no apparent signs that a woman had been in the room. All the women's clothes and shoes were gone. Natchez pointed to the flatiron. "How often does she use that?"

"Every day. I can't believe she left it. She will probably come back for it when she realizes she forgot it." Bodhi said, still denying the gravity of the situation.

Bodhi and Natchez walked back to the porch. Natchez looked at Bodhi. "I have Bobby in the back of my car. He told me a story. I think Ellie is in trouble."

Bodhi's daze shifted to anger. "What? Did Bobby do something to her?"

"No. I don't think so. I'm not sure what happened. Did your aunt talk to Ellie today?" Natchez asked.

"Danny, the motel owner said she came over after I left and that Bobby was here before that. It is probably that little fucker, Bobby!" Bodhi shouted.

"Bodhi! Hold on. Darrel, do you know him? Do you know where he is?" Natchez asked.

"Of course, we know Darrel. He lives just up the street," Ley said as he stood up. "We can take you there."

There was a bright flash of lightning, indicating the storm upon the island. "I will follow. Let's go."

Ley jumped in his truck and pulled out, followed closely by Natchez with Bobby in the back seat. They made the short drive to Darrel's house just behind the Big Tree. The rain was building, and the winds were already pushing thirty knots. Natchez pulled a raincoat out from behind the seat and pulled it over his shoulders.

Bodhi and Ley jumped out of the car and walked Natchez to the door. They hurried their way through the rain and rapped on the door. Darrel slowly opened it and saw Natchez standing there.

"Hi. Detective Natchez, NC SBI, can I come in?"

Darrel's heart throbbed at those words. What the hell was he doing here? Darrel stood there shirtless with his Glock-19 tucked into the waistband of his jeans. "Come in. How can I help you?" Darrel asked.

"I was wondering if you have seen Ellie? You know her, right? I was just wondering if you saw her today?" Natchez asked.

Bodhi and Ley made their way into the house behind Natchez. Darrel saw them, but his focus was on the detective. Bodhi looked at Darrel. Not exactly sure why they had come there. Then he glanced at Darrel and saw something on the kitchen table. It was lighter. Not any lighter. A BIC lighter was inserted into a custom sleeve that sparkled with rhinestones. Bodhi immediately recognized the lighter. It was Kristy's.

Bodhi interjected, "Why do you have Kristy's lighter?"

Natchez and Darrel both stopped and looked at Bodhi. Natchez paused his questions and asked Bodhi, "What do you mean?"

"That lighter on the table. Right there," he said, extending a finger in the direction of the kitchen table. "I would know that lighter anywhere. You can't buy them around here. Kristy gets them sent here from her sister-in-law in Texas. There is a lady there who puts the rhinestones on by hand. They are one of a kind."

Natchez's instincts seemed to be playing out. That kid in the back of the car was telling the truth. He had now connected Kristy and Darrel, but it didn't help connect where Ellie was. "Can you explain that lighter?" he asked Darrel.

Darrel stuttered and began to sweat. "She stopped over yesterday. We are old friends. She must have left it here."

Bingo! Natchez just corroborated Bobby's story. "When did she stop by? You didn't see her today, did you?"

"No, no. I didn't see Kristy today. I don't know what time she was here, but it was dark. Maybe ten or a little after."

"What did you two talk about?" Natchez asked.

"You know—old times. I hadn't seen her in a long time. We were just catching up." Darrel tried to explain away the visit.

"Darrel, I am going to ask you again. Have you seen Ellie today? She has gone missing, and Kristy was the last to visit her. Do you know where Ellie is?" Natchez asked one last time.

"I told you I didn't see her. Have you asked Kristy?" Darrel's voice elevated, hoping that it would help take control of the situation.

"Right now, we are here talking to you. Would you be willing to come down to the police station so I can ask you some more questions?" Natchez thought he had enough between Bobby's story and Darrel's admission to make him a suspect in Ellie's disappearance, and the fire.

Darrel pondered his next move. He had never felt that feeling of panic and anger together before. He was cornered. "Let me grab a shirt," Darrel said. As he turned, he drew his pistol and fired a shot whizzing past Ley's ear and lodging in the window frame.

Natchez, Ley, and Bodhi instinctively dropped down, and Natchez drew his weapon. Darrel sprinted out the backdoor, moving faster than he ever had. If he could get to the woods before Natchez, he could disappear into the thickets. The rain outside was coming in sheets. It streamed down with flashes of lightning in the distance. The treetops were bending from the gusts that were quickly building. Darrel made it to the woods and was gone into the tangles.

"Everyone, okay?" Natchez shouted.

"Holy fuck! What was that?" Ley asked.

"That's our guy. He just confirmed it," Natchez said. "Bodhi, I just have to say this because we don't have time. He and Kristy burned your house, and they probably took Ellie to cover it up. We have to find him."

"What, why would he take Ellie? Why would you say that?" Bodhi asked.

"Bobby came to my house tonight. He scared the shit out of me. He told me a story he heard last night between Kristy and Darrel. They burned your house. I didn't believe it, but Darrel just confirmed it when he said Kristy was here last night. And then, taking the shot at us. He is our guy," Natchez finished.

Bodhi felt his chest tighten and his breath being pushed out of him. His mind wobbled like a top being struck by a child but then quickly righted itself, focusing on the problem. He could not do anything for his family, and if Natchez was right, Ellie was in danger. He had to find her fast. His emotion ran away, and he could only think about how to find Ellie. "We gotta get him," Bodhi said, and before Natchez could respond, Ley and Bodhi bolted out the backdoor in pursuit.

They ran onto the back deck and looked into the rain-soaked night. Natchez came out behind them. "You need to stay here. He is armed; we need to get a search party out here."

"Detective. There is a hurricane sitting right out there," Ley said, pointing toward the ocean. "Those bridges are going to close any minute. You know as well as me; we are on our own."

Natchez said, "Let me get Burns out here, too. He should have a deputy on duty as well." Natchez picked up his phone and dialed the number for the Salter Path Police Department. The line was dead. The storm had already taken down the cell phone towers. The wind gusted, nearly knocking them off their feet. "Nothing, the phones are dead."

"It's us then. Wait. Get Bobby! He can help. He knows his way around," Ley said.

"Right." Natchez headed back to the car to let Bobby out of the back as he was no longer the prime suspect.

As Natchez walked away, Bodhi said to Ley, "This is hide-and-seek like when we were kids. Where was the best place to hide?"

Ley paused, "It was an outside game, so you hid inside. No one ever found you."

"Darrel went to DJ's. He knows he can't spend the night out in this storm," Bodhi said.

Ley and Bodhi jumped from the porch and bolted down the path toward DJ's trailer. It didn't take more than a minute or two to get there at a full sprint, but by the time Natchez returned with Bobby, they were long gone.

Ley pounded his oversized fist on the door. The lights were on, and DJ or someone began moving about inside. Ley and Bodhi moved away from the door opening in case Darrel answered. The door pushed out, and DJ's face peered through the opening. "What are y'all doing out in this? Get your asses in here."

"Is your dad here?" Bodhi asked.

"What the hell is wrong with y'all being out in this weather? Yeah, he showed up two minutes ago. Said he wanted to go off the island for the storm and asked if I would take him," DJ said as his father walked down the corridor with his Glock in his hand.

"Shit. DJ, I didn't want you getting caught up in this. I don't want to hurt anyone. Let me leave, and there won't be a problem," Darrel said, raising the pistol toward Ley and Bodhi.

"What the hell is going on?" DJ asked.

"Ellie's missing. He knows where she is," Bodhi said.

"Shut the fuck up. I didn't tell you to talk. DJ, get your keys, and let's go." Darrel had lost control of the situation, and he knew he had to run.

"What does that mean? Did you do something to her?" DJ asked Darrel.

"They don't know what they are saying. I am not going to jail for something someone else did. I need to get out of here. Let's go." He waved his gun at Ley and Bodhi.

DJ reached for his truck keys. "Take it easy; let's just get out of here.

You don't have to do anything crazy." DJ was trying to soothe his father.

Ley and Bodhi backed away from the trailer door. DJ walked out the door to start the car, and Darrel slowly made his way toward the door. As he neared Ley and Bodhi, a gust of wind burst across the island, slamming the open trailer door shut. Darrel instinctively looked at the door, and Ley leaped across the room, carrying his large frame into Darrel, knocking him to the ground and throwing the gun from his hand. They had him.

36

Storm Damage

Hurricane Adrian was hitting the island. If you have never experienced a hurricane up close and in person, you cannot appreciate the forceful blow of the storm against the land. The trees hissed as the wind began stripping the leaves from the trees. The violence of the storm was picking up quickly. It would not be long until venturing into the storm might be too big of a risk.

Ley was on top of Darrel. The former football player squeezed Darrel tight, holding him still. DJ opened the trailer door, hearing the shouting of Ley, Bodhi, and Darrel as Ley subdued Darrel with crushing strength.

Bodhi saw DJ at the door. "DJ, go find Bobby and Natchez! They were at your dad's house."

"Who is Natchez?" DJ asked.

"He's a detective. Find them! They might be driving around in a car," Bodhi said.

DJ knew Salter Path as well as anyone. He headed to his dad's house and shouted inside, "Bobby! You in here!" He continued walking through the house and saw the back door open. He yelled outside again, "Bobby, where you at? I need to find Natchez!" Nothing.

DJ thought, "If they need help, they probably are going to find Chief Burns." DJ jumped back into his truck and headed to the police station. Parked outside was an unfamiliar car; DJ knew it must be Natchez.

DJ ducked his head as the rain streamed down. It was being driven sideways by the constant wind. He pushed open the door to the station. Bobby was standing next to an older man he did not know. "Are you Natchez?"

"Yes. I am Detective Natchez."

"We got Darrel. He's at my place. Come quick, Ley and Bodhi are holding him."

In no time, they were pulling into DJ's front yard. The door to the trailer was still swinging in the wind. Natchez pulled his weapon and headed for the door as the rain soaked him. "SBI! I am coming in!" he yelled as he pushed through the doorway.

Ley and Bodhi were holding Darrel down, waiting for Natchez.

"Darrel. I am Detective Natchez. If these boys get off of you, are you going to be calm?"

"Yes. Yeah."

"Come on, get off him slowly. Darrel, you stay on the ground!" Natchez directed. Flashing blue lights were now pulling up as Chief Burns arrived.

Natchez put the handcuffs on Darrel and rolled him into a seated position. "Where is she? We will get you on the fire, don't let the girl be on you, too. Where is she?"

"I don't know. I haven't seen her," Darrel said.

"I have a missing girl that was supposed to be with Kristy. Kristy was with you. And she knew about the fire and what happened. It sounds like you are covering your tracks. So, where is she?" Natchez laid it out.

"I told you. I don't know."

Natchez squatted down to look Darrel in the eyes. "Darrel, you are not a criminal. You are a businessman. You don't know what you are doing here on the floor with cuffs on. I'm giving you a way out. You just need to help yourself. Tell me where the girl is, and we can help her."

Darrel's lip began to quiver, and tears came to his eyes. He did not want to go to jail. He wanted out of this. "Fi..."

"What was that?" Natchez asked.

Darrel shook his head as though he was trying to shake a memory from his mind. "Fish house. She is in the fish house."

"In the sound?" Bodhi asked.

"Yes," Darrel said.

"We have to get her. That place won't last the night. Maybe not even much longer. The winds are already blowing fifty miles per hour. We need to get there now!" Bodhi said.

Chief Burns was standing there and listening to the entire conversation. "We can't help. We are shut down once the winds hit forty-five miles per hour," Chief Burns said.

"You are just going to leave her?!" Bodhi exclaimed.

Burns looked at Bodhi. "We can't. It's a state of emergency, and we have to stand down until after the storm."

"That's horseshit! If you won't get her, we will," Ley said. "Let's go."

"Ley!" Burns yelled. "If you go out there, you are on your own. We can't do anything for you."

"You made that clear already. We got this. Let's go, boys." Ley, Bodhi, DJ, and Bobby headed to the boats.

They made their way to the dock where the *Lady B* was tied. The winds were everything of fifty miles per hour sustained with gusts pushing over seventy-five. The *Lady B* was already straining on her moorings but holding tight. The rain stung as it struck their skin, but they needed to try to make it to Ellie at the fish house. The fish house may be gone by now, but they needed to try. Ley climbed aboard and fired up the diesel engine. A puff of black smoke belched from the exhaust, and the engine began to rumble.

"Bodhi!" Ley yelled to get his attention. "It's going to be tight getting there. I am not sure there is enough water." Ley had been thinking this but did not know what to tell his friend that they might not be able to get there.

"How much water do you need?" Bodhi asked as the rain continued to pound down.

"At least two feet, and with these waves, maybe three or four," Ley said.

Bodhi knew there wasn't even two feet of water at the fish house, let alone three or four feet. They would be lucky to get within 500 yards on the *Lady B*. Bodhi jumped off her and ran to the skiff where it was cinched tight in its lift. He took out his pocket knife and started cutting the lines to free it. He began lowering the skiff, and waves pounded the bottom of the small boat. He fired up the motor and ran the engine hard in reverse, pulling it off the lift. Waves crashed over the stern, nearly sinking the boat as Bodhi backed away.

"Wait! Wait! I will go with you!" DJ yelled.

"Help Ley get *Lady B* out. We might need you if the skiff doesn't make it!" Bodhi yelled over the howling wind and pounding rain. A wind gust of maybe eighty miles per hour came from nowhere and almost knocked Bodhi overboard. He stumbled, grabbed the center console, and regained his footing. He took to the helm and throttled up, pushing the boat through the building seas.

The small skiff was not designed for the heavy seas that now covered the sound. The wind blew over the island, and as Bodhi ventured into the sound, the waves grew larger. It was dark, and he had no lights. He needed to find the fish house without the help of navigation. When he was young, he knew how to navigate by the onshore lights, but many new homes and lights had sprung up since he was last on the sound at night. The heavy rain made it so that he could no longer see the lights lining the sound. The storm was too much. He could only see the water tower on the island and used that as his guide. He squinted, trying to keep the rain and saltwater out of his eyes.

The skiff rose up and then slapped down, going over wave after wave. Even though it was no more than a mile to the fish house, the seas, wind, and rain made the journey happen in slow motion. Each breaking wave sloshed water into the boat. The waves broke over the bow causing the boat to become unstable and nearly capsize.

Bodhi was risking his life, hoping Ellie was still there in the fish house.

———————-

Ellie woke slowly inside a dark room. It was the roaring wind and crashing waves that brought her out of the drug-induced fog. She did not know where she was at first and did not remember how she got there. Her head was throbbing and bleeding. There was a goose egg on the back of her head, and what she thought at first was water in her hair, was actually blood. The room swayed, and she was not sure if it was actually swaying or if she was just feeling it sway. She sat up and looked around, straining her eyes in the utterly black space.

Ellie could see a window. She stood carefully and groped her way toward it. She peered out and saw nothing except a vast blackness with rain pumping down and the wind howling. She could make out the waves crashing below and the small deck. She realized she was in the fish house. She tried to make sense of what was happening with the fog of drugs still making her mind function slowly.

The fish house door slammed open, banging loudly against the wall as it opened. A gust of wind nearly ripped the door from its hinges, and the blast drove the rain inside. The loud noise caused a rush of adrenaline that focused Ellie's mind. She moved across the small room to push the door shut.

Her thoughts were coming more clearly, and she tried to talk her way through the situation, "I am in the fish house. The hurricane must be here. I am not going to survive here. I have to get back to the land." There was a thud on the bottom of the small building as the waves started beating on the building's bottom. The building creaked, and boards broke off the small deck and knocked against the house.

It was one thing to be on a sinking boat and another thing to be in a sinking house. Ellie could do nothing but pray that the building would survive. She dropped to her knees and began praying that this was not her time.

There was a cracking and tearing sound, and the roof began to lift and drop back down with a mighty BANG. The fish house was nearing its limits, and Ellie was getting ready to fight the raging water. The door slammed open again, and when Ellie looked up, a man was standing in the frame.

"ELLIE!" Bodhi yelled.

"BODHI! Here! I am here! Are you real? How did you get here?" Ellie thought she might be imagining him at the door.

Bodhi moved across the room and took Ellie in his arms, falling to the floor. He ran his hands through her hair, feeling the bump and cut on the back of her head. "Are you okay?" Bodhi asked.

"I am okay. We have to get out of here! This place is coming apart." Ellie said, not understanding why they were waiting.

"Ellie. We can't. We have to wait."

"How did you get here?" Ellie was confused.

"I came in the skiff, but the waves smashed it into the pilings when I got here. I barely made it. Ley is coming with the *Lady B*. He should get to us." Bodhi told Ellie that with all the confidence he could muster. He knew that the *Lady B* could not make it through the shallow water.

Bodhi knew precisely how dire the situation was. Having crossed the sound to the fish house, he knew the power of the building storm.

He held Ellie tightly. She was another victim in his twisted family drama. He thought that it was the end for another person he loved, but he would be there this time when the moment came. He pressed his face against Ellie's, and he couldn't hold back the tears. He spoke to her and thought this might be the last memory they shared, "You are my angel. You gave me the courage to come and face my fears here. If we don't get to share another day, know that you are everything to me. Know that you make me stronger. You make me better. I love you."

Ellie began to cry hearing these words. She leaned back and took his face in her hands, and said, "We are getting out of here. We have too much to live for. We will make it." Ellie had nothing but faith to make those words come out of her mouth.

Bodhi and Ellie sat holding each other on the floor. The roof lifted and banged back down again, making Bodhi jump. The roof lifted again but did not bang back down. Instead, it continued to rise on one end until it was nearly vertical and then flew away like a playing card thrown into the wind. The rain poured in, and the howling wind had grown to a roaring wind. The walls shook, and the fish house began to slump to one side like an old man falling asleep in his chair. There was a spinning and sliding sensation as the house finally gave up and slid into the water.

They plunged into the water and grabbed at anything they could. Bodhi managed to grab a piling leaning over at forty-five degrees. He reached for Ellie, grabbing her hand. He pulled her up close to him and held onto the piling as the waves beat them. With each wave, Bodhi held on with all his strength. His arms tired, and Ellie threatened to slip from his grip. They struggled to hold on and stay above the water. There was no reference point in the world other than leaning piling.

37

The End

Hurricanes whip the Carolina coast reshaping the dunes and channels. Every year, mariners spend time learning where new channels open and where sandbars have arrived. The first hurricane of 2021 would carve a new channel through the Bogue Sound. It would wash the sand from under the fish house and push it up, bringing back Dog Island.

The blackness surrounding Bodhi and Ellie was pierced by powerful white lights from high in the air. From the water's surface, Bodhi thought it might be a helicopter. Then, more lights nearer the water beamed forth. The *Lady B* made her way through the new channel created by the hurricane shifting the sands.

The boat rocked in the high seas, but Ley guided her expertly. He saw the pilings of the fish house sticking out of the water. Ley's stomach sank when he saw the fish house missing. He was too late. The house and Ellie were gone. There was no sign of Bodhi or the skiff. He powered forward to look closer, with DJ and Bobby on the bow looking for their friends.

"Nothing. We are too late," Ley muttered to himself. Ley did not know what to do next. He was getting ready to turn the boat back to the dock.

Bodhi could see DJ and Bobby on the bow. He clung on tight, waiting for them to come closer and throw him a line. Then, he saw DJ turn away and head back to the wheelhouse. They didn't see him. They were going to turn around. Bobby lingered a moment longer, and Bodhi kicked with all his might and lifted out of the water just enough to hopefully catch Bobby's eyes. In almost the same instance, Bobby turned away.

The *Lady B* paused, floating, bobbing, almost in a time warp. Then, she moved forward, getting closer! DJ and Bobby appeared with a life ring and rope, throwing it to Bodhi. He grabbed the ring and slung it over an exhausted Ellie. DJ and Bobby hoisted her aboard. They came back for Bodhi moments later, heaving him aboard.

They were safe on board the *Lady B* as she began chugging into the storm back to the dock.

Epilogue

I pulled up into a stone driveway of a new coastal house built one row back from the sound. The front porch extended across the width of the house and had a roof covering its length. The house was one story and painted a sky blue color with green trim. The house was quintessential coastal living. The stilts below the house held it high above the water, creating protection from rising floodwaters during hurricanes. Underneath the house was Bodhi's pickup truck next to Ellie's Four Runner. I parked my car and climbed the steps to the porch. I took a moment to look out over the sound from this perch. The sun was high in the clear sky. The wind was just enough to create a cooling breeze and small ripples on the sound.

After getting married, Bodhi and Ellie decided to build a new house on the land left to Bodhi. The pandemic had given them the chance to work from home, and this allowed them to move to Bodhi's hometown. They even bought a boat they kept behind Nana B's house on a boat lift.

I turned and knocked on the front door.

"Alice! I'm so glad you made it!" Ellie said.

"Ellie! Sooo good to see you! Your house is beautiful! I can't believe that you live here now!" I said.

"It has been so good. Bodhi is so happy to be where he grew up. Everyone has welcomed us back into the town. After everything that happened, I wasn't sure what it would be like, but it has been terrific," Ellie explained.

After Bodhi, Ley, Bobby, and DJ rescued Ellie from the fish house, Kristy and Darrel were arrested for the murder of Bodhi's family. The police were able to locate old police records showing Kristy was visited by the police on her way back to Raleigh the night of the fire. This information, along with Bobby's testimony and Darrel eventually turning on Kristy to save himself, put both of them in prison. Kristy was sentenced to twenty-five years after taking a plea deal which eliminated the chance for the death penalty and gave her a chance to be someday free. Darrel would receive fifteen years for his role in the fire. The town of Salter Path had peace fall over it once it realized that the feud was within the Salter family and not between the families of Salter Path.

Bodhi came out from the backroom. "Alice! Welcome, it's so good to see you again. Was your trip okay?"

"The drive was fine. I love this place. It is so open and airy. The deck out front gives you an amazing view."

"This was where I grew up, right here, on this piece of land. My parents left it for me. Ellie and I decided to build the house here." Bodhi was telling me things I already knew.

"I haven't seen either of you since the wedding. What has been going on?" I asked.

Ellie looked at Bodhi, Bodhi looked at Ellie. Ellie started, "We have been busy moving and getting settled in here. With our jobs being remote, we can live here full-time now. Bodhi has been spending time with old friends, and we have been starting to put down some roots here. "

"After everything that has happened in my life, I somehow feel complete coming back here." Bodhi smiled a bit and shook his head. "It's like I had to go through so much, but in the end, it seems I got what I wanted."

"How are you? What's new with you?" Ellie asked me.

"Just working away in Raleigh." A smile slipped across my face.

Ellie noticed the change in my face. "What is that?"

"Well, I have met someone, and I think it could be serious," I said.

Ellie came across the room to hug me. She knows that I haven't been able to connect with a partner since college. She was genuinely happy for me, and that was something I loved about her.

"I can't wait to meet him," Ellie whispered as she hugged me.

"Bodhi! You home?" Ley bellowed, leaning through the front door.

"Ley! Come on in. I want you to meet Alice. She is one of Ellie's friends from home." Bodhi gestured toward me.

Ley's face turned red, and he started to mutter something. I could not exactly understand what he said, but he seemed suddenly confused. I decided to walk across the room and help him out of his momentary lack of ability to speak.

"Nice to meet you. Are you from here?" I asked Ley.

He snapped out of his daze long enough to say, "My entire life. I wouldn't live anywhere else."

"It seems nice here. I think I could live here, especially since Ellie lives here now. I could live right next door." Even though I had someone, it felt good to see Ley's interest in me.

"You'll need to get down here more. I would be happy to take you on my boat," Ley said, not knowing exactly why he said that.

"Is it the same one that you rescued Ellie with?"

"Well, I could take you on that one, too, but it smells like shrimp. I got a new skiff after the storm. Insurance paid for another one after Bodhi sank it in the storm."

"Give me a break." Bodhi walked over and hugged Ellie from behind. "I had to get this." He kissed her on the back of the neck.

"I think I am going to visit more," I said to Ellie, ignoring Ley.

About the Author

Joel J. Pawlak was born in Holland, New York. He moved to North Carolina to become a faculty member at NC State University. He has spent his summers at the North Carolina Crystal Coast for the past twenty years. *Salter's Path* is his first novel. His stories center around people's secret lives, blending idealized life with painful realities. The tales vividly depict beautiful surroundings with people and characters that overcome their history to emerge renewed. He and his wife raised their three children in the salt and sand of Indian Beach, NC. While they live full-time in Raleigh, the beach is where they feel most at home. In the summers, you will likely find them sitting on an uninhabited island in the Bogue sound.

You can connect with me on:
- http://jjpawlak.com
- https://twitter.com/joelpawlak
- https://www.facebook.com/jjpawlak

Made in the USA
Columbia, SC
16 August 2022

65402494R10191